again,

ig him tighter

this was in-
evitable, this kiss and what would come after. She'd wanted
him for a long time. His hands on her. His mouth breathing
hotly against her skin. She wanted to finally satisfy that curiosity that seemed to swell low in her belly and tease certain
long-neglected regions of her body.

"You sure you want to kiss me like this?" Dev's words were
jagged, cautionary. But for once she wouldn't run scared.

"I'm sure." For the moment, Bodie was taken care of.
She'd told her mom she had a few errands to run, and Tammi
had told her to take her time. But taking her time would require more control than she currently had. Her patience had
run out. The ache yawning through her had to be remedied,
and at the moment she could think of only one way to do
that. "Let me show you how sure I am." She pulled him up
to stand with her, placed her palms against his chest, and
backed him down the hall into his bedroom.

HOMETOWN COWBOY

"Filled with humor, heart, and love, this page-turner is one wild ride."

—Jennifer Ryan, *New York Times* bestselling author

"An emotional ride with characters that come alive on every single page. Sara brings real feelings to every scene she writes."

—Carolyn Brown, *New York Times* bestselling author

"This will satisfy Richardson's fans while welcoming new readers to a sweeping land of mountains, cowboys, and romance."

—*Publishers Weekly*

MORE THAN A FEELING

"Ruby is the kind of heroine you can't help but love and root for. Fans of Robyn Carr will undoubtedly enjoy the Heart of the Rockies series."

—*RT Book Reviews*

SOMETHING LIKE LOVE

"The author's compassion shines through her beautifully flawed and earnest characters and takes readers on an emotionally wrenching journey to the elusive goal of love."

—*Publishers Weekly*

ALSO BY SARA RICHARDSON

Heart of the Rockies Series

No Better Man
Something Like Love
"One Christmas Wish" (short story)
More Than a Feeling
"Rocky Mountain Wedding" (short story)

Rocky Mountain Riders Series

Hometown Cowboy
Comeback Cowboy
Renegade Cowboy
"Rocky Mountain Cowboy" (short story)
True-Blue Cowboy
"Rocky Mountain Cowboy Christmas" (short story)

Colorado Cowboy

A ROCKY MOUNTAIN RIDERS NOVEL

SARA RICHARDSON

FOREVER
New York Boston

Copyright © 2019 by Sara Richardson
Preview of *A Cowboy for Christmas* copyright © 2019 by Sara Richardson
Unbroken copyright © 2019 by Jennifer M. Voorhees
Preview of *Justified* copyright © 2019 by Jennifer M. Voorhees

Cover design by Elizabeth Turner Stokes
Cover copyright © 2019 by Hachette Book Group, Inc.

Forever
Hachette Book Group
1290 Avenue of the Americas, New York, NY 10104
forever-romance.com
twitter.com/foreverromance

First Edition: April 2019

Forever is an imprint of Grand Central Publishing. The Forever name and logo are trademarks of Hachette Book Group, Inc.

The publisher is not responsible for websites (or their content) that are not owned by the publisher.

The Hachette Speakers Bureau provides a wide range of authors for speaking events. To find out more, go to www.hachettespeakersbureau.com or call (866) 376-6591.

ISBNs: 978-1-5387-1227-6 (mass market), 978-1-5387-1226-9 (ebook)

Printed in the United States of America

OPM

10 9 8 7 6 5 4 3 2 1

To my anchors:
Will, AJ, and Kaleb

Acknowledgments

"Thank you" never seems like enough to offer the dedicated team at Forever who works so tirelessly on my behalf: Amy Pierpont, Gabi Kelly, Siri Silleck, Estelle Hallick. Working with you all continues to make me a better writer.

I also would not be able to do what I love without the fabulous team behind me at New Leaf Literary. Thank you Suzie Townsend and Cassandra Baim for your incredible support.

Without my amazing community of family and friends, I'm afraid I would get permanently stuck in one of my imaginary worlds. Thank you for inviting me to experience life and love instead of simply writing about it. I am blessed.

Chapter One

Charity Stone really wasn't in the mood to get arrested tonight.

For some rodeo champions, showing up at the local watering hole after a big win meant parading through the crowd, slapping high fives—or swats on the butt—while you accepted congrats and free drinks from the fans.

For Charity, however, showing up at the Tumble Inn after shaving two seconds off her best barrel racing time meant tipping her Stetson farther down on her forehead and moving swiftly enough that none of the rowdy spectators from earlier—or her other competitors, for that matter—could ask if she was interested in riding something else later. Thankfully, the last guy who'd asked her that hadn't pressed charges, but tonight she might not be so lucky.

The Tumble Inn happened to be a classier establishment than a lot of the bars she found herself in when she traveled the circuit. It was more of a sports bar and it wasn't uncommon to see families there together, eating wings and nachos and Gil's specialty burgers. Back in the day, the place had been an auto body shop, and it still had that homespun feel—the square brick structure, the concrete floors, the garage doors that had been upgraded with glass windows so they could open to the patio in the summer.

On a normal night, Charity loved to hang out here, but tonight the place was packed. Everyone and their grandmas had turned out for the big Topaz Falls Rodeo Days. And she did mean that literally. Elbowing her way through the crowd, Charity waved at Gracie Sullivan and her grandmother, Evie, who were seated at a bar-top table near the old jukebox.

"Ohmygawd!" The girl bounced off her stool and came running. "You were amazing tonight! Can you come over sometime and sign my saddle? I'm gonna be a barrel racer someday too!"

"That's what your mom told me." Naomi Cortez, one of Charity's good friends, had mentioned how terrified she was of her daughter learning how to race. Charity had reminded her there were much worse things a thirteen-year-old girl could be learning how to do. Trust her, she would know. Thus the reason she'd offered to help. "I told her I'd be happy to give you some pointers sometime."

"Really?" Gracie's red ringlets and expressive green eyes made it impossible to believe she had recently become a teenager.

"Really," Charity confirmed. "In fact, we're doing a youth clinic after the season winds down, and I'll make sure to save a spot for you." During the off-season, she and her posse—which included Gracie's uncle, Levi Cortez, along with Ty Forrester and Mateo Torres—planned to do a few mentoring clinics for kids who were interested in competing.

"Awesome!" Gracie threw her arms around Charity's shoulders, trapping her in a spastic hug. At least the girl had some serious upper body strength. That would work to her advantage as a racer.

"Ohmygawd, I can't wait! I'm already growing out my hair so it'll look just like yours does when you race, flowing behind you on the breeze." She fluffed her curls—curls Charity would've given anything for at one point in her life. Back when she'd actually given a damn about how she looked. Nowadays she kept her blond hair long so she could braid it down her back and keep it out of her way.

"Your hair is perfect the way it is," Charity said with the same sternness she used on her horse. "Got that? Looks have nothing to do with barrel racing." Having good genes had done her no favors in the sport, that was for sure. If she had a shiny penny for every time she'd been mistaken for the rodeo queen or a buckle bunny instead of an actual athlete, she'd be the ruler of her own ranch instead of working at the Cortezes' place in between competitions. "If you want to be a champion someday, you focus here"—she placed her hand over her heart—"and here." With her other hand she tapped her head. "That's all you need. You race smart and you race fierce and nothing will stop—"

"Excuse me." A waitress balancing a small tray slipped in between Charity and Gracie. "That gentleman over there wanted to send you a drink." The woman's eyes shone with delight. "It's a strawberry daiquiri."

A strawberry daiquiri? Charity let out a threadbare laugh and looked over to where the woman pointed. Ah, yes. The new guy on the scene. The bull rider who'd neglected to qualify for a score in tonight's competition. She should've anticipated this. New guys never seemed to get the memo that she wasn't interested in dating a cowboy. She wasn't interested in dating period.

"He must be into you!" Gracie hung on her shoulder. "Look at him! He's so hot!"

Hot if you liked a walking rubber stamp. Charity had met a hundred men just like him—the worn but expensive jeans, the black button-down western shirt with the sleeves rolled up to expose the thorny tattoo on his forearm. Then there was that suggestive smirk on his face, the one that swore he could make all her dreams come true.

Only she didn't need a man to help her with that. She did just fine on her own, thank you very much.

Charity turned back to the waitress. "Tell him I don't drink alcohol with fruit in it."

"Are you sure?" Disappointment crowded out the woman's smile. "It's kind of sweet, really. You see it all the time in the movies, but I've never been asked to deliver a pickup drink before."

That was because it worked only in the movies. "I'm sure." Charity smiled politely at the woman. "I don't want the drink." She had other things to do, like somehow convince Gracie that cowboys weren't the best part about competing on the circuit.

"Okay." The waitress drew out the word with a pained grimace and then scurried away.

"I bet he would've asked you on a date," Gracie said through a dreamy sigh. "He probably would've made a picnic dinner and taken you up to the mountains."

Charity could all but see the stars shining in the girl's eyes. What kind of romantic crap had she been watching?

"Oh! He probably has a truck too. So you guys could drive up to Topaz Peak and put blankets in the back and stare up at the stars." Gracie visibly swooned.

Yeah. Sure. Stare up at the stars. That had to be right at the top of Don Juan Bull Rider's agenda. "Listen, sweetie."

Charity put her arm around Gracie's shoulders. "If you really want to focus on becoming the best racer you can be, you'll have to put romance on the back burner for a while." Preferably until she was at least twenty-five and able to make healthy, informed choices. "That kind of goal is going to take all you've got—"

"You must be a martini kind of gal."

The deep, suave voice behind them immediately sent Charity into a whirl. Don Juan Bull Rider stood right behind her, holding out a murky-looking drink.

"I bet a woman like you wants it dirty instead of sweet." He dragged his gaze south and paused at each of the buttons on her plaid shirt as though he was imagining himself ripping them off.

Was this jerk for real? Charity looked around to see if her friends were playing a prank on her, but Mateo, Ty, and Levi stood near the bar talking to Dev Jenkins, one of Topaz Falls's finest. They didn't seem to be watching. Gracie, on the other hand? Her eyes were glued to the cowboy and her cheeks had turned a spellbound shade of red.

Charity's face had to be red too. Red hot. Molten. Anger churned from the very pit of her stomach up into her throat, but Gracie stood right next to her, so she tempered it with an indifferent shrug of her shoulders. "Thanks, but I don't drink." *Walk away.* He obviously wasn't going to, which meant she'd better before she lost her temper again.

"Maybe she wants it." The scumbag nodded toward Gracie, giving Charity's stomach a hard lurch.

"You mean the *thirteen-year-old*?"

"She sure don't look thirteen." The man's eyes had fixated on Gracie, weakening the feeble hold Charity had on her temper. Men had stared at her like that when she'd been thirteen too. Her mother's revolving door of boyfriends who'd looked exactly like this sleazeball. And she might've been helpless to do anything about it back then, but she sure as hell wasn't helpless anymore. "Gracie..." She gently directed the girl in the opposite direction. "Go sit with your grandma."

This suddenly seemed like the perfect night to get herself arrested.

In his six years on the force, Officer Dev Jenkins had learned there was no such thing as an off-duty cop. He'd been trained to keep watch, to notice things when no one else did, and he did not like what he saw unfolding over by the jukebox.

On a typical night, he enjoyed running into Charity Stone. He liked to see her laugh with her friends. Liked to see her long blond hair loose down around her shoulders. He liked to see her ride the way she had a few hours ago—fully in control, caught up in something she loved. But he did not like seeing her having to fend for herself when some jerk was obviously making her uncomfortable.

"Do you know that guy?" Dev asked Ty, Mateo, and Levi.

"What guy?" Ty set his beer on the bar and turned around.

"The dude with Charity?" Mateo asked.

"Yeah. That one." Dev couldn't look away. The man's sneer at Charity triggered every protective instinct he had and then some.

"He's the new kid," Levi said with a laugh. "Obviously. The only one stupid enough around here to hit on Charity."

"You think he hit on her?" Dev assessed the situation unfolding across the bar. If the arm waving was any indication, Charity had gotten riled about something, and the dumbass in question didn't seem to be backing down. In fact, he'd moved in even closer and touched her arm.

"Fifty bucks says she knocks him on his ass." Levi pulled out his wallet and found some cash.

"Hell no." Mateo shoved the money aside. "I'm not betting against Calamity Jane. I've seen her do some serious damage."

"We should find someone else to bet against her," Ty suggested. "Someone who doesn't know her."

"Seriously?" Dev shot them all a look. "She's fending off unwanted advances and all you yahoos can do is place bets?"

"Charity wouldn't want us to get involved." Levi clapped him on the back. "Trust us. She can handle herself."

"I don't doubt she can handle herself." He'd seen enough to know she was a strong woman. "But why should she have to?" They'd likely witnessed her sticking up for herself countless times out on the road, but she wasn't out on the road. She was home. In Topaz Falls. Seemed to him someone should have her back. He glanced over at her again. She'd officially invaded the guy's personal space and had the collar of his shirt twisted up in her fist. *Shit.* He handed his beer to Mateo. "I'm gonna take care of this before I have to arrest her for disturbing the peace."

"Oh boy," Mateo muttered. "This ought to be good."

"Try not to touch her," Ty called to his back. "She has some freakishly good reflexes."

"Fifty bucks says he has to arrest her for assaulting a police officer," Dev heard Levi say behind him.

Shaking his head, Dev made his way through the crowd until he'd reached Charity, who now had the dumbass pinned against the wall.

"You want to say that to me again?" she asked through clenched teeth.

Dev didn't give the man a chance to say anything. "Hey Charity..." He moved in next to her. "Can I talk to you for a minute?"

"Not now, Dev." She didn't look at him. Her eyes were focused, on fire. She tightened her forearm against the guy's neck.

"She's insane," the man whined, wriggling like a hog-tied calf trying to get free. "The woman is batshit crazy."

"Oh, you haven't seen anything yet," Charity threatened.

Dev rested his hand on her shoulder. "Let's take a walk." Under his fingertips, he thought he felt her muscles go soft. This time she did turn to look at him, full on in the face.

"He was hitting on Gracie Cortez," she said, her jaw trembling. "He offered her a *drink*." Dev wasn't prepared for the trauma in her expression—her blue eyes had opened too wide, dilated with a look of fear, and her mouth strained against emotion, reaching for anger but faltering. He'd seen the same look on the faces of countless victims when he'd come to their rescue. He had to get her out of here. "He's an asshole," Dev confirmed, keeping his eyes trained on hers. "But he's not worth the trouble." Slowly, he moved his hand to her wrist and tugged it away from the guy's neck. "Now let's take a walk."

She didn't fight him as he led her away, through the small crowd that had gathered, and out into the night air. Only when they'd cleared the sidewalk outside the doors did Charity wrench away from him. "What'd you do that for?" Her breath came fast and hard.

"What'd you mean, what did I do that for?" he demanded. "You were about to lose it in there. I don't want to have to make any arrests on my night off." That and he couldn't stand seeing the way that man had been staring at her with greedy eyes. Now that Dev had her outside, away from the scumbag, he'd definitely go in and give the cowboy a good scare.

"I don't need your help." Defiance reinforced her glare. "I'm *fine*."

"I never said you weren't." But he'd seen fine and he'd seen traumatized, and he knew the difference.

"You should be in there talking to that creep." Charity leaned her back against the brick wall, folding her arms, curling her fingers around the exposed flesh under the sleeves of her shirt. "He's the one who was soliciting a thirteen-year-old girl."

"I'll talk to him." He had no problem letting the man know that kind of idiot behavior wouldn't be tolerated in his town. "But I figured you should get some air." It had already helped. Her eyes were fiery again instead of wild, and the red splotches on her face had faded. Damn. For the life of him, he couldn't seem to look away.

She had no idea how much power she had over him, with that stubborn lift to her chin and the traces of righteous anger still evident in her features. Every time her eyes met his he felt his heart stutter. They were as blue as the topaz gems his dad found hidden in the mountains at the edge of town. Blue and mesmerizing. As always, Charity looked away too soon. He'd noticed that about her whenever they happened to be hanging out with their mutual friends. She always tried to hide, even when she was standing a foot away from him.

Dev had noticed a lot about her since she'd moved to town over two years ago. She said what she thought and stood her ground and carried herself with an air of impenetrable armor. But he'd also seen her cry at Mateo and Everly's wedding. And she always signed autographs at the local competitions, not caring that the line of kids waiting to see her typically stretched on and on along the fence. She would stay as long as it took, kneeling down to greet all of them on their level, taking the time to learn their names, to answer their questions, to pose for pictures. He'd noticed that was when she smiled the biggest. When she was sharing her passion with kids.

Now, though, she didn't smile. Her face had paled and dark circles seemed to spread under her eyes as she stood in the shadows of the bar.

That protective fight surged in him again, but he approached her slowly, stopping himself before he got too close. "You want to talk about anything?" Like why her hands still gripped her arms so tight. Or why that confrontation in there had drained the color from her face. Far as he knew, Charity didn't talk much about her past. There was likely a reason for that.

Even before she shook her head, he knew she'd refuse. "Nope. I'm perfectly fine." Her eyes steered clear of his.

Dev accepted the refusal with a nod. "Let me know if you ever change your mind."

Her face tensed, indicating that she wouldn't confide in him, even if he interrogated her, even if he gave her truth serum; she'd keep her secrets to herself.

He could've walked away, but he waited until her eyes met his once more. "Just so you know, if I wasn't a cop, I would've let you kick his ass."

Surprise bowed her eyebrows. "You think I could've?"

He had to laugh. "Oh yeah."

A trace of a smile perked up her mouth.

He smiled back and started to walk away.

"Dev?" Uncertainty quieted her voice.

He stopped. "Yeah?"

"Thanks for getting me out of there." Charity walked over to him and shocked him with a squeeze on his hand.

Chapter Two

Dev's hand was warmer than she'd anticipated. Warm and strong. His fingers brushed over Charity's knuckles, setting off a trill that went skimming all the way down her spine. "I should go." She quickly dropped his hand and backed up a step. "Gotta be up early tomorrow. Ace likes training in the mornings best. He's always raring to go. Right after sunup." As if Dev cared about her horse's training preferences.

What was it about this man that always made her babble? Charity wouldn't classify herself as bubbly and talkative. She didn't know what to do with Dev, that was the problem. He didn't treat her like one of the guys. Didn't look at her like Levi, Ty, and Mateo did. To be fair, she didn't look at him like one of the guys either. She could pick out her colleagues' flaws from ten feet away, but that was much harder to do with Dev. His eyes always seemed to draw her in. They were a deep shade of brown, calming and vigilant. They held a quiet wisdom and always seemed to be keeping watch.

She did her best to avoid those eyes. They did things. Made her feel things.

And his eyes weren't the only feature she did her best not to notice. She might not be interested in dating, but she could still appreciate a man's best features, and Dev had plenty of them. A powerful jaw. Light brown hair that never seemed to muss whether he'd been wearing his cowboy hat or not. Then there was his body...strong and broad. Taller than most of the cowboys she hung around with. And the way he filled out a pair of jeans or those uniform pants he wore...well, let's just say she always had to look at least twice.

"You okay?" Dev asked, tilting his head as though seeking out her gaze. He had this quiet confidence that unnerved her and intrigued her at the same time.

"I'm great." Totally and one hundred percent together. Not flustered at all. "Just tired. It's been a helluva day."

"I can give you a ride home." He gestured to his shined-up sheriff's department SUV across the parking lot.

"Oh. No thanks." Heat flashed across her face. She never should've touched his hand. Never should've reached out. Something had changed in the air between them.

"I walked." She busted out a smile. "We're only a few blocks from home. Actually, I like walking. It's good exercise. Energizing. Really gets the blood pumping. I read that walking modifies your nervous system so much that it can decrease anger and hostility." Jeezum. *Shut the hell up, Charity.* Everyone already knew she had anger issues. Didn't have to remind Dev after what had happened in the bar. Instead of making fun of her like her friends, though, he'd somehow defused her, which had been really...sweet.

Oh crap, she'd looked him in the eyes—those soothing reassuring eyes—and now she was trapped. She couldn't make herself look away.

"I like walking too," Dev said, obviously doing his best to take the edge off the awkwardness she'd managed to wedge between them with all of the random facts and weird staring.

Giving herself a slight head shake, Charity set out into the parking lot before she could continue to prattle on about the benefits of walking. "Thanks again, Dev," she muttered on her way past him. "You probably saved me a trip to the slammer. I owe you big."

"You don't owe me anything, Charity."

She paused to peek back over her shoulder.

Dev stood there and watched her walk away, but she couldn't read the look on his face. Was that a small smile? Maybe intrigue? Amusement? Didn't matter. She had to get out of here. Her thoughts and emotions never jumbled together this way. It was Don Juan Bull Rider's fault. He'd had to go and make eyes at Gracie, which in turn had knocked Charity back a good fifteen years into a past she rarely allowed herself to visit.

Doing her best to shrug off the evening, she walked through the abandoned field behind the Tumble Inn and made it to the sidewalk at the edge of Main Street, already feeling some of the tension melt away. The sun had started to set over the peaks to the west, swirling the sky with orange and pink and, on the very fringes, a purplish glow that signaled night was coming. A long sigh expelled the rest of her hostility toward Don Juan Bull Rider. She swore those mountains had magical powers.

Topaz Falls was a world away from the flat plains of Oklahoma—and the colorless memories of her past. When Levi Cortez had first invited her out here for an event a few years ago, she hadn't planned on falling in love with the place. She'd been a lot of places in her career, and she'd never fallen in love with any of them. But the ridiculous beauty here somehow worked its way under her skin and made a place for itself in her heart.

Charity slowed her pace when she turned onto Main Street. It was like stepping onto the set of one of those Hallmark movies. Not that she watched them. Okay, she'd watched one. *Once.* It came on and she couldn't find the remote, thanks to hosting a poker game with the guys the night before. They'd been fighting over whether to watch baseball or NASCAR, and in the struggle, somehow they'd cued up the Hallmark Channel and then they'd gone and lost the remote. It took her a whole day to find it stuffed deep into the couch, and in the meantime, she'd manually turned on the TV for some background noise. The movie hadn't been *that* bad. A small-town love story where everything got seriously complicated but worked out in the end. And, sure, okay, it had made her tear up a little.

Anyway, downtown Topaz Falls had that same Hallmarky feel—cobblestone sidewalks, iron lampposts that were decorated for each season. Currently they were adorned with banners touting the Topaz Falls Rodeo Days along with cheesy props like horseshoes and saddles. Nostalgic little shops like the ice cream parlor and general store were intermixed with more modern establishments, like her friend Darla's wine bar and chocolate confectionary. But all of them had that same welcoming appeal with their large storefront windows and striped awnings stretching overhead. Being that it was nearly summer, flowers plumed from hanging pots that were clustered around small dwarfed trees growing right out of the sidewalks in the middle of every block.

She'd never imagined herself living in a quintessential town—or becoming attached to it—but now that she was here, she couldn't picture herself leaving.

After passing the Chocolate Therapist, Charity veered left onto Columbine Drive, where she'd lucked out with one of the best rentals in town. It sat in a sprawling neighborhood, among older custom homes with large, half-acre lots. Hers had been built at the end of the street, backing to the river. It wasn't a palace by any means, just a simple A-frame log structure. But the floor-to-ceiling windows on the backside of the house had the best view of Topaz Mountain towering beyond the river in the distance. In fact, that's where she'd sit now. In her overstuffed chair positioned right next to the window so she could watch the sunset—

Wait. Charity squinted against the sun's glare. Was that a car in her driveway? She jogged around the bend in the street until she could get a better view. Yes. There was a beat-up Honda Civic sitting in her driveway. With Oklahoma plates.

Dread seeped in and drowned all the good feelings her walk home had filled her with. She sprinted the rest of the way and cut across the green lawn. When the driver's side came into view, Charity stopped cold. What on earth was her sister doing here?

The door swung open and Melody popped out. "Surprise!" she called as though it was the most normal thing in the world for her to stop by.

Charity couldn't move. She hadn't seen her sister in ten years, but it could've easily been twenty with the way those years had changed Melody. Her once full-bodied blond hair hung limply around her shoulders. And she'd lost weight. Even with that big smile, her face seemed sunken, almost skeletal.

Charity shifted her gaze back to the car, her eyes searching. "Oh god." Bodie, her thirteen-year-old nephew, sat in the passenger seat, staring out the window at them.

"Well, aren't you going to say something?" Melody demanded, holding out her arms like she wanted a hug.

A hug? Was this some kind of sick joke? The last time they'd stood face-to-face Melody had told Charity she never wanted to see her again. She'd cut Charity off from the nephew she'd adored. She'd insisted she didn't want Charity's help or opinion on anything having to do with raising a child.

"What're you doing here?" The words tripped out of Charity's mouth. Even with the setting sun beaming on her face, a hollow coldness settled in her stomach.

"What do you mean?" Melody kept that phony smile intact. "I wanted to see my little sis! And Bodie wanted to see his auntie!" She swung her head toward the car. "Come on out, Bodes! Say hi to Auntie Charity!"

The kid took his time getting out of the car, which gave Charity the opportunity to face her sister. "You said you never wanted to see me again." Because she'd confronted Melody about her lifestyle. Charity had worried about Bodie back then. He'd been only three, and Melody kept moving around, living with whoever she happened to be dating at the time, just like their mom. Charity had seen the same evidence of neglect she'd experienced in her own childhood. The constant parties in the house—the drugs and alcohol lying around. "So what's changed, Mel?" she asked. "Do you need money or something? Are you in some kind of trouble?"

Her sister sighed loudly. "Of course not. Everything's fine. Can't we just forget about the past?" There was an emptiness to the words, but Charity didn't have time to address it before Bodie joined them.

At the sight of her nephew, Charity's heart swelled. Good god. He'd grown up. The little cherub she remembered still hid in Bodie's features, but his dark hair had grown out, feathering down around his jaw, and he stood only a few inches shorter than her. Back when she used to babysit him, he'd grinned all the time—a big open-mouthed grin that had radiated pure delight. But now his face held a cold hardness, and those blue eyes that looked so much like her own drooped with disinterest. "Bodie..." her eyes stung. So much for never crying. One sight of this boy she'd loved was all it took. "God, it's good to see you." Did he remember her? Did he remember how she used to carry him around everywhere when he was a toddler? How she'd take him to the house Charity shared with her mother for days at a time while her sister was off getting high with her friends?

"Say hi to your aunt." Melody poked him in the ribs.

"Hey." He raised his head but didn't look at her directly.

"He's shy," Melody said, brushing aside his indifference. "But such a looker, right? He definitely inherited our genes."

Charity's throat tightened. She couldn't stop looking at him. How could this be little Bodie? *I'm sorry.* The words got stuck. She was sorry she hadn't been able to help him, to give him a different life from the one she'd known. But after she'd confronted Melody, Charity hadn't been able to find her sister.

"We were hoping we could bunk up with you for a night." Melody slung an arm around her son. "We're on our way out west. I got a lead on a job in California, so we're making a road trip out of it. Right, Bodes?"

"Right," he muttered, staring a hole through his black combat boots.

Charity assessed her sister. "You got a job?"

Melody laughed. "Don't sound so surprised. You're not the only one who can be successful, you know."

"I know." But success required staying clean and avoiding the kinds of losers her sister couldn't seem to live without. At least back then. Maybe she'd changed. "What's the job?" she asked, hoping for Bodie's sake her sister had an answer.

"A friend of mine works at a winery in Napa. She said they'd hire me no problem. Doesn't it sound perfect? Selling wine? Meeting hot guys who come in for a tasting?"

"Sure. Yeah. That sounds great." Charity couldn't seem to smile back at her sister. It might've sounded great if it hadn't been for the comment about hot guys. Her sister had a pattern of searching for a man to rescue her. The problem was, most of the men she ended up with weren't exactly white knights.

"So can we stay tonight or what?" Melody demanded.

"Of course you can stay." Charity finally caught Bodie's gaze and smiled at him. Maybe it was good they were moving away from Oklahoma. Maybe her sister needed a new start. If she really wanted to try, Charity would offer all of her support. "You can stay as long as you want."

"Thanks, sis!" Melody did hug her then, squeezing tight enough that Charity could smell the lingering scent of pot emanating from her sister's hair.

That was all it took to remind her she definitely didn't live in a Hallmark movie.

Chapter Three

Charity had never considered herself the hostess with the mostest but even she could make a mean batch of blueberry pancakes. She eyed the small puddles of batter she'd poured onto the griddle, and stood at the ready to flip them as soon as those tiny bubbles appeared.

Normally this cooking breakfast gig wasn't her thing. Heck, she couldn't remember the last time she'd even had company. For her, the term *guest room* meant storage for her extra saddles and ropes and other gear she would've kept in a barn, if she had one. But she hadn't minded the company as much as she'd initially thought she would.

Sure, last night had been a little awkward. She'd thrown some burgers on the grill and she, Melody, and Bodie had sat down to a late dinner. Communication from her nephew had been sparse, consisting mainly of grunted answers to questions, but she supposed that was to be expected of a thirteen-year-old kid who didn't know her from the clerk at the grocery store. Melody had chatted on and on about their childhood as though it had been nothing short of a grand adventure—the frequent moves, the glamorous men their mother had dated. Not quite the way Charity remembered it, but she had to give her sister credit for trying to put a positive spin on things.

After dinner, she'd cleared enough space in the guest room for Melody, and then blew up her camping mattress and stuck it in her office for Bodie. Before they'd said good night, her sister had grown suddenly serious when she thanked Charity for letting them stay. Instead of the flighty act, Melody had looked her in the eyes. *No, really. Thank you, Char. It's so good to see you,* she'd said.

That was the sole reason Charity stood in the kitchen flipping pancakes. That was the reason she'd texted Levi, Mateo, and Ty to tell them she wouldn't make it to their morning training session. The look on her sister's face last night had given her hope. Maybe Mel had really changed. Maybe she was truly trying to seek out a better life for her and her son. God, she hoped so.

Steam rose off the pancakes and Charity flipped them over, admiring the golden brown crust. They looked exactly like the pancakes her friend Everly Brooks made at the Farm Café every day, though they wouldn't taste the same. Everly refused to give up the secret ingredient that had made her pancakes famous.

Tapping the spatula against the tiled countertop, Charity glanced at the clock. Already almost nine. If she let Mel and Bodie sleep in anymore, the pancakes would get cold. Besides that, last night her sister had said they needed to get an early start this morning.

Leaving the spatula next to the stove, she crossed through the open-concept kitchen and living room to the hall where the two extra bedrooms were. Melody's door stood open, so she peeked inside.

It was dark. "Mel?" Charity stepped into the room. The beginnings of panic prickled across her skin. Where was her sister's suitcase? Why was the bed made?

She walked to the dresser, her eyes fixated on a small scrap of paper sitting in the very center. The flashes of panic all merged into a searing heat that rose straight to her chest.

Char—I need you to watch Bodie for a while. Until I get some things figured out. I know you'll take care of him. It won't be long. I promise. Tell him I'll be back soon.—Mel

She promised? She *promised*? If she remembered right, Melody's promises didn't exactly count for much. She'd wanted to believe her sister had changed, but this was exactly the kind of thing she used to pull when Bodie was a baby. She'd show up unannounced and tell Charity she needed to run errands. A few days—or in some cases a week—later she'd come back to pick him up and explain that she'd met up with some friends and they'd gone out partying. A familiar anger snaked through her. Charity never would've minded watching him, but the manipulation—the similarity to their mom's treatment of them—got to her.

"Where's my mom?"

The groggy voice behind her turned her spine to steel. Charity placed her hand over the note and slid it against her palm before crumpling it in her fist.

"Did she already pack up the car?" Bodie asked, suddenly sounding more alert. "Why didn't she wake me up?"

A hard swallow knotted Charity's throat. She turned to face her nephew, still seeing that little boy she'd wanted so badly to protect all those years ago. He might act tough and indifferent now, but his hair was mussed and his mouth drooped with worry, and she couldn't do it. She couldn't tell him Melody dumped him off with her. "She had some errands to run." Before he could see the anger on her face, she slipped past him and booked it back to the kitchen.

"What errands?" Bodie followed behind her.

Smoke billowed off the now-blackened pancakes on the griddle, allowing her to buy a few seconds while she scraped them into the sink. When she turned back around, Bodie stood a few feet away, a knowing scowl on his face. "She's gone, isn't she?" His blue eyes were steeled, stone cold.

How many times had she worn that same look when her mother had left them a note? *Won't be home tonight! Make sure you get off to school on time in the morning.* Or the classic *Had the chance to go away for the weekend! There's food in the refrigerator.* It didn't matter if Charity had been in first grade or sixth. She'd wanted her mom there. She'd wanted to be worth sticking around for. And most of the time her mom decided she wasn't.

Avoiding Bodie's questioning glare, Charity went to turn off the stove top. "It's okay. Your mom will be back soon." She would make sure. She would track Melody down and drag her back here. There was no way she would let her sister get away with leaving her son while she went off and partied or whatever. He deserved better. He deserved to have a parent who put him first.

Rushing back to the sink, Charity doused the pile of blackened pancakes and the griddle, steam rising up to her face. "Why don't you get your shoes on?" she called to Bodie over her shoulder. She had no idea how long Melody had been gone, but it didn't matter. Charity knew exactly who could help find her.

Bodie didn't move. "Where are we going?"

"Out for breakfast." She wrangled a smile. "Obviously my pancakes didn't turn out so hot, but you'll love the ones my friend makes at the local café." That's where Dev hung out most mornings. "Come on," Charity prodded, waving her nephew toward the front door. "I'll even let you order chocolate milk."

"I'm not three anymore," Bodie snapped. "I don't like chocolate milk."

Oh, that anger. He held on to it the same way she did— like a shield. That's what you did when you felt abandoned. It's what she had done. In some ways, the anger had saved her. But she also knew what hid underneath it. Fear. If he pushed her away first, she wouldn't have the chance to reject him.

"Fine. Don't get chocolate milk." Charity shoved her wallet into her back pocket and opened the front door, pausing to wait for him to lace up his boots. "But I feel it's my duty to inform you that this particular chocolate milk is Everly's special blend with real cocoa and a dash of vanilla in the creamiest organic whole milk you're ever tasted. Trust me. Everyone in this town loves chocolate milk."

Bodie grunted something inaudible as he tied his boots in jerky motions.

"What was that?" Charity asked.

Her nephew stood. "I said I might try it," he muttered on his way out the door.

"Great." After locking the deadbolt, she traipsed along after him. When they'd both climbed into her truck and their seat belts were securely fastened, she backed down the driveway. "This'll be fun. Us spending the day together." She tried to keep her tone optimistic instead of panicked. What was she supposed to do with a brooding thirteen-year-old all day? "We used to do that all the time when you were little." It had been easier back then. She'd hand the kid a Matchbox car and take him outside and they'd be content for hours, building tracks in the dirt for their miniature Grand Prix. Something told her Bodie had outgrown innocent fun a long time ago.

"I don't remember." Her nephew glared out the passenger's window, his shoulders so stiff it had to put a crick in his neck.

"We used to have a great time together." A wistfulness sighed through the words. She couldn't help it. Emotion welled up inside of her. "I used to take you to the park. The one by the river back home," she murmured, lost in the memory. "It had the tallest slide I've ever seen. But you weren't afraid of it. You'd beg me to take you down, over and over. We'd laugh the whole way—"

"Can we cut the crap?" Her nephew had finally turned his face to hers. A brazen resentment clenched his jaw. "I don't know you. Haven't seen you in ten years. So don't pretend you care about me. Mom should've brought me to Grandma's house instead."

Oh yeah. That would've been great. Her mother could give grandparent hugs and kisses with the best of them but when it came to actually being responsible and supervising a child, she tended to flounder. But it seemed Bodie actually loved his grandma. He definitely didn't love Charity. That much was obvious. She tightened her grip on the steering wheel and pulled into a parking spot at the café. "I didn't know where you and your mom were." She struggled to hold back the threatening tears.

Bodie ignored her. "Like you said, my mom'll come back. She never stays away long. So you don't have to pretend you're happy we just showed up on your doorstep. I can take care of myself until she comes back." Without giving her the chance to respond, he got out of the truck.

"I thought cops ate doughnuts."

Dev wasn't sure if he should shake his head or roll his eyes at the worn-out adage courtesy of his friend Ty Forrester, so he did both. "I'm a mountain cop. I can't eat doughnuts." Hell, just last week, he'd had to chase Pauly Gleeson's drunk brother half a mile up a mountain when he'd pulled him over for speeding. Then after he'd arrested him he had to haul his butt all the way back to his SUV. If he ate too many doughnuts, that kind of thing would be impossible.

"Doughnuts sure look a hell of a lot better than that." Ty slid into the booth across from him. As usual, the Farm Café was packed. Even with the upgrades his friends Mateo Torres and Everly Brooks had made to the farmhouse-turned-restaurant, nearly every table was occupied except for a few in the back. Dev folded up his newspaper and tossed it on the bench next to him to make room for the large breakfast Ty would inevitably order. From what he'd seen, bull riders tended to burn a lot of calories.

"What is that anyway?" His friend eyed the food on Dev's plate.

"It's Everly's specialty—quinoa egg scramble." And she always threw in some meat for him too. Sometimes bacon, but today it was her special fennel sausage.

His friend grimaced. "It looks like something that came out of the garbage disposal."

"I heard that." Everly hovered nearby, refilling coffee mugs over at the Cortez brothers' table.

"Watch out," Mateo called from behind the dinerlike counter. "My wife doesn't serve customers who insult her cooking."

Ty immediately raised his hands. "No one's insulting anything." He shot Everly a grin. "You know I love your cooking."

"Yeah, yeah, yeah." She passed them by with a smile too sweet to be sassy. "I'll be right with you, Ty."

Dev had to laugh. Everly might be sweet, but she had no problem making Ty wait for his breakfast. He finished off the last few bites of his scramble and pushed away the plate, keeping an eye on his watch. "So, what's up, Forrester?" He had to start his shift at nine, but in his experience, Ty joined him for breakfast only when he had something to discuss. "You got something on your mind?"

"Actually, I do." His friend leaned in. "We need to talk about your campaign."

Here we go. Dev sipped his coffee, fueling up for a day of discussions exactly like this one. Lately he couldn't walk down the street without someone bringing up the county sheriff election. When his boss had told Dev he planned to retire, he'd encouraged the deputy to throw his hat into the ring as his successor, but Dev had never dreamed it would be a possibility. Now the election was only a few months away, and, according to the unofficial polls conducted by the local newspaper, he was the frontrunner. "What'd you mean my campaign?"

"It's time to get serious," Ty told him. "We need to ramp things up. Take the publicity to a higher level."

"That shouldn't be too difficult considering I haven't exactly run a campaign." Other than his friends posting signs on their land. "Actually, I don't plan to do anything else before the election. I figure most people around here already know me. They don't need help deciding whether they think I'm right for the job." He didn't want the job if the people didn't have confidence in him anyway.

"That's it?" Ty turned around to the Cortez brothers. "Did you hear that? He's giving in. Going down without a fight."

"Going down?" Levi held up the most recent edition of the local paper. "Didn't you read the opinion section? According to Betty Osterman, Dev Jenkins is—and I quote—not only devastatingly handsome, he's also the right man for the job."

Everyone seated at the nearby tables cracked up.

Yeah, yeah, yeah. This was exactly why he didn't love discussing the election. While his friends supported him, they also used it as an opportunity to razz him. "Can I help it if the over-sixty female demographic finds me charming?" At least he knew he'd get a couple of votes. "Why do you care so much about the election anyway?" he asked Ty. His friend had never shown an interest in local politics.

"I figure if you become the county sheriff you can make all my parking tickets go away."

"You're serious?" He let his expression do the talking.

"Hell, yeah, I'm serious. Those suckers are expensive."

"Then maybe you shouldn't park your truck illegally any-more," Dev suggested pleasantly.

"Come on, man—"

Thankfully, Everly chose that moment to scurry over to the table. "Hey, Ty. Sorry for the wait. Can I get you some-thing to eat?"

He eyed what was left of Dev's scramble. "I'll go with two eggs over easy and as much bacon as you're willing to put on the plate."

"Got it." She jotted down the order with a grin. "What about you, Dev? Want a refill on your coffee?"

"Thanks, but I'll be heading out pretty quick." Even quicker now that the election had come up. If he did get elected, he'd be honored to serve, but all the attention was starting to get old.

"Here's your check." She handed him the small receipt with the typical discount she gave him for being a public officer. He used to try to talk her out of it, but she insisted, so he left the difference in the tip.

"Have a good day," Everly said before rushing off to the next table.

As soon as she was gone, Ty started in again on the campaign thing, but the door opened across the room and Charity walked in, which meant all Dev heard from his friend was *blah, blah, blah.*

Charity seemed to scan the restaurant nervously. A kid trudged behind her like he was marching death row. He seemed to be dressed like it too—black T-shirt, black jeans, and tall black boots. Quite the contrast from the other kids in this town with their big belt buckles and cowboy boots.

Charity gestured for the kid to sit in a booth over by the windows. Everly greeted them both and handed them menus, but Charity simply set hers on the table and continued standing.

"Are you listening to me?" Ty asked.

"No." He was too busy watching Charity. Her eyes landed on him then, and she said something to Bodie before heading over.

Dev watched her the whole way. She had that walk...the one that stirred hunger. It was those tight jeans she wore, ripped and faded, conformed to the curve of her hips, her thighs...

"Dev, I need to talk to you." She stopped at the end of their table.

He glanced at Ty. "Guess you need to find another place to sit."

Confusion crumpled his friend's face. "What could you two possibly have to talk about that requires privacy?"

Charity leaned in, her long blond braid spilling down over her shoulder. She likely meant to look menacing, but Dev picked up on a touch of worry pulling at her mouth.

"Take a walk, Ty." She said it like a warning.

"Fine." The man scooted his way out of the booth, but pointed at Dev. "Think about that campaign. Okay? I could help get you some publicity."

Dev gave Ty a noncommittal nod and drained the rest of his coffee while Charity slid in across from him.

For the second time in two days she didn't have the strong, in-control look about her. He set down his mug and leaned into the table. "What's up?"

"I need you to find my sister." She sat straight and tall, chin cocked up, but a tremble hid in her voice.

"Your sister?" Charity had family around these parts? He'd obviously missed something.

"Yes. My older sister. Melody." It came out in a whisper. "She showed up at my house last night with my thirteen-year-old nephew and then sometime while I was asleep she took off."

Dev let that register. Charity had a sister. And a nephew. It reminded him there was a lot he didn't know about her. "Why would she take off?"

"Because she's a mess." The words ended in a deep, heartsick sigh. "It doesn't matter why. I just need you to find her for me."

If only life were that easy. He'd looked for his own birth mother for years, and even with all of the resources at his disposal, he had yet to find her. "Did your sister say anything? Like where she was going or when she'd be back?"

Charity pulled a crumpled piece of paper out of her pocket and slid it across the table like she didn't want anyone to see it. "She left this note and asked me to take care of Bodie for a while."

Dev glanced at the scrawled words. At least she'd left a note. That was more than his mother had done.

"I'm not sure what to do with him." Charity peeked over her shoulder in the direction of her nephew again. "The kid hates me. I think he hates everyone."

Dev did a quick assessment. Everything about Bodie seemed dark—his clothes, his mood. He sat in one of the best spots to see the view of the mountains out the window, but still he glowered with what seemed to be worse than typical teenaged angst. "Thirteen-year-old boys aren't known for being sunshine and roses." He hadn't been, that was for damn sure. Of course he hadn't looked like he'd just stepped off the set of *The Walking Dead* either. He refocused on the woman sitting across from him. "He has no idea where his mom would've gone?"

"No. She didn't tell him anything." The expression of soft concern on her face hardened into that same determined look she wore when she rode. "We need to file a missing persons report. Get everyone out there looking for her."

Oh, man. She wasn't gonna want to hear this. He braced himself. "I can't do that."

"Why not?" Her glare deepened, but it didn't scare him. That glare held his attention.

"Melody left a note. Said she's coming back. She asked you to watch her kid." All of which was perfectly legal and normal for a family member to do. "Technically, she's not missing. In fact, it sounds like she wanted a vacation."

Judging from the red hue on Charity's face, that was the wrong thing to say.

"Well, she can't do that. She can't take a vacation from her kid without telling anyone. She can't just dump him off with a relative he doesn't even know. It's not right."

"I agree with you." Dev raised his hands to remind her they were on the same side. "But I can't officially file a missing persons report." He couldn't waste police resources because Charity was pissed at her sister.

"Then what am I supposed to do?" she demanded. "I travel. I have to train. He should be in school right now..."

She had a point. If her sister hadn't gotten the boy's absence excused, they could always go the truancy route. But that could get ugly too. "We could call social services, but if they can't locate her, they'll want him to stay with you anyway."

"Why?" This seemed to be news to her. Not surprising. Most people didn't understand how social services worked.

"The state believes it's better for him to be with family. That's always their first option."

"But he doesn't want to be here." Her cheeks caved. "He doesn't want to be with me."

Dev took in the redness in her eyes, the very slight quiver in her lower lip. Holy shit...Charity looked like she was about to cry. That proved only one thing. She cared a whole lot more than she was admitting. "Maybe he needs to be with you," he said, being careful with his tone. He didn't want to overstep, but he'd seen plenty of situations like this. "If we call social services and you refuse temporary custody, he'll go into the foster care system."

"Maybe that would be better." She looked down at the table. "Maybe he'd end up with a good family. Maybe he'd get what he needed."

Was she being serious? Dev stared at her in disbelief. "It's not better. I was in two foster homes before my parents adopted me. The people were decent enough, but I was never part of their families. I never had a connection with any of them." He'd spent those two years trying not to screw up, trying not to get attached to anyone, trying to be invisible so he wouldn't have to move again.

Charity leaned over the table and gaped at him. "You're adopted?"

He didn't know why she looked so surprised. "My parents adopted me out of the foster care system when I was six." Young enough he could still bond with them. That would be much harder for a thirteen-year-old.

Charity simply stared at him for a minute, as though digesting that information. "Why did you have to go into foster care?" she finally asked.

"I don't remember much. According to my parents, my birth mother couldn't take care of me. She abandoned me at a fire station when I was four." He tried so hard to see those memories—but they were blank. He had no recollection of his mom's face, or the day she'd dropped him off and drove away. He'd pieced things together from what the social worker and his own parents had told him, but that was it.

"But they're good to you? Your parents?" Charity asked. "You're glad you got adopted, right?"

"Yes." He met her eyes. "They're amazing. I love my parents. But it doesn't happen that way for most foster kids, Charity. Most foster kids bounce around from home to home until they're eighteen and then they're on their own. They have no one." His had been one of the few miracle stories. "My parents were older. They'd tried to have a baby for years, but never could. My mom was a second cousin of my social worker, and that's how I got placed."

Charity seemed to consider what he'd shared.

"But maybe you won't even have to worry about it. Maybe your sister will come back in a few days." Or maybe she wouldn't come back at all. He didn't say it. "Can you figure out any reason she'd want to up and leave?"

"She's probably in trouble." Charity didn't hesitate with her answer. "It wouldn't be the first time. As far as I know, she's been living in Oklahoma. I haven't seen either of them in ten years. She showed up last night and said they were on their way to California so she could get a new job. Start over."

It would've sounded reasonable except for the rush. If she'd given Charity no warning, maybe there was a reason she'd had to leave so fast. "Would she have wanted to start over without Bodie?"

"I don't know. I don't think so." The words held no conviction. Charity's uncertain gaze locked with his. "When he was younger, she used to leave him at my mom's sometimes without telling anyone where she was going. But she always came back for him. I do believe she cares for him."

Dev nodded. "Could she be staying with friends or relatives? Maybe at your mom's place?"

"My mom lives in Texas with her new husband," Charity muttered. "And Melody has never been one to make solid plans. So I don't even know if she's really on her way to California." Her lost gaze drifted back to her nephew. "Please help me find her, Dev," she murmured. "Bodie needs her."

He wasn't so sure about that. If Charity's sister was the hot mess she sounded like, going home might not be the best place for him. "I don't know that we can find her. But I can do some checking around."

"Thank you." For the second time in less than twenty-four hours, she touched his hand.

The feel of her skin sparked that same slow burn it had in the parking lot at the bar last night. Maybe this was his chance to convince her to give him a shot. She needed help, and he needed her to see he wasn't some jackass cowboy. "I'm happy to hang out with Bodie too," he said. "If you need someone to keep an eye on him once in a while. I could bring him out to the ranch. Might be good for him."

Right on cue, her expression tightened. "No. Thanks, but it's okay. I can manage on my own for a few days."

"I'm sure you can." Like Mateo, Levi, and Ty had said last night, she was used to handling things on her own. But maybe that was because no one had ever been there for her. Maybe all she needed was someone to remind her she didn't have to do everything alone. Dev gathered up his newspaper and slid out of the booth. "If you ever change your mind, you know where to find me." He brushed a light touch across her shoulder so she'd know he meant it, and then he left for work.

Chapter Four

What *in the Sam Hill?* Charity thrashed out from under her quilt and blinked until she could get a look at the clock on her dresser. Two o'clock in the morning and one of her neighbors was gunning his diesel engine.

It had to be that old biker dude on the corner. The man partied hard and was known for tearing up and down the street on his Harley at all hours of the night. She was all for living it up in your later years, but seriously. "Some of us aren't retired," she muttered, scrambling to get out of bed. She stalked to the window and threw the curtain aside.

High-powered headlights cut across her vision, temporarily blinding her. Tires screeched against concrete. She rubbed the explosion of colorful dots out of her vision and squinted. Wait just one minute...

That was her truck!

It lurched backward, the tires squealing again, and then shot forward across her front lawn, cutting grooves into the grass and passing by her window close enough that she could see her nephew behind the wheel before it stalled again.

"Bodie!" What the hell was he doing behind the wheel of her truck? She cranked open the window. "Stop!" This had to be a nightmare. There was no way her nephew was driving across her lawn right now. Actually, he wasn't driving because he'd killed the engine. "Stay there!" she yelled, before snatching a sweatshirt off the dresser. She booked it through the house and paused to thrust her feet into a pair of flip-flops before rushing through the front door.

The engine started and truck stuttered forward again. "Bodie!" she yelled, sprinting behind the truck as it bounced across the lawn and back into the street. "Have you lost your mind? Stop!" Maybe he was sleepwalking...

Across the street a door opened. "What's all the noise?" Mrs. Lummens screeched.

"Nothing! Everything's under control!" Charity rushed alongside the truck, but before she made it to the driver's side, Bodie peeled out and the truck lurched its way down the street.

"You've got to be kidding me." Charity shuffle-ran back to the garage and threw it open. She hadn't been biking since her friend Cassidy had forced her to ride up a mountain last fall, but right now the bike was her only option. Scraping her toes on the concrete, she ran her hardly used mountain bike down the driveway and hopped on, pedaling hard enough that her quads cramped almost immediately. What was Bodie thinking? He was only thirteen years old! He couldn't drive a freaking truck down the street at two o'clock in the morning.

Actually, it appeared he *could* drive the truck, Charity realized when she came around the bend in the road. Bodie seemed to be getting the hang of it. The truck picked up speed and took a hard right at the end of the street, disappearing from sight.

Charity pedaled faster, her legs stiff from the cold. "Come on, come on." She was in good shape. She could catch him. She *had* to catch him and stop him before someone else did.

Thankfully, there was no traffic. The bike whizzed past the shops on Main Street, her reflection speeding from window to window. Oh god, she looked like a lunatic! Wild hair, half dressed, wearing flip-flops in what had to be forty-degree temperatures. "I'm gonna kill him." But truthfully, she couldn't blame this on him.

She should've been paying attention. All afternoon, he'd acted fine. She should've known better. She'd had some of those same wounds inflicted on her by her own mom, and she'd always acted fine too. At dinnertime she made him a sandwich—it was either that or boxed macaroni and cheese—and he'd taken it into the guest room. Before she'd gone to bed, she'd stuck her head in to check on him but he'd simply grunted that he was fine.

Of course he wasn't fine. His mom had left him.

Sorrow squeezed in to edge out the anger. She took another hard right turn and sped past the ice cream shop just in time to see the truck reel around the corner at the end of the street. Instead of tailing him, Charity cut across the small park next to the theater. He had to be headed toward the highway. If she crossed through the alley, she could easily catch him near the rodeo grounds.

Puffing out heavy breaths, she coasted between the restaurants and shops. Everything was dark and deserted. Quiet except for the occasional screech of tires somewhere nearby. Her legs ached but she forced them to keep cycling. *Faster.* She had to cut him off before he got out of town or she'd have no choice but to sic Dev on him.

Just as she neared the end of the alleyway, there was a crash—the sound of steel cracking, breaking. *Oh god. Dear god.* She accelerated down another block until the view opened up. There was her truck mashed into the copper statue of famed bull rider Luis Cortez in the parking lot of the rodeo grounds. The sculpture now leaned dangerously low, threatening to topple into the dirt.

"Bodie!" Charity ditched the bike and ran the rest of the way, a hit of nausea bringing on a cold sweat.

Steam rose up from the crumpled hood of her truck with a hiss, snaking into the air. The windshield had shattered. Right as she reached the truck, the driver's door groaned and opened. Bodie scrambled out. "Oh god, oh god, oh god." He raked his hand through his hair.

"Are you okay?" Charity wheezed, out of breath from the ride and the horror of imagining him slumped over the wheel unconscious. Or dead. *Don't throw up. Do. Not. Throw. Up.* Her stomach always rebelled against adrenaline. It was a common practice for her to throw up before and after a competition, but she never did it in front of anyone. "Are you hurt?"

"Don't think so." He looked down at his body as though he couldn't believe it. "I'm fine."

Well, she was not fine. Her bones shook. Everything shook. "What were you thinking, stealing my truck?"

"I wasn't gonna steal it. I was only borrowing it." Bodie's wide worried eyes made him look like a little boy again. "I swear. I was only gonna use it to go find my mom. Then I was gonna bring it back."

"You can't borrow someone's car. You're *thirteen*!" Charity shouted. She could hardly hear anything over the rush of blood in her ears. "You could've been killed. You could've killed someone else!" Her stomach heaved again, but she gagged back the nausea.

"My mom lets me drive sometimes," he shot back. He probably meant to sound angry, but his voice was still too ragged with fear.

Charity paced away from him to calm herself down. How many times had she been forced to handle things on her own when her mom was busy working a cowboy on the circuit?

"I'm sorry about your truck," he muttered behind her. "I didn't mean to hit that thing. I tried to turn but I was going too fast..."

"It's okay." A slow, steady inhale brought clarity. He was okay. That was all that mattered. He was okay...

Sirens whirred in the distance. Damn it, that was not okay. Bodie didn't need this on his record.

"The cops." Fear hollowed his voice. "This is gonna be bad, isn't it?"

Without answering, Charity jogged back to where she'd dropped the bike and awkwardly lifted it off the ground. Staggering against the weight of it, she hoisted it into the back of her pickup.

Bodie came over to join her. "What're you doing?"

"When they ask you what happened, tell them I was driving." Charity looked at him sternly. For once, the kid didn't look away. "Understand? No matter what they say. No matter what questions they ask. You tell them you were riding with me."

"Really?" Her nephew's eyes went round again before narrowing into a look of disbelief. "You're gonna cover for me?"

"I have to." Maybe it wasn't the most responsible thing. to do, but she couldn't let him take this on by himself. He already had enough to deal with. "I don't even want to know what they'll do to you if they find out you did this." God, that statue was the town's pride and joy. It had taken years to raise the funds to have it made, and her nephew had turned it into a crumpled heap. She stared him down again. "When the cops get here, I don't want you to say a word. Got that? Not a word."

Dev rarely had the opportunity to triple the town's twenty-five-mile-per-hour speed limit. But with one phone call, his night had gone from quiet paperwork at the station to some hoodlum crashing into the town's prized statue of Luis Cortez out at the rodeo grounds.

Hot damn, now we're talkin'.

It'd been a while since he'd gotten any real police action. Of course, this was likely a DUI, but for just a second Dev let himself fantasize that it might be some dangerous perp he'd get to take down.

His SUV whipped around the corner and fishtailed like they always did in the movies. That was a first for him though. At least he had an excuse for driving like a maniac. Imogen O'Connell—who lived less than a block from the rodeo grounds—had called in the crash and told him the driver was "either higher than a kite or as mad as a March hare," and Dev had better get out there before the idiot caused any more damage.

He accelerated down the block until the rodeo grounds materialized in front of him. Sure enough, a big truck had tangled with the bronze statue of Luis Cortez sitting on the back of a bull.

Hold on. His eyes strained, and he slammed on the brakes, bringing the SUV to a swift stop in the parking lot. Wasn't that Charity's truck?

She and her nephew walked out from the shadows.

That got him moving. He scrambled out of the car and jogged over, visually evaluating them both for potential injuries. "Everyone okay?"

"We're fine." Charity almost sounded bored. "Just a little mishap."

"You're sure?" It came out gruffer than he'd intended, but hell, he hadn't anticipated seeing her here. Hadn't anticipated seeing her in pajama shorts either. Had he ever seen her wear anything except for jeans?

"Of course I'm sure," she said with a hint of annoyance. "Like I said, it was a little mishap."

"A *little* mishap?" Dev eyed the damage again. A little mishap was a fender bender on Main Street. Her truck had just mowed down the town's only $75,000 statue. Which definitely seemed odd. In all the time Charity had lived here, he'd never had to pull her over once for speeding. In fact, he'd often admired her careful driving habits. She handled the hefty truck she drove like a pro. "What the hell happened?" He shifted his gaze to Bodie, who hadn't looked up from the ground once.

"I got distracted," Charity said, drawing his attention back to her. "My phone rang and I went to answer it and completely missed the turn, but by the time I realized what was happening, it was too late to correct."

Her phone rang? At two o'clock in the morning? Dev eyed Bodie again, but the kid still wouldn't look at him. *Oh yeah.* Something was definitely off. "And what're you doing out here at two o'clock in the morning?" Wearing only those shorts, a sweatshirt, and flip-flops? "It's the middle of the night." He not-so-subtly shifted into his stern cop voice.

"We were...hungry." Charity shot a quick look at Bodie, who nodded encouragingly. "Yep. Uh-huh. We were hungry." She gave Dev a tight smile. "I don't have many groceries in the house. We couldn't sleep so we thought we would go get a snack."

Damn, she was a bad liar. Of course, that only made him like her more. He let her squirm in silence a few minutes while he considered his response. It was pretty obvious something else was going on. This definitely wasn't his first rodeo with a suspicious crash, but playing the bad cop wouldn't get him anywhere. So he opted for the alternative approach. Logic. "Okay, so you were hungry and wanted a snack." He frowned at them both. "But nothing's open this time of night."

"Right." The woman's head bobbed in a slow nod, an obvious cue she was buying time.

"That gas station," Bodie said suddenly. "The one down the highway. It's twenty-four hours. That's where we were going." He still refused to meet Dev's eyes.

Dev struggled to keep from shaking his head at them. Didn't these two know you could get in serious trouble for lying to a cop?

"Right. Yes. The gas station," Charity echoed. Her smile turned smug. "They have the best nachos there."

Ha. Leave it to Charity Stone to get overconfident. Didn't matter what she said to him, none of this added up. Letting her sweat, Dev walked the length of the truck, taking his time to look over every inch. "Why is your bike in the back?" he finally asked, turning to Charity.

Her lips pressed into a firm line. "I keep it back there sometimes. So I can ride it whenever I want."

"Strange that the bike didn't get ejected on impact," Dev mused, peering into the bed of the truck again. "Judging from the damage to the front end of your truck, you had to be going, what? Forty miles an hour? And yet the bike didn't even dent the side of the truck bed." Which it definitely would have had the bike been in the back of the truck at the time of the crash.

"It's a heavy bike." Worry finally started to cloud her eyes. "Really heavy-duty. Very good quality. It's one of the best brands you can buy—great for hills and rocks. There was this one time I hit a rock and went flying over the handlebars…"

Dev ignored her and focused on her nephew. "The person who called in the accident said the truck was driving erratically. Was your aunt driving erratically, Bodie?"

Panic gripped the kid's expression. "Uh, maybe? I guess. Kind of." He shot Charity a desperate look.

She stepped in front of him. "I was distracted. Like I said, my phone rang."

Wow, she was really committed to this whole story. Didn't take a genius to figure out she was covering for the kid. And while Dev admired her loyalty, he couldn't let her get away with it. He couldn't let Bodie get away with it. "Who was on the phone?" he asked with a glare that wouldn't let her hide.

She shrugged and looked away. "Wrong number."

"Mind if I take look at your phone?"

"Yes, I mind." Charity stumbled back a step. "My phone is none of your damn business, Dev. You need a warrant for that kind of thing." And there was the fierce Charity everyone knew and loved.

He simply stared back. Her iciest glare didn't ruffle him. "I'm gonna need you to give me a few minutes alone with your nephew," he informed her. "I'd like to ask him a few questions."

"You can't interrogate him." She guided her nephew to stand behind her. "He's a minor. You have no reason to question him. I already told you what happened."

"I'm not interrogating him. I just want to ask a few simple questions."

"Fine." She crossed her arms, still blocking him from looking at the kid. "You can ask him anything with me standing here."

"Okay." If that's how she wanted to play it. He side-stepped her. "Bodie, were you the one driving the truck when it crashed?"

"I already told you he wasn't," Charity answered for him. "It was my fault. I crashed. So just give me the damn ticket and we can all go back to bed."

See, this is why he'd wanted to get Bodie alone. If that guilty expression on the kid's face was any indication, he would crumble faster than the sugar-free, whole-grain muffins Everly sold at the café. Dev looked past her. "Bodie, do you know what the penalties are for lying to a police officer?"

"He's not lying!" Charity stepped up toe-to-toe with Dev. She stood so close he could smell a subtle hint of tart cherry mixed with something sweeter.

"Let. It. Go." Her eyes blazed.

Dev shifted his gaze to Bodie, who now looked down-right scared. His hands had squeezed into fists at his sides and the poor kid seemed to be hyperventilating.

Damn it. During his training he'd always assumed that, when he got out on the field, things would be either right or wrong, black or white, legal or illegal, but that was before he'd considered the gray areas caused by desperate people who were stuck in situations he couldn't possibly imagine. He'd faced it more times than he cared to admit—that feeling of indecision, that dilemma between upholding the law and leniency. It never got easier.

He assessed Charity again. She was a force, that was for sure. And he usually admired her grit...except for when it was directed at him. "Can I have a word with you?" He nodded toward the truck.

"I'll be right back, Bodie." She gave the boy's shoulder a quick squeeze before marching to the other side of the truck.

Dev followed her, already feeling a chink in his armor. He wanted to help people—sometimes to a fault—but with Charity that tendency ran even deeper.

"I need you to let this go," she said as soon as he stood across from her. "Give me a ticket and move on."

"I have to do my job, Charity." He brought his face in line with hers so she'd see he meant no harm. "Covering for him won't help him in life. You know that, right?"

"No one has ever covered for him." She stared straight ahead. "No one has ever helped him. No one has ever given him a chance. He drew the joker card when he got stuck with my sister."

Well, she might suck at lying, but she sure knew her way around guilt trips. "I know he's had it rough." He softened his voice. "But he has to be held accountable or he'll never learn anything."

"I was driving the truck." Her gaze drove straight into his. "Please, Dev. I need you to trust me."

"Then I need you to trust me, too." She might insist she didn't need his help, but from the looks of things here, she was in over her head. "I can—"

Headlights careened around the corner and came straight for them. Dev shielded his eyes, trying to see past the glare.

Charity spun toward the car, which had screeched to a stop near the downed statue. "Who is it?"

With the headlights now off, Dev didn't even have to squint. He knew only one person who drove an ancient Oldsmobile that big. "That would be our fine mayor." Which meant things were about to get a lot more complicated for them both.

Chapter Five

Hank Green was absolutely the last person on earth Charity wanted to see right now. And considering how many disreputable men she'd met on the circuit, that was saying a lot.

She made a quick scan of the scene and winced at the damage to the statue. If there was one thing the mayor hated, it was anyone messing with his town. Last year, when a group of teenagers had spray-painted the bathrooms at the city park, Hank had launched an all-out inquisition, getting the town so riled up that the teens finally confessed out of fear they'd be sent to the gallows if they got caught. Now the man was walking toward her and Dev wearing a vulturelike scowl.

"Do you trust me?" Dev turned her to face him, his eyes searching hers.

Now was not a good time for loaded questions. Everything she'd seen had told her Dev was a trustworthy person, but life had already taught her she couldn't trust anyone. "Why?" she asked instead of answering.

"I need you to trust me, Charity." The deputy whipped his handcuffs off his belt. "Turn around."

"What?" Her heart lurched, forcing her back a step. "Are you serious? You're arresting me?"

"Not arresting," Dev corrected. "Detaining. Trust me," he said again.

"But—"

"What the hell happened out here?" Hank Green demanded, his voice booming.

"Everything's under control." Dev's voice held firm. "Turn around, Ms. Stone, and clasp your hands behind your back."

He was serious. He wanted to cuff her!

"It'll be in your best interest to cooperate while I conduct the investigation." Dev gave her shoulder a careful nudge. "Trust me." The whisper was so faint she almost didn't hear it. "Now please turn around and clasp your hands behind your back." His voice went all official again.

Every fight instinct she'd so carefully honed went crazy, but she gritted her teeth and did what he said.

Dev cinched the cuffs around her wrists. "This shouldn't take long, Ms. Stone. But seeing as how there's significant damage to public property, we need to cover all our bases. I'm sure you understand."

The only thing she understood was that Dev would hear about this later. Pretty much the second Hank Green left, Dev would hear about this.

"Aunt Charity?" Bodie jogged over. "What's going on?"

Dev took her arm and prodded her away from Hank Green and toward his SUV. "I'm detaining the driver while I conduct a thorough search of the vehicle."

"It's okay, Bodie." Charity peered over her shoulder and tried to smile, so her nephew wouldn't confess that he'd been the one driving. Calm. She had to stay calm, even though her heart hammered with the need to rip away from the deputy. No one confined her. No one forced her into anything...

"You're damned right you'll conduct a thorough investigation." Hank Green followed behind them as though supervising Dev's every move. "That statue was a landmark in this town. Took us two years to raise the funds to have it made."

"It was an accident. I already told you. I missed the turn." Charity pulled out of Dev's grasp so she could walk by herself. "I'll pay for the stupid statue."

Dev went ahead of her and opened the back door of his SUV. "Let me handle this," he said, his voice low and cautioning. He guided her to slide into the back seat. "I need you to wait here until I've searched your truck."

Another round of resistance sparked her temper. "Search my truck? What the heck are you looking for, Dev?"

"Isn't it obvious?" Hank answered for him. "Drugs. Alcohol. No one hits a statue that big unless they're under the influence."

Or unless they're thirteen. "I'll have you know that I have never been drunk. Not once." She wriggled to the edge of the seat and dangled her legs out the door, ready to stand up and get in Hank's face. "And even when I broke my collarbone, I refused any painkillers and took over-the-counter medications instead. So you can kiss my—"

"Enough." Dev stepped between her and Hank. "From everything I've seen, this looks like an innocent accident." He faced the mayor. "Most likely a case of distracted driving, but I will do my job and make sure." He shot Charity a look that clearly told her to keep her mouth shut and slammed the car door.

Of course the man's car would have to smell absolutely divine. A lot like him, actually. It had to be some kind of cologne. A heady mix of spice and something outdoorsy...masculine. No wonder some of the women in town purposely entrapped him by speeding so he would pull them over.

Charity squirmed to loosen the tension that had built low between her shoulder blades. He'd actually cuffed her. The man had put her in handcuffs and stashed her in the back seat of his car like some kind of criminal. Her temper flared. She had half a mind to completely trash the neat interior of his little justice mobile—she could do a lot of damage with her legs. But if she got officially arrested, what would Bodie do? He couldn't be left on his own overnight. *Hold it together.* She peered out the window.

Bodie had stationed himself right next to the SUV and was peering into the window with a worried expression. He looked too grown-up. She could still see traces of the chubby toddler she'd held on her hip. Back then he used to giggle and clap and sing and find joy in the smallest things. Now he was standing at the scene of an accident because he'd stolen her truck. It shouldn't be like this. He shouldn't be standing out there on his own, worried and afraid. *Grrr.* Why couldn't Dev see that Bodie just needed someone to stand with him? She fisted her hands and strained against the cuffs, but Dev had locked those things on tight.

Helpless to do anything but stare out, Charity scooted closer to the window. Hank stood next to her truck with his arms crossed while Dev searched inside. They wouldn't find anything. She kept her truck much cleaner than she kept her house. Tapping her foot, she waited for the inspection to end. Finally, Dev emerged and said something to Hank. The two of them walked to Hank's car. After another lengthy discussion, the mayor climbed into his Oldsmobile and drove away.

Charity leaned against the leather seat with a sigh. With Hank out of the way, maybe she could finally convince Dev to let Bodie off the hook for this. She watched the deputy saunter back to the SUV. As a matter of principle, she purposely ignored the way his body moved, the way it filled out his uniform so that the button-down shirt stretched tight across his broad shoulders. She would not appreciate it. Not when she was sitting handcuffed in the back of his SUV.

When the door opened, she snapped her head forward and looked straight ahead, bracing herself for the possibility that Dev would tell her he'd decided to charge Bodie.

Without saying a word, Dev opened the door, reached in, and took a hold of her arm, gently tugging until she slid out of the car.

When he stepped behind her to unlock the handcuffs, she peered over her shoulder. "What're you doing?"

"I'm taking off the cuffs." He pulled them away from her wrists and clicked them back onto his belt. "And then I'm going to write you a ticket." He moved away from her, opened the passenger's side door, and pulled out a clipboard.

Charity slid a surreptitious glance over to Bodie, who kept his distance. Wait, was that a smile on his face? She'd expected that scared expression he'd worn earlier, but instead he gave her a thumbs-up. "So you believe me? About Bodie not driving the truck?"

"Not even a little bit." Dev focused on filling out a form on the clipboard, his handwriting neat and precise.

Right. Because Dev wasn't stupid. "But you're not going to do anything about it?"

"What can I do?" He paused from writing to look up at her. "Bodie gave me the same story you did. There are no witnesses to refute it. So I guess I have to trust you."

The way he said it—like he knew he couldn't trust her in this case—stung. She'd always been trustworthy. She'd made sure she'd risen above her own mother's lies and deception. But tonight, she didn't have a choice. She couldn't let Bodie take the consequences for this. "Well, good," she muttered, finding it hard to look at Dev. "I'm glad you finally believe us."

Amusement perked up the corners of the deputy's mouth. "I didn't say I believed you. I said I have no choice but to trust you." He scrawled a signature on the bottom of the form and handed it over to her. "This one's gonna hurt, though. Destroying public property is a serious offense."

"That's fine. I can handle it." She'd never even gotten so much as a traffic ticket before. One infraction wasn't going to take away her license.

Dev still looked amused. "I doubt your insurance will think it's fine once they realize they have to pay for the statue."

"Then I'll find new insurance," she said defiantly.

The man sighed and looked at her. "I do trust you, you know. You're a good person, Charity."

And there went all of those hostile feelings for the whole handcuff thing.

"I know you're trying to do what's best for the kid," Dev went on. "But driving without a license—and destroying public property—is a big deal. I'd hate to see him try it again because there were no consequences this time."

"It won't happen again. Because you're going to find my sister and she's going to come back and get him. And they'll go back to Oklahoma." She hadn't realized her voice had gotten shaky until that last sentence. In fact, her whole body had started to shake again. She couldn't do this. She couldn't be a parent. She didn't know the first thing about nurturing a child. She wasn't enough for him.

Dev looked at her in his thoughtful, considering way. "Are you sure going back to his mom is the best for him?"

"Yes." Look at what had happened in twenty-four hours with him being under her supervision. If she hadn't woken up, he'd probably be on his way to juvie.

"All right then," Dev murmured, turning back to his SUV. "I'll go ahead and call out the tow truck. Then I'll give you two a ride home."

"Thank you." If Dev heard the sincerity in her voice, he didn't acknowledge it. He simply walked away and pulled out his phone.

Guilt chased her across the parking lot to where Bodie stood. It was a new feeling. Typically, she made sure she had nothing to feel guilty about.

"Did he buy it?" her nephew asked, as if they were co-conspirators in some dangerous scheme.

"No." Charity paused to freak him out a little. She wasn't sure she liked the excitement beaming from his eyes. That wasn't the point of this cover-up. The point was to make sure he didn't have to deal with legal trouble on top of being abandoned by his mother. "But he's letting it go. He wrote me a ticket."

"It's bad, isn't it?" Bodie turned to look at the statue. "It'll cost you a lot of money."

"That's an understatement." Not to mention, her truck was likely totaled as well, which meant her premiums would go through the roof.

"I'm sorry, Aunt Charity." There was the remorse she'd been looking for. His eyes were as repentant as a puppy's. And *aunt*. He'd called her *aunt*.

"I wasn't thinking," he mumbled. "I want to go home, that's all. I want to be with my friends. I never wanted to leave in the first place."

"I know." She knew what it felt like to get uprooted with no warning. Her own mother had done it every time she broke up with one of her boyfriends. Charity waited until Bodie looked at her. "But you messed up, Bodie." She was supposed to be in charge here, so she'd better act like it. "I bailed you out this time. But it won't happen again. And if you ever lie to the cops—*ever*—I will personally make sure you regret it. Got that?"

"Got it," he said solemnly.

"And," she continued while she was on a roll, "there are a few things you could help me with around the house to pay off some of the debt you now owe me."

"I will," he promised. "I'll help."

"You two ready to get home?" Dev sauntered over. "Tow truck'll be here in about an hour, but I gave him your information, and he said you can deal with it tomorrow."

"We're ready." Ready for this night to be over. Though things hadn't been nearly as horrible as they could have, thanks to Dev. "Come on, Bodie." She put her arm around him and he didn't try to shrug her away.

They all climbed into the car in silence. Bodie's uncertain expression had returned. Hopefully this whole fiasco would be enough to scare him away from any more criminal acts in the future.

Charity moved to strap on her seat belt while Dev started the car. He looked so official sitting there in his uniform. She couldn't help but slide her gaze down from his broad shoulders to his firm waist, where his gun sat snugly in its holster.

"It's a Glock 22," Dev informed her, guiding the SUV out of the parking lot and onto the road.

"Oh." She startled. He'd caught her looking. "It's...nice." Yeah, sure. She was totally checking out the gun and not his body.

"I actually prefer the old Smith and Wesson, but the boss likes the new ones."

"Have you ever had to use it?" Bodie asked from the back seat.

"Yeah, I've drawn a couple times." Dev glanced in the rearview mirror. "There've been a few domestic disturbances that got a little dicey."

"Have you ever shot anyone?" her nephew pressed. It almost sounded like an accusation. Charity winced.

"No. I haven't had to." The question didn't appear to faze Dev. Not much seemed to. "Firing your weapon is always a last resort."

"Not where I come from," Bodie muttered.

"I live over on Columbine Drive," Charity broke in before her nephew could expand. She didn't need him starting something right now. Not after Dev has just saved him from juvie. "It's the one right after the curve. Up there on the left," she said after he turned onto her street.

Dev pulled into the driveway and left the engine idling.

Charity turned to her nephew. "Why don't you go on inside? I'll be there in a few minutes."

Without a word—or even a thank-you—to the deputy, her nephew climbed out of the SUV and slammed the door hard. She watched him all the way to the front door to make sure he went inside, then she faced Dev. "I'm sorry. He's so angry right now."

"And what about you?" The deputy put the SUV into *park.* "You still mad about the handcuffs?"

How could she be when he'd done so much for her? For them? The fact that he always seemed to step up when she needed someone made it hard to stay mad at Dev for long. To keep up appearances, she shot him a smirk. "I'm still not sure that was totally necessary."

"I figured it was best to give Hank the whole dog and pony show. Especially considering the county sheriff election coming up." The election. She'd hadn't even thought about what could happen to Dev if someone found out he helped her tonight. That had the potential to hurt his chances in the election. Yet he'd done it anyway. "Thank you for being there when I needed you," she whispered.

Dev dropped his gaze to her lips, a new awareness rising to his face. He reached over and skimmed his fingers up her neck, gently guiding her face to his.

Tiny knots of pleasure pulled tighter and tighter in her stomach until it felt like they would break her open. Her eyes fell closed, her lungs suspended in wild anticipation of his kiss. The scent of spice came first, taking over her senses mere seconds before his lips touched hers with a jolt of electricity that reverberated through her body and hit all of the right notes. Notes no one else had ever managed to hit with a simple touch of the lips. Notes that strummed low in her belly before plunging down to more erogenous regions.

Sweet Jesus, she was in trouble.

Dev's lips guided hers open, and he stroked his tongue against hers, kindling a heat so intense she found it difficult to breathe. Their mouths fell into a rhythm—opening to each other, exploring, tasting with an extravagance she'd never experienced. Charity's eyelids fluttered, opened. She pulled back, her lungs full of a new ache. She didn't do this. Didn't kiss like this. Didn't feel things like this. Need. Longing.

The deputy stared back at her, eyes wide, lips still parted like he didn't quite know what to say.

"Whoa." Charity gasped. Parts of her still strummed too hard for her to fight against the emotions. Dev had made her hot for him. So. Damn. Hot. She narrowed her eyes into a glare. "First you handcuff me, then you give me a ticket, and then you *kiss* me?"

"Yeah..." He still had his gaze trained on hers as though he couldn't quite shake himself awake. "That was probably inappropriate—"

But hot. Too hot to ignore. Charity fisted his uniform shirt and pulled him back to her. "Just so you know...I'm not totally against inappropriate." She barely got out the words before her lips brushed his again.

This time it wasn't just a kiss...it was a sensual proposition. His hand palmed the back of her head roughly, fingers tangling in her hair. His obvious greed for her drove her own urges deeper. If the damn console wasn't in the way, she'd climb into his lap. Instead, Charity bit his lower lip lightly, teasingly, and smiled when a deep groan resounded in his throat. She responded with a sultry moan against his lips and worked her hands down the front of his uniform, toying with the buttons.

A knock on the window broke through the steady hum of pleasure. Charity pushed away from Dev, raised her head, and found herself staring directly into Mayor Hank Green's eyes.

Chapter Six

Dev didn't usually rely on coffee to wake him up, but the second he walked into his parents' house and sat down at their breakfast table, he poured himself a full mug.

"You look done worn out, son." Even after forty years in Colorado, his mother's Texas twang still came through. She leaned over and piled enough biscuits and gravy on his plate that he wouldn't need to eat lunch. "You been sleepin' all right?"

"Sure. I've been sleeping fine." Minus last night. After last night, he may never sleep again. Kissing Charity hadn't been the smartest move he'd ever made. Hank Green had pointed that out numerous times after Charity had hurried inside her house. The man claimed he'd simply swung by because he wanted to make sure everyone had gotten home all right, but Dev had a feeling Hank had wanted to check up on him. Granted, it had been with good reason. If Hank hadn't come when he did, Dev could've kissed her all night. Instead, he'd endured a lengthy lecture about what was at stake with the upcoming election. Didn't he know he couldn't be seen "fraternizing" with a woman who'd just "broken the law" and "ruined a town landmark"? According to Hank, it made him look bad. It sent the message that he wouldn't be tough on crime. He hadn't reminded Hank that Charity's ticket was technically only a Class 1 misdemeanor. Who hadn't gotten one of those?

"Did you have a busy night?" his mom asked.

"You could call it busy." Despite Hank's best efforts, Dev couldn't seem to make himself regret the kiss. He'd known he shouldn't touch Charity—not in his patrol car, not when he'd handcuffed her and given her a ticket less than a half hour before—but he couldn't stop himself. He'd wanted her so hard for so long and she'd always pushed him away. But not last night. Last night she'd seemed to want him as much as he wanted her.

Just so you know, I'm not totally against inappropriate.

"Dev? Hello? You there, son?" His father was looking at him over the top of his newspaper.

"Oh. Yeah." He shook himself. "Sorry. Did you say something?"

His parents exchanged concerned frowns. After being married for over fifty years, Dev swore the two of them were starting to look alike.

"I said, you must've had a hell of a night last night." His dad set down the paper. "I haven't seen you drink coffee since you worked the night shift."

"It was a late one." He'd best leave it at that. Sharing additional details about the statue would only get his parents riled and inevitably they'd end up deliberating how this would impact his chances of becoming the county sheriff. His parents were even more excited about the election than most people in town. They never missed a chance to tell him how proud they were, how this was the absolute best thing he could do with his life. Sometimes he wondered, though. If he was county sheriff, that meant he'd have even less time to help his dad on the ranch.

"I heard someone crashed into the statue of Luis Cortez in the middle of the night." Across the table, his mother buttered her toast. "I'll bet that kept you busy."

Why was he not surprised they'd already heard? "News sure travels fast." How long would it take for word to get out about the kiss? He downed more coffee. Hank had told him it would be their secret—as long as it didn't happen again— but what if one of Charity's neighbors had seen? The last thing he needed was an editorial about how he kissed his suspects showing up in the newspaper.

"Betty Osterman sent out a text to our walking group," his mom went on. "She said someone mowed the thing right down. Said most of the town is fit to be tied over the whole situation."

That's what he'd been worried about. Word would likely get out that the town's favorite barrel racer was behind the accident, but it wouldn't be him sharing the details. "It's taken care of," he said vaguely. And yet that wasn't exactly true. Taken care of would mean he'd been able to hold the right person accountable, but Charity hadn't given him that option. She'd asked him to trust her, and he was trying, but he still worried that Bodie didn't understand the seriousness of what he'd done.

His parents were both staring at him like they expected more details on the statue, so he steered them in another direction. "What do you two have going on today?"

His father shoveled in a spoonful of gravy. "Got some fences down over on the west side. Bordering the Cortez place. Thought I'd head over and see about rebuilding that section."

"Why don't you wait until I'm off my shift?" Dev did his best to tread lightly. His dad wouldn't appreciate the insinuation that he needed assistance. Even if it was the truth. "I can help out."

"Nah. I got it." The old man waved him off. "Want to get it done before any of them steers get fancy ideas about wandering off."

Okay, subtle hadn't worked. It was time to bring in the big guns. Dev shared a look with his mom. They'd already agreed his father shouldn't be out there on his own.

"Can't the fences wait?" MaryElla Jenkins could sound as sweet as her fresh-baked oatmeal chocolate chip cookies when she wanted to. She leaned over to refill his father's coffee. "I thought we could go on over to that new antique shop down the highway."

"New antique shop?" Nothing distracted his father like the prospect of looking through old crap.

"It's more like an emporium from what I hear," Dev said, playing up his mother's ploy. "The place has two floors of merchandise."

"You don't say." His father frowned thoughtfully.

"They've probably got all kinds of old tools there." That would do it. His father had a whole shed of antique tools he liked to tinker with.

"I guess we could take a look," he mumbled, bringing his mug back to his lips. "But I can't be gone all day, MaryElla. I've got a whole heap of work to do around here."

"Oh, we won't be gone all day," she promised.

Dev concentrated on eating his breakfast so he wouldn't chuckle at the twinkle in his mother's eye. She'd likely make sure they didn't get home until Dev got off his shift.

"What about you, son?" she asked. "You got a busy day ahead? I heard things are really heating up with the election.

Oh, that reminds me!" His mom jumped up from the table and hurried to the desk in the corner of the kitchen. "Did you see that wonderful article Betty wrote about you in the paper?"

"Yeah." Unfortunately. It'd take the guys a good long while to get over that "devastatingly handsome" bit.

"I had it framed!" She presented one of his dad's handmade wooden frames, and sure enough, there was Betty Osterman's glowing endorsement preserved in the glass.

"When you get elected, you'll be the youngest sheriff the county has ever had," his dad reminded him.

"*If* I get elected." Dev pushed away his plate. Lately he'd been wondering if he even wanted to get elected. Everyone else had been so enthusiastic about him running, he'd gotten swept up in the hoopla, but lately doubts had started to niggle at him. "I should get going." Before he had to witness his mom hanging that framed article on the wall. "Busy day ahead." That wasn't a total lie. After what had happened with Bodie last night, he intended to spend the day making good on his promise to look for Charity's sister. It'd be nice to focus on something besides the election. "Thanks for breakfast, Mom." He rose and planted a quick kiss on her cheek. Not giving her a chance to comment on his half-eaten plate of biscuits and gravy, he booked it out the door. "Have fun at the antique mall," he called over his shoulder.

Whew. Dev hotfooted it to his SUV and drove to his favorite hiding spot on the highway just outside of town.

He backed into the alcove in the mountain where the speed limit dropped from fifty-five to thirty-five miles per hour. Most everyone knew he parked here on a regular basis, so he could focus on doing some research instead of actually having to pull anyone over.

Once he was satisfied he was out of sight from traffic, he cut the engine and fired up his laptop. In his estimation, there were only a few reasons Charity's sister would skip town so fast. She might be running from an abusive relationship. According to Charity, Melody ran with a rough crowd, and domestic violence was not uncommon in those circles. The other possibility, which he hated to even entertain, was that she'd gotten herself into some kind of trouble and needed to hide. While that was the least appealing option, it also happened to be the simplest to research.

He looked up crime briefings in Oklahoma, scrolling through the typical petty thefts, domestic disputes, and an article about a carjacking before a headline caught his eye. CONVENIENCE STORE CLERK SHOT DURING ROBBERY NEAR STILLWATER.

Dev glanced at the date. The article had been posted four days ago. Interesting timing with Melody's arrival, if you asked him. He clicked on the link.

A local man was hospitalized after a midday robbery at a convenience store in nearby Morrison. Witnesses say two masked suspects, one male and one female, entered the store at 11:15 a.m. and held the clerk at gunpoint. When he reached for the phone, the male suspect fired the gun and cleaned out the register before exiting the store. A stolen Ford pickup truck used in the robbery was found abandoned a short time later.

Dev squinted at the grainy surveillance image of two perps as they stood across the counter. Hard to see much, but he could make out blond hair curling from under one of their ski masks. That wasn't good. He didn't believe in coincidences, and he never liked to speculate, but based on the woman's build and that long hair, she sure bore a startling resemblance to a certain blond barrel racer. Dev bookmarked the article and pulled out his phone. Looked like he needed to have a chat with his comrades in Oklahoma.

Faster. Charity crouched her upper body lower and steered Ace into the tight turn around the third barrel. "Yah!" She clicked her heels into the thoroughbred's wide girth as the horse accelerated out of the turn, kicking up dirt clods behind them.

"Yah! Yah!" Charity leaned over the horse's mane, urging Ace on with her heels. The wind brought a resistance, making her eyes tear up as they tore across the arena to the gate. Ace sailed through and then slowed to a trot, grunting from his efforts.

"Good boy, Ace." Charity gave him a good scrub with her fist, which made the horse prance proudly.

"Not so fast. No swaggering until we see if we beat our record." She steered the horse over to where Bodie hung out by the fence. "How'd we do?" she asked, giving the horse more love.

"Oh." Her nephew tapped the screen on his phone. "Don't know. Sorry. I was texting a friend."

Charity did her best not to groan. Usually she had Levi, Ty, or Mateo track time for her, but she'd wanted to make Bodie feel involved. All day, they'd worked on chores around her house. Well…she'd worked. He'd pitched in here and there in between texting his friends. She eyed his phone, tempted to throw it under Ace's hooves and take off again, but that would sever Bodie's only communication with his friends back home.

Patience. She had to have patience with him. He was going through a tough time. "Do you think you could pay attention this time? All I need you to do is start the timer when I yell go and focus for twenty seconds." She and Ace would finish in under eighteen, hopefully.

"Fine," the kid grumbled with a hearty eye roll he seemed to reserve especially for lame adults. She'd been trying not to take it personally, but her heart took a hit every time he looked at her like that—like he hated her. It only proved she had no idea what she was doing. She didn't know how to get through to him. She loved him but it didn't seem to matter. He needed a real parent.

Charity inhaled deeply. "I would really appreciate it if you would—"

"Hey you two."

Dev. Her joints went soft. All of them. Elbows, knees, hips... it was amazing she didn't topple right off Ace.

The deputy rode over to them on a beautiful horse—a paint with dark brown spots scattered over its clean white coat. He wasn't in his uniform. In fact, it was possible that he looked even better in worn jeans and a threadbare T-shirt than he'd looked in his crisp ensemble last night.

Oh, god. Last night... It all came hurtling back at her—the kiss, that horrible moment Hank Green had knocked on the window. She'd be the first to admit she was spooked. After quickly thanking Dev for the ride, she'd hightailed it inside and had proceeded to worry about him all night.

"How's it going?" Dev asked in that easy way of his.

"Fine." It didn't matter how she was doing, she was dying to know what had happened with Hank. "What about you?" She watched his face for any sign of turmoil. "Everything okay?" Had Hank fired him? Did Hank have the power to fire him?

"Everything's..." It seemed to take an extra second for him to settle on the right word. "Fine."

She waited in rapt attention for him to expand but instead he turned his attention to Bodie. "How's the training going? Looks like you've got a pro running time for you." He shot a peace-offering smile to her nephew, who promptly plugged up his ears with headphones and walked away. The kid managed to project so much attitude that giving Dev the finger would've been a subtler move.

Charity sighed. She had no idea what to do with him when he acted like that. She wasn't his mom—she hadn't earned the right to discipline him. She wouldn't even know how to discipline a thirteen-year-old. It wasn't like she could ground him. He had no life here. No friends. For all intents and purposes, he already was grounded. Her sister had basically taken everything good away from him when she'd abandoned him on Charity's doorstep.

She watched her nephew sit against the barn and drum his fingers on his knees like he was listening to music. Well, at least that'd give her a chance to talk to Dev. "Did you lose your job?" she blurted, channeling every bit of concern she'd harbored all night.

"No." Dev patted his strong hand over his horse's withers. "I'm not going to lose my job for kissing someone."

Clearly he wasn't nearly as worried as she had been. Maybe it was because he'd covered for her and now she felt like she owed him. If something bad happened to him because he'd helped her, she'd never forgive herself. "What about the election?"

Something flickered in his eyes, but she couldn't read the emotion before his expression changed to amusement. "What about it?"

"If people find out—"

"I'll let you in on a little secret. I don't care that much about the election. And anyway, Hank won't say anything. He wants me in that position."

Everyone wanted Dev to be the county sheriff. And you know what? He'd be great at it. No matter what happened, he always seemed to have rock-solid steadiness. He always seemed to know what to say, what to do.

"What about you? Are you two doing okay?" Dev glanced over to where Bodie was still slumped against the barn. "Maybe I should've had him checked out by paramedics last night."

"He's fine. Physically, at least." He hadn't even complained of being sore that morning. "Instead of just being angry about his mom leaving, he's now officially bored too." As he'd told her numerous times while she was prepping Ace for the training run. "He helped me with some chores around the house earlier but I have to get some training in." Both for her mental state and her riding abilities. The competition she'd been in the night Dev had rescued her at the bar hadn't counted for anything. It had simply been a fun warm-up show for the upcoming season. But her race schedule would really heat up come June, and she had to keep herself in top shape. Besides that, whenever she didn't know what to do, she rode. It was her coping mechanism, her freedom, her peace. Riding was about the only thing in the world she did well.

Dev eased his horse closer, and both animals lowered their heads to munch on some of the grain she'd spread out earlier. "If he's bored maybe you should put him in school," the deputy said quietly.

"School?" Charity dismounted and walked a few steps away, giving Ace space to enjoy his snack. It was pretty clear she wasn't going to get any more training in today anyway. She should take Bodie home and see about dinner. "I can't enroll him in school here. When my sister gets back—"

Dev dismounted too. "You don't know when or *if* she's coming back."

"She's coming back." Charity frowned at him. When had he suddenly become an expert on her sister? "Melody wouldn't abandon him forever." The conviction in those words shook as much as her hands. Her sister *couldn't* abandon him. She couldn't do that to him. God, don't let her do that to him.

Dev eased closer, keeping a close eye on Bodie. "Has she ever been in trouble with the law?"

Was that a trace of sympathy in his tone? What wasn't he telling her? "Melody is irresponsible. And spontaneous. And I used to think she was unstable, but she's always wanted to be with her son." She had to believe Melody loved Bodie, even if she didn't know how to show it. "As far as I know, she's never been in any real trouble. Not like that. Why?"

He suddenly looked away. "It seems like she's running from something. Like maybe she brought Bodie to you so she could hide from the authorities."

"Authorities?" Did he have any idea how ridiculous he sounded? "Melody may be unreliable, but she's not a criminal."

"What if she is?" Dev said in that grave cop tone she'd heard him use occasionally.

Okay. Whoa nelly. That fight inside of her had boiled up—building like those black funnel clouds used to do back home. *Count to ten. Breathe.* Even with the mental commands, her jaw clenched. "I didn't ask for your help so you could accuse my sister of breaking the law. You said yourself it's not illegal to leave your kid with family."

"I'm not accusing her of anything. All I'm saying is it's strange that she would uproot her son with no warning. In the middle of the school year." He glanced in Bodie's direction again. "She must've had a reason to run. To pull him out of school. She's obviously trying to protect him. Or herself. Or maybe both of them. But no one just up and leaves for no good reason."

"You're right. Maybe she had a reason. Maybe she's really trying to get her life on track." That's what Charity was clinging to. She couldn't consider the alternative. Couldn't even think about what it would do to Bodie. She couldn't raise him. He didn't want to be with her. "You know what, Dev?" Charity turned back to her horse, gathering the reins in her hands before she stepped into the stirrup and hoisted herself up to the saddle. "Forget it. I don't want your help anymore. I'll find her myself. I don't need you."

Dev looked up at her with a scorching expression that brought all of those feelings she'd had during their kiss bubbling back to the surface.

"That's not how you made it seem last night."

That damned reckless kiss. "Last night was a mistake. But don't worry. It's not a mistake I'll make again."

Chapter Seven

Dev surveyed his friends who were all milling around Levi's kitchen dressed up in khakis and collared dress shirts that were accessorized with bow ties and suspenders. And don't get him started on the derby and plaid newsboy hats the women had forced on their men's heads.

He slipped his off—a flannel plaid number that Darla had given him because "everyone who shows up at my birthday party is required to be in costume." He'd thought about not showing up at all, but Charity would be there, and the thought of her wearing a flapper dress was too much for him to resist.

"Better put that hat back on before we get to the party or Darla'll have your balls." Mateo handed Dev a glass tumbler with a few shots of whiskey. Since the women had all gathered at Darla's place to deck themselves out like Roaring Twenties bombshells, the men had decided to gear up for the big soiree with a pregame libation so they could pretend they still maintained a shred of their dignity.

"Why'd she have to hand out flannel hats in May?" Dev rubbed a hand over his head.

"Hell, I don't know." Mateo threw back a gulp of whiskey. "Can't say I care though. You should see what Everly's wearing tonight." He whistled low. "A bow tie and suspenders are a small price to pay. Trust me. Everly laid out her dress earlier just to torture me. It'll be a long couple of hours before I can get her home, if you know what I mean."

Oh, he knew. He had a feeling he'd be undergoing a similar torture when he saw Charity all dressed up like some vintage fantasy. The difference was he likely wouldn't get to mess around with her later. Not after the last time they'd talked. He hadn't even told her everything he suspected about Melody and she'd lashed out at him. He'd hate to see what would happen if he told her he'd called the precinct in Oklahoma to talk to the detective handling the robbery case. The man had been very interested to learn more about Melody Stone. Maybe Charity's sister hadn't been involved in the robbery but the detective agreed it seemed like quite the coincidence, and he said he would be checking into her background.

"You got a date for the party tonight?" Mateo asked him.

"No." Though he and Charity would be about the only single adults there, minus Darla and a few of her out-of-town friends. So he figured he might get a dance or two with Charity by default.

Mateo shot him a sly grin. "Why don't you just screw her already?"

"Screw who?" Playing dumb was always a safe bet when you didn't know what to say.

"Charity." His friend was apparently onto him. "If any other man had tried to talk her out of a fight the way you did at the bar the other night, she would've kicked him aside. But she followed you outside like a puppy. I think she's into you."

According to the kiss they'd shared, she was definitely into him, but right now she also happened to be pissed at him. And she'd be even more pissed if he told her about his conversation with the detective. "Things with Charity are complicated right now."

"Then maybe you should let it go," his friend suggested. "You don't exactly need that kind of distraction with the election coming up."

Not this again. "What does that have to do with anything?"

"Well, for one thing, everyone's watching you right now. A lot of folks aren't too happy with her for taking out the statue."

"I don't care." If running for county sheriff meant he had to live his life based on what everyone else thought, he'd be happy to withdraw from consideration right now. "If people don't vote for me just because of who I'm spending my time with, I don't want the job anyway." What would it be like to live his life under that kind of scrutiny? He wasn't sure he wanted to find out.

"You guys about ready to head?" Ty asked, walking over with Levi.

"Sure." Dev thunked the damn hat back on his head, ready to bail out on more election talk. "I'll drive." He set his untouched glass of whiskey on the counter. Being a cop meant usually being the designated driver, but he never minded. At least then he knew everyone would be safe out on the roads.

They all filed out the door with posture as enthusiastic as that of a convicted felon walking toward a prison sentence. Once they were all piled into his truck, Dev started down the long driveway.

"I can't remember the last time I wasn't allowed to wear boots," Levi grumbled, staring down at the shiny shoes his wife had obviously made him wear.

"See? That's why I'm not married." Ty leaned up from the back seat of the extended cab. "No woman is going to tell me what to wear."

"And yet you let Darla talk you into suspenders," Mateo pointed out.

"I don't half mind suspenders." Ty tugged on the elastic straps. "They'll be easier to maneuver out of than a brass belt buckle later."

"Yeah, like you're gonna be maneuvering out of anything tonight." Levi laughed. "Me and Mateo? We're gonna get real lucky later." He turned around with a grin. "That, my friend, is why you wear what your woman tells you. It's all about compromise."

"Hell, yeah it is." Mateo agreed. "Give and take. If you're willing to take on a measly few hours of humiliation, they're willing to give."

Dev shared a look with Ty in the rearview mirror. "Again with the married talk." He didn't have anything against marriage. But now all of a sudden, these two thought of themselves as the relationship experts in the group.

"I prefer to have options for who I'm going to get lucky with," Ty said. "Ain't that right, Dev? We've got unlimited possibilities."

"Sure." Keeping things casual with women had worked for him in the past. He had to admit though...that kiss with Charity had been anything but casual.

"You gonna make a move tonight?" Mateo asked, as though he'd read his thoughts.

"On who?" Levi demanded.

Dev shot Mateo a look that clearly told him he would use his gun if he breathed another word. "I'm not making a move on anyone." It wasn't like that with Charity. He liked her, and yes he was attracted to her, but he also happened to have a lot of respect for the woman. He didn't need moves. He just needed to show her he wasn't going anywhere, no matter how many times she tried to push him away.

He pulled up in front of the curb a few blocks down from the Chocolate Therapist and hastily parallel-parked his truck. They all piled out.

"I bet Darla has some hot single friends." Ty led the way down the sidewalk in front of the storefronts. He turned around and looked at Dev. "You want me to be your wingman tonight?"

"Not particularly." He already had his thoughts on a specific woman.

As they approached Darla's wine and chocolate bar, the sounds of music and laughter drifted toward them.

Levi suddenly looked concerned. "Shit, we're late."

"Only ten minutes." Mateo waved it off. "I bet the women won't even notice," he said right before the door opened and his wife walked out, followed by Darla.

"Happy twenty-fifth birthday," Dev greeted Darla with a smirk. They all knew this was her thirty-ninth.

"Thanks." She shook her shoulders, making the gold fringe on her dress dance. "I swear I feel younger every year."

"You look it too." Ty swaggered up to her. "Not even a twenty-five-year-old could wear that dress like you do."

Levi elbowed Dev in the ribs and they both chuckled. Ty had had a thing for Darla since he'd moved to town, though he'd never admit it.

"It's about time you guys showed up." Everly directed a disapproving frown at Mateo.

"Sorry, babe." Mateo tugged on his bow tie, straightening it with an innocent look at his wife. "We just wanted to make sure we looked good enough to stand next to our hot wives."

Dev had to hand it to him—the man was pretty smooth.

The slight irritation on Everly's face melted away and she wrapped her arms around him. "I know an excuse when I hear one, but you *are* looking pretty hot in the bow tie, so I'll let it slide this time." She dragged him away. "Let's go in and dance."

Dev followed them inside. The place looked like an actual speakeasy from the twenties. Shimmery gold curtains draped the walls. The tables and chairs that typically took up most of the space in the restaurant had been pushed to the outskirts of the room and were decorated with black tablecloths that were covered with flickering candles and strings of pearls.

"She went all out," Ty said, taking a long glance around the room.

"Yeah, she did." Dev glanced around too, but he wasn't admiring the decorations anymore. There were maybe thirty people mingling, but he was looking for only one.

That one right there.

Charity stood near the bar along the back wall looking very much like a risqué flapper. Dev tightened his jaw so it wouldn't hang open in awe. Her long blond hair had been twisted and pinned up, making it look velvety soft. The emerald green dress she wore sparkled with beads and sequins. His eyes followed the plunging neckline all the way down to the slit that ran dangerously high up her thigh. He barely managed to trap the whimper at the sight of her legs in those fishnet stockings.

"Are you checking out *Charity*?" Ty demanded.

Yeah, there was no way to recover from this. "I don't think I've ever seen her wear anything but jeans."

"It's weird," his friend agreed, making a face. "She actually looks like a woman."

Not just a woman. Hands down, the sexiest woman Dev had ever seen. "I'm going to go talk to her." He'd talk to her as many times as he had to prove that kiss wasn't a mistake.

Fishnet stockings were pure evil. Seriously. She'd like to meet the guy who'd come up with the idea. It had to be a man. No woman would ever inflict this form of torture on her own kind.

Giving up on being discreet, Charity hiked the elastic waistband of the tights upward and tried to reposition them so they didn't make the tops of her thighs itch. She let out a sigh and straightened her fancy dress for the hundredth time in less than half an hour.

She shouldn't even be here. When she'd told her friends she wouldn't be able to make it to the party because of Bodie, Naomi had insisted she drop him off at her father-in-law's house so he could hang out with Gracie. It sounded like she and her grandparents were going to play games and watch a movie together while everyone else went to the party. But Charity couldn't stop worrying. Was he having a good time? Had he hit it off with Gracie? She hoped so, because it was looking more and more like she'd have to enroll him in the local middle school come Monday.

There had been no word from Melody. Charity had called everyone she could think of to ask if they'd heard from her, but each time it was the same answer. *I haven't talked to her in weeks.* Or months. She wasn't sure she liked the sound of that. What had made her sister distance herself from friends? Probably a man. No, definitely a man. And yet Bodie insisted his mom hadn't been dating anyone…

"Will you stop hiking up your dress?" Darla walked over. "You look like a two-year-old who has to pee." Of course, in contrast, her friend made this whole costume thing look effortlessly elegant.

"I'm not hiking up my dress," Charity insisted. "I'm trying to keep these damn tights where they belong. I still can't believe you tricked me into giving you my measurements." Darla had told Charity she was ordering a birthday present for a friend who was exactly her same size but she needed specific measurements and didn't want to ruin the surprise.

"If I didn't trick you, how else could I have ordered that gorgeous dress for you?" her friend asked sweetly. "It's perfect. At least Dev seems to think so."

"Dev?" Suddenly panicked, Charity did a one-eighty, wobbling on her heels.

The deputy was currently en route, moving toward her with an air of single-minded determination, and that unstable wobbling in her ankles seemed to spread all the way through her.

Hell-O. The Roaring Twenties looked good on him. He wore khaki pants and a white dress shirt underneath a plaid vest that matched the newsboy cap on his head. His body filled out every article of clothing like it had been made especially for him, all that brawn and virility...

"I see the feeling is mutual," Darla murmured with an amused sparkle in her eyes.

"What?" Charity snapped out of her reverie. "No. Nothing's mutual. There's nothing to be mutual." Even as she spoke, her insides mocked her with that telltale achy smolder thing they did when Dev had his eyes locked on her. She couldn't go there with him though. Not after Hank Green had busted them for making out in his police SUV after Dev had given her a ticket. She didn't need to see the mayor's scowl to know that had been a bad idea. Dev had a visible job in the community—even more so with the election coming up. He didn't need to develop a reputation for hooking up with the women he busted. Then there was this whole thing with her sister. He didn't even know Melody, and yet he'd already decided she was running from the law. "I don't have feelings for Dev."

"Mm-hmm. Okay." Her friend patted the top of her head the way she would've done to a child. "I'll give you two lovebirds a minute. I need to go check on the booze anyway." Just as Dev arrived, Darla slipped away.

"Hey." Charity gave him a cool look lest he get any ideas about kissing her or discussing her sister. Those two things were currently off-limits.

"Hey." His eyes swept over her. "You look incredible."

That kind of talk would make it more difficult to avoid any kissing. Once again, she became ultra-aware of the elastic band cinching her waist, but she resisted the urge to tug. "I feel ridiculous in this dress. I can't believe Darla talked me into wearing it."

Dev stared steadily into her eyes, the corners of his lips twitching like he was holding back a smile. "I'm serious, Charity. You look beautiful."

If anyone else had said that to her, she'd deflect the compliment with a joke, but Dev wasn't giving her a pickup line. He meant it. She could see it in the way he stared at her with an honest sincerity. He looked at her like that a lot, completely open and unfazed by the magnetism between them.

She, however, did happen to be fazed. She didn't do this—dress up and do her hair and wear makeup. And she sure as heck didn't swoon over cowboys. She might feel something for Dev, but she'd been fine on her own since she was old enough to make a grilled cheese sandwich, and that wasn't gonna change now. She didn't need him. She didn't need him being all sweet to her and helping her and getting all up in her business. Most of all, she didn't need him doing his cop thing with her sister—speculating, surmising, conjecturing.

Dev turned to face her, dialing up the heat between them by about 500 degrees. "Do you want to dance?"

Couples had gathered over near the DJ and were holding each other close, swaying to some love song that would've made her turn the station if it played on the radio in her truck. Her gaze landed on Mateo and Everly, who had their foreheads pressed intimately together. They were both smiling as they whispered back and forth—their faces and bodies and hearts so perfectly in sync. Longing expanded in her chest, encroaching on her heart. For only a second she let herself imagine it was possible for her to dance with someone like that. Someone she relied on. Someone she obviously loved. But the fear of not being loved back overpowered the fantasy.

"I don't feel like dancing." She reached for the steel metal tub that sat nearby and pulled out a beer, using the edge of the bar top to pop the lid before taking a long pull. If she ignored him long enough, maybe Dev would disappear.

He leaned in next to her. "Are you afraid to dance with me?"

That stood her up straighter. "I'm sorry, what?"

Dev looked around. "Pretty much everyone in this room is dancing except for you and me. Even Ty and Darla."

Charity glanced in their direction. "So? Darla loves to dance. She'll probably dance with every man here tonight." She pulled out a stool and sat down before taking another sip of her beer.

"Okay." Dev pulled out the stool next to her. "Then we can talk instead. Have you found your sister yet?"

She eyed him. "I'm not going to talk about Melody with you." She didn't need his opinions on the situation. "I don't even want to think about her. Okay? Please? I've got enough to worry about with Bodie right now." And she definitely didn't want to argue with Dev again. Not tonight. Not when they were supposed to be having fun.

"Fine." Something shadowed his face, but it was gone before she could pinpoint the expression. "We can talk about other things."

"What other things?"

The deputy dropped his gaze to her lips. "Things like that kiss."

Heat descended deep into her chest and surrounded her heart, making it pump harder. More beer. She needed more beer. Taking her time with another sip, she attempted to pull herself together. "I thought you said it was inappropriate."

A slow smile got a hold of Dev's wise, captivating eyes. "And I distinctly remember you saying you weren't totally opposed to inappropriate."

She couldn't be held responsible for what she'd said in that one wild moment.

"I liked kissing you, Charity."

This was new for her. The honest, direct approach. Usually men delivered clichéd lines she'd heard repeatedly on the circuit, but not Dev. He didn't try anything fancy. He went right for what he wanted.

"It was a fine kiss." She bluffed with a one-shouldered shrug.

"Fine?" He leaned in as though threatening to reenact it right then and there.

Knowing she wouldn't be able to resist if he went for it, Charity inched away. "Okay. It was better than average."

Dev laughed. "You can't admit you liked it."

That would be admitting she liked him. And she couldn't. Like him or admit it. She had to keep him out of her heart. It was easier. "Fine. I liked the kiss, but I'm not interested in pursuing it further. We're friends and that's all I want right now." So there. Wasn't much a guy could do if you friend-zoned him.

"Then it shouldn't be a big deal for you to dance with me." There was a challenge in his tone. Dev stood and pushed in his stool. "As long as we're friends. As long as you're not worried about falling for me."

The insinuation that she might be worried about it stoked her temper. "I'm not worried at all." To prove it, she stood up too. "So sure. Why not? Let's dance. Just don't complain when I step on your toes. When I said I didn't feel like dancing, what I really meant was I'm a terrible dancer." But it was on now. He'd asked for it.

"You don't have to be good at it. You just have to trust me. I'll make you look good." He tugged on her elbow, and she leaned into him, navigating the uneven floor in her heels.

Dev faced her and slipped his hand onto the curve of her hip. "Follow my lead." He clasped her hand in his and swayed her to the seductive rhythm of the music. It flowed softly through her, warm and captivating. Dev was right. He did seem to make her look good. He held her firmly, urging her body to move with his. The touch soothed the fight in her, softening all of her rough edges. Somehow the way he touched her made her feel beautiful and graceful instead of inept and awkward. The sudden vulnerability it brought tempted her to go back to her beer, but she couldn't wimp out now or he'd know how she felt about him.

"How's your nephew doing?" he asked the way a friend would. *Friend.* Charity inhaled and held her breath. They were only friends. She could do this, even if her face felt hot enough to boil water.

She focused on keeping her hand steady in his. "I'm not sure how to answer that. He doesn't say much."

Dev guided her hips into a turn. "It's tough feeling like the one person who's supposed to want you the most doesn't want you at all."

The words stirred her own suppressed memories, kicking them back up to the forefront of her mind. No one had wanted her. Not her mother, not the father she'd never known. "Is that how you felt before you got adopted?"

"Oh yeah. I remember wondering what I did wrong. I even told my social worker that I would be a better kid if my mom took me back."

Charity stopped moving. "It wasn't something you did."

"That's what everyone told me, but I didn't believe them." Dev urged her back into the dance. "All I knew was that she'd left me behind. I figured there had to be a reason."

"I worry that's how Bodie feels too." That no one wanted him. It was the same way she'd felt when her mom took off or when one of her boyfriends made a pass at Charity and her mom did nothing to protect her.

"My offer still stands." Dev squeezed her hand a bit harder. "I'm happy to talk to him. Or to spend some time with him if you think it would help."

"Thanks. I'll keep that in mind." She gazed up into his eyes. Oops. Big mistake. They were magic, those eyes. They had the power to silence her good judgment and get her into a lot of trouble. She steered her gaze over his shoulder instead. "How did you get past it? Feeling abandoned?"

He didn't answer right away. In fact, he waited until she looked at him. "I'm not sure you do. I guess you learn to live with something missing from your life, knowing you'll find something better along the way."

His eyes had trapped her and now she couldn't seem to look away. "Knowing you'll find something better?" she asked quietly. "Or hoping?" She'd given up on both, filling the holes in her heart with riding and competing instead of close relationships. Those two things had always been enough, but something about being held by Dev, something about the openness in his demeanor, made her long for more.

"I like to think hoping and knowing are the same thing." He drew her in closer and slipped one arm fully around her.

"I don't think this is how friends are supposed to dance," Charity whispered with a smirk, but she didn't back away. For once she didn't want to. It felt good to be held, to be close to someone, and Dev seemed so safe.

"Oops." His grin flared. "You make it really hard for me to remember we're only friends."

She was having the same problem. "It's hard to remember the rules when we're both dressed up in costumes. It's almost like we're two different people." She let herself fantasize that she was a different person. That she was capable of giving her heart to someone.

"That's true," Dev mused. "So if I kissed you again, it wouldn't be like Dev kissing Charity. It would be like two strangers who'd met in one of those secret prohibition-era bars."

Desire snaked up through her abdomen, coiling tighter and tighter. "Exactly." She clasped her hands behind his neck.

Dev abruptly changed their direction, dancing her closer to the small hallway behind the bar.

"Where are we going?" Before that sentence, she hadn't known she was capable of a husky drawl, but Dev had that effect on her. With him, she was likely capable of a lot of spontaneous wild things she'd never even considered.

"We're going somewhere quieter." In the dimness of the hallway he paused and gazed down into her eyes with a heart-stopping stare. "I can't stop thinking about how your lips tasted."

"I liked it," she confessed, inching her face closer to his. "You're a good kisser, Dev." A good kisser. A good man. A good cop.

"You sure about that?" He teased her with a brush of his lips. "Because earlier you said it was *okay*."

"It was better than okay." His lips were so close, but not touching hers, not bringing that rush of heat and desire she craved. "Fine. It was the hottest kiss I've ever had. And I want you to do it again."

"You want me to do what, Charity?" he teased.

"I want you to kiss me." There was something freeing about admitting it, about knowing he wanted it as much as she did.

Dev's thumb skimmed her lower lip as he studied her face before lowering his mouth to hers. Sparks flashed through her, gaining heat and momentum, bringing her hands to his shoulders, sliding them down his back so she could press his body to hers.

"Charity?" Naomi's voice broke her concentration.

She backed up a step, spotting her friend at the other end of the hallway. "Yeah?"

"Oh, there you are." She rushed over but slowed when she saw Dev against the wall. "I'm so sorry to interrupt. So, so, so sorry," she said looking back and forth between them. "But I just got a call from Luis. He said Bodie's not feeling well."

"Oh my god." Bodie. He was sick? And she'd left him with people he didn't even know very well...

"It doesn't sound serious, but I thought I should let you know," Naomi said. "I was going to leave soon anyway, so I can always check on him and give you an update if you want."

"No. I have to go pick him up." She never should've come anyway. Not when she had a thirteen-year-old kid to take care of.

"I'm so sorry," Naomi said again, this time directing the apology to Dev. "I'm guessing that was bad timing."

Or perfect timing, depending on how you looked at it. She'd gotten all wrapped up in the man again. Dev tempted her to do things she didn't do. He made her feel like someone else. Someone she could never be.

And there were plenty of other reasons she had to steer clear. There was his whole position on the situation with Melody. Somehow she'd forgotten she was still mad at him about how quickly he'd jumped to conclusions. And yet she'd almost made out with him in the middle of her friend's birthday party where anyone could've seen. God, the rumors that would fly around about them . . . she didn't even want to think about what would happen if it got back to the guys on the circuit. News like that would completely torch her reputation as a respectable competitor. She'd spent years proving herself and setting boundaries, but one racy public display of affection like that and she'd have to start all over. No matter that the men got away with it all the time.

"Come on, I'll walk you out." Dev went to slip his arm around Charity's waist but she darted away before he could touch her again.

"It's fine. I can walk out myself." She hurried to the coatrack near the door and snatched her purse.

"Maybe we could go out sometime." Dev followed behind her. "Pick up where we left off."

That was a bad idea. "Things are complicated right now. Bodie needs me around. I shouldn't have left him tonight." She rushed outside and down the block to where she'd parked her rental truck and climbed in.

Dev stayed on her heels the whole way and moved in before she could pull the door closed. "You still have to live your life."

She had been living her life. She'd been living it just fine before Bodie came, before Dev had kissed her. Everything had been nice and easy, because she'd been in control of making it that way. But now nothing seemed in her control. She couldn't control what happened with Bodie. She couldn't control the emotions and desires Dev teased out in her, and yet she couldn't give in to them either. She'd never given in. "Please, Dev. I need you to leave me alone. I can't add anything else to my life right now." Especially not a cowboy deputy who made her wish she were someone else.

Chapter Eight

Apparently Dev's eyes weren't the only part of him with magical powers. His lips had put a spell on her too. Her heart still pounded hard and her legs were shaky.

What was wrong with her? She'd never had a problem keeping boundaries before, but with Dev it seemed impossible. He looked at her differently—touched her differently—in a way that made her feel like something was missing. When it came to men, she'd always used her head, but Dev managed to reach straight for her heart. The problem was he'd never be able to grasp that whole part of her because her heart was already in pieces. There were too many fragments to pick up, to put back together. She didn't know where to start.

Charity maneuvered one hand on the truck's steering wheel while she pulled off her shoes and yanked on the fishnet tights with the other, struggling to slide them down one leg and then pulling her foot off the gas for a second so she could take them off, as if shedding the costume would somehow make her forget how she felt nestled in

Dev's arms. Whole and safe. Hopeful. Tears burned as she balled up the tights and tossed them into the back of her extended cab.

She had to forget Dev. She had to stop getting sucked into the fantasy world that man created. She didn't belong in dresses or heels. She didn't belong kissing dashing police officers. She was a cowgirl—a good one—and that was enough.

Charity went a good fifteen miles per hour over the speed limit all the way to Luis and Evie Cortez's humble log house on the Cortez family ranch. Though they were nearly seventy, the two were newlyweds, and happened to be the most adorable older married couple Charity had ever seen. They were both friendly and easygoing, which was the only reason she'd even considered leaving Bodie there. She knew they'd welcome him like one of their own grandchildren, but now she regretted leaving him at all. Instead of getting carried away with Dev, she had to focus on Bodie. That was a situation she could actually do something about. She could help him. Right now that needed to be her sole focus.

After shoving her feet back into the dreaded heels, she scrambled out of the truck, wobbled her way up to the door, and knocked.

"Charity!" Evie let her in and stole a quick hug. "My goodness, you look like you just walked out of a movie." She appraised Charity's attire. "How was the party? I'm so sorry you had to leave early. I really do think Bodie is fine, but when I mentioned his headache to Naomi she thought it was best to tell you."

"It's no problem at all." Truthfully, she was thankful to get away from all those emotions Dev had stirred up. "I'm so glad you called Naomi. I was ready to go anyway." She followed Evie into the living room.

"Wowzers!" Gracie popped off the couch, where she had been sitting next to Bodie. "That dress is killer." The girl stared at her in awe. "Did you dance? I bet you danced with Dev!"

Bodie's expression went from subdued to stony.

Charity did her best to play down the accusation. "Why would you say that?"

"Because of that night at the Tumble Inn," the girl bubbled. "And because he's superhot. Especially when he wears his uniform. Don't you think?"

"Oh, I don't know. He's okay, I suppose." She turned to Bodie before anyone could get a good look at her face. "How are you? Feeling better?"

"I only had a headache," he muttered, as though the attention embarrassed him. "You didn't have to leave early."

"I wanted to. Are you ready to go?"

He nodded, and then to her surprise, glanced at Luis and Evie. "Thanks for letting me hang out tonight." He looked in Gracie's direction, though not directly at her. "I guess you're right. *The Empire Strikes Back* really is the best *Star Wars* movie."

The girl beamed. "Told you! Sometime maybe we can watch the rest of them. I've seen them all a million times. My dad is still a huge fan, even though he's, like, forty-five."

Bodie actually cracked a smile. "Sounds good."

Hope sparked in the midst of Charity's worry for the kid. It seemed he'd at least connected with Gracie on a *Star Wars* level.

Charity thanked Luis and Evie again and then led Bodie out to the truck. When they were both belted in, she turned to him. "Are you sure you're okay?" Not that he ever looked especially happy, but when she'd heard he wasn't feeling well, worry had crammed itself tightly into her chest. She didn't even know where it had come from.

"I'm fine," Bodie grumbled. "I barely mentioned I had a headache and the next thing I knew, Mrs. Cortez was calling Naomi."

Charity started the engine and pulled out of the driveway. "I was worried about you."

He kept his chin tucked, his head down. "I don't need you to worry about me."

Actually, he did. He needed someone to worry about him, to think about him, to put his needs above hers. Because it was pretty obvious Melody wasn't doing a stellar job of that. She tightened her grip on the steering wheel. He needed someone to protect him, to be there for him. Why didn't her sister realize that?

"Have you heard from Mom yet?" She thought she detected a waver in Bodie's voice, but he'd turned his head to the passenger's window.

"Not yet." Charity pulled over to the side of the road and rested her hand on his shoulder. "But we'll find her. I promise. She loves you so much, Bodie. You've always been the most important person in her heart." Even if she wasn't capable of showing it.

"Then why'd she'd leave?" He shook his head and looked down at his fisted hands, and Charity had to steel her chest against the heartbreak. She didn't have an answer.

"I need you to give me a list of all the people your mom knows back in Oklahoma." She'd called all of the old friends she could remember, but her sister likely had other acquaintances. "I need phone numbers, if you have them." They'd waited on Melody long enough. If her sister refused to come back, Charity would simply have to track her down and make her come back. She would fix this for Bodie.

"I've already called everyone," her nephew muttered. "No one knows where she is. She hasn't gone back home."

"Well, I'll call again. I'll keep calling until we get some answers. And if anyone is still in touch with her, they can tell her to check in with us." Because she had plenty of things to say to her sister. The most important one being that she was screwing up the best thing in her life.

"Aunt Charity?"

"Yeah?" She glanced over, expecting to see the kid's cold expression. Instead, Bodie bit his bottom lip uncertainly.

"Thanks for leaving the party early to pick me up," he finally said. "I've never had anyone to call."

Tears welled up, making the road in front of her swim. "Well, from now on, you can always call me, Bodie. Always."

Dev had completely tuned out of the party. Instead of joining everyone on the dance floor, he sat at the bar deliberating. He probably should've told Charity what he'd learned about the robbery back in Oklahoma. He almost had, but she'd shut him down. A weariness had taken over her mannerisms when she told him she didn't want to talk about Melody, and he hadn't wanted to ruin her night. He didn't want to make the situation with Bodie any harder on her than it already seemed to be, so maybe it was best to keep the whole thing to himself. Until he knew more. Until the PD back in Oklahoma had evidence to support his theory...

"You look like you could use a beer." Without waiting for an answer, Darla thunked an IPA down on the bar in front of Dev.

"Thanks." He definitely needed a beer. He and Darla had known each other a long time. Ever since she'd moved here ten years ago after her husband died. Though he wouldn't call her a close friend, they'd hung out occasionally. She always seemed to know when someone needed a pick-me-up.

"Anything you want to talk about?" She leaned on the bar across from him. "You know what they say about bartenders. We're the best listeners."

He took a long pull on the beer, already knowing it wouldn't take the edge off of Charity's disappearing act. "You shouldn't be tending bar tonight. It's your party."

"And we all know what a control freak I am." She poured a glass of red wine for herself. "Does the scowl have anything to do with Charity taking off?"

"Not exactly." It wasn't the reason she'd had to go that had him scowling. It was the exchange between them right before she'd left. "She had to pick up Bodie. He wasn't feeling well."

Darla came around the bar and sat next to him. "Then why do you look like you're about ready to take down a felon?"

"It's a long story." One he didn't feel like telling. But Darla knew Charity better than most people. "Let me ask you something." He spun the stool to face her. "Charity told me to leave her alone. Do you think she means it?" Because he wasn't about to pursue a woman who wasn't interested. He'd spent enough of his life wondering why he wasn't good enough. Didn't need to go down that road again.

"If she said it, my guess would be she means it." Darla gave him an apologetic look. "At least for now."

"Got it." That was it then. He wouldn't call, wouldn't drop by, wouldn't go out of his way to see if he could run into her. "Thanks." He tipped his beer toward Darla. "Appreciate the honesty."

"You know me. I don't hide from the truth." She clanked her wineglass against his beer in a toast. "Can I get you anything else?"

"Nope. I'm good." Well, not good exactly... more like resigned.

"Then I have to go check on the chocolate supply." Darla stood and gave him a squeeze on the shoulder. "Why don't you save me a dance later?"

"Will do." If he stuck around, that was. Since Charity had left, he didn't see much of a point. Though he doubted any of his friends were ready to leave. Since he was the designated driver, he might be here all night.

Searching for a distraction from his thoughts, he turned the stool so he could watch the rest of the party. Both Levi and Mateo were currently dancing with their wives and seemed to be enjoying themselves just fine. He panned his gaze to the outskirts of the crowd. Ty caught him looking and hurried over. "Dude, there're hot twins from Aspen over there."

"And?" Dev nursed his beer and resisted the temptation to get himself another. The one night he actually wanted to indulge and yet he'd volunteered to drive. He should've made one of the married guys be DD.

"I need my wingman." Ty slid onto the stool next to him. "Come on. A bull rider and a public servant? We'll be unstoppable."

"I'm not interested in twins from Aspen." The one woman he was interested in had run out on him. Again.

Ty gave him a suspicious once-over. "Does this have anything to do with the way you were dancing with Charity?"

Dev let his silence speak for him.

"All right, man. As your friend, I'm going to give you three reasons you should steer clear of that woman." He held up a finger. "One, she has a fiery hot temper."

"From what I've seen, she has a temper only when it's necessary." Like when that cowboy at the bar had hit on Gracie. Or when she'd been trying to protect her nephew after he crashed her truck. Sure, she had a temper, but she got worked up only about important things. Things that mattered. If anything, that only made her more appealing.

Ty didn't acknowledge the argument. "Reason number two to steer clear of Charity—she's a workaholic. Trust me, you've never seen anything like it. Trains every day, rain or shine. Up at the crack of dawn. I've even seen her work herself so hard she passed out."

Dev gave in and helped himself to another beer from the steel tub on the bar. "So I'm supposed to steer clear because she wants to be the best at what she does? Isn't that the point of your profession? To compete?" Seemed to him that was called dedication.

"Oh boy." Ty hopped off the stool. "You're a lost cause. You've already gone to the dark side, haven't you?" He grabbed Dev's collar in his fist. "It's not too late to come back. You can fight this, man. Don't give in. Bachelors are a dying breed around here. You can't leave me all by myself."

Rolling his eyes at the theatrics, Dev shook Ty's hand off him and set down his beer bottle. "Relax. I can still be your wingman. It's not like Charity wants to be with me anyway." She'd made that pretty clear before she left.

"So you're in?" Ty seemed to have frozen in disbelief.

"Sure. Why not?" If he was going to be stuck at this party for another three hours, he might as well have some fun.

Chapter Nine

Charity slathered a thick coating of Nutella on the French toast she'd made for Bodie. That was the best way to reach a teen boy, right? Through his stomach? She added a layer of cut-up strawberries on top for good measure.

Sunlight poured in through the window over her sink, bathing her in warmth, but it wasn't enough to reach inside of her. She'd spent all day yesterday making phone calls to the list Bodie had given her. Supposedly, none of her sister's acquaintances had heard a word from Melody since she'd left town. None of them knew where she had gone either. One friend her sister had known since high school mentioned something about a boyfriend named Cody, but when Charity had asked Bodie about it, he said he'd never met a Cody, so who knew if that was some recent man in her life or one of the many who had come and gone.

Uttering a heart-sinking sigh, Charity arranged the food on the plate and brought it to the kitchen table. Then she went to the refrigerator and poured Bodie a big glass of orange juice. Any minute now, he would come out of his room and after breakfast she would drive him over to the middle school.

He'd had a conniption fit last night when Charity had told him he had to start going to school, and she didn't blame him. But he'd already missed the better part of a week back in Oklahoma, and Dev was right. She couldn't let him get behind. They didn't need to add that to the long list of challenges he already had to face. So she'd gotten all the paperwork together, ordered his transcripts from Oklahoma, and now she had to bring him to a place where he didn't know one single person, except for Gracie, and leave him there all day. Nerves rolled through her stomach the same way they had back on her first day of middle school. She remembered all too well how much it had sucked.

Across the great room, there were sounds—a door opening, rustling, footsteps. Charity rushed back to the sink and busied herself with doing the dishes. She'd hardly slept all night fearing that the kid would try to run away again. She'd checked on him at least every hour, opening the door silently and poking her head into the room to make sure he was still there and not off joyriding in her loaner truck. Thankfully, the crash had seemed to discourage his plans to take off and go find his mom.

"Good morning," she sang in a chipper voice when he walked into the kitchen.

He grunted a response.

Charity turned off the faucet and assessed his attire. Black T-shirt, black jeans, black combat boots. This outfit appeared to be the full extent of the wardrobe he'd brought with him. That would make it pretty tough to fit in with kids who wore brass belt buckles and cowboy boots. Not that she wanted to tell him that.

Much to her relief, Bodie went and sat at the table right away, and even started to eat the French toast.

Gathering courage, she sat across from him. "So are you ready for school?"

He kept his head down. "Does it matter?"

Don't flinch. She couldn't let him see how much his hateful tone hurt. "I know this isn't ideal," she said patiently. "But it's only temporary. Just until your mom comes back. I don't want you to miss out on any learning."

His eyes got that stormy look again—like any minute lightning would flash out of them—but he didn't say anything.

"I've heard great things about the school." She'd called Naomi to ask some questions, and her friend had only positive things to say. "I know it'll be different, but Gracie will be there. I'm sure you'll run into her."

"Great." He dropped his fork and pushed away the plate of half-eaten French toast.

Charity ignored his sarcastic tone and forged ahead. "I found a backpack. And some supplies." She pointed to where she'd laid everything out by the front door. "And I talked to the principal earlier this morning. She said they're looking forward to meeting you."

Anger masked every feature on his face, but she recognized it for what it was. Fear. He covered it up the same way she did, and god, it made her heart ache for him. "It's going to be fine." All of it. School. His mom. Her. Him. It had to be fine. She couldn't consider the alternative, what it would do to all of them if Melody didn't come back. She wouldn't consider it. "We need to get going. Don't want to be late for your first day." Quickly, she cleared the table and dumped everything in the sink.

Her nephew took his time getting his things together, but eventually they made it out to the truck. Bodie didn't speak all the way to the middle school, and every word she thought of to say sounded too trite. This wouldn't be easy for him, so in the end she didn't try to sugarcoat it.

The school actually had a certain appeal to it, at least on the outside. It was an older brick building, but it had obviously been well cared for. The landscaping made it fit right in among the mountains and forests with the lush blue spruce clustered here and there and the mountain wildflowers dotting a large garden near the entrance.

Charity parked the truck in a space reserved for visitors. "Well, I guess this is it." Nerves swam through her stomach.

"Guess we should go in." She tried to keep a positive bounce in her step as they walked up to the main entrance. They were early, so only a few kids were hanging around. Charity tried to smile at them to compensate for Bodie's scowl. The office right inside the front door wasn't all that welcoming, but the admin assistant seemed friendly. "Mrs. Lockwood will be right out," the woman said after Charity had signed them in.

Bodie stewed in the corner while Charity glanced at the accolades hanging on the walls. There were certificates for academics and an antibullying campaign that had been led by students. Before she could point them out to her nephew, the principal emerged and greeted them warmly.

Mrs. Lockwood welcomed them with a genuine smile. She had long brown hair divided into two braids and calming brown eyes. Charity liked her instantly. Little by little, her anxiety eased as Mrs. Lockwood took them on a brief tour, pointing out Bodie's locker, the cafeteria, library, gymnasium, and art room. For the first time, Charity thought she noticed a flicker of interest on Bodie's face when the principal talked about the different projects the students worked on in art class.

When they got back to the office, Mrs. Lockwood handed Bodie a schedule. "Here are your classes. Everything is very easy to find since we're a small school. But if you do have any questions or need help finding something, just ask any of the teachers or other students. We pride ourselves on creating a friendly, open environment for all students here."

"Thank you," Charity said for her nephew, who was focused on cramming the schedule into his backpack. "Bodie, do you have any questions for Mrs. Lockwood?"

"Nope."

Oh, wow! A whole word. Not even a grunt this time. That was progress. "I guess I should get going then, huh?" The nerves in her stomach now churned into a cesspool of worries. Would he make friends? Would anyone talk to him? Would the other kids ostracize him for his sullen bad-boy look? A rise of tears burned against her eyes. How did parents do this? Leave their kids and not keel over from a heart attack due to the stress?

"Bodie, why don't you go put away your things in your locker?" Mrs. Lockwood suggested pleasantly.

This time he did grunt before he started to walk away.

"You can call me," Charity said quickly. "If you need anything at all. I'll keep my phone on me all day."

"I'll be fine," her nephew muttered, not even turning around to say goodbye.

Right. She had to play it as cool as he was. But she wanted so badly to chase him down and hug him to remind him he wasn't alone in the world. "Have a good day," she yelled instead.

Bodie immediately ducked his chin to his chest, slipped in his earbuds, and trudged down the hall.

"He'll be fine," Mrs. Lockwood said kindly.

"I know he will." And yet a few tears slipped out anyway. He had no friends here. No mom at home right now. His dad had never been a part of his life. She remembered that feeling—that you were so alone even when you were surrounded by people.

"I'll call you if anything comes up. We'll take great care of him." Mrs. Lockwood reached out to shake her hand and then disappeared back into the office.

Charity took the hint and got a move on. She'd originally planned to go directly over to the Cortez ranch so she could ride out all of her anxieties, but instead she veered off course and drove to Everly's Farm Café, where she knew at least some of her friends would be having breakfast. Sure enough, Darla and Naomi were sitting at a table with Everly near the kitchen.

"Hey!" Each of her friends offered her a warm hug.

"How'd it go this morning?" Naomi asked.

"I'm freaking out a little," Charity admitted.

Naomi nodded in solidarity. "Dropping them off the first day is always the hardest. I remember when I took Gracie to kindergarten. I cried all the way home."

"She was six." And Bodie was thirteen. But she'd never had to do this before.

Naomi stirred her coffee wearing a knowing look. "Well, it sure doesn't get much easier. I still worry. I still miss her when she's gone all day."

Yeah, that was weird. That missing feeling. Charity had been alone so long she'd forgotten how it felt to have someone in the house, but it was . . . nice. Even though her nephew didn't exactly exude cheer and warm fuzzies, she was getting used to having him around.

"I know how we can take your mind off it." Darla held up her iPad. "Let's look at pictures from the party."

"Oohh, fun." Naomi leaned over the table. "I'll bet you got some good ones."

Charity doubted the pictures would take her mind off Bodie, but she glanced at them as Darla swiped through. She had to admit, she was shocked by her own appearance. She actually looked like she was having a good time.

"It was such a fun party." Everly turned to Charity. "Why'd you have to leave early? I hardly even got to see you."

She hadn't seen much of anyone that night...mostly because she'd been too occupied with a certain deputy. "Bodie wasn't feeling well," she said quickly. Over the last few days she'd done her best not to think about Dev. About how he'd held her close when they'd danced or how he'd looked at her like he saw something special.

"Oh, man, I felt so bad," Naomi said across the table.

Uh-oh. Charity knew where this was going. She tried to signal for Naomi to zip it, but her friend continued.

"I hated to interrupt you and Dev."

"Interrupt?" Darla paused the picture slideshow. "What exactly did you interrupt?"

"Well...I'm not entirely sure." Her friend raised her eyebrows in Charity's direction. "But it looked like *something*."

"We were talking," Charity lied. She couldn't do the squeals and questions right now.

"Mm-hmm," Darla murmured. She swiped through a few more pictures and stopped on one that had caught Charity and Dev in the middle of their dance. Someone had snapped it right when he'd had his hand low on her back...

Charity's legs got all tingly again just looking at it.

"Whoa, baby." Everly leaned in closer. "Look at his eyes in this one. He's totally captivated."

"No. It's the lighting." Charity reached over and swiped to the next picture, which happened to be another of her and

Dev. "Geez, what creepy person was going around taking close-up shots like this anyway?"

"Me." Darla took back control of the iPad. "It was my birthday. I wanted to capture the memories." She shot Charity a brassy grin. "Not my fault if you'd rather not hold on to the memories. I for one had a great time. It'll be tough to top it next year." She scrolled through more pictures.

"Wait." Another image of Dev caught Charity's eye. "Go back to that one."

"Which one?" Darla swiped back a few and stopped on one where Dev was dancing with some woman Charity had never seen. She didn't care. Okay, she shouldn't care, but she couldn't stop herself from asking, "Who's that?"

"That's my friend Reba. From Aspen. She's awesome. Works as a sous chef at a fabulous new restaurant there."

Charity's gaze sharpened on the picture. In addition to being a sous chef, Reba from Aspen was also the kind of gorgeous that made *her* jaw drop. "And I thought my dress was low-cut," she muttered, rolling her eyes at the woman's generous cleavage. "She's really putting herself out there, huh? Trolling for cowboys?"

"Actually, she's gorgeous and smart and funny." Darla set down the iPad and folded her hands neatly on the table. "Did you or did you not tell Dev to leave you alone?"

"Yes. I did." She just hadn't thought he'd go off and find the next woman less than a half hour later.

"Then what's the problem?"

"There's no problem." Red-hot jealousy reared to life inside her. But she had no reason to be jealous. She didn't have feelings for Dev. Not real feelings. "Actually, it's a relief to see him dancing with someone. Maybe he really will leave me alone then." Like she wanted. Then things in her life could go back to normal. She could stop thinking about him and get her head back in the game with her training. Since Bodie had shown up and all this kissing business had started she'd already lost too much time, and the competition season wasn't that far off.

"You do realize your face is redder than a smacked bum right now, don't you?" Naomi asked gently.

"It is not." She reached up to touch her cheeks. "I got sunburned the other day."

Everly gazed at her with a look of sympathy. "If you like Dev, why did you tell him to leave you alone?"

Because the man terrified her. Actually, maybe that wasn't exactly true. The things he made her feel terrified her. "I don't like Dev. Not that way."

Unfortunately, Darla always managed to see right through her. "He asked me if I thought you meant it, and I told him yes." Her friend tilted her head. "Did you mean it?"

How was she supposed to know? Things in her life weren't exactly smooth sailing right now. Her sister was gone. She'd gone from living alone to having a thirteen-year-old to take care of. Dev had kissed her twice, and now suddenly she felt like something was missing from her life, but instead of trying to figure out what it might be, she wanted to run, to feel free. So even if she didn't quite mean it yet, she would eventually. "Yes. I meant it."

"Then do me a favor and don't bitch when you see more pictures of Dev and Reba," Darla said, all snippy-like.

More pictures? How many more were there? Charity couldn't keep her mouth shut. "Dev *and* Reba. So what, they're an item now?" He met the love of his life right after he kissed *her*?

Darla answered with an exasperated glare.

Yes, it was ridiculous. She had no business getting pissy because Dev had enjoyed himself with a woman at Darla's party. But it turned out jealousy was more like a reflex than a manageable emotion. She'd never experienced it quite like this before.

"If it makes you feel any better, he didn't seem that into her," Naomi offered. "They danced and hung out for a while, but at the end of the night they went their separate ways."

It did help, but Charity didn't want to explore why.

"Yeah, you can see it in the pictures," Everly added. "He doesn't exactly look thrilled."

"And look at this one." Darla swiped through a few more, stopping on one where Dev was looking away from the woman he was dancing with. "If you ask me, it looks like he'd rather be with someone else."

"Totally," Everly agreed. "Look at this one." She shuffled through more pictures, but Charity had had enough.

"I don't have time to look at any more pictures." She needed to get her mind off Dev and this wasn't helping. "I have to get out to the ranch and get in some training hours before Bodie comes home from school." She had to get back on her horse, where everything made sense.

Just when she thought the day couldn't get any worse, she found Levi, Ty, and Mateo standing outside of the corral chitchatting like a group of old biddies when she arrived at the Cortez ranch. She wasn't in the mood to chitchat. She wanted to climb onto Ace's back and ride until the overabundance of worries she'd suddenly accumulated rolled off her in drops of sweat.

Hoping they would take the hint, Charity kept her head down and her eyes focused on the stables beyond them.

"Hey Calamity Jane." Ty had never been particularly skilled at taking hints. "How's it going?"

She kept right on moving, sweeping past them. "Not my best day." It wasn't even nine o'clock and she'd already had her heart ripped out twice. Once when she had to leave Bodie at school and again when she'd seen those pictures of Dev cozying up to that woman.

"What's up?" Levi asked, walking over. He was married. Hadn't he learned when to steer clear of a woman?

"Rough morning with the kid?" Mateo asked, coming to join them.

Lovely. It looked like she would be forced into a round of chitchat after all.

"I had to drop him off at school this morning. And he definitely wasn't excited about it."

"Can't say I blame him." Ty ambled over to join the circle. "Middle school is about as fun as prison."

"Well, if he doesn't go to school he'll likely end up in prison someday." And she couldn't let that happen. If Melody wasn't going to guide him to a better path, she'd have to do it herself.

Levi's eyes narrowed. "So dropping your nephew off at school sucked, but you look pissed. You sure that's all it is? Or did some poor schmuck hit on you at the bar again?"

"Yeah, that looks more like your man-hating glare," Mateo agreed.

"You need us to rough the guy up for you?" Ty asked, pushing up his shirtsleeves.

"No thanks." That would be difficult, because she wasn't mad at a man. She was only mad at herself. But it was better to let them think she'd merely had another encounter at the bar. They could never find out about her and Dev. She'd never hear the end of it. "I can handle things myself."

"Okay. Sure. Yeah. You're fine all right." A healthy dose of sarcasm laced Levi's tone.

"What's that supposed to mean?"

Levi glanced at Ty, who glanced at Mateo.

"You've seemed more stressed lately, that's all," Mateo said, taking a healthy step back.

Ty gave her some space too. "There's a lot going on. We know you're tough and all, but sometimes it's okay to let people help—"

"I don't need help." They were as bad as Dev. "What I need is for people to stop—"

Her phone buzzed in her back pocket, sending a rush of panic through her. Was it Bodie? She yanked it out and stared at the screen, but it simply said *unavailable*.

"Bodie?" she answered breathlessly, darting away from the guys.

A pause stretched on too long, making her heart leap for her throat. "Hello? Bodie? Is that you?"

"Char?"

A weight fell on her chest, crushing the air from her lungs. She wasn't sure if it was relief or fear. "Melody."

Static blipped on the line. "Yeah. Hi."

Hi? Charity braced her free hand on the fence and gazed out at the peaks towering in the distance, trying to let the view fill her with a sense of calm. "Where are you?" Hearing her sister's voice, she now realized that was all that really mattered. Charity's sole focus had been on Bodie, but she'd been worried about Melody too. "Are you okay?"

"I'm fine." The words had a hollow ring. "Just calling to check in. Is Bodie okay? How's he doing?"

For a second, Charity was too stunned to respond. How could her sister call and chat like this was something they'd planned? Like she'd taken a vacation and Charity was babysitting for her? "How do you think he is?" The ache in her heart put a rasp in her voice. "God, Mel, you left him on my doorstep with no explanation. What is he supposed to think?"

"I needed time to figure out a couple of things, but I'll come back for him. I swear. Tell him that, okay?"

"Why don't *you* tell him?" He needed to hear that from his mom. That she hadn't abandoned him, that she loved him. "Where are you?" Charity asked before Mel could hang up. "Do you need help? I can come and get you. I can help you figure out whatever you're dealing with."

"I just wanted to get a few details straightened out before Bodie and I move," Melody said. "I should've talked to you first, but I didn't know if you'd take him, and—"

"Of course I would take him. He's my nephew." Emotion rattled her throat. "And you're my sister. I want to help. Tell me what I can do."

"Just take care of him for me." Desperation edged into her tone. "I'm not sure when I'll be able to come back for him. But I will. I have to. Tell him I love him. Please. Tell him everything will be okay soon." Before Charity could respond, the line went dead.

She shoved the phone back into her pocket and rested her forearms on the fence, hunching slightly while she took a few deep breaths. It didn't help to relieve the sudden queasiness.

Boots clomped nearby, kicking up dust, and Charity didn't have to turn her head to know that Levi, Mateo, and Ty were headed her way.

They gathered around her in a supportive formation, but still gave her a wide berth.

"Everything good?" Levi asked, edging closer to her.

That was a complicated question, so she opted to answer with, "It was Melody." She looked out at the mountains again, not wanting any of them to see evidence of tears in her eyes.

"What'd she say?" Ty asked, stuffing his hands into his pockets.

"That things are fine and she'll be back for Bodie soon."

Mateo awkwardly patted her shoulder. "That's good, right?"

"You don't believe her," Levi said when Charity remained silent.

"Things aren't fine." She knew from the bad feeling that had burrowed itself deep inside her chest. All those years of fending for herself had taught her to rely on instinct and intuition, and she just knew.

"So she's not coming back?" Ty asked.

"She wants to." Charity had heard that longing in her sister's voice. She straightened and turned around so she could lean her back against the fence.

"But you don't think she'll actually do it." Levi didn't phrase it as a question.

"I don't have high hopes that she'll be able to." What if Dev was right? What if her sister was in some kind of trouble? So many what-ifs, and she couldn't do anything about them. She definitely wouldn't tell Bodie about the phone call. It wasn't fair. She didn't want the kid waiting around the same way she had all those years. For her mom to show up, to step up, to be who she needed her to be. Look what all that waiting had done to her. Eventually she'd given up hope that anyone would step up, so she'd walled off her heart from the rest of the world. Now it was impossible to let anyone in.

"What're you going to do?" Mateo asked.

"I'm going to take care of Bodie." And she was going to do everything in her power to make sure her nephew didn't end up as damaged as she had.

Chapter Ten

*N*ot this again.

From his hiding spot off the west side of the highway, Dev watched a familiar blue Buick sedan steadily increase in speed as it approached his SUV. Sure enough, the car flew past him going at least twenty miles per hour over the limit.

Tempting as it was to let Vera McDougal continue on at her high rate of speed, he sighed, flicked on his lights, and tore out after her. He wasn't about to give her the siren though. She'd enjoy that a little too much.

He tailed her until she pulled onto the dirt shoulder and then brought the SUV to a stop behind her. He'd pulled her over three times in the last two weeks. The funny part was she only started to speed when she saw his car. And then every time he stopped her, it was the same thing—a friendly chat while she tried to flirt with him. She was pretty good at pouring on the charm, which shouldn't be surprising. She was in her seventies, and clearly had had a lot of practice.

Dev bumped open his door with his shoulder and took his time getting out of the car. Vera had already cut the engine and was waiting for him with her window down. It looked like she'd just come from the beauty shop. Her white hair was styled and stiff, completely intact, even with the breeze.

"Hi there, sugar." A glossy coat of red lipstick overpowered her lips...and a few teeth. "Was I goin' a little too fast back there?"

"We've been through this, Vera," he started, striving to hit the note between stern and polite. "You can't speed because you want to chat. One of these times I'm gonna have to give you a ticket." If he wasn't so worried about her plowing into someone, he wouldn't even bother to pull her over anymore.

The woman flicked down her cat-eye sunglasses and trailed her gaze over him. "Well, I wouldn't have to speed if you'd take me up on my offer to come over for those fresh chocolate chip cookies I've promised to bake you." She shot him a sultry gaze. "It'd be a good way to secure my vote for the election, if you know what I mean."

Not her too. "I'm not concerned about votes." Maybe he should be but he couldn't seem to make himself care. "And I don't think Chuck would like me coming over to see you." Although knowing her husband, he'd be relieved to have the time to himself.

"Oh, I don't think it would be a problem." A lengthy sigh made her shoulders sag. "Chuck and I aren't making love anymore."

"Uh..." Suddenly his uniform felt like an oven. They were not having this conversation. He'd gone through firearms training, self-defense training, defensive driving training, but he wasn't trained to discuss a senior citizen's sex life. "That sounds like a personal matter, and—"

"I want to," Vera interrupted miserably. "But it seems like he's not interested anymore. I mean, I know I'm not twenty-five, but the girls are still perky." She shimmied her chest and Dev averted his eyes to the ground at his boots. Lots of nice dirt. Some shiny rocks. Damn it to blue blazes. He really had to consider a move to the big city, where he could storm buildings and take down drug lords and murderers instead of offering little old ladies sex advice on the side of the highway.

"What do men want anyway?" the woman lamented. "I've cooked and cleaned and taken care of his kids, and now after all that, it's like he doesn't even want to touch me!" Those last words dissolved into tears.

"All right now, Vera. Don't cry." Dev patted her shoulder in what he hoped was a benign, friendly way. "You need to talk to Chuck." Not that he was qualified to be giving relationship advice, but it seemed to him a whole lot could be solved by talking through things.

"You really think I should talk to him?" Vera peered up at him, her mascara running down her cheeks.

"You have to." That would be a hell of a lot better than her talking to Dev about these things. "Maybe he doesn't know how you feel."

She considered this with a frown. "But we've been married for fifty years. He should know."

"I'm gonna let you in on a little secret." Dev leaned down conspiratorially. "Men aren't mind readers. Even after fifty years, I would assume. You have to tell him what you want."

Images of a certain blond barrel racer drifted through his mind, shimmery and tempting and untouchable. Why was it so hard for Charity to admit she wanted him? She'd let him get close and then take the first opportunity she could find to cast him out...

"I guess I could *try* talking to him," Vera muttered, directing her gaze out the front windshield. A look of confusion narrowed her eyes. "Well, that's odd. We don't get many hitchhikers around here this time of year. And that one looks like a real hoodlum."

Dev stood up taller and looked over to where she was staring. Down the highway, about a quarter of a mile, a kid wearing a backpack walked along the shoulder sticking up his thumb at every car that drove past. Aw, hell. He'd recognize those black clothes anywhere.

According to Naomi, Bodie had started school this morning. Looked like he hadn't quite made it through the whole day. Dev muttered a curse under his breath. "You go on home and talk to Chuck," he said to Vera, backing away from the car.

"I will." She started up the Buick with a look of determination. "Maybe I'll stop by that boutique and get some new lingerie too."

Dev pretended he hadn't heard. Hearing things like that made him want to stick his fingers in his ears and sing *la la la* like a little kid. He jogged back to his car and drove down the road, pulling up alongside Bodie.

The kid obviously saw him, but evidently decided to ignore him and stared straight ahead with those damn earbuds firmly fastened to his ears.

Dev swung the car in front of him on the shoulder and stopped. He got out and walked back, gesturing for Bodie to remove the headphones, which the kid did with a huff of irritation.

"What're you doing out here?" he asked when he was sure Bodie could hear him.

"Nothing," the kid muttered. "It's not against the law to go for a walk."

"That's true, but I heard you were supposed to start school today." He'd been surprised to hear that Charity had enrolled the kid in school. She sure hadn't seemed to think it was a good idea when he'd mentioned it. Dev glanced at his watch. "As far as I can tell, school's not out for another two hours."

Bodie's eyes darted around like he was searching for a way to bail on the conversation.

"Get in the car," Dev said before the kid got any fancy ideas. He really wasn't in the mood for a foot chase.

"What if I don't?"

"Then I guess I'll have to keep tailing you all the way down the highway." He wasn't about to let him hitchhike his way back to Oklahoma. Bodie didn't want to think about the kind of people who would pick up a kid off the highway.

With a look seemingly meant to incinerate him, Bodie climbed into the back seat of Dev's SUV and slammed the door hard.

Well, at least he hadn't had to chase him down. Dev climbed into the driver's seat and buckled up.

"Just take me back to my aunt's house," the kid ordered like he'd climbed into a cab instead of a police vehicle.

Had to hand it to him, Bodie had nerve. "Actually, I can't. Because I happen to know your aunt is not home right now." She'd be out at Levi's place training, and this kid had already proven multiple times he required some intense supervision.

"So?" Bodie demanded. "I'm by myself all the time back home."

Dev didn't doubt that. "Well, now you're in Colorado." And from what he could tell, the kid had better get used to it. After his lengthy conversation with the investigator back in Oklahoma, he was even more convinced that Melody had been involved in the robbery.

With that in mind, Dev pulled out onto the highway and headed for the Cortez ranch. "So what happened at school? Why'd you leave?" Maybe the kid actually had a good reason. For Charity's sake, Dev hoped so.

"I didn't like it," Bodie muttered.

And maybe he didn't have a good reason. "You should give it a chance. Can't tell much after only a few hours."

"Whatever." Bodie turned to stare out the window. "Not like I'm gonna be here long anyway." Because he planned to leave on his own or he really thought his mom would come back? Dev didn't ask. "Well, while you are here, it wouldn't hurt to make an effort," he said with a glance in the rearview mirror. "For your aunt at least." God knew she'd have her hands full with an angry teenage boy living in her house.

No answer. Not that he'd really expected one. Letting the conversation die, Dev turned onto the Cortezes' winding drive. He hadn't even seen Charity yet, and already anticipation snaked through his veins.

He parked in front of the corral and cut the engine. Bodie scrambled to get out of the SUV before Dev had even released his seat belt. When he finally got out of the car, Bodie was already marching over to his aunt, who had ridden Ace to meet them.

"What's wrong?" She dismounted and hurried over to Bodie, her mouth twisted with worry.

"This was the worst day of my life." Suddenly, the kid sounded like he was on the verge of tears.

Yep. Dev remembered middle school angst. Everything always seemed worse than it was. He tried to figure out the best way to break the news to Charity. "He left school. I found him on the highway. Hitchhiking."

"Hitchhiking?" Now worry took over her pretty blue eyes too.

"I was only trying to get back to your house," Bodie muttered. "No one at school was nice to me. They made fun of me. One kid even said he wanted to fight me."

"Oh my god. I'm so sorry." Charity slipped off her helmet and tossed it on the ground. "Why didn't you call me? You didn't have to hitchhike home. I would've come to pick you up right away if I'd known what was going on."

Dev eased a step closer to her. While he understood it was rough at a new school, Bodie had to learn to handle things like this. He was a smart kid, not to mention strong. "If you're being bullied, you can always go to a teacher or the principal." After the school violence that had taken place elsewhere in Colorado, the administration had a zero-tolerance policy on bullying. Every incident was taken seriously. "But you can't leave school grounds without permission. For one thing, it's a closed campus, and for another, there are consequences for ditching."

"I don't know any of the teachers," Bodie snapped. "And the principal wasn't even around during lunch."

"Well, I know every teacher at that school, and I know they all care about the students' safety and well-being. Any one of them would've stepped in to intervene."

"He didn't know that." Charity hadn't looked at Dev directly once since she'd walked over. She was solely focused on her nephew. "I totally understand why you left. Come on." She laid her hand on Bodie's shoulder. "I'll take you home."

Home? But then the kids who'd bullied him wouldn't be held accountable. It would likely keep happening.

They both turned to walk away.

"Maybe we should take him back to school and meet with the principal," Dev called. He didn't want to overstep, but Bodie would have to go back to school eventually. He couldn't avoid those kids forever.

Charity squared up her shoulders. "He's not going back to school today." *And you can't make him*, her posture seemed to add. But a threatening look had never stopped him before. He could help. That's what he did for a living, that's who he was as a person. She might not want anything to do with him, but that didn't mean he couldn't help Bodie. Dev remembered that feeling of insecurity after his mom had left all too well. He'd lacked the confidence to stand up for himself the same way Bodie seemed to. That's what the kid needed right now—a way to develop some self-confidence, and maybe another friend to talk to sometimes. Someone who understood a lot of what he was going through. He'd offered that to Charity on more than one occasion, but maybe he should be offering it to her nephew directly.

"Hey, Bodie," he called over, just as the two of them were climbing into Charity's rental.

The kid paused, but didn't acknowledge him.

"You interested in one of those brand-new PlayStation things?"

Bodie's eyes seemed to open a tad bit wider. Yeah, now they were speaking the same language. Dev sauntered over. "Because my parents got me one for my birthday months ago, and it's still in the box." Yes, it was embarrassing to admit his parents still bought him things like that, but his mom thought playing video games would be a good "stress reliever" to give him a break from his job. Only he didn't have time to play video games. "I'd be willing to part with it if you'd be willing to help me out with some work on the ranch. I've even got a few games to go with it."

"That's okay." Charity stuck her head out the window. "He doesn't need a Play—"

"What kind of work?" Bodie slammed the passenger's door shut and walked back to meet Dev. "And how much time are we talking?"

"I'd say all the work could be done in a couple of Saturdays. We've got some fences that need fixing, a few trees to take down." Dev glanced past him to Charity, but he couldn't read the look on her face. "If it's all right with your aunt." He had a feeling he already knew the answer to that question.

Bodie spun. "Please, Aunt Charity? I've never had a PlayStation."

When she hesitated, Dev walked over to her window and leaned in. "It might be good for him. To spend some time outside. To have something to work toward. When I said I'd like to help, I meant it."

For the first time since he'd brought Bodie to her, Charity's worried frown seemed to soften. "You're right. It would be good for him. Thank you." Her gaze crossed Dev's but didn't linger. "What time should I bring him over?"

"I'll be ready whenever you guys are." Dev smiled to reinforce the truce they'd seemed to form. Maybe she was finally starting to believe that he really would be there for both her and Bodie, as long as she would let him.

Dev slammed the blade of the shovel into the soft dirt surrounding the fence post and jammed the heel of his boot into the step. Getting leverage on the handle, he dug out a wide circle around the rotted wood, heaving and hauling dirt off to the side until sweat rolled down his temples. At this rate, he'd be done working on the fence before Charity and Bodie showed up.

He hadn't meant to get such an early start, but he'd been wide awake since before sunup. Charity had that effect on him. As much as he'd reminded himself she was coming only for Bodie's sake, he still couldn't wait to see her. The anticipation buzzed through him, which made him antsy for some manual labor.

Dev tossed his shovel aside and ripped the fence post the rest of the way out of the ground. He'd loaded up the ATV with everything they'd need to fix the fence posts his dad had mentioned, and then had driven down the driveway to where Charity and Bodie would easily spot him.

He snatched up one of the new fence posts and plunked it into the hole he'd dug before packing the dirt around it. Fifteen more to go and he'd be able to check this off his list.

A diesel engine droned behind him and sent his heart plummeting. Dev watched Charity's rental truck roll up the drive in a plume of dust. He picked up the shovel where he'd dropped it and walked over to meet them on the road.

Bodie opened the door and slowly slunk out of the truck like he was still half asleep. Yeah, Dev remembered those days—sleeping in until noon whenever he could get the chance. That was before girls had made his life complicated. The thought prompted a grin.

"What time should I pick him up?" Charity called out the window. She'd certainly mastered the art of keeping her distance.

"You're welcome to stay if you want. To supervise."

"I can't." Though the truck was currently in *park*, she kept her eyes on the road in front of her as though she had to concentrate. "I really need to get some training in."

"Right." And she likely didn't want to be within two feet of him. She was scared. He could see it every time he got close to her. The way her body stiffened and her face flushed. The way she guarded herself so carefully. Talk about fences. She'd put up plenty around her heart. He'd managed to get past them a few times, but it wouldn't be as easy as working these posts out of the ground. Dev backed off, giving her the space she seemed to crave. "I think we'll quit about noon." Four hours of manual labor was a good start for the kid. He didn't want to work Bodie too hard their first day, especially since he didn't know how much experience the kid had with yard work.

"I'll be back then." Charity slipped the truck in *drive.* "Bodie, I'll be over at the Cortez ranch if you need anything."

The kid's shoulders sagged into an indifferent hunch, but he gave her a nod.

"Thanks, Dev," Charity muttered as she rolled past. He didn't even have time to say *you're welcome* before she was gone.

"Okay. Well." The deputy made his way back to Bodie, who now stood by the ATV, ogling the machine like he wanted to climb on and speed away.

"You ever driven one?" Dev asked.

"No." Bodie rested his hand on one of the handlebars. "They look pretty fun though."

"They are." Though Dev drove them a lot more conservatively now than he had when he was a kid. As a deputy, he'd been called to the scene of too many ATV accidents around here. "I'll tell you what. You work hard for the next few hours and I'll let you drive it back up to the house when we're done."

The kid's mouth lost the angsty teen scowl, and for a few seconds he looked like any other kid—happy, unburdened. "Seriously?"

"Sure." Dev unloaded more fence posts out of the small trailer and lined them up along the ground. "I mean, I'll ride on the back." Just to make sure he got the hang of it. "But you can drive."

The kid narrowed his eyes in a suspicious glare. "I know you're only doing this because you like my aunt."

"I do like your aunt." It's not like that was any big secret to anyone who'd been paying attention. "But I also happen to think you're a great kid." A kid with a lot of potential if he could get more stability in his life.

"That's not how you made it seem when we hit the statue," Bodie muttered.

And therein would lie their biggest obstacle to any kind of friendship. "I'm a cop, Bodie. I have to do my job." Though he liked to think he did it with some level of compassion, he still had to enforce rules. "You made a few bad decisions, but that doesn't mean I don't like you." It meant he had to help the kid get on the right path before one of those bad decisions cost him everything. Dev had seen it too many times. Last year, he'd had to arrest a "good kid" for driving drunk and killing a classmate. "I know it's hard to believe, but the choices you make now can impact the rest of your life." He handed the kid a shovel.

Bodie rolled his eyes at the lecture and walked away.

Right. Dev blew out a sigh. Words wouldn't be enough. Not for Charity and not for Bodie either. Rather than giving him more advice he wouldn't want to hear, Dev gave Bodie the lowdown on what they were working on and got him started on digging out the next rotted fence post.

"How was the rest of your week at school?" he asked as they slammed the shovels into the ground side by side.

Bodie paused to shed his black sweatshirt and tossed it aside. "It sucked."

Yep, Dev remembered that too. He'd definitely gone through a phase where everything had sucked. "Going to a new school isn't easy." He kept his tone light, so it didn't sound like a lecture. "But you're strong enough to handle it." Maybe he didn't have the confidence quite yet, but they could work on that.

"I hate it here." The kid drove the blade of the shovel into the ground harder. Maybe he needed the same outlet Dev did. If they kept up this pace, they might be done in an hour.

"What's it like back in Oklahoma?" he asked, ditching his shovel and working the fence post out of the ground with his hands.

"I don't know...it's different." Bodie swiped sweat off his forehead with his arm. "I know everyone. People like me there."

Dev tossed the rotted fence post aside and brought over a new one. "People like you here too. Your aunt. Me."

Bodie didn't say anything, but he kept a wary eye on the deputy while Dev shoved the post into the hole. He didn't trust him. Not yet. That was understandable given his history. Dev would have to prove to the kid that he had his best interests in mind.

"Go ahead and pack dirt around it." While he held the post in place, Dev watched the kid work. Bodie definitely had a toughness about him. It appeared manual labor wasn't exactly new to him. "You've got some serious skills with that shovel," he said, trying to wobble the post. It wouldn't budge. "Do you live on a ranch back in Oklahoma?"

"No." Bodie stomped over to start digging around the next post. "We rented a trailer. But I put up a fence to keep some crazy dogs out of our yard."

"*You* put it up? By yourself?" He tried to wrangle his surprise. Not that he didn't think Bodie was capable, but that was some hard work for a kid to handle by himself.

"Mom helped when she could, but she had to work too." Bodie tossed a heaping pile of dirt aside. "The fence was before she got fired, so she didn't have much time."

Dev stopped working so he could get a good look at the kid's face. If Melody had lost her job, there'd likely been money problems. Bad enough to motivate her to hold up a convenience store? "When did she get fired?" Sometimes he hated that his job made him so suspicious of people.

Bodie shrugged like he couldn't exactly remember. "A month ago, I guess."

So the timing was right. Dev started to dig again, trying to plot out his next words carefully. "I guess money was tight then, huh? It definitely was for us when I was growing up." This time he handed the new fence post to Bodie and let him do the honors.

"We've never had any money, but a few weeks ago Mom said someone gave her some to help us out." He jammed the post into the hole and held it straight while Dev packed the earth in around it. "That's probably why she wanted to move and start over somewhere else. We're going to California." His expression dared Dev to disagree. "She's coming back to get me and we're moving there. She probably went to find us a place first. I guess it won't be all bad since the ocean's there."

"Uh, yeah. California's great." Dev couldn't look at him. Someone had *given* them money? *Shit.* He'd like to think maybe it was a relative, or some kind of nonprofit or something, but that gut-twisting instinct of his never lied.

"Hey, how come I'm the one doing all the work?" Bodie demanded, already well over halfway to digging out the next post.

"Right. Sorry." Dev lumbered over in a fog. They worked silently, but his mind was running fast with the information he'd learned. Melody had the motivation to commit the theft, and she'd gotten what sounded like a significant sum of money from an unknown source. So she was likely hiding out and waiting to make sure the robbery investigation went cold before she came back for Bodie. At least that was his informed theory.

For the kid's sake, he hoped he was wrong.

Chapter Eleven

Friday. Thank. God. It. Was. Friday. Charity collapsed on her living room sofa as though she'd just run a marathon in record time. In some ways, she had.

Friday meant she and Bodie had made it through a whole week with no issues at school. Friday meant two days of not rushing around in the mornings when Bodie realized again that he'd forgotten to do a homework assignment the night before.

His first week of school had gotten off to the wrong start with the ditching issue, but this week, he'd made it through—they'd both made it through—and her nephew had even made some friends at school. One of them had invited him over tonight, so for her, Friday also meant book club. And boy did she need it. Her friends. Laughter.

On the other side of the great room, the guest room door opened and Bodie stepped out.

She sat up straight. He wasn't wearing black! Well, not all black anyway. He had on a gray shirt with his black jeans and combat boots. That was progress, right?

He slipped on his backpack and made a beeline for the front door. "I'm gonna head over to Jett's house."

"Right. Sure." Charity dragged herself off the couch and stood, searching for her keys. "I can drive you."

"You don't have to drive me. It's, like, five blocks away."

"Yeah, but I should probably meet his parents."

"I'm not five years old," Bodie muttered. "This isn't some stupid playdate. No one's parents drop them off in this town. Everyone walks or rides their bikes."

He had a point. The last thing she wanted to do during this difficult time was embarrass him in front of the few friends he'd made. But still...she couldn't help but worry. "Are his parents home?"

"Of course they're home. Not like there's anywhere to go on a Friday night in this town." He opened the front door. "I already texted you their address and phone number."

A hint of pride shone through her worries. That was very responsible of him. "And you're sure you want to spend the night? Because I could pick you up later."

"Nah, I'll stay there. We're gonna watch movies and play video games and stuff. Probably stay up late."

He actually looked excited for once, though he was trying to hide it behind that cool kid smile. "You'll have your phone, right?" Naomi had shown her how to track him via Find My iPhone so she'd always know exactly where he was.

"Yeah. I'll keep it with me all night. Right here in my pocket." His tone was almost teasing. As if her protectiveness amused him.

Well, he'd better get used to it. She might be a newbie, but she wasn't half bad at this parenting stuff. Thank god for online parenting articles. She'd read at least a hundred of them this week, and they had all outlined the importance of asking questions and communicating with your teen.

She walked over to the door to see him out. "No hitchhiking, right?"

He grinned again. "No hitchhiking. I swear. That was stupid. Trust me, it won't happen again."

Well, she didn't exactly trust him—not yet—but they were moving in that direction. "If you need anything, or you just want to come home—back to the house, I mean—call me. It doesn't matter what time."

"I will," he overemphasized the words, his wide eyes calling her out with a look of exasperation.

Okay, okay. She could take a hint. He wasn't used to having a parent fuss over him like this. She got it. She'd been independent at his age too.

She followed Bodie out onto the front porch. "Have fun," she called to his retreating back. "Let me know if you need anything." Had she already said that? Oh well. At least he'd know she meant it.

The kid didn't turn around, but at least he waved once more before he disappeared around the corner.

Charity went back inside and closed the door. After having Bodie there for almost three weeks, it felt emptier somehow. Even though he talked as much as a typical thirteen-year-old boy, she'd gotten used to having him around, to sitting down at the dinner table with him at night. Charity went to the kitchen and stuffed her wallet into her back pocket before snatching her keys. Book club wasn't supposed to start for another hour, but she doubted Jessa would mind if she showed up early. It was better than sitting around here and worrying about Bodie and her sister, or thinking about Dev, which had still been happening more than she'd care to admit. It didn't help that Bodie had been talking about him. About how Dev had let him drive the ATV all over their ranch. About how they'd had a race to see who could replace a fence post the fastest, and how Bodie had kicked Dev's butt. She'd tried to keep her feelings for Dev in check, but hearing Bodie talk about the man made it almost impossible. His kindness to Bodie meant more to her than he could ever know.

Before her thoughts of the deputy could take a more romantic turn, she jogged out the door, locked up, and got into her truck. On her way through town, she swung by the address Bodie had given her. It was a modest square modular unit with peeling siding. There were two cars in the driveway, which likely belonged to Jett's parents. The sight made her breathe a little easier. Maybe she could actually enjoy herself tonight instead of worrying. She quickly blazed down the street and got out of there before Bodie caught her spying.

On the drive over to Jessa's, she finally began to relax. Things had gotten off to a rocky start with Bodie, but he seemed to be adjusting. Which was good, since she'd been unable to find her sister. After the phone call, Charity was starting to lose hope that Mel would come back. She'd started to think about the future. Bodie was doing well, so maybe he could stay with her. She had no idea how that would work with her upcoming travel schedule, but she'd figure it out if that's what needed to happen.

Again, she wouldn't worry about it tonight. She'd let herself relax and enjoy being with her friends. Tomorrow morning, she could pick up all of the worrying again.

Doing her best to shut out thoughts of her sister, Charity turned onto the Cortez ranch and followed the winding drive up to the houses. Lance and Jessa had a nice place at the top of the hill near the corral and stables. At one time, Naomi had lived on the property too, but now she and Lucas ran the Hidden Gem Inn on the edge of town. They lived in a large apartment adjacent to the inn with Gracie and her little sister, Charlotte.

Charity parked next to the driveway and got out, admiring Lance and Jessa's gorgeous house. It was all timber and stone, with high vaulted ceilings and beautiful bay windows. Even before she reached the front door to knock, she heard chaos inside. That would be courtesy of the triplets. Declan, Cole, and Paisley were almost a year old. Charity had never been into babies, but even she had to admit they were cuties.

Knowing there was no way Jessa would hear the doorbell, Charity simply walked inside.

Whoa. Paisley was lying on her back on the living room floor, screaming and kicking her legs in the air. Declan was in the middle of the room dumping out a toy box, and she couldn't see Cole, but judging from Jessa's firm "No, no," he had to be up to no good as well.

"Oh my god!" Her harried friend stood in the kitchen looking like she'd just gone to battle. "I'm so glad you're here!" She ran over to Charity, dodging the minefield of toys on the floor. "Lance has been gone all afternoon, and things have really gone crazy around here."

"I can see that." Now Charity spotted Cole. He was sitting in one of the high chairs throwing orange mushy food at the wall. And she thought living with a thirteen-year-old was hard. "Wow. Good thing I came early. It looks like you could use some backup."

"That would be great." Jessa rushed back to the kitchen. "Can you pick up Paisley and try to calm her down?" Her friend lifted Cole out of the high chair and set him gently on the floor.

Calm her down? Jessa wanted Charity to calm down a baby? "Uh. Sure." Though *calm* and *babies* didn't exactly fall within her realm of talents. She crossed the room and assessed the situation, giving it a few minutes before she scooped the tantrum-throwing angel into her arms. "Hi there, Paisley," she murmured, bouncing her lightly.

The baby immediately stopped crying and gazed at her with huge blue eyes.

"Cole, no!" Jessa ran to the other side of the kitchen. "Oh dear lord. He's eating dog food again. I took the time to steam him sweet potatoes, but no...he wants dog food."

Charity laughed and brought Paisley over to where Declan was trashing the living room. "Maybe he likes the taste." She knelt and set the baby girl in front of the toy pile and went to work cleaning up the mess. Grinning at Declan, she tossed the toys into the basket, making a game out of it, and within seconds he'd joined her.

Jessa walked over with Cole and plopped down on the floor across from Charity. "You're really good with them."

Charity continued her game with Declan. "I don't know much about babies." Didn't know much about kids period. One-year-olds or thirteen-year-olds.

"They like you though." Her friend tossed a few stuffed animals into the basket.

"I like them too." Over the past few years she hadn't been around kids much, but that did happen to be one of her favorite parts about traveling to competitions. Meeting the kids, signing autographs, hearing about the dreams they wanted to chase someday. "I definitely don't think I could handle triplets, though." From the look of things, that was a whole other level of insane.

"Oh, it's not so bad—"

The front door swung open and Lance rushed in looking every bit as harried as his wife. "Babe, I'm so sorry I was out that long."

Charity didn't know Lance well. She wasn't sure she'd ever had a real conversation with him, but she could read the love on his face when he walked over and picked up Paisley and Declan, one in each arm, giving them both kisses on their chubby cheeks. The babies cooed and giggled and made a chorus of "dada" noises.

"No worries, hon. We're fine." Jessa stood with Cole and wrapped her arms around Lance, and the five of them hovered like that for a few seconds, clinging to one another in the midst of the mess surrounding them.

A strange sense of longing gripped Charity at the way Lance and Jessa seemed to rely on each other. She envied Jessa's openness. Her friend didn't push anyone away. Somehow, even in the chaos of what Charity had walked into, the two of them seemed even stronger together.

Still holding two of his babies, Lance leaned down and gave Jessa a long, savoring kiss. "Since you've got book club tonight, I'll take these rascals over to Levi's and force him to help me feed them dinner." Somehow he made room for Cole in his arms too, then hauled all three babies to the front door.

"Thank you, my love." Jessa hooked the strap of a diaper bag onto his shoulder and gave him one more kiss. This time, Char had to turn away. She'd never wanted this. The domestic life. The kissing. The babies. And yet an undeniable envy still tugged at her heart.

While Lance and Jessa finished their goodbyes, Charity knelt on the floor and continued picking up toys. They were everywhere—under the couch, in front of the fireplace, on top of the coffee table. Wow, those little cuties left a trail of destruction wherever they went.

"Whew." With her kids and husband gone, Jessa trudged over to join Charity. "I'm exhausted." And yet her eyes still had their happy sparkle.

Charity tossed yet another stuffed animal into a nearby basket. "That was definitely intense. I don't know how you do it all." In addition to having triplets, the woman also ran the local animal rescue from the ranch. Charity grinned. Come to think of it, taking care of the animals probably wasn't so different from taking care of those three babies.

"I don't do any of it alone," her friend said, stacking up the board books Declan had strewn about. She paused and looked up at Charity. "You know you don't have to either, right? Do it alone? I'm sure things are tough right now with Bodie, but we're all here for you."

"Yeah." Charity rocked to her heels and stood to fold one of the blankets that had been hiding under the toys. Though she'd repeatedly told Dev she wanted to handle things alone.

"I think we're starting to figure things out," Charity said. "I've been taking it one day at a time."

"Taking what one day at a time?" Naomi appeared in the doorway.

"Bodie," Jessa informed her sister-in-law. "And you're early." She walked over to greet Naomi.

The woman took one look around the room and her face broke into a wide smile. "I figured you could use a little help getting ready."

"How'd you guess?" Jessa muttered, bending down to straighten three of the most adorable pairs of cowboy boots Naomi had ever seen.

"So what's this about Bodie?" Naomi joined Charity near the sofa. "Did he have an okay week?"

"I think so," Charity answered with a sigh. "Though it's hard to tell much. Communication isn't exactly his strong suit."

"Typical teenager." Jessa dumped another handful of toys back into the basket.

"Well, I'm glad to hear he's adjusting." Naomi reached down to snatch yet another toddler-sized blanket off the floor. "I was surprised to hear you were coming. Where is he tonight?"

"At a friend's house, actually." A friend. Bodie had a friend. That alone had made her feel more at ease with his situation at school.

"That's great!" Jessa paused from picking up a pile of barnyard animals.

"Who is it?" Naomi asked. "Maybe I know him."

"His name is Jett. I think they've been hanging out at lunch."

"Jett?" Naomi repeated, her smile going slack. "As in Jett Lewis?"

"Oh lord." Jessa dropped the plastic cow she'd been holding and the thing broke out into an obnoxious rendition of "The Farmer in the Dell."

"Yes. Jett Lewis." A nervous tremor started in Charity's shoulders. She did not like the way her friends were looking at her right now. "Why?"

Jessa and Naomi frowned at each other as though debating what they should say, but Charity didn't have all night. "What the heck is wrong with Jett Lewis?"

"The Lewis family doesn't exactly have the best reputation around town, that's all," Jessa said carefully.

"Mostly because the parents are hardly ever around. They take a lot of weekend trips and leave their sixteen-year-old son in charge most of the time."

"No. Bodie told me Jett's parents would be home." She knew enough to ask that much.

Naomi and Jessa shared yet another pained glance. "You didn't take him over there and meet the parents?" Naomi asked.

She knew she should've driven him over there! "I wanted to, but he got all huffy with me..."

"Yeah, because they're not there." Jessa gave up on cleaning and walked over. "Trust me. They're never there."

"But..." He'd lied to her? After she'd specifically asked him all of those important questions? "Maybe they stayed home this weekend." Please let that be it. She didn't want to deal with the alternative. What would she do? Ground him? Send him to his room?

"Maybe." Jessa obviously tried to say it encouragingly, but her eyes were full of concern.

"But if not, that house is definitely not a place you want Bodie to be." Naomi said. "I've heard about the parties Jett's older brother has. I think his parents are the ones who buy the alcohol for them."

"Unbelievable." Charity dug out her keys and sprinted for the door.

"You want me to come with you?" Naomi called after her.

"No. You should stay and help Jessa." She needed to handle this alone.

Charity raced back to town in her truck, almost hoping Dev was hiding out in his patrol car somewhere so he would follow her to the Lewis's house with his lights flashing and gun blazing.

If Dev was there, maybe she wouldn't get arrested for murder.

Bodie had lied to her face. So easily. He'd even made fun of her concerns when she'd questioned him. All along he'd known Jett's parents wouldn't be home. He'd probably even known all of the kids would be drinking and partying. Her fingertips dug deeper into the leather steering wheel. There were so many ways she could punish him—ground him to solitary confinement in his room until he stopped making stupid choices. Oh, better yet, she should force him to sit through every scientific documentary ever made on how alcohol affects the body. Didn't he care that he was killing brain cells? As a thirteen-year-old boy, he needed all the help he could get in that department.

Maybe that was what got to her more than the lying. The fact that Bodie didn't see his value, didn't see the point in taking care of himself or striving for anything. No dreams. Just anger and bitterness. Instead of trying to build a better future for himself, he was partying like his future didn't matter.

But that was on her.

She'd excused everything he'd done since her nephew had arrived at her house, and he had taken advantage of it. Anger burned, but underneath it simmered a fear she'd never known. She was responsible for this boy. This life. If anything happened to him, it was all on her. She wasn't his babysitter or his friend or even his aunt right now. She was his guardian. And she might be his guardian for a very long time.

The term *mama bear* had never meant anything to her, but when she pulled up in front of the Lewis's house, that was the only way to describe the anger. Bearlike. Dangerous. Threatening.

She screeched the truck to a stop behind one of eight cars parked along the street. As soon as she got out, she heard it—music thumping, people laughing.

They wouldn't be laughing in a few minutes. Charity jogged up the front walkway and didn't even bother knocking. She barged right in, nearly taking out a young high school–aged couple who were kissing in the entryway.

"I'm looking for Bodie," she growled at their shocked faces. "Thirteen-year-old kid. Black pants and a gray shirt."

The boy pointed down a hallway and then ducked out the front door as if he knew all hell was about to break loose.

He didn't even know the half of it. Charity marched down the hallway and found herself standing in a cramped living room. A few kids sat around on the sagging sofas with beer bottles in their hands, barely even looking up when she entered.

"Dude, it's the barrel racer chick," a young punk said from the couch. "What're you doing here?"

"I'm looking for my nephew," she ground out. "Bodie. He's *thirteen*. And if he's been drinking, so help me god, every single one of you is going to regret it." That was all it took to clear the room. Everyone scattered as though they'd been through this routine before. It likely wasn't their first time running from a pissed-off parent.

"Bodie!" Charity yelled, continuing on into the kitchen. The smell of pot hung thick in the air, filtering in through an open window. Outside. He had to be outside. She slammed through a flimsy screen door, nearly breaking the thing off its hinges, and stopped cold. There was her nephew, standing by a small firepit with a joint between his fingers.

"Hi there, auntie." Bodie took a few wobbling steps. "What're you doing here?"

"What am I doing here?" she repeated in a whisper. She couldn't move. Couldn't even take one step toward him. She had no clue what she was doing. Obviously. She had no business raising a kid. His eyes were bloodshot and his mouth couldn't seem to lose the grin.

"What're *you* doing?" she demanded, though the answer was obvious. Throwing away his future. Drinking and smoking himself stupid.

"We're just having some fun," he slurred, looking down at the joint between his fingers. He quickly threw it into the fire as if he'd just remembered he shouldn't be holding it.

"Fun?" The control she'd had over her voice had started to crack. "How much have you had to drink?"

"I dunno." His shoulders arched into an exaggerated shrug and that dumb grin grew bigger. "Tasted like juice though."

She turned to the delinquent standing next to him, presumably Jett. "What has he had to drink?"

The kid had the balls to look bored. "I don't know."

She got in his face. "You'd better tell me exactly what you gave him, or I will call the cops right now."

"Chill," Jett said like he had no idea why she was so upset. "He had some vodka. Hardly any."

"So my thirteen-year-old nephew has been drinking vodka and smoking pot."

Again, Jett seemed to appear as though this was an everyday occurrence in his world. "Yeah. But like I said, he hardly had anything."

"Hardly anything? He can barely stand up." She pushed past Jett and took Bodie's hand. "Come on. We're going."

"Aw, man." He stumbled a few steps. "Do we hafta? I like it here."

She ignored his whines and marched him inside through the now-empty house and out to the truck. He was so inebriated, she actually had to help him climb in.

"Put your seat belt on," she snapped. He wasn't getting off easy this time. There were serious consequences for underage drinking. If he wouldn't listen to her, she had to find a way to get through to him. And maybe give him a little bit of a scare in the process. Dev might be on friendly terms with Bodie, but he was still a cop. He would know exactly what to say.

Chapter Twelve

Dev closed the email from the investigator back in Oklahoma and shut down his laptop. Melody Stone was officially a person of interest in the robbery. Thanks to him. While they hadn't issued a warrant for her arrest yet, they likely would as soon as they found any scrap of evidence, and he still hadn't found a way to tell Charity. Well, that wasn't exactly true. He hadn't had the opportunity to tell her. It was hard to tell someone something when they made it a point to avoid you.

He walked into the kitchen and got a beer out of the fridge. It might be better to wait to tell Charity anyway. The longer Melody was gone, the smaller the chance she'd come back, and Charity already had enough to deal with right now. He didn't want to—

An engine hummed outside his cabin. Dev glanced at the clock. Almost nine. That surely couldn't be his parents going somewhere. Not at this time of the night. Far as he knew they'd been hitting the hay around eight. He moved through the living room so he could look out the window, but someone started banging on his front door.

"Dev? Are you there?"

The panicked ring in Charity's voice gave him a good kick in the chest.

"Please! I need your—"

He had the door open before she could finish. He meant to say something, but the tears running down her cheeks rendered him completely speechless. Charity Stone didn't cry.

"Oh, thank god." She was out of breath. "It's Bodie. He's in the truck. He was at a party drinking and now I can't wake him up."

"How much has he had to drink?" he asked, shoving his feet into his boots. If the kid had alcohol poisoning, Dev could easily call dispatch and get an ambulance out here within a few minutes.

"I don't know." She sniffled and wiped her cheeks with the edge of her sleeve. "All I could get out of his friend was that he'd had some vodka. And they were smoking pot too."

Dev followed her to the passenger's side of her truck and opened the door. "Let me guess, he was at Jett Lewis's house."

"Yes." Her voice wobbled. "I didn't know. I had no idea that kid was trouble. Oh my god." Her hands gripped Dev's arm. "Will he be okay? If anything happens to him—"

"He's fine." In fact, the kid was sacked out on the seat, snoring peacefully. He'd definitely had too much to drink, but he wasn't in distress. "He's only passed out." She probably could've woken him if she'd tried hard enough. Maybe with a bullhorn and a bucket of ice-cold water...

"Are you sure?" Charity asked, still hanging on to him. Her body shook.

Dev drew her in and slipped his arm around her. "I'm sure. Trust me, I've seen more than one drunk kid." Unfortunately.

It was never one of his favorite things to issue underage drinking tickets, seeing as how he'd been on the other side of it a few times in his life. "Most of them have been at Jett Lewis's house," he added.

"Why does everyone know that kid is trouble except for me?" Surprisingly, Charity stayed nestled in the crook of his arm.

Even though he hated to, Dev moved away from her and undid Bodie's seat belt. He hoisted the boy out of the truck, cradling him like he would a little kid. "I've busted more than one party at that house," he said, making his way back to his front door.

"Well, I had no idea." She followed him inside. "I was just happy he'd started to make friends. If it weren't for Naomi and Jessa informing me about Jett's family situation, I would've left Bodie there all night. He probably would've been dead by morning." Tears flooded her eyes again.

"I doubt it. My guess is he only had a drink or two before passing out. Most thirteen-year-olds are lightweights."

That didn't seem to make her feel much better. "Why don't you take a seat?" Dev gestured to the couch. "I'll get him settled in my bed so he can sleep it off."

"Thank you." Charity sank to the couch while he maneuvered into his room and eased Bodie to the bed. After checking the kid's breathing one more time, Dev moved a trash can by the bed for the inevitable puking session that would happen later and then slipped out of the room, closing the door behind him.

By the time he got back to the living room, Charity had hunched over and was hiding her face in her hands.

Damn. He'd never seen her like this. "Hey." Dev sat next to her. "It's all right. He just needs to sleep it off."

"It's not all right." She laid her head back and stared up at the ceiling. "I can't do this. I can't raise a kid. I can't keep him out of trouble."

That lost look on her face drew him closer to her. Screw what she'd said about not wanting his help. Right now, she needed it.

"I didn't even take him over there," she went on. "I didn't push to meet the kid's parents. I completely trusted everything he said. But that's obviously not working." She turned her face to his. "He needs to be held accountable. And I can't do it. I can't hold him accountable. I can't give him consequences."

"How come?" He stroked her silky hair, letting the ends fall through his fingers.

"Because I know what it's like." The words came out in a garbled whisper. "I know what it's like to have to fend for yourself all the time. And it makes me want to rescue him. I go crazy with this feeling that I have to protect him from anything that might hurt him. It's like instinct takes over and I can't think clearly."

That was the most she'd ever revealed to him, the most she'd ever let him see. He wanted to be careful with it, to guard her vulnerability, but he also wanted to know more. He wanted to know her. After the scene with that cowboy at the bar a few weeks ago, he'd seen an obvious fear in her eyes. "Is it because you couldn't protect yourself when you were his age?" he asked quietly.

The question seemed to surprise her, and for a minute he thought she wouldn't answer it, that she would retreat again, but then her gaze dropped to her lap. "My mom dated a lot of men." She stared at her knees, chewing furiously on her bottom lip. "They were always saying things. Trying to touch me." She raised her eyes to his. He'd seen that look before— the night he'd pulled her out of the bar. Blank, wild eyes.

The hum of anger started in his chest, spreading in scorching pulses, but he said nothing. Asked no more questions. Only waited and braced himself for what he knew was coming.

"When I was twelve, one of her boyfriends used to run his hand up the back of my shirt." Her shoulders twitched as if the memory still made her skin crawl. "Another one would kiss me on the lips. Hard. It always made me feel like I couldn't breathe."

Dev's hands fisted. The thought of someone violating her like that...he could've punched a hole through a steel wall.

"They'd make comments about my butt and my breasts," Charity went on. "They'd buy me slutty clothes and make me wear them." A choppy sigh spluttered through her lips. "I know they didn't abuse me, but—"

"Like hell they didn't," he growled. If he could, he'd go back and track down every single asshole that had ever laid a hand on her—every man that had made her feel small and had taken advantage of her vulnerability.

Charity's eyes flared wider.

She really didn't know. "That's abuse," he said quietly. Carefully. "You were a child, Charity. Any sexual advances. Any touch. Any time one of them made you feel uncomfortable and took away your voice. That's abuse."

Her lips pursed together, trembling violently. "You're right. They took advantage of me. But the worst part is, my mom never stopped it. She was too afraid it would ruin things with whatever guy she happened to be dating at the time."

"So you learned to protect yourself." That's why she pushed him away. The person who was supposed to take care of her had failed her, and now she didn't trust anyone.

"Now I see Bodie acting the same way I did." She wiped away tears. "I see the anger covering up his fears. I see how he keeps his distance. He'll start to open up to me and then two minutes later he'll completely shut down again."

Exactly like she did. Dev fought the urge to touch her, to take her in his arms and hold her so she'd know she wasn't alone in this, but he forced himself to give her space.

Charity turned her face to his, her eyes shimmering with a sad vulnerability. "He's exactly like me, Dev. And I hate watching it."

"You're not so bad..." He cracked a smile, doing his best to lure out hers. "A terrible driver, maybe, but you've got your good qualities too."

The diversion seemed to work. She didn't give him a real smile, but her mouth perked up. "All I seem to recognize in him are my bad qualities. The things I don't exactly love about myself."

"Then let me tell you what I see." Dev brought his face in line with hers so she wouldn't look away. "I see a kid who's exactly like his aunt. He's tough and determined. Loyal." Even to a mother who'd abandoned him. "He's a hard worker, and yes, he has a lot of fears, but he's got a lot of heart too." He slid his hand forward on the couch cushion and brushed his fingers over her knuckles. "Best of all, he's got an aunt who's stubborn enough to do whatever it takes to make sure he gets exactly what he needs to live a good, happy life."

Charity couldn't remember the last time she'd cried. And she definitely hadn't cried in front of another person since she was a kid—not even when she'd broken her collarbone during a race, even though her eyes had stung as bad as the break. She'd always forced herself to hold back tears. Now, though, she couldn't seem to stop them.

"I don't know how to help him." Dev's hand was still close, resting on the cushion inches away from hers. Needing a lifeline, she reached for it, craving the faith this man always seemed to kindle in her. "What if I'm not enough? What if I mess up?"

Dev leaned closer. He gathered both of her hands in his, holding them tightly, fully capable and steadfast. "What if everything you've been through up until now has made you the perfect person to be exactly what Bodie needs?"

He let go of her hands and touched her cheek. "You know better than anyone what he's experienced, Charity. You know what's hurt him. What saved you?"

She didn't hesitate. "Riding."

"Because it gave you a purpose. Made you realize you had something to offer the world." Dev smiled. "That's all you have to do. Help him find his purpose. Help him see how much he has to offer. You're resilient and determined. You have a huge heart. Those are all things he needs right now."

His words eased her worries, somehow making them seem more manageable. It didn't matter if she was enough or not. She had to do this. And she would put everything she had into it. "Thank you." Charity lightly pressed her palm against his jaw, drawing his face closer.

She needed him to take her away from the past, from the worry, from the isolation. Dev made her feel softer and open. Lovable.

Their lips touched in a frenzy of heat that ignited the hollow spot deep inside of her. The glow radiated all the way through, casting its vivid light into her darkest places. This was a kiss. Something shared and mysterious. Like a secret only their lips knew.

Dev opened his mouth to hers and stroked her tongue with his, sharpening the edges of that heat so it sliced through every hesitation that had made her retreat from him before.

Charity raised her other hand to his jaw to hold him there, to hold on to this kiss that told her he understood so much— what she needed, what she feared. She let herself get lost in it, not fully surrendered, but edging closer, clinging to the rhythm of his lips and the way they claimed hers.

When Dev pulled back, her whole chest ached, suddenly laden with disappointment.

"He's going to be fine," the deputy assured her. "You both are." He pushed off the couch and reached out to help her up. "Come on. Let's go check on him. See if he's regretting the last four hours of his life yet."

For the first time, the kiss didn't tempt her to run out the door and spend the next week avoiding him. Instead, Charity put her hand in his, and then held on to him all the way down the hall. Together, they stepped into his bedroom, where Bodie lay in the middle of a massive king-size bed, still snoring away.

The room was much larger than she'd anticipated. It had that rustic look with tall ceilings and log beams. A stone fireplace was nestled in one corner, giving the whole space a romantic ambiance. Under different circumstances, she might've been tempted to pull Dev over to the bed so they could continue that kiss. Probably not wise, given her current emotional state, but that didn't stop her from considering it.

"Still sound asleep." Dev leaned over to adjust the pillows under Bodie's head.

Her nephew groaned a little, but then turned over and started to snore again.

She gazed down at him and every worry Dev had just soothed came bubbling back to the surface. "I don't know what I'm going to do with him."

Dev slipped his hand in hers again. "You're going to keep caring about him. You're going to do whatever you have to do to show him how much you care about him."

She did care. She might not know him well, but she loved that kid. Hopefully that was enough.

After one last look at Bodie, she quietly ducked through the door. Dev followed, closing it behind him. They stood face-to-face in the cramped hallway.

"You haven't heard any more about your sister?" Dev asked.

"No." She hadn't mentioned the phone call to him. It would only reinforce his suspicions about Melody and, while she was starting to fear he might be onto something, she couldn't do anything about her sister right now. She had to figure out how to handle this crisis with Bodie. "What would you do if you were me? If you caught the kid you were in charge of drinking at a party?" She didn't have any clue what consequence would fit that kind of crime.

"You really want my advice?" There was a warning in his tone, like it might not be easy for her to hear.

Well, easy wasn't exactly working out so well for her at the moment. "Yes. I really want to know." Dev had seen a lot of kids in trouble. She couldn't let Bodie end up that way.

"I think you have two options. If you want, I can bring him down to the station and give him an underage drinking ticket, which'll mean a hefty fine, court appearance, and likely community service."

"That's probably what I have to do, right?" Even if it killed her. "That's a consequence." For both of them, since she'd likely have to front the money. But hopefully it would be enough to make him learn his lesson so this didn't happen again.

"I think there's another option," Dev said thoughtfully. "Leave him here tonight. I'll sleep on the couch, check on him every so often. Then I'll wake him up at the crack of dawn and put him to work on my parents' ranch again. Still the hard work of community service, but it won't go against him on his record."

Charity's mouth dropped open. "You would do that for him?"

"I would do it for both of you." Dev edged his body closer to hers. "We'd planned to work anyway. We'll just get an earlier start." He chuckled. "That was my father's favorite form of punishment after I'd had too much fun drinking on a Friday night back in the day. He'd wake me up before the sun and hand me a list of my least favorite jobs on the ranch."

The pained look on Dev's face prompted a laugh. "It must've been effective."

"Oh yeah." He whistled low. "It happened only a couple of times before I learned I didn't want to spend my Saturday mornings mucking out stables with a serious hangover."

The fact that Dev had experimented with alcohol made her feel at least a little bit better. After all, he'd turned out pretty good. There wasn't a better man Bodie could be spending time with right now. But she couldn't put it all on Dev's shoulders. "I'll come back in the morning," she told him. "Then the three of us can work together."

"You sure?" Dev led her out to the living room. "What about training?"

"Right now this is more important." For a long time, she'd used her riding as a means of escape. Training and competing allowed her to stay too busy to form any kind of real relationship, but Bodie needed her to be present. He needed to know she'd make him a priority. And while she was at it, maybe she could figure out how to stop running from Dev too.

Chapter Thirteen

Rise and shine." Dev threw open the curtains in his east-facing bedroom, knowing full well the early-morning sun would hit Bodie square in the eyes.

The kid groaned and rolled over, burrowing his head under a pillow.

Dev had been afraid that's how this would go, so he'd come prepared. He lifted the bullhorn to his mouth and clicked the button. "I said rise and shine." The words echoed loud enough to make him wince, and he'd been ready for them.

Bodie shot straight up in the bed. "What the hell? Where am I?" The kid scrambled out from under Dev's comforter, but when the sunrays hit him in the face, his upper body collapsed and his head went straight into his hands. "Owwww."

"Got a little headache, do ya?" Dev asked cheerfully.

"Is this your house?" Bodie squinted at him. "Is this your *bed*?"

"Relax, desperado." He whipped the covers the rest of the way off the bed in case the kid puked. "I didn't kidnap you or anything. Your aunt brought you here after you passed out last night. She was worried." It had surprised him when Charity agreed to leave Bodie at his place. But then again, a lot of things about last night had surprised him. The way she'd opened up to him, the kiss. It still simmered on his lips.

"Ugggg." The kid hunched again, squeezing his forehead with his hand. "Shit. The party." He peered up at Dev, having the decency to look worried. "How bad was it? Did she send you over there to bust everyone? Oh my god, they're gonna hate me. They're never gonna talk to me again."

Dev sat down next to him. "Maybe this is just me, but I wouldn't consider Jett Lewis a big loss."

"He's my friend." Bodie likely tried to scowl, but he was too pale and sleepy-eyed to look all that menacing. He almost looked like a little kid, probably because he had the worst case of bedhead the deputy had ever seen.

"How's being friends with Jett Lewis working out for you?" he asked.

Bodie wisely ignored the question and inched to the edge of the bed, looking paler and paler by the second. "Where're my boots?" he demanded, wobbling to his feet.

"By the front door." Dev stood too, stepping aside so Bodie could move past him. The kid made it three steps before he darted to the trash can, which still sat at the side of the bed. He hit his knees and upchucked what appeared to be all the contents of his stomach and then some.

Dev stood behind him and waited patiently for the convulsions to stop. "You done?" he finally asked after a few minutes of silence.

"I don't think I'll ever be done." The kid groaned.

"That's okay. We'll be outside anyway. You can throw up wherever you want."

"Outside?" Bodie staggered to his feet. "I'm not gonna be outside. I'm going back to my aunt's house. I need to go back to bed."

"You're not going anywhere." Dev followed him out to the living room. "Here's how the rest of your morning is gonna go down." Luckily his stern voice had gotten a lot of practice. "You get a choice. Option A? You stay here for a few hours and do the work we'd planned to do. But it won't count toward the PlayStation."

"Are you crazy?" Bodie gaped at him. "I can't work right now. I just threw up! You can't make me stay."

"You're right," Dev agreed. "You don't have to stay. I can't make you. So if you choose option B, you and I will head on down to the station, where I'll issue you a real official-looking underage drinking ticket that will likely result in a court appearance, some hefty fines, and a hell of a lot of community service, depending on how friendly the judge feels that day." Dev leaned in closer to share a little secret. "Just an FYI, most of the judges in this county aren't very friendly."

"You can't do this. My aunt won't let you." Bodie patted his pockets, desperately searching for his phone, Dev had to assume. "I'm gonna call her. She'll come get me right now."

"Actually, your aunt thought this was a good plan. She'll be over to join us shortly." Yet another surprise from last night. Instead of avoiding him, she'd volunteered to come. Maybe he was getting through to her. "By the way, I haven't seen your phone. My guess is you left it at your good friend Jett's house."

"I'll walk home then." The kid's resolve had obviously started to weaken. The look on his face gave him away. He knew he was in deep shit, and it was only getting deeper.

"Fine with me," the deputy said easily. "Walk home. But you'll still get the ticket. You'll have to work it off anyway. And you will be the one who has to show up in court." He leaned casually against the wall. "Trust me, working on my ranch would be a lot more pleasant than some of the court-assigned community service opportunities one of our fine judges will offer you." If he refused, Bodie would likely find himself picking up the nasty trash all along the highway. The kid didn't want to know what kinds of things people threw out on the side of the road. "Totally up to you," he said with a grin. "Just let me know what you decide." He started to walk away to give the kid a few minutes to think.

"Wait."

Huh. That didn't take quite as long as he'd expected.

"We're just taking down that one tree, right?" Bodie asked. "The one you showed me last week?"

"We'll do that after we muck out the horse stables." He knew from experience the smell alone would be enough to deter Bodie from making the same mistake again. "After the tree, we'll mow down some of the grasses that have grown too tall in the pastures."

Bodie had started to look a little overwhelmed. "You got a tractor?" the kid almost growled.

"Of course I have a tractor." Dev held off a threatening grin. "But there're plenty of spots I can't get to. You'll have to use the push mower." If the horse manure didn't take care of the problem, pushing that mower over a couple of acres of wild grass might be enough to convince him drinking wasn't worth it. "You ready to get started?"

Bodie didn't budge. "What about breakfast? I'm starving."

Dev went to his closet and tossed him a jacket. "Breakfast will be at ten. After the work's done." He'd already made himself a cup of coffee and a hearty bowl of oatmeal, but he figured he'd let Bodie sleep in until seven.

Yeah, he was a softie. "Besides, I don't want you puking again."

"If you don't feed me, I might pass out," the kid grumbled, pulling on the coat.

"Fine with me. I'll just bring over one of the cows so it can lick your face until you wake up."

"I don't get it." The kid sank to the couch and started to put on his boots. "What's the big deal? I went to a party and drank. Kids do it all the time. Who cares?"

"Your aunt cares." Dev had never seen her like that. So terrified and lost. "I care too." As much as Bodie tried to hide it, the kid had the smarts and the grit to go far in life. He might pretend he didn't care what happened to him, but Dev could see through the act.

"Yeah, right." Bodie stomped past him. "You just like busting people. That's probably why you became a cop in the first place. So you could look all important and give people tickets and arrest them."

"Actually, I like shooting people," Dev said with a straight face. "That's why I became a cop."

Bodie did a double take, and Dev busted out laughing. "That was a joke."

Now that he was more awake the kid's scowl had started to come back. "It was a stupid joke."

"I'm full of stupid jokes." Dev clapped him on the back. "Consider it part of your punishment."

Bodie jerked away. "Great. I can't wait to hear more."

"Then let's get started." Dev led the way outside.

"Hold on, I've got another one." Dev rested the blade of his ax on the ground. Before he could deliver the joke, Charity paused from stacking the logs Bodie and Dev had split and looked at her nephew. They both groaned.

For the last hour, in between chopping up the tree they'd brought down, Dev had been sharing his vast knowledge of bad police jokes. Charity had no idea so many terrible cheesy jokes existed in the world. Of course, knowing Dev, he was making them up as he went along just to distract them from the work.

"No, this one's good. I swear." The deputy placed his hand over his heart in a solemn pose.

"None of them have been good." Bodie dropped his ax too. Sweat drenched his forehead and his T-shirt, but instead of making him surly, the physical activity seemed to energize him.

It had energized her too. Being outside, doing something productive, watching Bodie bond with Dev. It was so good for him. Charity almost couldn't believe how hard he'd worked under Dev's instruction, how much he'd responded when Dev told him he was doing a great job.

"What happened after the Energizer Bunny was arrested?" Dev didn't wait for them to guess. "He was charged with battery."

Bodie clutched at his chest and made choking sounds like he was dying. Charity couldn't help but laugh.

"Just when you think they couldn't get any worse," her nephew said. "You come up with something like—"

A horse whinnied behind them. Charity turned and watched as Gracie rode over on her speckled appaloosa, looking like a rodeo princess in her jean leggings, sparkly T-shirt, and glittering white cowgirl hat.

"Hey." Charity walked to meet her. "What're you doing here?"

"Mom told me you guys would be here." Charity and Naomi had talked last night after she'd left Bodie at Dev's. Even though she'd been nervous about it, her friend had insisted she'd done the right thing by letting him sleep it off at the deputy's house.

"She said I could ride over to say hi," Gracie went on. That was so like Charity's friend. Naomi had probably sent Gracie over so her nephew would feel like he had at least one friend left after last night.

"How's it going?" The girl dismounted and smiled shyly at Bodie. "Looks like you've been working hard this morning, huh?"

"Yeah." He did one of those cool-guy no-biggie shrugs, which sparked a chuckle deep within Charity. She didn't dare let it out.

"Dev needed my help with some things around here." The kid's voice lowered into something gruff and badass.

Oh god, it was adorable.

Dev didn't seem to think so, however. A solid scowl cracked open his mouth, but before he could say anything, Charity clamped her hand onto his arm. "We'll be back in a sec," she announced, dragging him away.

Once they were out of earshot, Dev chuckled. "I needed *his* help? I guess I shouldn't mention he was the one puking in my bedroom this morning."

Charity stopped and turned to face him. "Probably not. He's only trying to impress her." Based on the way Gracie offered Bodie her rapt, undivided attention, it seemed to be working.

"I'm not sure that's a great idea." The longer Dev stared over at them, the more his eyes narrowed. "Bodie was drinking at a party last night and Gracie just started watching PG-13 movies, like, a month ago."

"So?" Was he really saying he didn't want Bodie around Gracie? "Gracie is exactly the kind of kid he needs to be hanging out with right now." A kid who wouldn't get him in trouble. A kid who actually had his best interests in mind.

Gracie was sweet and genuine and, yes, innocent. Bodie needed more of that in his life.

"I'm sure there are a lot of other kids who don't party," Dev grumbled. "He could hang out with them."

"Naomi is fine with the two of them developing a friendship," she informed him. "You said you wanted to help him." He'd said he wanted to help *her*.

"I'm trying to help him." Frustration ground into the words. "But I also know thirteen-year-old boys. I've known Gracie since she was baby, and I don't think they should hang out."

Ha. As if he held all the control in this situation. "What do you plan to do? Follow her around school and make sure she doesn't talk to him? That's the most ridiculous thing I've ever—"

"Hi there, y'all."

The honey in that voice snapped Charity's mouth shut. She peered over her shoulder almost expecting to see Aunt Bee standing there behind her. She'd loved that lady on *The Andy Griffith Show*.

Instead of Aunt Bee, Dev's mom stood on the front porch of her house, her hands resting on cushioned hips. She looked nothing like everyone's favorite aunt from television, though she did have a wholesome grace about her— the coiffed white hair, the slick of red lipstick, the sensible polyester pants and flowered cardigan.

"Hey, Mom." Dev quickly sidestepped Charity and walked over to meet her on the sidewalk in front of the house.

"Looks like a party out here." The woman took her son's arm and ambled over to Charity, smiling the whole way. "Why, Charity Stone. You're even prettier up close."

Charity could feel herself blushing. "Thank you, Mrs. Jenkins." She waved her nephew over. "This is my nephew,

Bodie. And obviously you know Gracie." The girl had followed the object of her affection right over.

"Of course I know Gracie." The woman wrapped her in a
hug. "How are ya, girl? It's been a while since you've ridden
over here to see us."

"I know. I'm sorry, Mrs. Jenkins." A bright smile showed
off the girl's dimples. "I've been so busy with riding lessons
and homework. You wouldn't believe the homework at our
school. It's out of control." She turned to Bodie and elbowed
him. "Right?"

Charity's nephew agreed with a nod. "It sucks."

Dev's jaw tightened back up, but before he could say anything, Charity smiled at his mom. "Dev has told me a lot
about you, Mrs. Jenkins. It's so nice to meet you in person."
She offered her hand, but instead, Dev's mom ambushed her
with a hug. "The pleasure is all mine." She pulled back and
beamed. "I've watched some of your races, honey, and don't
mind if I say, you have a real talent."

Now that was a compliment she felt more comfortable
receiving. "Thank you."

"Y'all are stayin' for brunch, right?" Mrs. Jenkins asked
with a hopefulness that immediately made Charity want to
tell her yes, of course they were staying. But how could they
stay when Dev had already decided he didn't want Bodie
and Gracie to develop a friendship? "Thanks for the offer,
but we should—"

"I'm starving," Bodie interrupted.

"I'm hungry too." Gracie edged closer to Bodie and
tossed her hair over her shoulder in a flirtatious little maneuver Charity recognized from her own middle school days.
Dear lord, this girl had it bad. Dev would have his work cut
out for him if he planned to keep them apart. She'd like to
see him try to dissuade that girl.

"Then it's settled. Food's already on." The older woman ushered them up the porch steps. "We'd best hurry up before it gets cold."

Welcome. That was the only way to describe the feeling that came over Charity when she walked into Dev's parents' house. Welcome and instantly comfortable. The house smelled like breakfast, like fried bacon and fresh banana bread.

It seemed either furniture or memorabilia took every square inch of wall space in the small living room, but the area was also tidy and well cared for. Charity wandered a bit, to the back of the room where rows of photographs hung in precise patterns. An homage to Dev's various sports pursuits, it appeared. She studied the photographs of him in his uniform, with his team, holding trophies. One in particular held her. It was a picture of him standing between his parents, both of them beaming with a poignant blend of love and pride. Stadium lights glittered above their heads, and, behind them, the green field stretched out for what seemed to be miles.

Dev was their everything. You could see it on their faces.

"Oh, but I worried for him out there." Mrs. Jenkins came up alongside her. "Every time he collided with one of those boys on the football field or basketball court, I had to turn away."

"Sports can be brutal." She could attest to that.

"That's true," Mrs. Jenkins agreed. "But it also gave him something we couldn't. Discipline. Perseverance. Camaraderie. Those boys on his teams were like brothers, and he needed that back then."

Charity nodded, seeking out Bodie. He and Gracie were chatting near the couch. There was so much wisdom in Mrs. Jenkins's words. Bodie needed those things too, and no, Charity couldn't give them to him. Not on her own. He needed support. A community to rally around him.

"Come on." Dev's mom collected Charity under her arm and they all drifted into a small dining room tucked into a corner behind the kitchen. A man—Dev's dad, she would presume—already sat at the head of a dark cherry pedestal table, a newspaper hiding his face.

"Carl, we have company," Mrs. Jenkins said loudly.

The newspaper rustled and then came down. "Well, I'll be." Mr. Jenkins quickly folded up the paper and stood, straightening his flannel shirt. The first thing Charity noticed about him was his eyes. They were deep set and a wise brown, almost identical to Dev's, even though there was no blood relation. Wrinkles crosshatched the man's face in a distinguished pattern, making him seem approachable and perceptive.

Dev started in on the introductions. "Dad, this is Charity, her nephew, Bodie, and you know—"

"Gracie girl. It's been ages." Mr. Jenkins edged around the table and gave the girl's shoulder a squeeze before offering Bodie a hearty handshake. "That's quite a grip you've got there, son. Dev said you and he were gonna take down that old pine tree that was being eaten up by beetles."

"Yes, sir." There was a respect in Bodie's tone that he didn't offer to just anyone. "Wasn't easy, but we managed to get it down."

Charity smiled. That was it, what she'd needed to see, especially after last night. That glimpse of pride in what he'd done to help Dev this morning. Bodie cared. He cared far more than he let anyone see.

"Well, I have to thank you for that, then." The older man clapped her nephew's shoulder. "Can't do the work around here like I used to with my arthritis. I really appreciate you helpin' out."

"Uh, sure. Yeah." Her nephew seemed to struggle to find words. "Of course, sir. I was happy to help."

"And Charity Stone." Dev's father lumbered over and hugged her the same way his mom had. "Not every day we get a celebrity in the house."

"And it's not every day that I'm welcomed into such a lovely place." A place that seemed to wrap its welcoming arms around her.

"Now that we're acquainted, why don't y'all take your seats?" Mrs. Jenkins walked over and pulled out a stack of plates from an antique hutch along the side wall, setting them gingerly in the center of the large table. "Bodie and Gracie, you two sit over there." She gestured to the other side of the table by the window.

"Actually, I'll sit here." Dev muscled his way in between the two kids and pulled out the chair, dropping down before anyone could tell him otherwise.

Typically, Charity didn't resort to rolling her eyes, but she made an exception, waiting until he looked at her and then adding a shake of her head for good measure. The man might be sexier than sin and heroic and strong and noble, but he had a lot to learn when it came to middle school girls and their crushes.

Chapter Fourteen

If Gracie made gaga eyes at Bodie one more time, he'd...well, hell, Dev had no clue what he'd do.

He'd tried everything—leaning forward and back to block her view of the kid, rudely interrupting their conversation as often as he could, in between deflecting glares from both Charity and his own mother, of course. Didn't matter what he'd tried, Gracie had simply outmaneuvered him during the entire breakfast.

The girl had some quick reflexes, and it appeared she was on a mission to cast a spell on Bodie. If the kid's slightly improved attitude was any indication, it had started to work.

The frown Dev couldn't seem to shake went deeper. He wasn't loving the way these two kids had started to look at each other. Or the flirty tone Gracie kept using. It would only lead to trouble. Flirtatious giggle one day and the next he'd be busting them for making out in the car somewhere. Or maybe a barn since neither one of them could drive...

"Bodie, that's hilarious!" Gracie reached around behind Dev and patted Bodie's shoulder.

Hilarious? The kid had only told a story about the time his neighbor's chickens had gotten into his bathroom and one got stuck in the toilet. Dev didn't see what was so funny. There was nothing fun or funny about this breakfast, in his opinion. Good thing they were wrapping it up. Bodie was a good kid and all, but he still had some issues to work through. Issues Gracie Cortez knew nothing about.

"I love chickens." Gracie leaned past Dev to look at Bodie for the five millionth time. "I keep begging my parents to get some, but they said they don't think the guests at the inn would like a bunch of squawking hens running around."

"Well, we've got a whole flock." Dev's mom balled up her napkin and tossed it onto her empty plate. "In fact, we've got a few new chicks and a couple of piglets down in the barn."

"Piglets?" Gracie gasped. "I'd love to see piglets!" She was already scrambling out of her seat. "Don't you want to see piglets, Bodie?"

The kid finished off the last of his bacon and shrugged. "Yeah. Sure."

Dev stood too. There was no way those two were walking down to the barn alone. "Don't you think you should get back to your uncle's ranch, Gracie?" he asked firmly. He'd be more than happy to escort her home. "I wouldn't want your mom to worry."

"Nah." She traipsed to the other side of the table. "Mom's helping Aunt Jessa with the triplets this afternoon. They told me I could stay over here if it was all right with you."

Great. So she had all the time in the world to charm the pants off Bodie. Literally. Well, not on his watch. He'd make sure everyone's pants stayed exactly where they belonged. "I'll walk you down to the barn," Dev said.

Across from him, Charity stood abruptly. "Actually, Dev, I thought we could do the dishes together." She glared at him with a tight smile. "How does that sound?"

"Uh." Based on her expression, this was one of the times when he didn't have a choice but to say it sounded great.

"Oh, honey, I couldn't let you do my dishes," his mother gushed. "I'm the hostess, after all."

"Please. I insist." Charity reached in and took the stack of plates right out of his mom's hands. "You all go down and see the animals. We'll join you in a few minutes."

Okay. Fine. A few minutes. Bodie and Gracie couldn't get into trouble in a few minutes, could they? Just in case, Dev stacked the rest of the dishes scattered around the table in record time.

"Well, I don't know—" his mom started, but his father steered her toward the living room. "Come on, MaryElla. If she wants to do the dishes, let her do the dishes." He gestured for Gracie and Bodie to follow them. "Y'all might even be able to hold those piglets we got down there."

Gracie squealed with excitement as the group paraded through the living room and out of sight.

"Make sure you all stay together," Dev yelled.

Charity shot him a death glare over the table. Then, without a word, she carted the dishes to the sink and set them on the counter.

Dev assessed the rigidity in her movements. Yeah, she definitely wasn't happy with him. She opened the dishwasher and continued to ignore him as she turned on the faucet.

Guess he had to be the one to break the cold snap howling between them. He walked over and leaned against the counter next to her. "You glared at me a lot during brunch."

Charity paused from rinsing a plate. "You were being a jerk."

That baited a laugh. "Tell me how you really feel."

"I don't think I have to." She bent and nestled the plate into the dishwasher between the others, then straightened and faced him directly. "It was pretty obvious to the entire room. I wasn't the only one glaring." She snatched another plate. "Your mom glared. Gracie and Bodie both should've glared."

"Fine. Maybe I went a little overboard." He couldn't help it. "I'm protective of Gracie. I mean, I still think of her as a little girl. She hasn't experienced half of what Bodie has. I guess I'd like to do my part in keeping her happy bubble intact."

Charity secured the plate in the dishwasher and shut off the faucet. She turned to him and seemed to think for a few minutes before speaking. "No one wants to live in a bubble, Dev." The anger in her tone gave way to something else. Sadness? "When I first walked into your parents' house, you know what I noticed right away?"

"The weird Beanie Baby collection my mom has on those vintage 1970s bookshelves?" He noticed it every time and it never failed to make him cringe.

"No." Her small smile scolded him. "I noticed that you're the very center of their world. The pictures, the memorabilia, even the Beanie Babies." She playfully narrowed her eyes as though she was on the hunt for information. "You know you loved those things when you were little. I'll bet you slept with some of them."

"The koala and the monkey," he confessed. "Those were my favorites." Until he realized how creepy they were. Staring at you with the glassy, lifeless eyes? Yikes.

Charity's face sobered. "Bodie doesn't have that. He hasn't had parents telling him he matters. He hasn't had parents *showing* him he matters. He needs friends, Dev. He needs to believe he's lovable. If you try to keep Gracie away from him, you'll only be reinforcing his insecurities. The self-doubt is what makes him act out in the first place. He's testing me—testing all of us—to see if we'll abandon him like everyone else has."

The words hit him hard enough to knock out most of the concerns he had regarding Gracie and Bodie. Most, but not all. "You're right," he said to Charity. "It's easy to forget that."

"I know he's hard." She eased closer. "Trust me. I get it. But I'm trying to look for glimpses of the good in him. Like when your dad thanked him for helping with the tree. He lit up from the inside. I haven't seen him respond that like to anyone."

"Yeah." He'd noticed it too. His dad was good at that—at seeing what people needed to hear.

"I'm not trying to make you feel bad," Charity said. "You've done a lot for him too. And I can already tell it's helping. I'm just saying you shouldn't automatically think he'll ruin Gracie's innocence."

"Good point." She made a lot of good points, and she wasn't afraid to share them, which was one of the things he liked the most about her. Unable to resist, Dev slipped his hand onto the curve of her hip and hitched her closer, searching as deep in her eyes as she would let him.

"What?" Her gaze shied away.

"I'm just trying to figure out what's wrong with you."

Her head tipped back. "What's wrong with *me*?"

"Yeah." He swept his gaze from those captivating eyes down to her lips, and then all the way down her body. "You're smart as a whip, as my dad mentioned numerous times during breakfast." He caught her eyes again. "You're strong and brave. Funny. Pretty much the perfect woman."

She belted out a laugh, completely unfiltered, and he loved hearing it, loved the way she didn't try to edit herself around him.

"I'm not perfect," she insisted. "For one thing, I have no filter."

"You're honest," he murmured, moving as close as he dared.

"I'm selfish." Her breath caught in the words.

He shook his head. "I don't buy that. Ambitious maybe. Hardworking and focused, but not selfish."

"Okay, fine." Her voice had noticeably weakened. "I push people away and try to do everything on my own."

"Being independent isn't necessarily a bad thing. You know who you are." And she didn't apologize for it. She didn't try to be who everyone else wanted her to be. "Trusting people takes time. Especially when you've never had someone to rely on."

"How do you do that?" She asked, her eyes intent on his.

"Do what?"

"Make me have faith in things I've never believed?"

"That's not me, Charity. That's you. Maybe you're ready to believe."

She caved against his chest, bringing the sweet heat of her mouth to his. *Finally.* The kiss loosened every ounce of control he thought he'd had. He brought his other hand to her hip, urging her closer but not forcing her.

She moved on her own, fitting her body tightly to his. She seduced him with her lips, drifting over his in light fleeting touches before pressing in harder and opening her mouth to him. Her tongue sought his, and all the wetness and heat of her nearly drove him over the edge. He inched his hands higher, sliding them along her hips, then waist, under her shirt and up her ribs, moving them slowly, giving her the space to tell him to stop.

Instead, she arched into his touch. "Your hands," she murmured into his mouth. "Oh god, Dev. Your hands."

She was silky soft, every inch of her; every spot he touched made him want to feel more of her. "You can tell me to stop," he reminded her gruffly. "I would never take more than you want to give."

She pulled back and brought her hands to his face, cupping them around either side of his jaw. Her gaze settled in his, so comfortable and open. "I know you wouldn't." She kissed him softly again, her hands drifting down to his elbows and applying pressure to prod his hands higher on her body.

His fingers grazed the satin edge of her bra, and he felt a hitch in her breath. His own breath hitched too, ragged with anticipation. He glided his hands up to hold her breasts and took their kiss deeper. Her nipples responded, hardening into tight buds against his palms. "Damn, I want you," he uttered against her lips. "I've never wanted anyone like I want you."

"You can have me—"

Somewhere, a door banged open.

Charity whirled away from him, flailing to turn on the faucet. She grabbed a plate just as his father walked into the kitchen.

Dev's arms fell heavy at his sides, his heart still pounding hard enough to put him off balance.

"Did Bodie and Gracie come back here?" his dad asked, seemingly oblivious to the awkwardness that had driven Dev and Charity to opposite sides of the room.

"Uh. No." Dev watched Charity at the sink, her posture rigid and her hands bordering on frantic as she rinsed and stashed the plates. "Why?"

His dad glanced out the window with a furrowed brow. "Your mom and I took a detour to get the mail. Said we'd meet them at the chicken coops, but we couldn't find them out there anywhere."

"Did you check the barn?" Blood still rushed through him so fast all he could think about was being alone with Charity again. "I'm sure they're around somewhere. They couldn't have gone too far."

"We checked the barn. Even called out for them a few times," his dad said. "And Gracie's horse is gone."

"Her horse?" That got Dev's attention. "Maybe they headed back over to the Cortez place."

"I'm sure that's it." Charity had shut off the water and turned around to face them. "I'll call over there and ask Naomi if she's seen them."

Dev waited as she dug out her phone and made the call. Judging from her end of the conversation, Naomi hadn't seen them either.

"Maybe they went for a ride," his dad suggested when Charity hung up.

"Bodie doesn't know how to ride." The flush that had brought her face alive only moments before had paled. "And Gracie's still learning. It's one thing for her to ride over here on the road, but I'm not sure either one of them is qualified to go much farther."

Dev felt the same worry creep over him, but he hid it underneath a casual shrug. "We can go out and look around. Like I said, I doubt they could've gone too far." Beyond the meadows on his dad's property, the hills turned into mountains with steep, unforgiving terrain. There were no trails, and unless you'd spent a lot of time out there, it was easy to get lost. Rather than think about that scenario, Dev walked over and took Charity's hand, leading her out the backdoor behind his father. "We'll find them," he said, making her a promise. Hopefully they'd find them before they got into any trouble.

She was going to ground him. Charity stomped back up the road from the stables where the Jenkinses housed their animals. She'd been so sure Bodie and Gracie had to be there somewhere, given how much they both seemed to like the idea of chicks and piglets. But she'd been through every square millimeter of the stables and the surrounding meadow while Dev and Mr. Jenkins searched other areas of the property, along with Lucas. Gracie's stepdad had come right over after she'd called Naomi. But there was no trace of Bodie and Gracie anywhere.

Actually, grounding Bodie would not be nearly enough. Oh, no. She would Google the absolute worst possible punishment you could inflict on a thirteen-year-old boy legally and that's what she would do.

As she crested the hill, her consternation quickly iced over into the panic she'd been trying to keep at bay. Dev, Lucas, and Mr. Jenkins all stood in front of the house deliberating.

"Any sign of them?" she called, jogging over.

They didn't need to shake their heads; their grim frowns told her enough.

"We've combed the land around the house and barn, all the way to the edge of the woods." Dev's voice had taken on a more official tone. He seemed worried too. "We have to assume that's where they went."

"Why would they go into the woods alone? Without telling anyone?" Charity had never seen Lucas's jaw so tense. He was the mellow Cortez brother, the quiet one. But right now, he looked like he could boil over any second. She didn't blame him.

"They're probably just out having some fun," Mr. Jenkins suggested. "You two boys used to do that all the time back in the day."

Dev and Lucas shared a pained look. That likely wasn't all they were doing when they were sneaking away as teen boys. Not that she wanted to know what they were up to. She did not need any help conjuring up worst-case scenarios at the moment. "How are we going to find them in thousands of acres?"

"We'll take the ATVs and split up," Dev said definitively. "We can each head a different direction. Neither one of them know the property very well."

"Oh my god." Charity's stomach rolled. "Lucas...I'm so sorry about this." She wished she could say it wasn't like Bodie, but that would be a lie. He'd tried sneaking out of her house. He didn't seem to care about authority at all, and now he had gotten Gracie into trouble. He might've even put her in danger.

Lucas's frown deepened. "If anything happens to Gracie—"

"Hey." Dev stepped up to him. "As far as we know right now they're two kids going for a ride. Let's not overreact. That won't help us find them." He directed Lucas toward the barn. "Why don't you head up into the north section of the woods?

Lucas gave a brisk nod and jogged away.

Dev turned to his father. "You can take one of the ATVs up over to the south side, and Charity and I will head west."

"Sounds good, son." Mr. Jenkins reached over and squeezed Charity's hand kindly. "I'm sure there's no reason to worry. Bodie seems to have a good head on his shoulders."

She couldn't even nod right now. She'd like to think her nephew was more responsible than he seemed, but then something like this happened and she had to wonder.

Dev walked away with his dad. "I'll bring the ATV around and come pick you up."

She nodded, grateful for the opportunity to pace out some of the fear that had circulated through her. Truthfully, it was easier to be mad at Bodie. She'd never been a fearful worst-case-scenario kind of person, but in the last couple of weeks, she'd learned that there was something about having a kid that made you the worst kind of fearful.

What if something happened to him? Her throat closed around an onslaught of tears. Even with the roar of the ATV engine behind her, she didn't turn around. Couldn't face Dev.

He pulled the ATV next to her and killed the engine. "You can climb on the back. The helmet's right there."

Instead of speaking, she nodded, but before she could get the helmet on, Dev turned around. His eyes met hers, and there was no hiding the tears.

"They're fine," he said firmly. "We'll find them. We won't stop looking until we find them."

"I can't believe he'd do something like this. I feel like I've failed him. Nothing I've done has made a difference at all."

Dev pushed himself off the ATV and faced her. He gently took the helmet out of her hands and set it on the seat. "Listen to me. Bodie is a kid. He's gonna make more stupid choices than you can count. Trust me. That's part of growing up." He rubbed his hands up and down the backs of her arms. "But you won't fail him, Charity. You've already given him more stability than he's known his whole life. That will mean something to him someday. Even if he doesn't realize it now. He needs you."

"I'm glad you're here." Charity leaned in until her head rested on his chest. Dev's arms came around her, holding her tightly, keeping her together. "I couldn't do this alone."

Chapter Fifteen

Dev steered the ATV around trees and undergrowth and rocks, taking it slow. They'd already searched the meadows, and were now headed up the steeper incline. Charity's hands clasped tightly around his waist, arms stiff, body rigid with the tension of worry.

Easing on the brake, he brought the machine to a stop and killed the engine. "It's too loud. We'll never be able to hear them if they call."

"Why haven't we found them yet?" Charity scrambled off the ATV and removed her helmet, her face flushed and her eyes wild with fear. "Where could they be?"

After ditching his own helmet, he collected her into his arms. "We've been out only about twenty minutes. And there's a lot of ground to cover." More acres than he cared to think about right now. "We need to stay calm and clearheaded."

"I wish I could." She looked up at him. "I didn't even know it was possible to worry like this. It's sickening. I feel like all of my nerve endings are on fire. Like I want to puke but also eat a whole pizza."

Dev smoothed his hand over her hair. "It's the adrenaline. But it's good. It gives you the instinct to fight instead of take flight."

She ducked out of his arms. "I'm not good at that. Standing to fight. It's easier to run."

He let her pace a few feet away. "You're good at it when it's something that matters." She'd done nothing but fight for that kid since he'd shown up at her house. "And when you're tempted to run, that's when you rely on your anchors."

"Anchors?" She stepped back, searching his face.

"The people who love you." Dev slipped his hand in hers and started walking. They had to keep looking. "The people who'll stand and fight with you."

"I've never had anchors." Charity tugged him to a stop. "But now with you—"

A faint shout nearby cut her off.

"What was that?" She frantically looked around.

"Definitely a person." Dev squeezed her hand tighter and brought his finger to his lips, straining to hear...

"Help!"

He could barely make out the word, but it sounded like—

"Bodie!" Charity screamed, breaking away from Dev and running blind through the woods. Dev followed and finally caught her, pulling her to a stop. "We have to listen. To figure out what direction—"

Footsteps crashed through the brush behind him.

"Aunt Charity?" Her nephew sprinted to them, red-faced and out of breath.

"Where's Gracie?" Dev asked, adrenaline coursing through him.

"She's hurt," the kid wheezed. "The horse spooked and we fell off."

"What?" Charity swayed.

Dev put his arm around her to support her. "Where?" he asked roughly.

"She's not too far from here. I think she's okay." Now Bodie was in tears. "But her ankle hurts. She can't walk on it, and I didn't know what to do."

Dev put his hand on the boy's shoulder to calm him down. "Show us where."

Bodie ran in the direction he'd come from, and Dev and Charity jogged behind.

It took only a few minutes to reach her. She was sprawled on the ground, not far from a whole lot of boulders that could've done some serious damage if she'd landed there instead.

"Dev? Ohmygawd! I'm so glad you're here." She was half crying, half whimpering. "My ankle hurts. It twisted when I fell, and—" The words broke into sobs.

"It's okay." Dev knelt beside her. Relief washed through him. She seemed okay. At least she wasn't unconscious or anything. He quickly did a visual check on Charity behind him. Her face was a stark white, but other than that, she seemed to be holding up all right. "Can you call Lucas and Naomi?" he asked gently. "Tell them we found her. Tell Lucas we're about a hundred yards to the west of the log bridge over the river." He'd know exactly where to come. Dev and the Cortez brothers had built that bridge for fishing access when they were in high school.

Charity nodded and turned away.

Sobs still rattled Gracie. "Peaches took off and I don't know where she went."

"Peaches knows the way home," he told Gracie. "Horses are smart like that." He carefully straightened her left leg so he could get a look at that ankle. "I'm going to take off your boot." Before there was too much swelling.

"No! It'll hurt." She started to pull back, but Bodie took a knee next to her. "You can squeeze my hand."

Dev waited until she'd taken Bodie's hand, then he carefully inched the boot off her foot. Even through her sock, he could see the swelling. He couldn't say if it was broken or sprained, but she definitely shouldn't walk on it.

"It hurts so bad." Gracie gritted her teeth and started crying again. "What're we gonna do?" Panic squeaked through the words. "I can't walk back."

"You won't have to walk." Dev stood. "Charity called your mom. And your stepdad. I'm guessing he'll be here with the ATV soon."

"He's on his way," Charity called, the phone still attached to her ear.

"My stepdad's coming?" Gracie let out a wail. "He's mad, isn't he? He's gonna kill me for taking off without asking. I'm going to be in huge trouble. They'll probably take away my riding lessons."

Dev kept his mouth shut and looked at Bodie. "Let's not worry about any of that right now. You two want to tell me why you came out here in the first place?"

Gracie darted her gaze around like she thought the answer might be hidden somewhere in the rocks. "I don't know," she finally said. For a girl who liked to chat so much she was suddenly being suspiciously quiet. "I might as well jump off those rocks over there. I'll be grounded for the rest of my life anyway."

"I don't know about that," Dev teased. "Maybe just until you turn eighteen."

She gave him a stormy look. Okay, not in the mood for jokes. He decided to change the subject. "Have you ever ridden out here before?" He still couldn't get over the fact that they'd come here when they could've simply stayed on the road. Then they wouldn't be in trouble for sneaking away, and they likely wouldn't have gotten tossed either.

"No, I've never ridden back here," the girl muttered. "I'm supposed to ride on the road. I just wanted to have some fun. We weren't planning to go very far but—" Her mouth snapped shut at the sound of an ATV engine somewhere nearby. "Oh great. That's my stepdad. My life is officially over."

"It won't be that bad." But even Dev had to admit, Lucas looked as pissed as he'd ever seen him when he came to a stop and pulled off the helmet.

Bodie wisely drifted away to stand behind Charity.

"Everyone's fine," Dev yelled over. "Her left ankle's swollen, but we don't have any serious injuries." Which was lucky since neither one of them were wearing helmets...

"Her ankle?" Lucas rushed over and hit his knees next to Gracie. His face was as pale as Charity's.

"I'm so sorry, Dad." Gracie widened her eyes. "I told Bodie we shouldn't keep going, but he didn't listen."

Hmmm. That's not exactly what Gracie had said to him a minute ago. Dev gauged Bodie's expression. There was a split second of obvious surprise before the kid moved out from behind Charity.

"Uh. Yeah. It was my idea. I'm sorry."

"What were you thinking?" Lucas stood and got in Bodie's face. "Do you even know what could've happened? This is your fault. She's hurt because of your stupid decis—"

"All right." Dev stood too. "That'll do. You should get her back, take her to the doctor to get her ankle fixed up."

Without another word, Lucas lifted Gracie into his arms. Everyone remained quiet, while Lucas carted his stepdaughter over to the ATV and got her settled with the extra helmet.

Dev checked on Charity again. It looked like she'd gotten her color back. In fact, her cheeks blazed red.

Uh-oh...that was the same look she'd had on her face when he'd fake arrested her.

"How could you do this?" She whirled to face Bodie. "Everyone was worried sick. It was completely irresponsible for you to leave Mr. and Mrs. Jenkins without telling them where you went. You don't even know how to ride, Bodie."

"I'm sorry." Shoulders hunched, the kid darted a quick look at Gracie, but she stared straight ahead.

Huh. Interesting. Whenever Dev had seen them together before, Gracie couldn't seem to take her eyes off Bodie. He looked back and forth between the two of them. Something didn't sit right.

"Sorry's not good enough." Charity's voice shook. "Not this time."

Dev stepped between them before she said something she'd regret. "Why don't you drive our ATV back to the ranch?" He reached over and squeezed her hand. That'd give her a few minutes to cool off. "Bodie and I will walk."

Charity tilted her head and studied him. "Are you sure?"

"Yep. It's not far." And he wanted a few minutes alone with the kid. Something about this story wasn't adding up, and he intended to get to the bottom of it.

Without another word to any of them, Lucas blitzed off with Gracie on their ATV, and Charity headed in the direction where Dev had left his. When they were finally alone, he assessed the kid.

"Go ahead," Bodie said. "Tell me how stupid I am. Tell me what a big mistake I made and how everyone's pissed at me."

"That's not why I wanted to walk back with you." Dev started out at a steady pace. "Because I'm pretty sure it wasn't your idea to go on a horseback ride anyway." He snuck a glance over his shoulder, but Bodie kept his head down.

"You don't ride," Dev went on. "But Gracie does." And when he'd first asked, she'd said, *I just wanted to have some fun.* So he'd venture to guess the whole thing had been her idea in the first place. "What happened? How'd you two end up out here?" He stopped and faced the kid. "The truth this time."

Bodie looked him right in the eyes. "We were walking down to the barn, but then we passed her horse and I wanted to pet it. Gracie said we should go for a quick ride. She knew a really cool place that wasn't far away. I didn't think we'd be gone more than a few minutes. When we got out here the horse totally freaked out."

"Why didn't you tell everyone that?" Why would he let Charity think it was his fault?

"No one would've believed me." Bodie hiked past him. "And I didn't want to get Gracie in trouble. She's never in trouble, and I can handle it."

Dev watched him walk away with a stab of regret. The kid was used to handling things, used to taking the blame, used to living with a label. Troubled. Bad news. Bodie had likely realized Dev wasn't exactly excited about him hanging out with Gracie, based on their brunch together. So of course he assumed everyone would blame him.

"I'm sorry." He caught up to Bodie. "I wasn't being fair earlier. During breakfast. Trying to keep you and Gracie from hanging out."

Bodie looked over at him like he'd gone off his rocker.

"You're good kid. A great kid. Gracie would be lucky to have you as a friend."

Bodie deflected the compliment with a shrug. "You can't tell Aunt Charity it was Gracie's idea. You can't tell anyone."

That would mean Bodie taking the blame, getting punished for something he didn't do. "I won't," he finally said. He'd spent too much time trying to build Bodie's trust to ruin it all now. "But I think you should."

And even if the kid chose not to tell Charity...in Dev's experience the truth usually came out.

It was amazing Charity could drive at all with her hands still shaking so badly. Instead of dissipating, the swirl of adrenaline and fear and worry had gained strength. A nauseating heat swarmed inside the helmet, making the back of her throat itch. She hit the brakes and ripped off the helmet just in time to lean over and vomit.

Bodie could've been killed. Gracie could've been killed. Either one of them could've been thrown into those rocks, and they had no protection. She inhaled deeply, replacing the helmet, steadying her hands back on the handlebars. Bodie's choices didn't affect only him. They affected his friends. His friends' parents. Her.

The terrain jostled her, and she struggled to hang on in the midst of her weakening grip. Finally, she broke through into the meadow and drove over to where Lucas and Gracie had stopped in front of Mr. and Mrs. Jenkins's house. Everyone had gathered on the expansive front porch. Even Naomi was there.

Fighting the nausea, Charity killed the engine and hurried to get off the ATV so she could join them. On her way up the steps, she heard Lucas giving Gracie the third degree.

"Did that kid touch you? I swear to god if he touched you..."

"No! God, Dad." The girl's cheeks went pink. "Of course he didn't touch me! Bodie isn't like that!"

"How am I supposed to know what he's like? You two took off into the woods without bothering to get permission, and—"

"All right." Naomi tenderly took hold of her husband's arm and directed an apologetic smile at Charity. "Let's focus on what matters. No one got badly hurt—" She stopped suddenly and looked around. "Where's Bodie?"

"He's walking back with Dev," Charity said. She had no idea how she managed to form words with her head spinning like this. "They should be here any minute."

"I've brought out some lemonade." Mrs. Jenkins carried a tray through the door. "And an icepack for poor Gracie too." She set the tray on a small table next to where Gracie sat in a lounge chair. Charity looked at the girl's ankle, all swollen and black and blue. God, Bodie was lucky it hadn't been worse.

"Thank you, Mrs. Jenkins," Naomi said, taking a seat next to her daughter. She carefully tucked the icepack in a towel and wrapped it around Gracie's ankle. "We appreciate all of your help."

"It's no trouble at all." The older woman took her husband by the hand and led him back inside. "We're going to get some lunch on for everyone. I'm sure y'all are starvin'." The older couple disappeared inside, and Charity didn't know what to say. She was at a complete loss for how to deal with this.

"Well, at least things weren't worse." Naomi planted a kiss on Gracie's forehead. "Everything will be fine."

Charity didn't feel fine. She still felt like she was five seconds away from emptying her stomach again.

"Why would you go off like that without telling anyone?" Lucas demanded. He didn't seem to think things were fine either.

"It was Bodie's idea to go for a ride." Charity stepped forward. "I'm so sorry. I should've kept a better eye on them." Once again, she'd given her nephew too much freedom. But she would find a way to fix this. "He's definitely going to be grounded." She wouldn't be able to let him out of her sight.

"And he'll pay all the doctor's bills. He can work them off at the ranch and—"

"No, it was me," Gracie blurted through a sob. "It was all my idea to go riding instead of down to the barn. Bodie wanted to turn around but I didn't listen. I wanted him to like me. To think I was cool." She choked out another mournful sob. "So I made Peaches keep going. It was all my fault."

"*Your* fault?" Was she trying to protect Bodie? Charity lowered into the chair next to her. "You said it was Bodie's idea. I heard you."

"I know." Gracie sniffled. "I'm so so so so sorry." She peeked up at her parents. "I was afraid Mom would take away riding, so I lied. But I don't want Bodie to get in trouble. I'm sure he hates me now."

"Of course he doesn't hate you." Charity gave her hand a squeeze right as her own heart sank. She'd been so hard on Bodie. So angry. And he hadn't even tried to defend himself.

"I bet he'll never talk to me again," the girl whimpered. "He probably wishes he never met me."

Charity refocused on Gracie and tried to smile. "You've been so nice to him since he started school. And he obviously tried to protect you. Which means he likes you."

That seemed to stop her tears. "You think?"

"Yes." Her nephew definitely had a little crush on Gracie.

"I'm so sorry I said it was him." She swiped her nose with her shirtsleeve.

"Oh sweetie," Naomi said, studying her daughter's face. "Honey, you know the rules. You're only supposed to ride on the road."

"I know. It was a mistake." A hopeless sigh turned into a sob.

Lucas and Naomi shared a look. "It's okay. We'll talk about the consequences later," her stepfather said. "Right now we need to get you to the doctor." He leaned over and lifted

Gracie into his arms. On his way down the steps, Lucas glanced at Charity over his shoulder. "We'll come by your place later. So I can apologize to Bodie for how I acted."

"I need to apologize too," Gracie blubbered.

"Sure. That's fine. Anytime." Charity couldn't seem to stand up. She'd yelled at Bodie too. She'd been horrible to him. She hadn't even bothered to ask him for the truth. She'd simply assumed it was all his fault.

"You okay?" Naomi leaned down to hug her.

"Nope." No sense in lying. "I'm not sure I'm cut out for this parenting stuff."

"It's not for the faint of heart," her friend agreed. "I'll call you later. After we're finished at the doctor."

"Thanks." She watched Naomi follow Lucas to his truck. They both fussed over Gracie, getting her settled in the back seat, and then they drove away.

Charity kept her eyes trained on the very edge of the meadow, waiting and watching. When Dev and Bodie finally came into view, she slowly rose from the chair. By the time they'd made it up the porch steps, she was crying. Without saying anything, she walked over to her nephew and wrapped him in a hug. He was still shorter than her—it probably wouldn't be that way for long, but she took advantage of his height and planted a kiss on the top of his head.

"Uh…you okay, Aunt Charity?" Her shoulder muffled his voice, and she gave him a little more space to breathe. Only a little.

"I'm sorry," she whispered. "I should've asked *you* what happened." She pulled back so he could see her face. "Next time, I will."

"How did you—"

"Gracie told us the truth," she interrupted, desperate for his forgiveness.

"Well, good. I'm glad the truth is out." Dev stood a few feet away, as if he wanted to give them two of them some space.

"You told Dev the truth?" But not her. He'd simply taken the brunt of everyone's fear and frustration.

"I figured it out," Dev offered. "But I had a feeling Gracie would come clean eventually."

"Do her parents know?" It was sweet how Bodie's face got all concerned.

"Yes. They're all going to stop over later so they can apologize to you."

He brushed off the whole thing with a shrug. "They don't have to. It's no big deal."

Charity took his shoulders in her hands and directed him to face her. "Yes, it is. It's a big deal. Bodie...you have to trust me. You have to tell me things. So I can help you."

"Why?" Her nephew stared down at his boots. "What's the point? I'll probably never see you again after my mom comes back anyway."

"Of course you will." Charity staggered back a step. Before she could say more, the screen door opened and Mrs. Jenkins poked out her head. "Oh, Bodie, thank heavens you're back! Why don't you come on in? Get some water and have a little snack? I'm sure you're starving after such an ordeal."

"Thanks." He moved swiftly past Charity as though he couldn't wait to escape, and disappeared into the house. Mrs. Jenkins continued holding open the door, but Dev walked over and gently pushed it closed. "We'll be in soon."

"Of course." His mom smiled at them in a knowing way and scurried off.

Charity walked over to the railing, curled her fingers around the solid wood, and gazed out at the clouds building over the peaks on the horizon. She found it hard to breathe past the scorch marks Bodie's words had left on her heart. *I'll probably never see you again.*

"Hey." Dev came over and stood next to her. "He does trust you, you know. As much as he can trust anyone."

Charity went back to the chair and sank down. "That's the thing. He can't. He can't trust anyone. His life is in limbo right now." She glanced at Dev from behind a fresh curtain of tears. "Maybe I need to try harder to find Melody. Maybe he'd be better off with her. I mean, look at what's happened since he came to stay with me. He crashed my truck, ditched school, got drunk..." All in a couple of weeks. How was she going to help him when she couldn't get through to him?

Dev pulled over a chair and sat across from her. "He wouldn't be better off with Melody. I know that much."

She used her shirtsleeves to dry her eyes. "How do you know?" Because she was doing a pretty crappy job of being a parent. For all her sister's issues, Bodie seemed to love his mom. He seemed to trust her, even though she'd left him.

"There's something I have to tell you."

Charity raised her head to look at him, to see into his eyes. They were drawn and sad.

"I did some research, looked up crime reports in Oklahoma a while back," he said, holding her gaze. "A month ago, two suspects robbed a convenience store near Stillwater. One of them was a woman. With blond hair."

Not this again. "Are you serious? You're still looking for some crime to accuse her of? Why would she rob a convenience store?" Her sister was irresponsible, not violent.

Dev leaned closer, like he wanted her to listen carefully. "Bodie said she lost her job a month ago. Then he told me someone had given them money right before they left. To help them out."

Suddenly a chair seemed like the worst place to be. She couldn't sit still, not with the anger sending streaks of heat through her chest. "When did he tell you that?" She swiftly rose to her feet, standing over Dev. "And why? Were you trying to get information out of him?" Was that why he'd offered to spend time with Bodie?

"No. He just mentioned it. When we were working." Dev stood too. "But I couldn't let it go, Charity. I'm a cop. I called the detective working the case. Melody is a person of interest in the robbery. They'd like to find her so they can question her."

The news hollowed her out. Empty. Her body felt empty. Especially her heart, which had just only started to open up to this man. "How long have you known?" The words barely squeaked past the lump in her throat.

Dev hesitated. "A while," he finally said.

"And you didn't tell me. You kissed me, but you didn't want to tell me you were working on building a case against my sister behind my back."

"I'm not building a case. I was trying to help you find her. But I had an obligation to report what I learned. And I didn't want to tell you anything until they had evidence against her. I'm sorry." He reached out for her, his hands grazing her arms before she jolted back.

"Don't. Don't touch me. God, Dev. Do you even know what it'll do to Bodie if his mom goes to prison?"

"There's a chance she committed a crime." His arms dropped to his sides. "If she was really involved in something like that, Bodie will be better off with you. I did what I thought was best."

But that didn't change the fact that he'd lied to her. That he'd been lying to her for weeks. And to Bodie too. "We're done," she told him. "Bodie and I are going home and we're done."

Chapter Sixteen

Dev had never been any good at pretending. He sat up
on the stage at the old Episcopal Church, which had been
turned into the town hall, and folded his hands on the table
in front of him. Months ago, Hank Green had scheduled
an official question-and-answer session with the sheriff
candidate—trying to cast Dev in a friendly light for local
voters, he suspected. At the time, he'd agreed it might be a
good chance for people to get to know him, but tonight was
not the best night for him to stand up in front of the whole
town to declare how excited he was about the opportunity to
become their county sheriff.

He hadn't slept in a couple of nights, and he hadn't
thought about the election in even longer. Not since he'd
been distracted by everything that had happened with
Charity. Throughout the whole session, Dev had done his
best to answer the questions, and he even tried to muster
some enthusiasm, but based on Hank's furious glares, he
wasn't meeting expectations.

"We'll take another question," the mayor said, moderating from the podium off to the side of the stage. Dev had just struggled through an answer on how he would change the direction of the sheriff's office if elected. The truth was, he hadn't spent as much time thinking about that lately as he probably should have.

"I have a question." A woman near the back raised her hand. Dev didn't recognize her, but then again about half the people here were likely from other towns in the county. His friends and family took up one whole section on the right side of the audience, but he'd told them not to ask questions. God only knew what the guys would come up with. Probably something about why he was so devastatingly handsome. He still hadn't lived that down.

"Yes, ma'am." The mayor gestured for her to stand.

The woman appeared to be in the retired demographic, a segment Hank assured Dev he'd already won over. "Why do you want to be sheriff?" she asked politely before quickly sitting back down.

"Great question," Hank said, turning the floor over to Dev with a wave of his hand.

"Oh. Well..." Dev sat straighter and clenched his shoulder blades tightly together. A familiar tension burned at the base of his neck. Why? Why did he want to be sheriff? Everyone else had plenty of reasons—Hank because it would be good for the town, his parents because they were so proud, Ty because he thought Dev could magically make his parking tickets disappear...

"He's having a hard time narrowing down the many reasons," Hank quipped. A few people chuckled. "But let me remind you, deputy, we are on a bit of a schedule here. So why don't you pick your top three reasons?"

Three? Dev hoped no one else could see him squirm.

Shit, he was having a hard time coming up with one. "I guess I'd have to say ... I think being county sheriff would give me the best chance to help the most people." Even as the words sputtered out, he questioned their credibility. His boss was hardly ever out in the field anymore. It seemed the man's days were filled with meetings and phone calls and appearances and personnel issues.

"Great answer," Hank said proudly. "As I'm sure you all know, Deputy Jenkins has an outstanding record for service in the community."

That was because it had always been important to him. He liked being out there—not just on calls, but also on patrols. He liked knowing the people in town, getting to chat with them often about what was going on in their lives. He liked being part of that sense of community.

"What are your other top two reasons you're looking forward to this opportunity?" Hank prompted, making a lingering glance at his watch.

Dev scanned the crowd. His mom gave him a sneaky double thumbs-up from the front row where she sat next to his dad, both of them beaming with pride.

"It's really tough to pick only two more reasons," he fibbed. "I guess I would have to say that I would look forward to being a liaison between the community and the Sheriff's Department, and I am passionate about upholding the law." Talk about vague. Any of the other candidates could've said the same thing—probably better than he had.

"Thank you for keeping it brief." Hank's jaw seemed to have clenched. "We have time for one more question, and then we'll invite you all to stay for a small reception in the community room."

"I have a question." Betty Osterman didn't bother to raise

her hand. She simply stood up. "What's your relationship with Charity Stone?"

His heart took a punch. "I don't see how that's relevant." *We're done.* Those were the words that had been keeping him up at night.

"She's the one who took out the statue of Luis Cortez, at the fairgrounds, right?" The same woman who'd called him devastatingly handsome in an op-ed posted her hands on her hips and glared. "Rumor has it you're romantically involved. Does that have anything to do with why she got off so easy?"

Dev opened his mouth to speak, but Hank jumped in before he got the chance. "Deputy Jenkins conducted a thorough investigation. I was there to oversee it myself. We found that it was simply a case of distracted driving, and Ms. Stone was punished to the full extent of the law. Now, it appears our time is up. Why don't we all gather in the community room for refreshments? If anyone else has questions, Deputy Jenkins would be happy to address them then."

Everyone stood and started to gather their things, and even though he wanted to disappear, Dev made his way to the reception along with the crowd. He hated to admit it, but Betty had a point. He had gone easy on Charity that night. Or, more accurately, on Bodie. But wasn't that part of being a good cop? Evaluating each individual situation and blending compassion with discipline?

Some people would say no. A lot of those people were probably county sheriffs. When you were in charge—always being scrutinized—there likely weren't a lot of opportunities to exercise mercy...

"Whew, rough crowd." Ty sidled up next to him in the hallway. People murmured around them, likely judging every word Dev had said up there. Most of them probably weren't impressed.

"Yeah. I wasn't exactly stellar up there tonight." He said it quiet enough that hopefully no one else heard.

"I don't know..." Darla appeared on his other side. "I thought you came across as real."

"Yeah," Ty grumbled. "Real bummed about something. Would it have killed you to smile?"

"I smiled." At least he'd tried.

"Leave him alone." Darla reached past Dev and whacked Ty. "He's totally bummed out about Charity. Give the guy a break."

Dev stopped, leaving the crowd behind them only a small space to filter past. "Wow, word travels fast." It had been only a few days since Charity informed him she was done with him.

"I've talked to her," she said. "She's pretty pissed at you."

"For what?" Ty was never up on the latest gossip.

And Darla never hesitated to bring anyone up to speed. "Dev implicated Melody in a robbery back in Oklahoma and now the cops are looking for her."

"I didn't exactly implicate her," he clarified. "I called to talk to the detective to learn more about the robbery. And now Charity has pretty much written me off."

"Dude." Ty shook his head. "I warned you, man. Don't get too attached to Charity. And what did you do? Dove right in there, didn't ya? Well, my friend, let me tell you, life is much easier when you're unattached."

Solid advice from someone who clearly had an attachment to the woman currently standing next to Dev. Ty might pretend to be all autonomous, but it was common knowledge that he and Darla hooked up occasionally.

Darla gave a quick glance around before leaning close. "For what it's worth, I think Charity's pretty attached to you too."

"I'm not sure that helps." He'd been trying to protect her. She'd basically told him she didn't even want to think about Melody, but he should've told her about the robbery anyway. Her trust in him had already been tenuous, and he'd completely destroyed it.

"Listen…" Darla glanced around, waiting until the last stragglers of the crowd disappeared into the community room. "If you want to fix it, why don't you just find a way to help Melody? Show Charity that you're not against her."

"Or you could just let it go," Ty said. "Move on to the next woman. I find that's a much easier solution than—"

Darla cut him off with a raise of her eyebrows.

Yeah, Ty was just as much of a lost cause as Dev. Only he didn't know it yet. "I have no idea how to help Melody." Especially now that she was on the radar. Now that the detective knew about her, she might be beyond his help.

"Find her." Darla made it sound so easy. "Maybe if you get to her first, you can find a way to help her. Even if she is guilty."

If she was guilty, the only way he could help her would be to convince her to turn herself in. At least they might go easier on her then. "I've looked. The police are looking, and they haven't found her. She's definitely off the grid."

"Have you talked to their mom?" Ty asked. "Charity always used to say how her sister was much closer to their mom than her. Maybe their mom knows where she is."

Huh. It wasn't every day that Ty came up with helpful advice, but… "That's actually a good idea." From what she'd told him, it sounded like Charity didn't get along with her mom, but maybe Melody did.

"Why aren't we going to Dev's place?" Bodie peered out the window as they flew past the Jenkinses' ranch.

Charity kept her eyes on the highway, not allowing herself to even look toward Dev's cabin, which sat up on the hill. "I thought we'd do something different this morning." She hadn't told him about Melody and the robbery. She couldn't. She'd looked up everything she could find about it online, and she still couldn't believe Melody had been involved. She refused to believe.

"What about the PlayStation?" Bodie asked. "And Mr. Jenkins said something about needing help fixing a tractor." The kid sounded bummed, but he'd be a lot more bummed if he knew Dev had been working with him so he could pump him for information about his mom. He'd be crushed. That was the only way to describe it when you learned someone you'd actually started to care about had betrayed you.

But this was not about her. This wasn't about the twinge of pain that had settled just beneath her heart like a bruise. Today was about Bodie. "You can do chores around my house to earn a PlayStation." She had plenty of yard work she'd been putting off. "But today I thought we'd spend some time racing."

"Racing?" Her nephew finally quit staring out the window and gaped at her instead. "Like horse racing?"

"Barrel racing." She flicked on her blinker and slowed to turn into the Cortezes' driveway.

"Oh." Bodie's shoulders fell. "You mean like you're gonna train and I'll time you or something?"

"Nope. I mean you're going to train and I'll time you." She wasn't thinking about Dev right now, but if she were thinking about him, she would admit he was right. Bodie needed something to strive for—a pursuit that could help him develop discipline and goals. Something to drive him.

"You're gonna let me ride Ace?" Bodie almost looked like he was afraid to believe it.

"I'm not going to *let* you ride him." Charity pulled the truck to a stop in front of the stables where she boarded her horse. "I'm going to teach you how to ride him."

"No. Way." Her nephew scrambled to get out of the truck. She hadn't seen this much interest on his face since Dev had offered him a PlayStation.

Dev. For not thinking about him, he sure seemed to cross her mind a lot.

"I can't believe you're gonna teach me to race." Bodie rushed over to the driver's side door and pulled it open like he couldn't wait for her to get out. "It's what they do at all the rodeos, right? They steer the horse around the barrels going superfast?"

"Exactly." She climbed out of the truck and led him into the stables. Walking in to the dim, cool space always made her feel grounded. The sound of the horses breathing, the manure-tinged scent of the air. It was all so familiar and comfortable. She might not be an expert on relationships with people, but she knew horses. "You probably won't go superfast today," she warned Bodie. "Not until you get comfortable riding." This first lesson would cover only the basics—saddling up, walking, turning, halting. All things he'd need to know before she could let him loose.

"That's okay. I'd never ridden before I got on the horse with Gracie." Her nephew eyed the stalls as they passed. Most of the horses here belonged to the Cortez family and were used for work around the ranch. She stopped at the last stall, where her horse ambled over to meet her at the gate.

"Bodie, this is Ace." She reached up to give her boy a good pat. As always, Ace leaned his head into her touch.

"He's huge." A look of fear had replaced the excitement in her nephew's expression. "Way huger than he looks from far away."

"I like to think of him as a gentle giant." She unlatched the gate and coaxed her nephew into the stall. "Quarter horses are more even-tempered than thoroughbreds, and Ace here has the patience of a saint." She had no reservations about putting Bodie on this horse's back. But before they could do that, she had to teach him how to saddle up.

Going to the shelves at the rear of the stall, Charity collected the brush and the saddle pad, but left the saddle sitting on its stand. "First we have to give Ace a good brushing." She did a quick demonstration on the horse's back before handing the brush to Bodie.

"Okay." He stood as far away as he could get and still be able to touch the brush to Ace's back.

"It's okay to stand closer." Charity guided him next to the horse. "He knows the routine, so nothing you do will surprise him. Just run the brush over his sides and back." She covered Bodie's hand with hers and showed him again.

When she was satisfied that they'd removed all of the loose hair from Ace's coat, she quickly brushed the underside of the saddle pad and had Bodie help her position it on the horse's back. "Now for the saddle." She lugged it over, inhaling the scent of oiled leather, and arranged it over the pad. "You have to make sure the horn is right above the withers." She pointed. "That's most comfortable for Ace. And when he's comfortable, he's more motivated to keep you comfortable."

"Right." Bodie seemed to carefully examine the position and make a mental note.

"The next step is to string the tie strap through the ring on the girth strap." She bent to demonstrate while Bodie watched over her shoulder. "Then pull the strap up and loop it through the D ring from the front down." She peered behind her to make sure he was getting it, and laughed at his confused frown. "The last step is to loop the tie strap back through the girth ring front to back to front again," she said, finishing the motion. "I know it's kind of a lot, so I'll walk you through it the first few times."

He looked at her wide-eyed. "Yeah, that'd be good."

While Bodie continued to examine the straps at the base of the saddle, Charity slipped on Ace's bridle and then went back to the shelves and found him a helmet. "You ready to climb up?" she asked, plunking the helmet on his head.

"I guess." He still didn't seem too sure, but she had a feeling that would all change the moment he sat on the horse's back.

"Okay. First take the reins in your hands." Charity helped him find the right grip. "Then put your left foot into the stirrup."

Her nephew did as he was told, his balance teetering.

"Now you're just going to step up and swing your other leg over."

He went for it, and she gave him a little boost until he slowly sank into the saddle.

"Wow." A smile beamed from underneath the shadows of his helmet.

She smiled too. "How does it feel?"

"Like I'm really tall." He looked around the stables. "This is crazy." Only when he peered down at her again did his smile even out. "After all the mistakes I've made, why are you letting me do this?" he asked.

A sudden rise of emotion flooded her throat, but she did her best to swallow it back. "You deserve the best life, Bodie." It was true that mistakes would help him find his way, but so would victories. "I want you to believe that." All of the love she had for him made her chest ache, but she had to keep going. "No matter what. No matter what choices your mom makes or where you end up, you get to choose who you want to be. You get to choose what you go after." Melody had fallen into the same cycle of their mom's destructive patterns, but he didn't have to.

Bodie's gaze hardened into a glare. "Mom told me you never wanted to see us again," her nephew blurted. "That you thought you were too good for us, so you left us behind."

"No." Charity squeezed her eyes shut, but the tears came anyway. "That's not how it was at all. I worried about you. I questioned her ability to be a parent. So she hid from me. All those years...I didn't know where you were. I should've tried harder to find you." She shouldn't have let ten years pass without making sure Bodie had what he needed. "I hope you can forgive me for that." In a way she'd given up on her sister because it had been easier than dealing with the constant worry, the fear that something terrible would happen. That's what she did when things got hard. She ran. But she wouldn't do that to Bodie.

Bodie seemed to consider her words. "How did you do it?" he finally asked. "How did you escape and make something of yourself?"

"I had help." She'd had people who never gave up on her. "Gunner Raines brought me into his program and gave me a place to train." And then Levi, Mateo, and Ty had welcomed her onto their team. "I can help you too. Even when your mom comes back."

"What if she doesn't come back?" he whispered, and she could hear him holding back tears.

Charity reached for his hand, which still tightly clutched the reins. "If she doesn't come back, it's not because of you." She would tell him that every day of his life. As many days and as many times as it took for him to believe it. "You're not the reason she has problems. We had a tough time of it growing up." Before she'd talked about it with

Dev, she'd refused to let herself think about it. But he was right. She'd been abused. She and Melody both had. "But I want you to know, Bodie, if your mom doesn't come back, or if she can't come back, you will always have a place with me."

Chapter Seventeen

The pot roast came out of the oven with a charred crust, only proving that Charity was no domestic diva.

She poked the rubbery carrots and potatoes surrounding it with a fork. Well, it may not be the perfect meal, but it was the first roast she'd ever made, and she and Bodie were sitting down to a Friday night dinner together after a not-so-terrible week. *Take that, domestic goddess.*

She carted the roast over to the table, which she'd set with napkins and placemats. How was that for fancy? "Did you have a good day?" she asked, settling in across the table from Bodie.

"Yeah, it was good."

She did her best to temper a smile and play it cool, but that was the first time he'd ever responded to that question with anything other than a grunt or a roll of his eyes. Something positive must've happened. Not that she wanted to push it. "Your classes are going okay?" Nonchalance breezed through the words.

"Yeah." Bodie carved off a bite of the overdone roast. "We got to dissect a frog in science. It was pretty cool."

Cool was *really* positive, right? She did her best to keep the conversation going without sounding overly eager. "Doesn't sound cool to me. That sounds disgusting."

He grinned—a full-on grin, teeth and everything. She would've pressed the pause button if that were possible, to keep his face that bright with genuine happiness. He looked like a normal kid...not a kid whose mom abandoned him with someone he didn't know. Not a kid who'd likely been raising himself. Charity sucked back tears with a silent sniffle. Didn't need to go ruining this moment with a bunch of emotions. "So why did you have to dissect a frog? What're you supposed to learn from a bunch of blood and guts?"

Bodie shoveled the questionable potatoes and carrots into his mouth like a champ. "It's like a biology unit. So we can see what the organs look like. The intestines looked like worms," he informed her, somehow still eating with that visual hanging between them.

Pushing her plate away, Charity groaned. "There goes my appetite."

Bodie laughed. A real laugh! "You sound like Gracie. I thought she was gonna hurl."

Gracie? Charity's ears perked up again. "How is Gracie anyway?" she asked casually. "Is her ankle better?" When Lucas and Naomi had brought her over to apologize after taking her to the doctor, Charity and Bodie learned her ankle had been only sprained, but she'd still had to hobble around on crutches all week.

"Yeah. She said it's a lot better. I told her we've been riding a few days this week, and she said she wanted to practice with us as soon as the doctor says it's okay."

"Sure." Before she could ask how long that would be, someone knocked on the front door. "Hang on." She jumped up from the table intent on hurrying to shoo whoever it was away so she and Bodie could finish their very normal, pretty wonderful dinner. Unless it was Girl Scouts selling cookies. She never shooed Girl Scouts away.

Charity moved swiftly down the hall just as the person knocked again. She threw open the door ready to either send a salesperson packing or give a Girl Scout a huge hug, but instead she stopped and stared—no, gaped—at the one person she never in a million years would've expected to see. "Mom?"

"Char-Bear!" Tammi Stone flew at her and smothered her in a hug.

Charity stood frozen, her arms suspended out wide, and gagged on the smell of cheap perfume. This was not happening. She stepped away from her mom, but no matter how much she tried to deny it, Tammi Stone stood in front of her, dressed in a red chiffon pantsuit and glittering gold heels. Her face was lathered with enough makeup to fill in the creases and her bleached blond hair reached for the sky.

"I came as soon as I could get a flight out," she twanged, channeling a character from *Dallas*. "I had to drive all the way down to the big city to get a flight, and then they sent my connection through Los Angeles, which is so crazy, because it's all that way west and then I had to come back east to Denver, and goodness me, the flight was so turbulent the man sitting next to me kept getting sick." Her glossed red lips bent into a smile. "But not to worry. I'm here now and everything's going to be just fine."

"Why?" Charity squeaked. She did not need this right now. One more character in the after-school drama her life had suddenly become. "What are you doing here?" For the first time, Charity looked past her mother at the pile of suitcases stacked behind her. As in three suitcases. Big ones.

"What do you mean, what am I doing here? I came as soon as I heard that Melody was missing." Her mom clutched both hands against her chest. "I can't believe it. I can't believe your sister would leave Bodie here and take off to god only knows where—"

"Whoa, back up." Charity stopped her right there. "How did you find out about Melody?" After her sister had left Bodie, Charity had called her mother and casually asked if she'd heard from Melody. When her mother told her they hadn't spoken in a couple of weeks, she found an excuse to get off the phone without telling her what was going on. Mainly because she hadn't wanted her to do something like this—show up unannounced to make everything even more complicated.

"One of your friends called me. A nice boy. Dev, I think. He has a real deep, sexy voi—"

"You're telling me Dev called you?" That was impossible. He wouldn't go behind her back and do something like that...

"Yes, I'm sure his name was Dev. He said he was a friend of yours. He wanted to know if I'd seen or heard from Melody. Imagine my surprise when I learned what she'd done."

Anger lodged itself tightly beneath her ribs. What was he thinking? She'd told him they were done, which meant he should stay out of her life and her business. She and Bodie were settling, they were finding a rhythm and making progress, and now her mother had come to add to the drama.

"Grandma?" Bodie walked outside and pushed past Charity.

"Hi, baby." Tammi closed him in an airtight embrace. "I'm here! I came as soon as I heard. Oh, my dear sweet boy. Everything'll be all right. Don't you worry."

For a brief second Charity wondered where that affectionate loving motherly side of Tammi had been when she was growing up, but it didn't really matter. It was too late to matter.

Her mother bumped Charity out of the way and led Bodie inside. "Be a peach and get my suitcases," she called over her shoulder.

"Oh, I'll get your suitcases." And then she would tell them she had to run some errands so she could pay Dev a little visit.

Dev was not in the mood to lose money. He'd already lost enough this week—namely Charity. Now he was stuck hosting poker night for Lance, Lucas, Levi, Mateo, and Ty tonight. Had he not messed up things with Charity, he might be sitting here with her instead. Well, not at his dining room table. Maybe on the couch where they could talk...and he could kiss her again...

"Should we play another round?" Ty asked, shuffling the deck. One by one, Dev's friends all said they were in, so he did too. Not like he had anything more important to do right now.

"Have you found Melody yet?" Ty dealt another round of cards.

"No." As usual, Dev got a terrible hand. Still, he made a show of rearranging the cards like they were winners. "I called their mom, but she hadn't even heard what was going on." Tammi's shocked reaction had floored him.

"Yikes. I bet that was a fun conversation." Mateo helped himself to another beer from the fridge and came to sit back down across from him.

"Yeah. Tammi seemed pretty worried about the whole thing." If he'd realized Charity hadn't told her mom yet, Dev wouldn't have called, but it was too late to go back now. "If she doesn't know where Melody is, I doubt anyone does." What more evidence did they need that she was involved in the robbery? Why go underground like that if you didn't have anything to hide?

The table got quiet.

They all focused on their hands, shifting cards around, eyeing one another while they assessed their best moves. Dev didn't have anything to assess. It was a good thing he excelled at bluffing.

Always the first one ready with a strategy, Lucas laid his cards facedown on the table. "So it sounds like Bodie'll be sticking around and living with Charity then, huh?"

"I would assume so." Dev laid down his cards too. He wouldn't know for sure because Charity wasn't exactly speaking to him right now.

"I swear, Bodie is all Gracie talks about these days. 'Bodie said the funniest thing at school today,'" Lucas mimicked in a high voice that bore a striking resemblance to his dramatic stepdaughter's. "'Bodie did all of the work dissecting the frog so I didn't have to touch anything.'" He shook his head. "Should I be concerned?"

"Hell yeah, you should be," Lance said. "Don't you remember when we were in middle school? We were always trying to find ways to hook up with girls."

"You were probably the worst of all of us," Levi reminded his older brother with a laugh.

"I don't want to remember." Lucas grimaced. "Not now that Gracie is that age. I can't deal. I just want to stick her in a magic bubble to protect her from the jerks."

Dev thought back to the morning he'd spent with Bodie and Gracie. When most kids would've done everything they could to avoid getting in trouble, Bodie had tried to protect her. In his opinion that was a good sign. "Actually, Bodie is pretty mature for his age. He's had to raise himself." The kid had made plenty of mistakes since arriving in town, but he'd also handled the consequences well. "That's good to know." Lucas picked his cards back up as though he could relax. "Still, she's not allowed to date anyone until—"

A loud knock on Dev's front door broke the concentration in the room. "Dev?" Charity's voice may have been muffled, but it still had a sharp edge.

"Whoa. She sounds pissed," Ty said. "What'd you do?"

"Not sure." Dev stood and headed across the living room.

"Hello?" Her fist pummeled the wood. "Open this door!"

He did as he was told, fast enough that Charity's fist came flying toward him. He caught it in his hand and held on. "Hey. What's up?"

"Don't play dumb." She ripped her hand out of his grasp. "You know why I'm here." She peered past him, seeming to notice everyone else for the first time. "I need to talk to you. Alone."

Ah. Well, the only thing he'd done since he'd seen her last was call her mother. Obviously she didn't appreciate his help. "You heard her. The party's over." Dev walked back to the dining room table and started collecting beer bottles.

"Seriously?" Try tried to hold on to his IPA. "You're kicking us out because of a woman?"

"Yep." Dev snatched the beer out of his hand. "You can take the party somewhere else," he said, herding his friends to the door.

"Go easy on him, Calamity Jane." Mateo shot a teasing look at Charity, but wisely stayed out of range.

One by one, Dev all but shoved his friends out the door. "Night all. Thanks for coming. Drive safe now, ya hear?"

"You had no right to call my mom." Charity didn't even wait for the door to close fully before she started in on him. "You had no right to tell her what was going on with Melody and Bodie."

"I thought she knew." Call him crazy, but he thought daughters told their moms things like that. Sure, they weren't close, but Melody had been missing for almost a month. "I was trying to help. I was trying to find Melody so we could get to the bottom of everything."

"Why?" she demanded. "Why do you always have to help? Why can't you just leave things alone?"

Good question. He'd been asking himself the same thing lately. Why was it so important for him to make everyone else happy, even if he wasn't? That's the question that had haunted him since Hank Green had put him in the hot seat at the event the other night.

"My mother showed up at my house," Charity went on when he didn't answer. "You shouldn't have gone behind my back and called her."

"You're right. I'm sorry." Dev put his hands on her shoulders to remind her they were on the same side. "I only wanted to see if she'd heard from Melody. I didn't tell her to come out here. And I didn't give her many details. But I should've asked you first."

"Yes, you should've." She backed away from him, her eyes all fiery. "And you should've talked to me about the robbery investigation."

"I tried," he reminded her. "That night we danced. You told me you didn't want to talk about it with me. So I figured I wouldn't say anything else until I knew more."

"That's a total cop-out." She shook her head. "You had plenty of other chances to tell me."

He couldn't argue with that, but she had to know his motives were good. "I wanted to protect you," he said simply.

"What good has it done now that you know? You're worried and upset, but there's nothing we can do about it right now." He tried to see past the walls she was putting between them. It was like she *wanted* him to betray her, so she could walk away and leave him behind. But he wouldn't let her go that easily. "I know how tough you are. I know you're independent. I know you don't need me to protect you. But I want to anyway." Didn't she know by now? Hadn't he shown her? "I've never felt this way about anyone. You captivate me. I care about you, Charity. I admire you and I respect you, and maybe I screwed up by not telling you, but I've also been there every time you needed me. I'll always be there for you if you'll let me be."

She looked at him wide-eyed. A single tear slipped down her cheek.

"I thought if I could find Melody, if I could find a way to help her through this whole situation, you'd forgive me." Dev walked over and dropped to the couch. "I know it's messed up, but that's what I do. I try to fix everything for everyone else. I try to make everyone happy." Even when they didn't want his help.

"Why?" Charity came and sat next to him, tears still glowing in her eyes. "That sounds exhausting."

"I guess in some ways I'm still trying to prove myself to my birth mom. She didn't want me. I wasn't worth keeping." He couldn't look at Charity. He knew how pathetic it sounded. "So I have to prove my worth. All the time. By doing everything right. By taking care of my parents. By helping you and Bodie. By running for sheriff..." Even though that felt less and less like his dream and more like everyone else's.

"Dev..." Charity turned to him and gently took his face in her hands. For a second he thought she might kiss him, but she only stared, her eyes brimming over with tears. "You're already good enough," she murmured. "You're open and you're positive and you're wise and you're protective. You are a good man."

He closed his eyes to let those words soak in. He had no idea how much he needed to hear them until that moment. When he opened his eyes, he saw that tears had spilled down her cheeks.

"You completely messed things up for me by calling my mom, but I still like you." Her lips broke into the most beautiful smile he'd ever seen. "A lot. I like you a whole hell of a lot. More than I've ever let myself like anyone." She still held his face firmly, centered with hers, like she wanted to make sure he heard every word she said. "So you can stop trying so hard. It won't make any difference. I like you because of who you are."

Maybe a lot of people felt the same way, but no one had ever said it to him. No one had ever looked at him like Charity was looking at him either, with eyes so clear and blue he could see into the depths of her. "I like you too," Dev murmured. Then he carefully guided her face to his and leaned in to show her exactly how much.

Chapter Eighteen

This was the part when she usually started to fight. Fight the pull, the urgency, the no-holds-barred lust Dev's kiss stirred up in her. But she was tired of fighting. She'd been holding on to his deception so tightly, using it as another shield to protect her heart, but for once she wanted to lay the armor aside so she could accept the intimacy he offered her. Little by little, word by word, her heart had opened to him. Maybe the whole last month had been chipping away at her defenses—all the love she had for Bodie had started to change her. Dev was right...he had been there for her. She'd relied on him without even meaning to and he'd proven himself over and over no matter how many times she'd pushed him away. And she'd kept things from him too. She never told him Melody called...

Charity pulled away from the kiss. "My sister called a while ago," she blurted. "And I didn't tell you. Because she didn't sound good. The truth is, she really might be in trouble. I don't know."

"Okay." Dev ran his hands up and down her arms, and it was so comforting to be touched, to have someone she could share her worries with.

"What'd she say?"

"Just that she'd come back for him. She wanted to check on him, but she wouldn't tell me where she is or what she's doing."

"I'm sorry you have to deal with all of this." He pulled her close, giving her a place to rest, to let go. "I'll do whatever I can to help, but you have to tell me everything. You can trust me."

"I know." He was so good. She wanted to show him, to prove the words she'd spoken. In some ways Dev was as lost as her—trying to overcome the wounds of his past, and she could help him with that. They could help each other.

Charity raised her head to kiss him again, gliding her hands over his shoulders and pulling him tighter in against her. On some level, she'd known this was inevitable, this kiss and what would come after. She'd wanted him for a long time. His hands on her. His mouth breathing hotly against her skin. She wanted to finally satisfy that curiosity that seemed to swell low in her belly and tease certain long-neglected regions of her body.

"You sure you want to kiss me like this?" Dev's words were jagged, cautionary. But for once she wouldn't run scared.

"I'm sure." For the moment, Bodie was taken care of. She'd told her mom she had a few errands to run, and Tammi had told her to take her time. But taking her time would require more control than she currently had. Her patience had run out. The ache yawning through her had to be remedied, and at the moment she could think of only one way to do that. "Let me show you how sure I am." She pulled him up to stand with her, placed her palms against his chest, and backed him down the hall into his bedroom.

He stared at her, lips parted, eyes full of a heightened awareness as he dragged his gaze down her body. But he didn't touch her. He still didn't believe she was sure.

"Sit on the bed." Again, she pressed her hands against his shoulders, directing him back. His eyes never left her as he sank slowly to the mattress.

Charity lifted her shirt over her head and dropped it on the ground, leaving her bra on for the time being. She eased closer to him, wedging herself between his legs. "Touch me, Dev."

He brought his hand to the edge of the lacy satin, tracing his fingers lightly over her skin.

Goosebumps prickled the backs of her arms.

"You're so sexy." Dev brought his hands down to cup her breasts, teasing her through the material.

Charity's lungs tightened, laboring each breath. She eased forward and straddled his lap, bending her head to kiss his neck.

Dev brought his hands around her back and unclasped her bra, slowly sliding it down her shoulders.

She sat taller, anticipation boiling through her.

When her bra straps were at the tops of her arms, Dev paused. "We can stop. Anytime." His eyes were steady on hers.

She brought her face level with his. "We're not stopping until we're both extremely satisfied." She sealed the promise with a slow, seductive kiss, letting her lips linger over his.

"I'm going to make you feel so good, baby." He brushed the straps all the way down her arms, and then peeled the bra off, his eyes darkening in the dim light. His lips found their way to her skin, leaving kisses all the way down.

"That feels so good," she murmured, guiding his head to her other breast. "No one has ever kissed me like this. No one except for you." There'd been a few other men, but no tenderness, no mindfulness. Dev seemed determined to give her the control, to ignore his own desires and offer her what she needed.

More. What she needed was more.

His warm, wet tongue stroked her into sweet oblivion as she lowered her hands to the buttons on his shirt. His shoulders rose and fell, tensed and hard as though anticipating her touch. She pushed the shirt off him, taking her time to feel her way across the wall of muscle and skin that made up his chest. "So strong," she said, admiring the bends and curves.

"Damn, you turn me on," he murmured.

Charity spread her knees wider and rubbed up against the crotch of his jeans. "I can see that." She shifted her weight so she could work on that heavy-duty belt buckle at his waist, but Dev scooped his hands under her and lifted her up, standing. "Not so fast." He spun and laid her back on the mattress, hovering over her. "First, you. Always you first."

Charity opened her mouth to protest but he lowered his mouth to her breast again, grazing his teeth against the hardened peak of her nipple while he unbuttoned her jeans.

By the time he raised his head, she'd resorted to gasping, which seemed to amuse him. "Do you need a minute?" he asked, sliding her jeans down her legs.

"A minute won't help." She clawed at the waist of his jeans until she could get a good grip and pulled him down over her.

"What will help?" He murmured between soft kisses on her neck.

"You. Inside of me." Taking their connection deeper.

She turned on her side so they were face-to-face, chest-to-chest, hips-to-hips. Arching against him, she brought his lips back to hers. This time the kiss struck something deeper.

Dev stroked the skin on her hip and trailed his fingers lightly over her butt before nudging her legs apart so he could slip his fingers inside her underwear. His movements were slow and deliberate, which could only mean he had a hell of a lot more control than she did.

Impatiently, she wriggled her hips into his touch, breath shuddering hard when his fingers slid into her hot wetness.

"Mmmm." He stroked and teased. "You want me."

"Obviously." Charity realized she was digging her nails deep into his back. "You need to lose the pants. Now."

"Patience," he murmured in her ear. His thumb hooked the edge of her underwear and tugged it down her hip, then thigh. Rustling her legs, she impatiently kicked it off. "Patience is not one of my strengths," she informed him.

Dev grinned and directed her to lay on her back. "But I've been waiting a long time for this, Charity. And I want to see everything. I want to feel everything." He circled a finger over each of her breasts and then painstakingly slowly down her stomach.

"Is this what you want?" Dev worked his fingers into the folds between her legs, sliding them up to graze that magic spot before plunging them deeper inside of her. "Yes." Her head fell back and she pressed her heels into the mattress, bending her knees.

"What about this?" Dev leaned over her and took her breast in his mouth, while his fingers started a rhythm that made her hips arch off the bed.

"Oh my god, yes." She strained against the tightening, the pulsing that was pushing her closer to the edge of a monumental orgasm. *Not yet.* "I mean no. That's not what I want." She scrambled to her knees and unclasped his belt. "This is what I want." This is what she'd wanted since that first night he'd kissed her in his car.

His erection strained against the button fly of his jeans. Dev watched with rapt attention as she undid each button. *Ha.* Now it was her turn to torture him.

"Let me help." He yanked his jeans down and kicked them off onto the floor.

"Patience," she taunted, slipping her hand into his boxer briefs.

A groan of frustration rumbled in his chest. "It was easier to be patient when I was the one teasing you." He hastily pulled off his underwear, baring himself so she could get a better grip on him. She tightened her hand around his shaft and moved it up and down, grazing her fingers over the head.

"That's good," he breathed. "Jesus, Charity, that's so good."

"Good but not enough." She stretched out an arm, reaching for the drawer in the bedside table. "Do you have any—"

"Over here." Dev rolled to the other side of the bed and opened the drawer, pulling out a condom. By the time he came back to her, he already had it on.

"That was fast."

"Patience isn't one of my strengths either."

She straddled his lap again, situating her hips so she could come down on him and bring him deep inside of her. A moan hurtled out as he filled her, stretched her. "This," she whispered. "This is what I want."

"This is what I've wanted since the first night I kissed you." Dev's hands caught hers and he clasped their fingers together intimately. "You completely naked. Opening up for me. Your body wrapped tight around mine..."

"I've wanted it too." There was nothing between them in this moment. Nothing pulling them apart. Nothing except for their shared desire to give each other everything.

Charity moved against Dev, bending her upper body back in a graceful arch that lifted her hips and then lowered her back onto his lap, taking him even deeper into her. That motion, so fluid and smooth, built into an erotic pressure that throbbed through him. "That's it, baby. Just like that." He still had her hands clasped tightly into his, and couldn't resist rocking his hips under hers, joining her dance.

Charity's breathless pants deepened into long moaning sighs, the sound alone tempting him to come. He watched her move, watched her breasts rise and fall as she rode him, watched her blond hair spill past her shoulders and down her back.

She watched him too, her lips parted, those pleading sighs joining with the unashamed need simmering in her eyes.

"You, Charity Stone, amaze me." He let go of her hands and brought his arms around her, holding her against him while he thrust his hips to give her more—more friction, more heat, more intensity.

She kissed him, whimpering into his mouth. "You are so good, Dev. Such a good man." Her breath caught and her eyes closed, but a tear slipped down her cheek. "It's never been like this. I never want this to end."

"It doesn't have to end. I can promise you... we'll do it again." He shifted her in his lap, pumping into her at a higher angle, until her fingers dug into his skin like they had when he'd brought her to the edge before. The strain of holding himself back shuddered all the way in his lungs, but he would not give it up. He would not let go. Not yet.

"Hold me tighter." Charity opened her eyes and searched his. The curtain hiding her emotions had come down. They were all there for him to see. Tears clung to her long eyelashes but something like hope brightened those blue depths.

"I'll give you whatever you need." He cinched her in tighter so that her breasts pressed into his chest, soft and perfect. Together, they rocked and moved, lifting their hips. "I can't hold on," Charity said breathlessly.

"Let go." Dev thrust deeper, sliding out of her and crashing back in. "Let yourself go."

Her body responded, clenching tightly around him, pulling him right to the brink.

"Oh, Dev. Oh yes." Her gasping cries and enraptured shudders nudged him off the cliff and into a free fall. He was reeling, out of control, spilling out everything into her as he trembled under the power of his release.

Charity went limp against him, his arms holding her up, her forehead resting on his collarbone. Carefully, he eased his back to the mattress, still cradling her. For several silent minutes, Dev held her that way, his hand stroking her silky hair, breathing her in while they lay on his bed together. He would've been content to stay like that forever, but Charity rolled onto her side and peered over at him. "I never understood what was so great about it before."

"About what?" He quickly got up and discarded the condom before lying back down next to her on the bed.

"Sex." She said it with a straight face. "I never understood what was so great about sex."

"Never?" He did his best not to widen his eyes, but... "Really?"

She solemnly shook her head. "Not until now. Not until you."

Okay, he got that. They had something deeper than a physical attraction. Dev reached his hand over to her shoulder, sliding it down her back so he could feel her skin again. He couldn't not touch her when she was lying next to him naked. "What's so great about it with me?"

A devilish grin quirked her lips. "You mean other than the blinding rush?"

"There's more to it than that?" he teased.

"Ha." She was quiet for minute. "I guess it's how much I felt. Not your body, though I have to say, it is quite sexy." Her fingers traced circles around his pecs. "But there's way more. I felt you protecting me, caring for me, like no one else ever has."

"You're worth protecting, Charity." He swept her hair over her shoulder. "I know you're strong, but you don't have to take on everything alone. I promise not to butt in without your permission anymore, but I hope you'll ask me to be there when you need me."

"I'll do my best." She kissed him lightly. "It's new for me. Having someone to ask. So you'll have to be patient—"

A song blared from somewhere on the floor. Must be Charity's phone.

"I came in like a wrecking ball…"

"Who is it?" Dev asked, getting up to help her look for it.

Charity gave him a sheepish smile as she dug through the pile of their clothes next to the bed. "My mom."

He laughed. "Nice ringtone."

"Wait until you meet her." She finally found her jeans and dug her phone out of the back pocket.

Dev sat on the bed, watching her. He couldn't *not* watch her. She was exquisite. Long-limbed and curvy and strong and graceful. Beautiful, free-spirited, tough, honest, real. And she liked him…

"Hello?" When Charity brought the phone to her ear, her expression noticeably darkened. There was a long pause. "I don't keep wine in the house, Mom. I hardly ever drink."

The muscles in her back tensed, so Dev pushed off the bed and came up behind her, smoothing his hands over her shoulders and down the length of her spine. She sighed, her body caving in to his touch.

"No, I'm not stopping to get wine." Charity shoved her hand up into her hair, pushing it back from her forehead. "Bodie's what? No. He's not going out tonight. Why would you tell him that?"

Dev could hear Tammi's voice but he couldn't make out what she was saying.

"Forget it." Charity's jaw had tensed too. "I'll be home in a few minutes. You tell him to stay put. Understand?" She clicked the phone off and threw it on the bed. "I have to go."

"I know." Dev wrapped his arms around her, savoring the silkiness of her skin against his. "Just remember... I'm here when you need me."

Chapter Nineteen

Charity turned the truck onto her street and pulled up in front of her house, where she hit the brakes hard. Bodie was walking down the driveway wearing a backpack. "Where are you going?" She cut the engine and hopped out before he made it to the sidewalk.

"Grandma said I could go hang out with my friends." He kept right on walking.

Charity marched over and blocked his path. "Which friends?"

Her nephew's jaw suddenly went on lockdown.

That was all she needed to see. "You're not hanging out with Jett. There's no way I'm letting you go over to his house again."

"But Grandma said—"

"Grandma is not in charge." The irritation that had already started to simmer rolled into a full-on boil. "So you can go ahead and march yourself right back inside. You're not leaving to go anywhere right now. It's almost nine o'clock."

"Fine." He bit off the word like it had a bitter taste. "Geez. What're you so pissed about anyway?"

Before she could answer that loaded question, her mother traipsed out the front door. "What's all the ruckus out here?" She spotted Charity. "Oh, hi honey. I'm glad you're back. Did you happen to change your mind about picking up the wine? I need a nightcap."

The threads of anger pulled tighter, and there was no way around it. She was going to snap. "Go inside, Bodie," Charity ordered, so he wouldn't bear witness to the confrontation she'd waited years to have.

"Inside?" Her mother looked confused. "But I told him he could go to his friend's house."

"His friend's house." Charity marched up to her mother. "Just over a week ago I had to drag him out of this friend's house because he was so drunk he could hardly walk."

"Bodie," Tammi scolded like she was talking to a puppy. "You didn't tell me that."

"Of course he didn't tell you that," Charity nearly shouted. "You have to ask questions. You have to actually *pay attention*."

"God, it's no big deal," her nephew muttered, trudging up the porch steps. "I'll be in my room." He slammed the front door behind him.

Tammi turned to Charity. "How would a child get their hands on alcohol anyway?"

Seriously? Melody had started drinking in their house when she was twelve years old. But that wasn't the point. "You know nothing about what's happened since Melody abandoned her son on my doorstep." She hadn't seen the pain he'd tried to hide. The confusion, the depression, the fear. Charity had. She'd seen it all, and it was like looking into a mirror.

"I know. I know, honey," her mother purred. "But I'm here now. I want to help."

"Why now? Why are you here *now*? You've never helped me with anything."

"What's that supposed to mean?" Tammi demanded, looking wounded.

"I spent years fending off your boyfriends. *Years.* And I've been fending men off ever since." The words flew out like punches—fierce and calculated, intended to wound. "Which wasn't always a bad thing before. But now there's a good man. A man I like very much. A man who likes me, and I don't even know how to have a healthy relationship."

Tammi shook her head in a blatant denial. "You're blaming *me* for that?"

"It's not about blame." She wasn't blaming anyone. She was simply telling the truth. For the first time. "You knew what was happening when we were kids. You knew those men were hitting on me. On Melody too. She got the worst of it, being older." There were times her sister would tie a rope from their bedroom doorknob to the closet so no one could come into their room. "I used to wish I had an ugly face so they wouldn't look at me. I wore baggy shirts so they wouldn't make comments about my body. After we went to bed at night, we worried they'd come in our room, so Melody tied the door shut."

"That's ridiculous." Her mother's trembling lips refuted the statement. "I know I dated some jerks, but they never would've hurt you."

"They *did* hurt me." And now she had no idea what a healthy functioning relationship should look like. No idea how to build one, how to hold on to one. "They made me feel small and powerless." So she'd done everything she could to become independent and powerful and unaffected by all of it.

"Charity…sweetie…" Her mother reached for her hand. "I had no idea you felt that way. I made some mistakes. I know that. I was young. I didn't realize—"

"You were our *mom*." She withdrew her hand and cut off the excuses. She couldn't stomach them anymore. Tammi might've been young, but she didn't have to put men over her daughters. "It was your job to protect us." Despite her best efforts to hold on to anger, tears heated her eyes. "It was your job to fend people off. You let it happen. You looked the other way." Her jaw ached, but she couldn't stop herself. "And now you don't get another chance. Bodie is *my* responsibility. I'm going to do what's best for him. Even if he hates me for it. I'm going to protect him and make sure he knows that there is someone in the world who'll fight for him. So he never has to fight for himself the way I did."

"Okay." A mixture of tears and shock glazed Tammi's eyes. "Okay," she half-whispered. Then she turned around and crept back into the house.

Dev was smart enough to recognize a trap when he saw one. He'd walked into the Farm Café and headed for his usual table just before seven, exactly like he did most days, but today he had a whole crowd of women waiting for him.

Jessa, Naomi, Everly, and Darla all sat at *his* table, sipping from fancy teacups. They immediately quieted when they saw him, which couldn't be a good sign. An even worse sign was that Ty, Mateo, Levi, Lucas, and Lance sat all the way on the other side of the room looking guilty. *Here we go…*

"We saved a seat for you over here," Darla called.

"And your breakfast is already cooking," Everly added sweetly.

"Great." He took the long way around so he could swing by the guys. "Which one of you ratted me out about last night? That's what this is about, right? The scene with Charity?"

"Well, we all know it wasn't me," Ty said smugly. "I'm not married to any of them." Levi raised his hands. "My wife is working in Denver this week, so don't look at me."

Dev eyed the other three.

"You can't blame us," Mateo said. "It's that women's intuition thing."

"Yes." Lance pointed at Dev. "It's not our fault. They always just know whenever something goes down."

"After I got home Naomi gave me the third degree about why we'd quit on poker so early," Lucas added. "I never hold up well under questioning. Actually, you might want to think about hiring her down at the station. She's got some serious interrogation skills."

Ha. Dev shook his head at them to show what he thought of their excuses.

"Hey, Dev, your breakfast is up," Jessa announced, beckoning him over. In other words, get your butt over here so we can start the inquisition.

"Good luck, man." Ty gave him a salute.

"Don't look directly into Naomi's eyes," Lucas advised. "She reads minds."

"Thanks for the tip," he muttered, leaving them to their black coffee and talk about prize-winning bulls. If the women weren't holding his breakfast for ransom, he'd gladly take a place at the table with the cowboys.

"I haven't had to deal with an ambush since our last active shooter drill," he said when he approached the table.

"Ambush?" Everly waved him off. "We only wanted to chat. See how things are going."

"And what happened with Charity last night." Darla had never been one to mince words. "Since we haven't been able to get a hold of her, we thought we'd join you for breakfast."

Naomi set down her teacup. "So what's the deal? Why'd she show up at your house all upset?"

That didn't even matter anymore. Dev took the seat they'd saved for him at the head of the table. "I called her mom to see if she'd heard from Melody, and then Tammi made a surprise appearance at Charity's house last night."

The words were met with gasps and groans.

"Her mom? Seriously?" Jessa rolled her eyes. "She can't stand her mom."

"Yeah. She was upset at first but then we talked things through..." Those scenes from his bed flashed again, fully engulfing him in the same sensual blaze that had claimed them both last night...

"Oh my god." Naomi leaned in like she wanted a better look at him. "You had sex with her!"

Whoa. The woman really did read minds.

More gasps came at him, but this time they were interspersed with happy squeals. At least, he was pretty sure they were happy.

"I knew there was something between you two!" Everly clapped her hands.

"Thanks to my advice," Darla put in.

"So tell us everything." Jessa scooted her chair closer to the table. "I mean, this is huge news. I don't think Charity's ever really dated anyone."

Well, technically they hadn't exactly defined their relationship. They hadn't had much time to talk before she'd had to run out, and he sure wasn't going to talk through the details with these four before he and Charity had even figured things out themselves. He wasn't that stupid. "I'm not saying another word." He stood and picked up his plate. "If she wants to talk about it, that's fine by me, but I'm—"

His phone buzzed from his pocket, and he rushed to put down the plate and answer it on the off chance it was Charity.

"Hello?"

"Deputy Jenkins? This is Detective Barry."

His contact in Oklahoma. Dread snaked through him, coiling around his throat. "Yeah, hi." He walked swiftly away from the table and stepped outside, where no one would be able to overhear. A phone call before eight in the morning was never good. "What can I do for you?"

"I'm assuming your friend still hasn't heard from her sister?" the detective asked.

"No. She definitely hasn't." Charity would've told him.

"Well, I wanted to let you know that there's a warrant out for Melody Stone's arrest. We apprehended Cody Billings, who confessed to his role in the robbery. During the questioning he named Ms. Stone as the accomplice."

"Okay. Thanks for letting me know." That was it, then. All the evidence they needed. It would be an open-and-shut case. The news didn't surprise him, but it still made his heart hurt. For Bodie, and for Charity too.

"If you happen to see her, or if she comes to see her sister for any reason, you'll have to bring her in." The detective said it in a cautionary tone, as though he knew it wouldn't be easy.

It wouldn't, but Dev wasn't too worried. Melody already knew she was in trouble. He doubted she'd come back. "Of course. I'll keep in touch, let you know if I hear anything."

After a brisk thank-you and goodbye, the detective disconnected.

Dev stood there for a while, wishing he didn't have to tell Charity, that he didn't have to break her and Bodie's hearts.

But he'd made her a promise and he wouldn't keep something else from her. She deserved to know. Maybe he'd call her and ask her to meet him at the café when she got up.

That would give them some time to figure out how to tell the boy that his mom wasn't coming back.

Chapter Twenty

Something was burning.

Charity pulled on jeans and a sweatshirt and dashed out of her bedroom, ready to evacuate the house and call the fire department. Only there was no smoke, just an acrid haze in the air coming from the kitchen.

She hurried in that direction and walked in just in time to see her mother dump a whole skillet full of charred pancakes into the sink.

"Hey, Grandma makes pancakes exactly like you," Bodie said from his seat at the kitchen table.

Her heart continued to race because (a) she'd thought the house was burning down, and (b) it seemed she'd overslept. "Why didn't you two wake me up?" she demanded, looking at the clock. She never slept in.

"I said we should, but Grandma told me not to." The kid downed a cup of orange juice. "She wanted to make breakfast."

"And I failed at that too," her mom said miserably. "Like

everything else. All you have to do is add water and keep an eye on the stove, and I couldn't even manage it."

Oh boy. Charity swallowed a sigh. She supposed she deserved that. Last night had been one of the most confusing nights of her life—first the elation of her and Dev making love and then the tirade she'd went on with her mother. The emotions had ping-ponged back and forth most of the night, not allowing her to get any sleep until sometime this morning.

"Come on, Mom. It's no big deal." She went to the cupboard and pulled out Bodie's favorite cereal. "I've burned pancakes before too."

"She has," her nephew confirmed. "And I think there was even more smoke."

"I only wanted to help." Her mother plodded to the seat across from Bodie and slumped with defeat.

"You did help." Charity set a bowl of cereal in front of her nephew and pulled the milk out of the refrigerator. "If you hadn't made pancakes, I'd still be asleep." And she had a lot to do today—somehow find a way to smooth things over with her mom, take Bodie up to the Cortez ranch so they could continue their training. And see Dev. She had to see Dev again as soon as possible.

She put the milk down next to Bodie and tried to smile. "Thank you for trying." She owed Tammi more than that— a solid apology for blowing up at her—but she also didn't want to drag Bodie into the drama between them. "I appreciate the—"

The doorbell rang, only adding to the headache that had started to build in her temples. Last time her doorbell rang before eight, it was her neighbor coming over to complain about the weeds spreading into his yard.

"Bodie, will you get that, please?" Maybe Mr. Chan would go easier on a preteen.

Her nephew bounded away with a mouthful of Cocoa Puffs, giving her the perfect opportunity to grovel. "I'm sorry about last night, Mom." Charity took the chair next to her. "I didn't mean to hurt your feelings."

"It's fine." Instead of looking directly at her, Tammi cast a forlorn stare just above Charity's head. "I've already packed my things and I'll leave as soon as I can get a flight."

She supposed she deserved that too. "Don't leave like this. I don't want to fight." Especially not now, when she was on the verge of so much happiness. "I want things to be better between us." For the first time, she actually thought that could be a possibility. "Maybe everything had to come out so I could get past it. But I didn't mean to be so harsh. I know things were hard for you too, and—"

"Look who's here."

Charity didn't have to look. Not with the pure joy she heard in her nephew's tone. Her head turned slowly, slowly, slowly, and even though she braced herself, her entire upper body lurched when she saw her sister.

"Mellie!" Their mother flew from the table and pulled her eldest daughter into a sloppy hug. "Oh my god. Where on earth have you been? You've given us all such a scare!"

"She was in California." If Bodie's smile got any wider it would fall off his face. "Looking for a place to live. She found us an apartment. It's only ten minutes from the beach!"

Charity wanted to speak, to ask a thousand questions, but her throat had gotten gritty. She could only sit there and assess her sister. Melody looked better than she had when she'd dropped Bodie off. Cleaner. More rested, maybe? But that didn't mean anything. It didn't mean Dev's suspicions about her weren't true.

"Hey Char." Her sister approached her with a healthy caution, as though she knew she owed her an explanation. "I didn't want him to have to be in limbo while we searched for a place to rent," she said, giving her son a good scrub on the head. "I wanted to surprise him. I wanted to have everything settled before I came back for him."

"You found a place?" Charity swallowed the grit of emotions. "You actually moved into a place?"

"Yep." Mel's face beamed with pride. It wasn't an expression Charity had ever seen her sister wear. "Right outside of Santa Cruz." She slung an arm around her son. "You'll love it there, Bodes. There's the ocean, but there're also mountains and huge redwood forests."

"Oh, it sounds wonderful!" Tammi came back to the table too. "Doesn't it sound wonderful, Charity?"

"Yeah." And a little too good to be true. How did her sister find enough money to secure a rental in California? *Bodie said someone gave them a bunch of money.* Was Dev right? Had she really resorted to stealing?

"It's going to be amazing," Melody chirped. "A whole new start for us, Bodes. You'll love it there."

"I can't wait!" Bodie dug back into his cereal, looking more energized than he had since he'd ridden Ace the other day. But the protective instinct Charity had honed over the last month tore at her stomach. How could she let Bodie go with his mom when she still had so many concerns? She couldn't. She *wouldn't.* "Hey, Bodie, why don't you go get changed so we can head up to the ranch for our training session?" That would give her and Melody a chance to talk.

"Training session?" Melody studied her son.

"Aunt Charity's teaching me how to ride Ace. So I can be a barrel racer." Bodie finished off his cereal and downed the milk.

"Oh. That's great." Melody flashed a fake smile. "But I'm afraid we don't have time for training. We have to get on the road."

"You're leaving?" Pain spiked through Charity's chest, clutching at her heart. "Now?"

"It's a long drive." Melody grinned at Bodie. "I'm supposed to start working at the winery on Monday and I want to get you all settled before you start school out there."

"Sweet!" Her nephew hopped up and carted his bowl over to the sink. "I'm gonna go pack my things!"

Charity tried not to take his enthusiasm too personally. He loved his mom, she knew that, but she still wasn't convinced this would be a good move. "Mom, why don't you go help Bodie?" she asked. They didn't need their mother here for a tough conversation.

"Sure. I'd love to help." Tammi scurried off with Bodie as though eager to be useful.

Once they'd gone, Charity stood up and faced her sister. "Are you sure everything's okay?"

"Of course I'm sure. Why?"

Tone, Charity reminded herself. "I've been worried. You completely disappeared. You only called me once, and you didn't even talk to Bodie." If she was simply getting their happy new life all ready, why hadn't she been honest about it from the start?

"I knew leaving was tough on him," Melody said in a reasonable manner. "So I wanted to get things figured out and make the transition as easy as possible."

Okay, based on her sister's complete calm and practical explanation, it seemed Charity and Dev had both been wrong to be concerned. But she still had to come out and ask. "Are you in trouble? Are the police looking for you?"

"What?" Melody's laugh sounded genuine. "No. Are you serious? You think I'm *running from the law*?"

"I didn't know." For some reason, Charity couldn't seem to grasp relief. Maybe because she didn't want Bodie to go. "How was I supposed to know, Melody? You up and moved Bodie out of school and just showed up on my doorstep. Forgive me if I started thinking through some worst-case scenarios."

"I'm sorry." Her sister hugged her. A real, tight hug full of affection. She pulled back. "I should've handled everything differently. I know that. I just…I want things to change. I want everything to work out for me and Bodie this time. Things have never been good for us, but that's all going to change now. This is like a second chance."

"Okay." Charity had to fight the tears. She was so torn between happiness that her sister seemed to be getting her life on track and complete devastation that she was taking Bodie away. "You know I'll help you however I can. I don't want to lose touch with you two again."

"You won't. I promise." She said it with such sincerity that Charity had no choice but to believe her.

"Hey, why don't we all go out to breakfast together? Before Bodie and I get on the road? I'm dying for a huge stack of pancakes," her sister said. "It'll be my treat."

"Sure. That sounds good." Though she knew she wouldn't be able to eat anything. Not with the sorrow leaking into her stomach. "I'll just go check on Bodie. See if he's ready." Not wanting her sister to follow, she rushed down the hall and almost bumped into her mother.

"Bodie can't find his boots," Tammi said, scurrying past. "I told him I'd check the garage."

"Thanks, Mom." That was perfect. Then she would have a minute alone with him.

Charity quietly pushed open the door to his room and walked in. "How's it going?"

"Good. I think I got everything." He still hadn't stopped grinning, his face so full of hope.

She looked around what had become his room. It no longer felt like the guest room because it had become his. He belonged here. She had half a mind to barricade the door so she could keep him here. *But you have to let him go.* He would be back with his mom, and that was *really* where he belonged, but that didn't stop her heart from snapping in half. *Don't cry.* Whatever she did, she had to show him she was happy for them. "I'm gonna miss you a lot, kid." The burning in her throat intensified.

"You will?" Bodie slipped on his backpack and studied her.

"Oh yeah." *Screw it.* She gave up on fighting the tears. "I know I haven't been easy to live with, but I love you, Bodie. And I'll always be here for you. You can call me anytime. In fact, I hope you'll call a lot."

"I will. I promise." He patted her arm like he didn't know how else to make her feel better. "And you weren't so bad to live with. If I was gonna pick someone to live with besides Mom, it would *probably* be you."

She tilted her head. "Probably?"

"Okay, fine. I love you too, Aunt Charity." He gave her an affectionate, albeit quick, version of a hug. "But don't get all mushy about it."

"Too late," she whimpered, prying her arms away from him. God, maybe it was better he was leaving now. If she'd gotten this attached in a month, she'd hate to see herself when he left for college.

"Do you think you could say goodbye to Gracie for me?" It was the first time she'd ever heard him sound shy.

"I have a better idea. Why don't you write her a note? We can leave your phone number so you guys can stay in touch." The poor girl. She'd probably be devastated when she found out he'd left.

"You think she'd want to stay in touch?"

"I think she'll be sad if you don't."

That made him smile.

"Come on, come on, come on." Melody appeared in the doorway. "Let's get going. We'll eat at the Farm Café on our way out of town. It got five stars. I Yelped it."

"It's the best breakfast in town," Bodie said, trotting off with his mom. "Wait until you try the chocolate milk."

They all ambled down the hallway, where they met Tammi by the front door.

"Don't worry. I know where it is," Bodie told his mom. He took his boots from his grandma and turned to Charity. "We'll meet you guys over there."

"Sounds good," she said, choking back more tears. Wow, she really had to get herself together. Charity quickly gathered her purse and keys and led her mom out to her rental truck. After they'd climbed in, she couldn't find a way to break the sullen silence.

"All right," her mom finally said. "What's wrong?"

"I don't know." Charity backed down the driveway, but then paused before they'd made it to the street. She slipped the truck into *park*. "I can't help but feel like something is off with Melody." Or maybe she wanted something to be off. Maybe she wanted a reason to keep Bodie here with her.

"I worry about her too." Tammi faced her. "She's not strong like you. You survived so much all on your own." Guilt weighted the words. "Melody is too much like me. I thought about it all night, after what you said. You were right. We never had money and I was always afraid. I couldn't give you the safety or security you needed. I couldn't give you a mom to be proud of, or an example of what a strong woman looks like."

Charity closed her eyes. "I shouldn't have lost it like that. It wasn't fair. I'm sorry."

"I'm glad you did, honey. It had to come out. And it made me realize how proud I am. You made yourself better than me. You can't even imagine how deep my regrets go." Her jaw wobbled. "But I hope we can fix it. All of us together. You and Melody and me and Bodie. I hope we can figure out a way to be a family."

"We will." Charity had spent most of her life running from people when she should've run toward them. Bodie. Melody. Her mom. Dev. She'd been too afraid to fight for them, but she wouldn't let fear stop her anymore.

Chapter Twenty-One

Dev finished off his fourth cup of coffee and pushed the mug away.

Too bad Charity's friends had ditched him when they'd realized he wouldn't talk. They'd all moved to another table, which had left a seat open at his table for Hank Green to join him. Dev glanced down and checked his phone again. Why hadn't Charity called him back yet?

"I've decided we need to have a preparatory session before the next question-and-answer event," the man said, pulling up the calendar on his phone. "What nights are you available next week?"

"None." He didn't have plans yet, but he was going to leave every night open in case Charity could steal a few minutes away.

"Okay, the next week then." Hank squinted at his phone. "I have Wednesday open."

Dev didn't even have to check his phone. "That won't work for me." None of it was working for him. Charity was right—it had gotten exhausting trying to be what everyone else wanted or needed him to be. Talking with her—acknowledging those insecurities—had freed him in a way. He'd likely always have to battle that desire to earn his way into people's lives, but at least now he could stop himself before it took over.

Hank laid down his phone on the table between them and narrowed his eyes into what might've been an intimidating stare if it weren't for the plaid bow tie around his neck. That and the sweater vest. It didn't exactly scream tough guy.

"The election is only a few months away," Hank barked. "You need to get your head back in the game."

"Here's the thing." Dev folded his hands on the table and leaned into them. "I'm thinking about withdrawing from the election."

"You can't *withdraw*. You're the best man for the job."

"I'm glad you think so, but I'm not sure it's the best job for me." The settled feeling he got from saying the words out loud confirmed it wasn't the best job for him. "I like being out in the field. I like interacting with the community. I don't want to deal with all of the politics involved in running the department."

"But you can make a difference there," Hank argued. "A real difference. The policies are outdated and hardly ever enforced. You could have influence on the future of this county—of this town."

Dev could or Hank could? He didn't ask the question because the answer was obvious. "I appreciate your—"

"Hi." That voice. That soft sweet tone he heard Charity use only when she talked to him.

"Hey." Dev didn't know when she'd come in, only that she now stood next to his table looking radiant and happy at the sight of him. As happy as he was at the sight of her.

"I'm glad you're here," he said, pushing back his chair so he could stand. "We have to talk." He had to tell her about

Melody right away this time. So he gave Hank Green a look that clearly told him to move on.

"You think about what I said, Jenkins. We'll talk tomorrow." The man stood and lumbered away.

"Yes, we will." And he'd tell him the same thing then. But that was a concern for another day. Right now, he wanted to focus only on Charity. On helping her navigate the current situation with her sister. "Can you sit for a minute?" he asked, brushing his hand across hers.

"I'd love to, but I've got a whole crowd with me." She gestured to a booth across the room, where Bodie and Tammi and another woman sat. Another woman who looked a whole lot like Charity...

No. His heart dropped, giving him a hit of vertigo. "Is that Melody?"

"Yeah. She showed up this morning. It sounds like she's been in California finding a place to live. She and Bodie are leaving after breakfast."

The potent combination of adrenaline and dread put his body on heightened alert. Everything had tensed, from his jaw all the way down to his calves. Without turning his head, he eyed that booth again. Bodie sat next to his mom, pointing out things on the menu.

His mind sped ahead, trying to formulate a plan. "I need you to listen to me, but you can't react," he murmured to Charity. "You have to smile and nod like we're only chatting." If Melody sensed something was up she'd run, and he'd have no choice but to make a scene.

"What?" Charity's eyes searched his. "God, Dev, what's wrong?"

As much as he wanted to protect her, he couldn't. He simply had to tell her. "There's a warrant out for her arrest. I just heard this morning. They got the other suspect in the robbery. A man named Cody Billings. And he told them Melody was his accomplice."

"No." Her head shook in small fluid motions. "That's not right." Desperation edged her tone higher. "She came back for Bodie so they could start over. She told me everything's fine. I asked her. I asked if she was in trouble with the police and she laughed at me."

"Charity." He said her name with all of the tenderness he felt for her. "I have to bring her in. I need you to figure out a way to get her outside so Bodie doesn't have to see."

"I can't. I can't do that." The words were breathless. "Please, Dev. Don't make me do that to him. You don't have to arrest her. We could let her leave—"

"No. We can't. I don't have a choice." He crawled his fingers forward and clasped her hand in his. "*We* don't have a choice. But we can try to protect Bodie. Okay? You can tell Melody you want to show her something. Tell your mom and Bodie you'll be right back. I'll wait outside, and we can do this fast. Before Bodie even knows what's happening."

Tears streamed down her cheeks. "Oh my god. This'll break his heart. He was so happy to see her. He was so excited about starting a new life..."

Dev glanced across the room again. Now Charity's family all sat in the booth watching them. "You can't cry, Char. You have to be strong. For Bodie." He forced a smile. They had to pretend like nothing was wrong. "If she runs, I'll have to go after her. We can't let that happen. Okay?" It was asking so much—too much—he knew that, but there was no other way. "You're so strong. You can do this," he told her. "Just for a few minutes."

"And then what?" She staggered a step back. "What am I am supposed to tell her son when I come back in without her?"

It didn't matter how she told him, Bodie would be devastated. "I'm sorry. I'm so sorry, honey. If there were any other way, I'd do it. I just don't want to risk Bodie seeing her get arrested. I don't want him—"

"Aunt Charity?" Her nephew appeared next to them.

Dev had been so focused on Charity, he hadn't been watching.

"Mom says we don't have time for breakfast anymore." Bodie sounded apologetic. "She said we have a long drive and we have to go. She told me to meet her in the car."

Shit. She knew. Bodie probably told her he was a cop. Dev slipped past Charity and Bodie, moving swiftly toward the door. "Stay here," he called behind him. "Both of you. Stay here."

"What's going on?" Panic shrilled through the boy's voice.

"Everything's okay," Dev heard Charity say behind him.

But Dev already knew nothing would be okay. There was no way to contain the situation now, and he couldn't think about it—about what this would do to Bodie or Charity, he had to be a cop. He had to do his job.

Dev bolted out the doors and spotted an old Honda Civic he didn't recognize. He sprinted to the car just as Melody slid in behind the wheel.

Before she could start the engine, he ripped open the driver's side door. "Step out of the car."

"No." Her hand shook hard as she jammed the key into the ignition. "No! You don't understand! I didn't want to do it! He made me! Cody made me!"

"Don't say another word," Dev cautioned. "And don't make this harder on everyone. Your son is right inside that restaurant."

"Mom!" Bodie shot through the door with Charity and Tammi right behind him.

"Hold him back," Dev yelled.

"What're you doing? What the hell are you doing?" Charity's nephew screeched. Dev cast a quick glance over his shoulder. Charity and Tammi closed in on either side him, both wrapping their arms around him.

"No! Mom! What's happening?"

Dev blocked out the kid's cries before they made his knees buckle. He leaned down so Melody would look at him. "Step out of the car and come with me nice and easy, and I won't cuff you," he said quietly.

Tears stained her cheeks, but she kept the keys in the ignition.

Behind him, Bodie was sobbing. Dev had handled plenty of messy situations in his career, but none of them had made him want to sob. *I'm sorry, kid.* Damn, he hated this. There had to be a way to minimize the damage. If Melody could just understand what it was doing to her son...

"You can't run," he told her. "There's a warrant out. Even if you get away now, you'll always have to look over your shoulder. Is that what you want for your son?"

"No." Her hands covered her mouth and caught a sob. "I want him to be happy. He deserves to be happy." Dejection hunched her shoulders as she climbed out of the car and stood before Dev, her hands clasped behind her. "I'll go. I won't cause any trouble. I swear. Please don't cuff me in front of him."

"I won't," he promised. "We'll walk over to my car, and once we're at the station I'll read you your rights."

"Okay," she whispered.

Dev took her arm and prodded her across the parking lot.

"Where are you taking her?" Bodie screamed. "Don't take her away from me! Please, Dev! Let her go!"

He didn't turn around. He couldn't. He simply stared straight ahead and marched Melody to his SUV.

"I love you, Bodes," she called, tears streaming down her cheeks. "I love you, and I'm so sorry."

Only when Dev opened the back door of his car did he catch a glimpse of Charity. She still held on to her nephew, her arms wrapped tightly around his upper body, both of them shaking with wrenching sobs.

Charity careened through the kitchen, but she was too slow to keep up with Bodie. She hadn't even fully stopped the truck when he'd jumped out and run into the house.

Somewhere down the hall, a door slammed, the sound shuddering through her. She should've done what Dev had asked right away. She should've acted before Melody decided to leave. Then Bodie wouldn't have seen. He would've been hurt when she told him, but not so traumatized.

In the truck on the way back, Charity had told him what his mother had done—why Dev had to take her in—and Bodie had said nothing. He'd simply fixed a robotic stare out the window, giving no indication he heard or understood.

Heading down the hall, she pictured her nephew's smile again, that bright, brilliant smile. The glimpse of hope she'd seen on his face earlier. It had all been ripped away from him, but she would bring it back. Someday he would smile again like that, even though he'd been hurt. She would make sure.

She crept to the guest room and tried the knob. Locked. That's what he was used to doing. Retreating. Dealing with things on his own. But he didn't have to do that anymore. Every time he tried to hide, she would remind him that she was there for him. Always. "Hey, Bodie. Let me in." She rapped her fist lightly against the door.

There was nothing. No rustling or footsteps, or even an angry reply. "Come on. We need to talk about this."

When the silence threatened to stretch into forever, she jiggled and yanked on the door handle until the lock popped open.

The disturbance didn't seem to rattle Bodie. He had collapsed onto the bed, his arms over his head while he sobbed into a pillow.

Charity rushed to his side and knelt next to the bed. "It's okay." She squeezed his shoulder. "I promise you everything'll be okay." She would love him enough for a whole family. She would be whatever he needed.

"She doesn't care about me." Bodie didn't raise his head or move his arms or even glance in Charity's direction.

"That's not true." She struggled to keep her voice even. "I know she loves you, Bodie. How could she not? You're brilliant and funny and thoughtful. She came back for you, even though she knew she could get caught." Her composure broke. "She doesn't know how to take care of anyone. Not even herself." It was the same story as her own mother's. Always looking for a man to take care of her...doing whatever he told her, no matter how much it threatened the people she loved. "You're the best thing in her life, and you always will be."

Bodie pulled his arms away from his head. "She's going to jail for a long time. Isn't she?" His eyes were downcast, full of pain. Even though she wanted to, Charity couldn't lie to him.

"Most likely." She could only hope Melody would cooperate. Maybe then the authorities would go easy on her. "I'll do my best to help her. To make sure she gets a good lawyer." Though she didn't even know where to start.

"A lawyer won't matter," the kid mumbled. "She's been busted before. For drugs and stuff. She thinks I don't know, but I do." Anger laced his tone. "I'll never get to go home."

Charity's heart thumped harder as she eased onto the bed next to him. "This is your home too. As long as you want it to be." She glanced around at the white walls and bland navy curtains and generic down comforter on the bed. "I'm not much of a decorator." Obviously. "But we can redo this room and make it yours. So you'll have your own space. You're already familiar with the school. I know it's not perfect, but at least you get to dissect frogs."

The comment drew a tiny quirk in the corners of his lips.

"I travel a lot, but it's mostly in the summers, so you could come with me," she went on, not caring that she sounded like she was making a sales pitch. "And maybe you can start competing too. You've got the talent for it." When he rode Ace, he was strong and tough and determined.

"Really?" Bodie looked at her like he needed a lifeline. "You think I could compete? At a real rodeo?"

"I know you could. They have junior competitions all over the country." She would train him and give him everything he needed to pursue a passion. "I'll do my very best for you, Bodie." Tears filled her eyes again, but this time she didn't blink them away. "It won't be perfect. Or even easy to live with me, probably." She'd been on her own for so long, and she could be just as headstrong as him. "But I want you here. With me." More than anything else, she needed him to know that—he was wanted. "It doesn't matter where your mom is, we'll go see her. We'll be there for her too." Melody would need them. Somehow, like her mother had said, they'd have to find a way to be a family, even if they couldn't be together.

Bodie looked at her with bleary eyes. "I'm so mad at her. And Dev. He knew, didn't he? That's why he asked me questions about her. So he could bust her."

"No." She stroked his hair. "That's not why he asked you questions. He was trying to help us find her. He cares about you too. He wanted to try to protect you today, but everything happened too fast."

"He could've let her go." Her nephew's jaw tightened, pulling his mouth into a scowl.

"He had to do his job, Bodie." Dev would always have to do his job, even when it meant hurting someone. She'd seen the pain in the deputy's expression when he looked back at her before driving away. She felt it too. Pain. Shock. Disbelief...

"I hate him," Bodie whispered. "I—"

There was a light knock on the door and Charity's mother stuck her head in. "Can I talk to you for a minute?"

"I'll be right back," Charity said, giving her nephew's hand a squeeze.

In the hall, her mom led her away from the door. "Dev's car just pulled up out front. I thought I should tell you before Bodie realized he was here."

"Thank you," she whispered, barely holding on to her emotions.

"I'll go sit with Bodie." Her mother drifted past her, and Charity hurried to the front door.

She opened it quietly and slipped outside, not wanting Bodie to realize they had company.

"Hey." Dev walked up the porch steps and reached for her, but she jolted back, hands raised in the air between them, telling him to back off. This wasn't his fault. She knew that, but she didn't want to be touched or comforted or talked down. She wanted to scream.

"Is Bodie okay? I'm so sorry," he murmured, sounding less like the cop who'd arrested her sister and more like the man who'd kissed her. "I should've figured out another way. I should've been able to protect him." His shoulders fell and he lowered his head as if he felt the weight of it all as intensely as she did.

Charity didn't know what to do with him. Not right now. She couldn't fault him for doing his job, but the trauma of holding back her nephew while he screamed still shook her. "Bodie will be okay." She believed that. "But right now I think you should go. He's still so upset and—"

The door opened behind them with a sudden whoosh. Bodie peered out. "What're *you* doing here?"

"He was just leaving." Charity hurried to her nephew's side, taking his hand in hers. "Let's go inside."

He yanked out of her grasp. "I don't want to go inside. You lied to me! You pretended you were helping me but you really wanted to find out about my mom!"

"No." Dev backed up a couple of steps as though giving them space, but he seemed determined to stay. "I'm sorry, Bodie. I didn't lie. I wanted to help—"

"Where'd you take her? Where is my mom?" He aimed the questions over Charity's shoulder at Dev, but the deputy said nothing. He simply stood there steady and calm, hands clasped behind his back.

"Answer me!" Bodie yelled. "Where's my mom?"

"She'd being held at the county jail," Dev said. "And then she'll be extradited back to Oklahoma."

"Because of you!" Her nephew slashed an arm toward Dev. "It's your fault! She could've gotten away!"

Dev didn't deny it.

"It's not his fault," Charity said, falling to her knees in front of him. "Your mom made bad choices. There're consequences."

"But they never would've found her if it wasn't for you. We could've moved away!" He swiped at the tears running down his cheeks like they made him angry.

"I'm sorry, Bodie." Dev approached them. "I had to do my job. I know it's hard to understand but—"

"Get away from me!" Bodie bolted inside the house and slammed the door.

Dev started to follow. "I should talk to him."

"No." Charity blocked his path inside. "You need to go."

"You shouldn't have to deal with this yourself."

"I have to. From now on. He's my responsibility." And he would come first. Always.

"I can help." He took her shoulders in his hands and man, that look on his face tempted her to give in. "Please let me help."

"I can't. He doesn't want you here."

"What about you? What do you want?"

What she wanted no longer mattered. "Your being here will only make things worse. Please, Dev. Just go."

He stood there a moment longer, looking at her as though asking her to change her mind. She couldn't. It was so tempting to run over to him and collapse, to let him hold her up, but this would be her life for the foreseeable future—an angry teen who needed stability, not more drama and angst.

Dev must've seen the resolution on her face. He walked over and pulled her into a rough kiss, melting every joint in her body. Then he let her go, walked to his car, and drove away.

Chapter Twenty-Two

Dev turned in his weapon and went through the law enforcement security screening along with his assigned guard.

It had been a while since he'd visited the county detention center, but his reputation had preceded him. He'd already had three employees stop him to talk about the upcoming election. He'd played along, but he'd already made up his mind. First thing Monday morning, he'd officially withdraw from the election. Until then, though, he'd use the attention to pull some strings so he could meet with Melody Stone.

Your being here will only make things worse. Charity's words still stung, but he understood what was behind them. Since he couldn't be there to support Charity and Bodie right now, he'd been doing some digging on the best way to help Melody, and he'd found some good leads. With everything Charity would have to put in to care for her nephew, he figured this was one burden he could take off her shoulders.

The guard paused on the other side of the screening area, waiting for Dev to cinch his belt back around his waist and shove his wallet back into his pocket. He wasn't on duty today, but he'd worn his uniform anyway. Looking the part of the official would only help his cause.

"Won't be long and you'll be running things around here," the guard commented as they walked down a sterile hallway.

"I guess we'll see." Dev glanced around, viewing the place through new eyes. He'd never paid much attention to how desolate it was—the bleak white walls, beige linoleum floors, and harsh fluorescent lights buzzing overhead. Thankfully, the jail had done away with in-person visits for inmates' families, opting instead for video visitation. He'd hate for Bodie to have to see his mom in a place like this. With any luck, Melody would end up serving her sentence in a minimum-security facility. At least, that's what the lawyer Dev had hired said he would push for.

The guard paused next to a door and gestured for Dev to go past. "You can wait inside."

"Thank you." He stepped into the room and took a seat at the small table. That was the only furniture—the table and chairs. Otherwise it was as sterile as the rest of the facility. He'd met with a lot of inmates here, but never one whom he had a personal connection with. It changed things, made him more aware of how depressing it felt—like he'd stepped into a void.

The door opened again, and the guard led Melody in by the arm. Her hands were cuffed in front of her waist and leg irons shackled her feet. The orange jumpsuit she wore seemed to be three sizes too big, or maybe she simply looked defeated and small.

Dev stood when she walked to the table. The guard led her straight to a chair and then backed into the corner of the room and stood watch.

"What're you doing here?" Melody's dull blue eyes peered up at him, but she didn't raise her head.

Dev sat across from her. "Why did you come back to Topaz Falls?" He wanted to hear the answer before he told her about the lawyer—to make sure it hadn't been a mistake. "You could've stayed on the run. Maybe no one ever would've found you in California." She could've started a new life by herself. "But you came back."

Her long sigh wasn't angry, just weary. "I followed the news. Heard they caught Cody. So I knew if I didn't come back for Bodie now I'd never see him again. I thought I could grab him and disappear before anyone knew."

That was exactly what he'd hoped to hear her say. If she could use Bodie as motivation maybe she would be able to fight, to turn things around and focus on what she had to do to get to her son back. "I hired you a lawyer."

She finally raised her head. He'd seen that same narrow-eyed suspicion on Bodie's face plenty of times. "I already have a lawyer."

"I'm not talking about a public defender. This lawyer is one of the best in cases like this." He'd called around and everyone he'd talked to had recommended him. "I'll cover all of your legal costs."

"Wow." Amusement replaced the suspicion in her eyes. "You must really like my sister."

"I'm in love with her." Completely, one hundred percent head over heels. "But that's not why I'm here." He knew this wouldn't earn him a place in Charity's or Bodie's life. He still believed what Charity had said. She liked him for who he was, and he had to hold on to hope that, in time, it would be enough to bring her back to him. But he wasn't here to discuss Charity. "I believe in giving people a second chance. Or a third chance. Or as many chances as it takes to get it right. You still have time to get it right. Even if you go to prison, you can still get another chance."

"There is no *if*," Melody mumbled. "I'll serve time. You know the worst part? I hated my mom for how she treated us. But I'm a worse mom than she was. Even she never went to prison. It's probably better this way. Bodie'll be better off with Charity. I don't deserve him."

"Maybe not, but he still loves you. He still needs you." Dev reached out and touched her shoulder so she'd hold her head up. "My mom gave me up when I was young, and it's always felt like a piece of my life was missing. I don't want Bodie to grow up feeling the same way." Having a mother who was accepting responsibility for her actions in prison was better than having no mother at all.

Tears brightened her eyes, bringing their color back. "I don't want that either."

"So you take this opportunity to figure out how to be better," Dev said. "How to be there for him, even if you can't be *with* him for a while."

"I don't know if he'll ever want me to be there." A raw fear whispered through the words. "He'll probably forget all about me."

"No." Dev knew better than anyone that wasn't possible. "I haven't seen my birth mom since I was little, and I still haven't forgotten her." He looked into Melody's eyes, trying to offer her hope. "It's what you do now that matters. What you do today and tomorrow and the day after that. That's what will make the difference. He'll see. He'll know you're trying, and he'll try too." They had a bond, and no one could take it away or even replace it with something else.

Melody nodded, her eyes suddenly full of life again. "Do you think you could take him something for me? Can I write him a letter? I didn't even get to talk to him. I want to explain, to tell him how sorry I am."

Dev glanced at the guard. "I can't take anything out." It was against the rules. "But I might be able to do something even better."

"We're having ice cream for dinner." Charity hauled the grocery bags onto the counter. The last two days had been such an overwhelming, emotional whirlwind that she hadn't had any time to plan healthy meals. She'd gone to the grocery store while Bodie and her mom watched a movie and had wandered aimlessly until she made it to the frozen food section. "Rocky road and mint chocolate chip and cookie dough." She pulled each one out of the bag and then found the whipped cream, sprinkles, chocolate sauce, and cherries.

"Seriously?" Bodie wandered into the kitchen, his eyes wide. "Wow. Even Mom never let me have ice cream for dinner."

Tammi came in behind him. "That looks like a lot of sugar."

"It's a lot of sugar," Charity agreed. "A lot of chocolate, a lot of calories, a lot of fat, and we're going to enjoy every bite." Tomorrow she would become a responsible adult again. She would make a meal list for the week and go shopping in the health food aisle. But not today. Today they would eat away the stress of the last couple of days, and once they succumbed to the sugar coma, maybe they would have a *Back to the Future* movie marathon. "Bodie, please get out the bowls. Mom, find the ice cream scoop."

While they took care of their jobs, she lined up the ingredients on the counter, taking off lids and getting everything organized.

"I love mint chocolate chip." Bodie scooped himself out a generous portion.

"Don't forget the chocolate sauce and whipped cream." Charity handed them over. "The more calories the better."

Bodie grinned at her—a real grin. The first one she'd seen in two days. He snatched the can of whipped cream and started fidgeting with the lid, but the cap popped off and the stuff shot out everywhere—all over Charity's face.

She dropped her own bowl and staggered back, the white froth temporarily blinding her.

"Oh dear!" her mother squealed somewhere nearby. "I'll get a towel."

Charity couldn't see Bodie but she could hear him laughing hysterically, and it was music—the happiest music she'd ever heard. "You think that's funny?" She swiped the whipped cream out of her eyes—still seeing it stick in her eyelashes—and found the other bottle on the counter.

Before Bodie could dodge away, Charity had the lid off and she sprayed him everywhere she could manage.

"Hey!" He came after her with his can again, and they were both standing in the middle of the kitchen shooting each other with whipped cream, laughing like fools, while her mom screeched and scolded.

"Stop that! Look at the mess you're making!"

That only made them laugh harder.

"Where's the chocolate sauce?" Charity slipped and stumbled her way over to the counter and snatched the bottle.

"No!" Her mother took it away from her. "Have you lost your ever-loving mind?"

"Yes." Charity spun to face her and shot her mom with whipped cream right in the face.

Bodie howled with laughter.

Tammi's mouth formed a big O, which made her white face even funnier. Charity's upper body collapsed over the counter, her shoulders shaking with giggles.

"That's it!" Tammi popped the lid off the chocolate sauce, and dumped it over Charity's head.

Bodie sank to the floor, gasping and snorting. "She showed you!"

"Oh yeah?" Charity stole the syrup from her mom and sloshed through the mess on the floor ready to show him, but her phone buzzed in her back pocket.

Umm... She swiped her hand down her jeans to clean off the stickiness and pulled it out to check the screen.

Topaz County Detention Center.

That was all it took to suck the laughter clean out of her. She looked at Bodie and brought her phone to her ear. "Hello?"

"Char? It's me." Her sister sounded so far away. Or maybe that was because of the sudden buzzing in her ears.

"Melody?" She said her sister's name the same way she used to when she was small and afraid. "It's really you? They told me we couldn't call you. Not until you were back in Oklahoma." She'd tried more than once...

"Yes, it's me. I don't have much time. Is Bodie there? Can you put him on the phone?"

"He's here." Charity looked at her nephew, but he shook his head and backed away.

Tammi went and put her arm around him. "Don't walk away," she murmured. "She's still your mom."

"Please, Char," Melody sniffled. "I know he might not want to talk to me right now, but this is my only chance."

"Okay." She pulled the phone away from her ear and put it on speaker. "You can talk to him." But Charity couldn't guarantee he'd talk back.

No one seemed to know what to say first, so Charity broke the silence. "How did you find a way to call us?" They'd been so adamant that inmates were to have no contact with family...

"It was Dev," Melody said. "He came to see me. He got them to let me call you."

Dev. Hearing his name brought tears to her eyes. "He came to see you?" Of course he had. Because he knew she and Bodie couldn't. He knew they were probably worried sick.

"Yes, he was here this morning. He came to tell me he hired a lawyer. A good one. And he's paying all the bills."

"No." She couldn't let him. He was not going to pay her sister's legal fees. "I can pay," Charity said, the tears breaking free. "Tell the lawyer I'll pay all the fees."

"I think it's too late. Dev already has everything settled with him." There was a pause. "Listen, I only have a few minutes before I have to hang up. Bodie? Are you there?"

He grunted out a sullen, "Yeah."

"I'm so sorry, Bodes." Melody's voice broke. "I messed up. I just wanted to get away and start over, but I made a mistake. Dev told me it's not too late, that I can still fix things, and I'm hoping he's right."

"Why'd you do it?" An angry expression hid beneath the remnants of whipped cream on his face. "Why'd you have to mess everything up?"

"I was scared. We were out of money. But it wasn't right." Her sister's voice gained strength. "I know that. And things are going to change. *I'm* going to change. I'll prove it to you. I'm going to do everything I can to make it up to you. Okay?" She didn't give him a chance to respond. "I know I won't be able to be with you for a while, but I still want to be part of your life, if you'll let me. You don't have to decide right now. I know it'll take time, but I'm asking you to forgive me."

A silence stretched on while Bodie seemed to think. His eyes were downcast, his mouth strained. "I'm really mad at you right now," he finally said. "But I don't think I'll always be."

Oh, that kid. Charity moved in to hug him. For a quick second, he let his head rest against her shoulder.

"Thank you," Melody said softly. "I won't give you any more reasons to be mad at me. I swear." There was noise in the background, someone's voice. "I have to go. I'm so sorry. Char—take care of him for me. I know he'll be happy staying with you. I'll write as soon as I can. I love you both. And you too, Mom."

"We love you, baby," Tammi sobbed.

"We really do," Charity added, her tears carving a path through the dried cream on her face. "We won't give up on you, Mellie. We'll always be here for you." Because they were a family.

Chapter Twenty-Three

Whenever Dev told his mom he was coming for dinner, she went all out. He sat across from his parents in front of a spread that could've easily served his entire patrol division at work. She must've spent all day cooking. Between the roast, garlic mashed potatoes, creamed spinach, roasted brussels sprouts, and fresh-made rolls, they'd all be eating leftovers for a week. Especially because he wasn't exactly hungry at the moment. Nerves already filled his stomach, leaving little room for Friday dinner.

"Dig in, son." His mom passed him the platter of meat, watching like she wanted to make sure he took a generous portion.

Too bad he didn't have a dog under the table like they used to. He'd slipped their old border collie a heck of a lot of food back in the day.

"Have you heard from Charity?" his dad asked, slopping a pile of mashed potatoes onto his plate.

"No." Dev took a small helping of each side dish. But he

did keep hearing her words. *You being here will only make things worse. Please, Dev. Just go.*

"Well, don't worry," his mother said. "I'm sure she'll come around once things are a bit more settled. They've all been through such a lot."

That was putting it mildly. Every time he closed his eyes to go to sleep, he saw Bodie's face, his horrified expression frozen in shock. That would haunt him for a good long while. "I'm hoping I'll have a chance to talk to Bodie sometime soon, but I don't want to rush it." He wanted to apologize to the boy, even though saying he was sorry wouldn't be enough.

"You were doing your job, son." His father slathered butter onto a roll. "As hard as it is, you have an obligation. You can't go easy on a criminal. When you're the county sheriff, you'll set the tone for the rest of the department."

Yeah, about that. It was the opening he needed, but he still hadn't figured out how to tell them he planned to withdraw from the election.

"I don't care what anyone says." His mom set down her fork and pointed at him. "You were wonderful at that question-and-answer session. So personable and honest. People want someone real in those positions, someone they can relate to."

He wasn't so sure he'd agree with that statement. He hadn't exactly been honest. With them or anyone else. People wanted a face for the department, and he wasn't right for the job. That was the bottom line. "Actually, I wanted to talk to you about the election."

"You're still ahead in the polls," his dad said, handing over the folded local newspaper he'd probably memorized during breakfast that morning.

"The polls?" Dev glanced at the article it was open to. "You mean the informal questionnaire Hank sent out?"

"It's as good as anything else," his father assured him.

"Right." He'd learned better than to argue about the local newspaper. His dad was their biggest supporter. "Well, the thing is, it doesn't matter anyway. The polls, the numbers. Because I'm planning to officially withdraw from the election on Monday." Once the words were out, he braced himself.

"Withdraw?" His mom's fork froze halfway to her mouth. Her smile went slack. "Dev...why?"

"It's not what I want." That was the only way to say it. "I guess I thought it was because everyone else wants it so much, but I realized I don't want to give up being out on patrol for management." And meetings and press conferences and personnel issues—things he had no interest in dealing with.

Both of his parents gaped at him, setting down their silverware as they exchanged a look of utter surprise.

"If it's not what you want, why'd you run in the first place?" his dad finally asked.

It would've been easy to blame it on a whim, but it was time to stop hiding from his issues. He figured he'd get past them only if he owned them. "I knew how important it was to you," he forced himself to say. "How important it seemed to be to everyone in town. And I don't want to disappoint anyone." That had always been one of his biggest fears, because disappointing someone led to rejection. At least that's the lie he'd always believed. "But I also can't keep making decisions based on how they'll affect everyone else." Especially now, when he thought about pursuing a future with Charity.

"Oh, honey." His mom had tears in her eyes. "How could you think we'd be disappointed in you? You're everything to us. We only want you to be happy."

He knew that's what they'd say, and yet the words brought a surprising amount of relief anyway. "I know. I've always felt loved and accepted by you both, but it's still there. The knowledge that my birth mom didn't want me." Like he'd told Charity, he lived with something missing, but it didn't have to define him. It didn't have to drive all of his decisions.

"She might've given you up, but we wanted you." His mother held his dad's hand on the table. "We wanted you so much. You were our dream come true. You still are."

"I've always known that." Man, looking at his parents so concerned on the other side of the table got him a little misty-eyed too. "I couldn't have ended up in a better family. I'm so lucky to have you two as my parents." They'd given him everything and made him into the man he was.

"We're already proud of you, son," his dad said with a tremble in his voice. "We couldn't be more proud. You're a good man, and that's all that we've ever cared about."

"You pull out of that election on Monday, and don't worry about what anyone says." His mom had always been great at giving pep talks. "Find what makes you happy and go after that."

He'd already found it, but things with Charity happened to be complicated at the moment. "I'd like to go after it. Trust me. But it might have to wait for—"

His cell rang. Normally he wouldn't have it on at the dinner table, but he'd been waiting—hoping—for a call. He pulled it out of his pocket, and as soon as he saw the screen he popped up from the table. "Sorry, I have to take this." Hope had galloped into his heart by the time he made it into the kitchen. As he brought the phone to his ear, he stared at that spot right in front of the sink. That's where he'd held Charity in his arms, where he'd kissed her before Bodie and Gracie had wandered off…

"Hello? Dev?"

It seemed he'd forgotten to answer.

"Hey. I'm glad you called." The relief of hearing her voice allowed him to breathe—really breathe...deeper than he had since he'd left her house. "I've been worried about you two."

"I don't want you to worry," she murmured. "We'll be okay."

Damn, he wanted to have this conversation in person, so he could see her face and be sure.

"How's Bodie?" There was that image again—the pain on the kid's face. It gouged into Dev every time he remembered it. "He has every right to hate me. I think that might be the hardest thing I've ever done. Arresting a mother in front of her child." He still went over it in his mind every day— what he should've done differently.

"We understand," Charity told him firmly. "You had to do your job. It's over now. We'll move past it. And what you did for Melody...hiring that lawyer." Her voice turned weepy. "Well, um, it's beautiful. There's no other way to say it. I don't think anyone has ever bothered to see the good in her, the potential. No one has ever given her a break like that."

He'd asked her sister not to tell Charity about the lawyer, but it seemed Melody hadn't listened. "She loves Bodie, that's for sure. Every mom should have another chance to be there for her kid."

"Thank you," Charity whispered. "It was so good to talk to her. So good for Bodie to hear her tell him she was sorry." There was a sniffling pause. "You didn't have to do all of that, Dev. I want to make sure you know that. Your arresting my sister didn't change anything for me. I still like you."

"I know." But it was good to hear her say that. "I wanted to do it. For her. For Bodie." Something told him her nephew wouldn't be as forgiving as Charity.

* * *

Well, her life might be a mess right now, but at least her garage was clean. Charity stashed the broom next to the shelf that housed her saddle collection and glanced around. It was spotless. That's what happened when she needed to think. She cleaned, found something to obsess over besides the problems cramming her head. After Melody's phone call last night, Charity had plenty to think about. Mostly Dev.

She'd been dying to tell him in person she was sorry for sending him away when he'd come to see them, but she still wasn't sure how to approach the subject of Dev with her nephew. Everything felt so tenuous right now. With all Bodie had been through, she didn't want to make things harder for him. He would come first no matter what, but she was hoping he'd give Dev a chance. Especially after everything the deputy had done for Melody.

And yet...Bodie hadn't said much after they'd finished cleaning the kitchen last night, and then he'd slept until well after noon. She didn't want to push too hard, but she'd hidden in the garage long enough. She had to stop thinking, obsessing, deliberating. She simply had to come out and ask if he was willing to give Dev a chance.

That in mind, Charity went back inside the house.

Bodie sat on the couch doing homework. "Hey." She walked over to join him. "How's it—"

There was a crash in the kitchen followed by her mother's interpretation of taking the lord's name in vain.

"Judas Priest!"

"What's she making in there?" Charity asked, not sure if she wanted to hear the answer.

Bodie winced. "She said something about lasagna."

"Oh dear god." Charity sat taller, trying to get a good view of the kitchen and slowly, quietly, carefully pulled her phone out of her back pocket.

"What're you doing?"

She grinned at her nephew. "Ordering pizza."

There was another clatter, and Charity rushed to tell the pizza place their order without being heard.

"Bodie?" Her mother came scurrying out of the kitchen. "Oh! Charity, there you are. I knew you were busy out in the garage so I'm starting dinner."

She and Bodie shared a look. While she appreciated her mother trying, she would not subject her nephew to Tammi's cooking.

Her mother didn't seem to pick up on their lack of enthusiasm. "I was thinking maybe you'd want to invite Dev over."

"Oh." It was the perfect opening, but she still didn't know how Bodie would feel about spending time with him. "Um. Actually, I did want to hang out with him. So I could tell him thank you. For what he's done for Melody." She held her breath and waited for her nephew's reaction.

Bodie closed his book and set it on the coffee table. "Would you tell him thank you for me too? It's cool what he did for my mom."

Relief nearly overwhelmed her. "Of course. I'd be happy to tell him."

Tammi looked thoughtful. "Why don't you go over to his place?" her mother offered. "Bodie and I will have lasagna—"

"Pizza," Charity interrupted with a grin at her nephew. "You're having pizza. I called for delivery."

"Why would you go and do something like that?" Tammi demanded.

"Have you forgotten the great lasagna fiasco of 1996?" Charity widened her eyes at Bodie. "She'd never made lasagna before, and—"

"My mom never taught me how to cook," Tammi interrupted.

"Anyway," Charity went on. "She was determined to make lasagna for your mom's birthday dinner, but she didn't realize she had to cook the noodles first." The memory almost amazed her. Somehow she'd suppressed the good ones right along with the bad ones.

"The recipe wasn't clear," Tammi grumbled. "I swear it didn't say you had to cook the noodles."

"So she threw it together and popped it in the oven and then forgot about it," Charity continued.

Bodie laughed. "She forgot?"

"As I recall, the reason I forgot is because you girls left the hose on outside and it flooded the basement." Her mother slapped her hands on her hips like she used to when they sassed her.

"Anyway," Charity said with a teasing roll of her eyes, "when she finally remembered the lasagna, it had been in the oven for a good two hours and she couldn't even get a knife to cut through it."

"Yeah, I'm good with pizza." Bodie sent an apologetic look to his grandma. "Sorry."

"It's fine. We can have pizza." Her mother always could out-sigh any martyr. "But you should go, honey." She prodded Charity off the couch. "Bodie and I will be fine. We'll get his homework done, and then maybe we'll play a board game."

Charity glanced at her nephew.

"Yeah." He smiled. "Go ahead. It'll be good to spend time with Grandma."

"Okay." Charity tried not to seem too rushed, but she kind of couldn't wait to go spend some time alone with her favorite deputy. "Thanks."

Tammi gave her a hug and whispered, "We won't wait up."

Chapter Twenty-Four

Dev added a splash of olive oil to the pan, swirling it a few times like he'd seen Alton Brown do on television. For once he was glad his mom was obsessed with the Food Network—and mainly Alton Brown. *He's a tall drink of iced tea*, she'd always say while they watched. Not his taste, but he'd picked up a few pointers food-wise, so it hadn't been a complete waste of time.

Dev placed two steaks on the sizzling puddle of butter and oil.

A pitter-pattering knock that sounded a lot like his—

"Dev? I've brought you a rum cake," his mom called through the door. "Hot right out of the oven."

Yep. Right on time. He opened the door, already smirking. "Why would you do that?" The question wasn't necessary. He'd mentioned earlier that Charity might be stopping by tonight.

"A rum cake can't hurt your chances with her." His mom swept past him and set it on the kitchen counter.

He got a look at the dessert over her shoulder. "No, but it could upstage the dinner I'm working on." Could? More like it most definitely *would*.

"Well, since you mentioned dinner, I'd better take a look." His mom bustled over to the stove top and gave the steaks her critical eye. "Not bad. But we should add a little more thyme." She plucked a few of the leaves off the stem he had sitting next to the stove and sprinkled them in like magic fairy dust. "Otherwise, it smells divine. She's going to love—"

"Hello?" The door creaked open. In her haste to micromanage his dinner, his mom must've forgotten to close it all the way.

"Hey—"

"Charity!" Mrs. Subtle wasted no time upstaging his greeting. She hurried over and gave Charity a hug. "How's Bodie? Is he all right? I can't believe all he's been through. Poor boy. You tell him I'll bake another batch of chocolate chip cookies next time he comes over here, okay?"

"Will do." Charity gave Dev a quick smile before focusing on his mom. "And he's okay. We've officially decided he's going to stay with me. I'll be his legal guardian."

"Oh, how wonderful!" The news prompted yet another hug.

"We should have a party to officially welcome him to town," his mom insisted as though someone had just assigned her to be the social director. "We'd be happy to host it here. Wouldn't that be fun?"

"That sounds perfect." Charity suddenly inhaled and looked around. "Is something burning?"

Shit, the steaks. Dev flailed back to the kitchen and flipped them. A little charred but not too overdone.

"Dev made you dinner," his mom informed her. "And I brought over a rum cake for dessert. It's an old family recipe that my grandmother used to make."

"And it's delicious." Dev rushed back to them before his mom launched into the half-hour story about how they'd thought the recipe was lost in a house fire. "So...Mom... thanks for the cake. Charity and I have a lot to talk about. Hope you have a good night." Any other day he'd let her talk to Charity as much as she wanted, but he and Charity had an unfinished conversation lingering between them from a few days ago on her porch. She was right. Bodie would always come first in her life. Especially now when he was grieving. And Dev wasn't sure where that left him and Charity. He couldn't stand in the way of Bodie's healing, but he wasn't ready to give up and disappear from their lives either.

Thankfully, his mother only smiled. "Oh, yes. I'm going, I'm going. You have a good night too." She chuckled at herself. "What am I saying? Of course you'll have a good night." She scurried past Charity. "I'll get back to you about that party soon."

"I'll look forward to it, Mrs. Jenkins. Thanks for the cake."

"MaryElla. You call me MaryElla." She left in haste, and finally—*finally*—they were alone. Dev took a minute to simply look at Charity. She looked good. Nothing fancy, just darker jeans than usual and a simple white button-down shirt unbuttoned low enough to make his eyes linger there. The sight heated him right up. His gaze drifted to the duffel hanging off her shoulder. That was one big purse. "What's with the bag?"

Charity sashayed past him, shooting him a hot glance over her shoulder. "It's my overnight bag." She set it on the couch.

Hmmm. That sounded interesting. And promising. "What do you keep in there?"

"There are a few things I think you might like."

It took everything in him not to run over there and look for himself. But they did have something to discuss. "So

I take it Bodie was okay with you coming to see me? Because I don't want to cause any problems between you two." He'd wait, if that's what Bodie needed. It might kill him, but he'd wait.

"He said he knows what happened isn't your fault and he's fine with us hanging out." Charity's smile held relief. "He's thankful for what you did for his mom, but in typical teenage boy fashion, he doesn't want to make a big deal out of it. So don't expect a hug or anything."

"I won't expect one from him." But he wouldn't mind one from her right about now.

"So what're you making?" She walked over to him and stopped just out of reach.

Shit, the steaks. She made it too easy to forget things. He went back to the stove and pulled the skillet off, setting it on a hot pad on the counter. "Pan-seared rib eye with herb butter."

"Mmmm." She came up behind him, draping her arms over his shoulders. "It smells good."

"So do you." He turned so he could pull her against him. "You smell like cherries." And something subtly sweet. Something he wanted to taste.

"It's my shower gel." She raised her eyebrows. "I packed it in my bag."

He had no idea why someone would need gel in the shower, but hell, he was down with trying it out. "Maybe we should shower before dinner." The image of her wet, naked body against his completely hijacked his focus.

"No way," she teased. "I'm starving and that steak smells amazing."

"I'm starving too," he murmured, pressing his lips against her neck. "But not for steak." She'd aroused his curiosity, his hunger, his desire to hear her moan his name again.

"There'll be plenty of time after dinner, since I'm spending the night." She propped her hands on the countertop and hopped up to sit there. "Is there anything I can do to help?"

"Stop seducing me?" he asked futilely. That would be impossible.

Charity laughed. "If it makes you feel better, you look incredibly sexy standing at the stove."

"Saying that doesn't help." It made him want to haul her back to the bedroom. But...if she insisted on eating first... "You want something to drink? I'm sure there's a bottle of red wine around here somewhere."

Charity crossed her legs and leaned back into her hands in a pose that emphasized her chest. "I'll take a beer."

Now she was just torturing him. "I knew you were the perfect woman." He reached into the fridge and handed her an IPA. She popped the top and took a long pull, tilting her head back so that her blond hair spilled down her back just like it had when she rode him all the way to an orgasm.

Yeah, he wasn't gonna be able to eat dinner when he was this hard.

"That's it." Dev hastily covered the steaks with foil and turned off the stove. "We're having dessert first." He walked over, took the beer out of her hand, and then lifted Charity off the counter, securing his hands under her perfect ass.

A surprised squeak parted her lips, but he kissed her before she could say anything. Within seconds her legs wrapped tightly around his waist, and her hands were tangled in his hair. He pulled back to grin at her, to take in that rosy glow on her face.

"I thought you told your mom we had a lot to talk about," she murmured.

"That overnight bag told me all I needed to know."

* * *

Something shook Charity gently.

"Time to get up." Dev's voice was hushed and deep, radiating into her.

She forced her eyes open, too comfortable on his soft mattress and wedged up against his hard body to even think about moving. "Do we have to?"

Propped up on an elbow, he hovered over her. "I thought we'd sneak you back into your house and then take Bodie and your mom out for breakfast."

She stared up at him, taking in his mussed hair, those persuasive eyes. "You're so hot."

He grinned. "Last night was hot."

So hot they'd hardly slept. "And now you want to get up early."

"I don't want to keep you from Bodie too long." His fingers trailed down her bare arm. "I don't want him to think I'm going to occupy all of your time."

"You are very good at occupying my time," Charity assured him. "But thank you." She pulled him to lie down with her and wrapped herself around him. "I won't have as much freedom as I would've a month ago."

"I can't complain." He kissed her temple. "If it wasn't for Bodie, you might never have given me the time of day."

"This is true." She might never have realized how good Dev was. She might never have let him in. "I think he'd still like to work on the ranch sometimes."

"We could use the help." Dev leaned over to look into her eyes. "When he's ready. I don't want to get in the way of him bonding with you either."

Right. Even with Dev in her life, Bodie would be her priority. "I don't know what it should look like. Being his parent, his aunt, his guardian." It overwhelmed her.

"It's okay to figure things out as you go. Naomi and Jessa

are great resources. So are my parents, for that matter. And I'll be here whenever you need me to be."

Charity smoothed her hands up his chest. "I'm going to need you a lot. After last night, I have a feeling my bed is going to feel pretty boring."

"We'll get creative," he promised with a grin that sparked a sensuous passion. "Speaking of creative, last night you said something about shower gel?"

"Oh, right. I forgot all about my overnight bag." Despite her care in packing it, she really hadn't needed anything from it, not even the satin-and-lace nightie she'd never worn before. "Where'd it end up anyway?"

Dev rolled off the bed, and the sight of those strong sinewy muscles made her heart dance with anticipation.

He disappeared into the living room and came back carrying the bag. "Let's see." He unzipped it and pulled out the nightie. "Whoa, how did I miss this?"

She swiped it out of his hands and tossed it aside. "You never gave me time to put it on. You never gave me time to put *anything* on."

"Yeah, okay." His hand fished back in the bag. "This feels like shower gel." He pulled out the plastic bottle.

"That's it."

"Cherry vanilla," he read off the label. His eyes got bigger. "Warming shower gel."

"You're going to love it," she promised.

"I have no doubts." He pulled her up off the bed and started kissing her as they made their way into the master bathroom. Dev knew his way around a kiss. He started with a tease, then gradually made it more demanding, more passionate. In the bathroom, he nudged her up against the wall by the shower, and somehow got the water going without breaking their kiss. Steam rose into the air, clouding everything. Dev tugged on her hand, then eased his hands onto her hips and guided her to step into the shower with him.

Hot water sprayed down on her skin. "Mmmmm," she couldn't help moaning. Her head fell back as Dev held the bottle of shower gel over her breasts and let the cold drops fall to her skin. He caressed with his hands, working the gel into a warming lather that made her tingle. Before she lost herself completely, she stole the bottle and squirted a whole handful into her palm. She let the bottle fall to the tile and brought her hands to Dev's abs, spreading the gel lower until he was moaning too.

Their kisses grew more frantic, and she swore she would never get enough of his mouth, his tongue, the way he held her and teased her and turned her on. "I love you, Dev." It was so freeing to say it, to feel safe enough to tell him the truth. She wrapped her arms around his neck and hopped up, knowing he would catch her and hold her.

"I love you too." He kissed her shoulder, her neck, her chin, and then her lips, and moved his hands to her butt, positioning her just right to fit them together.

Shockwaves coursed through at the feel of him entering her. He filled her so completely. Without even one thrust she was already gasping. "Make love to me," she whispered, her tongue toying with his ear. "Make me yours."

"You are mine." He edged her back against the wall and started to move their bodies, letting her slide down below his hips before lifting her back up with long thrusts. Charity lifted her hips to meet him, her hands digging into his shoulders, giving her more leverage. Dev lowered his mouth to her breast and used his tongue to heighten every sensation until they completely took her over.

Charity clung to him tighter and tighter until she had no choice but to hand herself over to him, trembling with the powerful surge of emotion and pleasure and release that finally broke her apart, leaving her in pieces in Dev's powerful arms.

Charity slipped the key into the lock and quietly turned the knob. The door creaked open and she and Dev snuck into her house like two teenagers.

The living room and kitchen still sat dark and quiet. "I knew they wouldn't be up." She eyed Dev. "We could've stayed in bed longer."

"But then we wouldn't have gotten in the shower."

Oh god, the shower. Charity turned to him, stretching to her tiptoes to kiss his lips. What started out as a peck on the lips quickly escalated to include their tongues...

"Are you guys gonna do that all the time now?" Bodie asked in a bored voice. "Because you're gonna have to warn me."

Charity and Dev quickly separated, but it was too late. They were already busted. "Morning," she said, trying to recover. "Dev and I thought we'd take you and Grandma out for breakfast."

"That sure sounds better than Grandma's pancakes."

"I heard that," her mother called from down the hall. "Just let me finish teasing my hair, and I'll be right out."

Dev looked confused. "Teasing her hair?"

"Don't ask." Charity and Bodie said it at the same time, and then grinned at each other. Moments like these made her think they would be okay. Bodie would be okay. She would be okay. They would figure this out.

"So her pancakes are pretty bad?" Dev asked Bodie quietly.

"Like hockey pucks," the boy confirmed.

"Like burned hockey pucks," Charity corrected.

"Don't listen to them, Dev." Tammi came storming down the hall, her tall, teased hair bobbing. She wore a leopard-print blouse that Charity was sure she'd seen someone wear on *Jersey Shore*, but honestly, she had never loved her mother more. Somehow loving Dev made her love everyone else better.

"You used to love my pancakes," her mother said. "You used to beg me to make them."

"That was before I knew pancakes weren't supposed to be crunchy."

Dev and Bodie cracked up, but they tried to hide it behind coughs. Charity watched them, feeling a deep sense of belonging. Bodie might not want to talk about what happened with Dev yet, but eventually they'd get there. Until then, they could laugh and joke around.

"All right, all right." Tammi snatched up her huge purse and walked to the door in a huff. "Just you wait, Char-bear. Bodie'll be making fun of your cooking in no time."

"I already do," the kid said, sending himself and Dev into another round of hearty chuckling.

They all paraded out into the morning sunlight and piled into Dev's SUV.

"I thought we'd drive out to the diner on the highway." As he drove, Dev rested his hand on Charity's thigh, the simple touch filling her with a sense of belonging.

"Why?" Bodie asked.

Charity didn't have to ask. She knew Dev didn't want to remind him of what had happened at the Farm, but no one came out and answered his question.

"I want to go the Farm," her nephew said. "For chocolate chip pancakes and Everly's chocolate milk." He leaned over the seat and grinned at Charity. "That's where all of the locals go for breakfast, right? I'm a local now."

"Good point," Dev said, taking a quick turn onto Main Street.

As they drove through town, Charity pointed out the landmarks to her mother—the ice cream shop, Darla's wine bar, and some of the fun shops Tammi had yet to visit.

"This is a great town," her mom mused, watching the buildings pass by. "I'm really hoping to spend more time here."

There would've been a time that Charity would've cringed to hear her mother say that, but now she turned around and smiled. "You're welcome to visit whenever you want." Bodie would need as much family in his life as he could get. More than anything, she wanted to create a support system for him. Actually, she wanted to create a support system for them both. "And I was thinking maybe you could travel to some of my events with us this summer," Charity said to her mom. She'd need the extra help keeping an eye on Bodie while she competed.

Her mom's eyes got all teary. "I would love that."

"Here we are." Dev pulled the truck into the parking lot at the Farm. For a brief second, Charity wondered what everyone in town would think when she and Dev walked in together like a couple, along with her mom and nephew. Surely news about Melody had traveled fast. But then again, she didn't care what everyone thought. Ty, Mateo, and Levi might give her a hard time about her new relationship status, but her friends would be thrilled.

Her mom seemed to admire the exterior. "I didn't notice what a cute little place this was before."

"Wait until you taste the food." Dev came up behind Charity and wrapped her in his arms. They walked inside like that, and she couldn't stop smiling.

"This time I'm definitely getting the pancakes," Bodie said.

"And the chocolate milk," Charity added.

"Hi there!" Everly greeted them with a look of happy surprise. She winked at Charity, clearly telling her she wanted to hear about this later. "Table for four?" she asked, grabbing the menus.

"I like the sound of that." Dev brushed a kiss on Charity's cheek. "Table for four."

Epilogue

I wish my mom could be here."

Charity dabbed at the tears that had been well on their way before Bodie had gone and mentioned Melody. "I know, Bodes." She gave him a hug strong enough for two moms. "She wishes she could be here too." Melody had been sentenced to six years in a minimum-security prison. They'd gone out to visit her four times over the last year, and it truly seemed like her sister had changed. For one thing, she'd been sober since she'd been arrested. And for another, she'd started working in the kitchen, managing to send some money to Bodie every month. She and Bodie kept in close touch, writing letters and talking on the phone every week. But Charity knew it still hurt not having her at his first barrel racing competition. Melody would miss the rest of Bodie's childhood, his young adulthood. But Charity would be there. She was there for everything—even for chaperoning the middle school dance last winter, much to his embarrassment.

Bodie slipped on his cowboy hat. "Do you ever get nervous before a competition?"

She had to laugh. "Every time."

"What do you usually do about it?"

"You really want to know?" She figured she should warn him. No one had ever heard about her pregame routine, mostly because she'd always been too embarrassed to talk about it.

"I think so?" He didn't seem sure, but at least her embarrassment would distract him from his own nerves.

"I throw up," she blurted.

He gave her a grossed-out look. "Seriously?"

"Yes. When I get nervous I get nauseous, and I throw up." It never failed. "And it makes me feel better. Every time."

That clearly didn't sound appealing to Bodie. "I hate throwing up."

"Me too, but I don't have much of a choice." In fact, she was so nervous for him, she might have to visit the bathroom before he mounted his horse. "You can come up with your own pregame ritual, though. Maybe something a little less disgusting."

"Like what?"

Hmmm. She tried to think of things that would get the adrenaline going. "I don't know. Maybe fifty push-ups? Or burpees? That'd warm you up for sure."

He shook his head. "Push-ups aren't really my thing."

"How about—"

"How's it going back here?" Dev made his way to where they were standing just behind the bleachers at the Topaz Falls Rodeo Grounds.

Resisting the urge to answer for him, Charity looked to Bodie. It still killed her how much he'd grown in one year. He was nearly as tall as she was now. He'd likely pass her by in the next few months. But he looked so different. He smiled more. He dressed like a cowboy. He'd developed a passion for horses and racing very similar to her own. And, while they still butted heads on a regular basis over things like phone time and friends, they'd both learned a lot about what it means to be a family.

"It's okay," Bodie mumbled. His face had paled a lot like hers did before a competition. Maybe he had some of her in him after all.

"Bodie's feeling the nerves, so we were trying to figure out what he could do for a pregame warm-up ritual."

Dev's eyes lit with an idea. "Know what I used to do before a big game?"

"What?" her nephew asked hopefully.

Her hot deputy held out a brown paper bag. "I always ate one of my mom's chocolate chip cookies."

Bodie took the bag from his hand. "Always?"

"She brought me one before every game. And today she made some for you."

"Really?" The kid dug his hand into the bag and looked as touched as a fourteen-year-old boy could.

"She wanted to wish you luck," Dev said. "And I used to swear that her cookies had magic powers. Seriously. Once I bit into that doughy goodness, I felt like I was eight years old again and nothing scared me."

Bodie looked thoughtful. "That's it. That's what I want my pregame ritual to be." His face broke into a grin. "Eating cookies. But I can't do it with you two standing there watching me."

"Oh. Sorry." Charity gave him a quick hug and even a kiss on the cheek. "You're going to kill it out there today. Seriously. You've worked so hard, Bodie. I want you to try to enjoy it."

"I will." He all but shooed her away.

"We'll be watching right at the fence," Dev promised.

Charity still couldn't believe how quickly those two had bonded. Dev had been wise about giving them space, but he'd also stepped in and had been like a mentor to Bodie, taking him fishing and even inviting him to poker once in a while. Bodie liked to joke that he was friends with a bunch of old guys.

"Good luck." Dev gave the kid a salute and they walked into the arena.

Charity had to keep a tight grip on his hand to hold her own nerves in check. "I remember my first ride. God, I threw up like ten times before I walked out there. Gunner thought I had the flu, almost didn't let me compete."

"Bodie's ready for this." Dev led her to their seats in the very front row. "A few months ago, I wouldn't have said that, but you can see the confidence in him."

Charity leaned her head on his shoulder. "That's thanks to you, in part."

He eased his arm around her. "But mostly thanks to you."

"No." She turned to him so he could see her emotion. "I'm always tempted to baby him. Protect him. Shield him. You're the one who challenges him." Like when Bodie had talked about joining the basketball team, but then chickened out two days before tryouts. Charity had consoled him, telling him he didn't have to play basketball. Truthfully, she was worried he'd get made fun of since he'd never played on a team. But Dev had taken him down to the gym and they'd spent the whole day dribbling and shooting until he felt comfortable enough to walk out onto the court. And he'd made the team.

"He needs both of us then. The protector and the taskmaster."

"He does. He really does need both of us." Her heart pounded the way it had for months, ever since she first decided what she wanted to do. It had taken a long time for her to build up the courage, but she was finally ready. She reached under her seat for the shopping bag she'd brought along. "I have something for you."

"Yeah?" He tried to get a peek into the bag.

"Yeah." Not keeping him in suspense, she pulled out the tattered coil of rope and handed it to him.

He inspected it with confusion muddling his eyes. "It's a lasso."

"It was my *first* lasso," she corrected. "I got it when I was twelve. That's when I knew I wanted to ride."

"And you're giving it to me because...?"

The question didn't offend her. It wasn't your average everyday gift. "It's my most prized possession. And you're the most important person in my life." She moved in closer, her heart pounding, but also soaring. "You're the only person I've ever loved with my whole heart. The only person who has given me security and space because you know I need both." She clasped her hands in his, feeling them steady with surety. "I never thought I would fall in love, Dev. But I did. I am. It's pathetic. I wake up in the morning and think about you first. Before I think about anything else."

He grinned. "That's because of *how* I wake you up."

She whacked him playfully. "Even when you're not in my bed. I want to be with you. Always. I know the lasso might not mean much to you, but it's everything to me. And I want to give you everything. All of me. I want to marry you."

Though they'd been dating for a year, they'd never talked marriage. There had been so many other things to figure out with Bodie. And Charity knew why Dev never brought it up. He didn't want to push her. Didn't want to make her feel too confined. He was so good that way.

Now he was staring at her, his eyes so full of kindness and wisdom and love.

Charity wrapped her arms around his waist. "Will you marry me? So we can be together always? So you can be a bigger part of Bodie's life?"

She'd never seen Dev cry, but those were definitely tears in his eyes. "Hell, yes. Let's get hitched, baby." He held up the rope. "Do you want to lasso me or something? To make it official?"

Ha! He wished. "Maybe later," she murmured, going in for a kiss. "Actually, definitely later."

Right at that moment, the loudspeaker crackled. "Next up, Bodie Stone riding Macho!"

Charity broke away from their kiss and they both whooped and hollered, waving at Bodie like two crazed fans.

Her nephew completely ignored them, but under the shadows of his helmet, Charity saw him smile.

The best way to spend Christmas is in the arms of a cowboy!

Don't miss the next story in Sara Richardson's Rocky Mountain Riders series! Please turn the page for a preview of *A Cowboy for Christmas*.

Available Fall 2019!

Chapter One

Everyone had their dirty little secret, and Darla Michaels fully intended to keep hers under wraps.

She cinched the belt on her trench coat, pulled a long brunette wig over her black hair, slipped on her Jackie O sunglasses, and then climbed out of her cherry-red Mercedes Roadster, which she'd parked across the street just in case anyone she knew happened to drive by.

You'd think traveling an hour and twenty minutes—two towns away from her home in Topaz Falls, Colorado—made for a pretty safe bet that none of her friends or acquaintances would find her out, but one could never be too careful.

What if someone she knew back home had to make an impromptu Target run? Glenwood Springs would be the first place they'd come. They would likely take this very route, which meant they would inevitably recognize her car, because—hello—a cherry-red Mercedes Roadster stuck out like a sore thumb among the burly, big-tired, four-wheel-drive SUVs and diesel pickup trucks that typically cruised these mountain roads. But that was okay, because even if someone did happen to drive by and see her car, they wouldn't know where she'd gone.

For all they knew she could be shopping in one of these fine boutiques right here along the main drag. They'd never in a million years suspect she'd gone into the dingy basement of the nondescript brick building across the street. And that was good, because whatever she did, she had to make sure her life back in Topaz Falls never intersected with her purposes here.

After a quick visual scan of the street, Darla made her way across and ducked into the building through the glass door, which had been splattered with slush from the last early-season snowstorm.

Once she stepped inside, the space's familiar warmth brought a soothing comfort—the feel of the threadbare carpet beneath the soles of her boots, the hum of the old rickety furnace churning out heat. The first night she'd come here, she'd sworn it would be a one-time thing, but somehow, eight years later, here she stood yet again, getting ready to attend her eightieth meeting with her bereaved spouses' support group.

Before marching down the steps to join the others, Darla quickly removed the coat, then the wig, then the sunglasses, balling them all up and shoving them onto one of the cubby shelves the community center had built for children to store their belongings. The disguise was only for the outside world, not for this little posse she'd become part of.

When her husband had died nearly ten years ago at the age of thirty, there were all these steps she felt she had to take. Step one: make a ridiculously expensive and impractical purchase. Hello, Mercedes Roadster.

Step two: get a new job that would completely dominate all of her time and thoughts. Three weeks after Gray's funeral, she'd decided her job as pastry chef at an upscale restaurant in Denver wasn't nearly consuming enough, so she'd taken the insurance money, moved three hours away to Topaz Falls, Colorado, and started the Chocolate Therapist—a wine and chocolate bar on Main Street. Which had indeed dominated all of her thoughts and time.

Then there was step three: attend a bereaved spouses' support group. She'd found the group two towns away, lest anyone in Topaz Falls get the idea that she was still a poor, grieving widow who needed extra pity and emotional support, and had attended that first meeting only with the intention of crossing it off her list, a kind of *Look! I did it! I checked off all the boxes! I'm a healthy and happy widow.* But...well...for some reason she chose not to examine too closely, she hadn't quit coming yet.

"Darla? Is that you?" Josie Wilken lumbered up the concrete steps from the basement meeting room. "I thought I heard the door." Her smile went broad, the ends of her mouth accented with crescent-shaped dimples. Like everyone else in the group, Josie had gray hair, though she always wore it coiled on top of her head in a carefree knot that bobbed to one side and then the other when she walked.

"You're late," Josie announced with a glance at her watch. As the group's fearless leader, she'd always been a stickler for time. "You missed refreshments."

Darla grinned at her and fluffed her hair back into shape. "I don't need refreshments. I own a confectionary." She had a little too much access to refreshments, if you asked her. Her quality control procedures kept her about ten pounds heavier than she'd like to be.

"Speaking of...how'd the new recipe turn out?" Josie was always giving her ideas for new combinations to try. "For the lavender-infused truffles?"

"They turned out unbelievable." Darla unearthed a small box of them from her purse. "Seriously. I never would've thought to try it, but once again, brilliant." She handed the box to Josie.

"I knew it would turn out!" The woman opened the box and popped a truffle into her mouth, closing her eyes in obvious rapture. "Damn, I'm good."

Darla laughed and linked their arms together, guiding her friend back down the steps to the basement. "So how've you been?" Seeing these friends only once a month meant there was always plenty of gossip to catch up on. In fact, that's really what the group had turned into—a place to talk about life with people who knew what it meant to live with a missing piece.

"It's been a boring month," Josie complained. "The kids at school are doing all this crappy testing, so I haven't even been able to do any fun projects." As the art teacher at a local elementary school, fun projects were Josie's specialty. "What about you?" Her friend paused outside the door of the community meeting room. "How's your month been?"

Darla gave the same answer she usually did. "Good. Busy." Though she would've liked it to be busier. Topaz Falls didn't exactly see many tourists October through November. Things didn't usually pick up until the ski season started, and even that had been slower with the warm, dry winters they'd had the last few years. "Hopefully we'll have a busy Christmas season this year." God knew the town needed it. They'd already lost three businesses over the last several months.

"Yeah, I've been thinking about Christmas." Josie rested her hand on Darla's shoulder, giving it a compassionate squeeze. "You'll be comin' up on the big one-zero this year, huh?"

Darla was only half paying attention. Inside the room, she could hear Peter, Ralph, and Norman discussing Peter's latest date. "One-zero?" she asked, still trying to eavesdrop on the men's conversation.

"Yeah." Josie steered Darla's gaze back to hers. "You know, the ten-year anniversary."

The realization of what her friend meant sent her heart skidding. "Oh. Right." December 23. Ten years since Gray had died. "I guess I haven't really thought about it too much," she lied. The closer the holiday got, the more that date seemed to cross her mind.

"It's a tough one. That ten years," Josie said solemnly. She'd lost her partner twelve years ago, so she always liked to keep Darla informed on what to expect as time went on. "I don't why, but that one hit me the hardest. Almost had me a mental breakdown, I did. Made me reevaluate everything in my life." Josie and Karen had been together for almost twenty years, which was more than triple the time Darla had shared with Gray, but somehow that didn't seem to matter. A soul mate was a soul mate whether you'd spent six years with them or twenty.

"You got a plan for how you're gonna get through it?" Josie was big on plans.

"Like I said, I haven't thought about it too much," Darla said, brushing the whole thing off. "It's always such a busy time of year. And I don't usually mark the anniversary." In fact, she did everything she could to keep herself too occupied to think about it at all. That was her plan: avoidance through escapism. So far, it had worked pretty well for her. In fact, it could work for her right now. She peeked back into the meeting room. "We'd better get in there before we miss all the juicy details about Peter's date."

"What? That scoundrel! I told him to wait until I got back!" Josie took the bait and charged into the room with Darla at her heels.

"Hello, gentlemen." She dug into her purse and retrieved more boxes of truffles, handing one to each man.

"My god, I wish I was thirty years younger." Norman gave her a scandalous hug. At eighty, he was the oldest in the group, but also the most handsome, she'd say.

"Lookin' good, doll." Ralph took his turn next. "Thanks for the chocolate. You're my dream girl."

Darla smiled and placed a kiss on his cheek. Come to think of it, this could be why she hadn't left the group yet. It was good for her self-esteem.

"They'd have to fight me for you," Peter told her, forgoing the hug completely to give her a quick smooch on the lips.

"All a bunch of playboys," Josie mumbled behind them.

"And I love them." Darla gave her friend a wink. These men were actually decent and kind, and still loyal to the loves they'd lost. Not to mention, they all had the most wonderful distinct smell—Norman's with hints of pipe smoke in his sweater, Ralph's like the Tabasco sauce he poured on everything, and Peter's like cheap aftershave. There had been plenty of others in the group who had come and gone but the five of them had a special bond.

"What took so long?" Peter demanded, munching his way through his third truffle. "What were you two talking about in the hallway?" Chocolate crumbs sprinkled his chin.

"Darla's coming up on her ten-year," Josie informed the others.

Groans went all around.

Seriously? It was that bad? Dread crammed itself tightly into her chest. "It's really not a big deal."

Peter finished off the last truffle. "Oh, it's a big deal all right."

"There's something about a decade that makes you re-think your whole life," Ralph added.

Josie's head bobbed in a self-important nod. "That's exactly what I told her."

"And I'm telling you all, I'll be fine." She didn't want to hear any more about how hard it would be. This year was like any other. She had her business, she had her friends, and she'd plan a whole lot of festive events to keep her moving from one thing to the next.

Darla took Peter's hand and led the way over to the circle of chairs they usually sat in for their discussions. "Now how did that date go last month?"

For the next hour they discussed poor Peter's disastrous date. The woman had brought her cat to the restaurant in her purse. Peter had been caught unawares when the cat climbed up his leg and started to nibble. When the poor man had jumped out of his chair, the entire table had flipped over.

"I wish *you'd* agree to go out with me," he said to Darla as they were wrapping up.

"Sorry, Pete. You know I don't date." She went out with men—and sometimes hooked up with the very tempting specimens—but as far as a traditional dating relationship—that had always been off the table.

Josie sent a look to the others and at the exact same time, they all opened their mouths. "Ten years," they said in a chorus.

"Wow, did you guys practice that?" Darla stood and folded her chair. "Is that what you were doing before I came? Rehearsing?"

"Sorry, love." Norman swooped in and put her chair away

for her. "We just don't want you caught off guard. It's better to be prepared."

"And anyway, I don't understand why you don't date," Josie said, supervising while Norman took care of the rest of the chairs. "If your loss is no big deal and all."

Darla gave her a look. "Wow, it's such a bummer we're out of time tonight. Guess we'll have to save that topic for another time."

"Another time never comes," the woman muttered, but Darla pretended like she hadn't heard. "Can I give you a ride home tonight, Ms. Josie?"

That perked up her friend's sullen expression. "Sure." She never could resist a ride in the Roadster.

They all walked up the stairs together, filing out onto the street while they pulled on hats and gloves and coats. Darla went ahead and stuffed her wig and sunglasses into her purse since it was dark outside. Everyone exchanged more hugs and a few stolen kisses—Josie nearly slapped Peter when he snuck one onto her lips. After the hearty goodbyes, Darla and Josie crossed the street.

"Poor Peter. I was dying when he told us how the cat jumped the waiter." That had to be one of the best date stories Darla had ever heard.

"That's what you get when you use those online dating sites," Josie said. "A bunch of weirdos."

"And you wonder why I don't da—" A spray of ice-cold slush hit Darla's upper body seconds before a truck blazed past. *Cold.* She gasped and sputtered, trying to mop her face with the sleeve of her coat, which had been soaked clean through. Oh god, it was freezing. She glanced at Josie, who by some miracle had been spared. "Who the heck—?" The truck in question pulled over next to the curb ahead of them and stopped just behind her car.

It was a big truck. A black burly diesel extended cab with a familiar pro-rodeo bumper sticker.

Uh-oh...

"I'm sorry." Ty Forrester got out and came jogging down the sidewalk. "I didn't even see you there until it was too late."

Darla stopped dead in her soggy tracks. *No.* Not Ty. Anyone but Ty. "It's fine," she called, lowering her voice so he wouldn't recognize it. "No worries." *Leave. Turn around and get into your truck.* But Ty was a cowboy and if there was one thing a cowboy couldn't stand, it was leaving a damsel in distress.

"It's not fine," he said, making a fast approach. Of course he had to look good. Ty always looked good. He wasn't tall, but his upper body had a lot of brawn, which didn't seem to fit the classically handsome structure of his face. Maybe it was the perfect angle of his jaw or the inviting curve of his mouth, or the magnetic energy in his deep-set blue eyes. Yes, those eyes. They happened to be the perfect contrast to his dark hair.

"You're soaked—" Ty's eyes went wide when he stopped two feet away. "*Darla?* Is that you?"

Leave it to her to try to hide right under a streetlight. Now she wouldn't be able to vanish into the darkness like a mysterious mirage.

"Damn, it is you," he said when she remained silent. "I thought that looked like your car. What're you doing here?"

"Noth—" she started, but Josie butted in.

"We just finished our bereaved spouses' support group meeting," her friend offered. "I'm Josie Wilken, by the way. And you are?"

"Ty. Ty Forrester. I'm a friend of Darla's. From Topaz Falls." He quickly wriggled out of his winter coat and wrapped it around Darla. "I'm sorry. Did you say *bereaved spouses'* group?"

"Yep. As in dead spouses," Josie said helpfully.

"*Spouses?*" A look of pure shock bolted his gaze to Darla. "Wait. You were...? You're a...?"

"Yes," she huffed through a put-out sigh. And that overly sympathetic look on his face was the exact reason she didn't talk about it with anyone back home. Most of her friends knew she'd been married, but she hadn't offered many details.

"Wow." Ty diverted his disbelieving stare to the ground. "I'm so sorry for your loss. I had no idea."

"But you said you were a friend." Josie turned to Darla and crossed her arms. "Surely you tell your friends about your dead husband."

"*Friend* can mean a lot of different things." In her and Ty's case, it was a bit more complicated than she'd like. He happened to be one of the more tempting varieties of men. Combine that with the fact that he was single, she was single—and it was slim pickings in Topaz Falls—so of course certain things had happened between them. A few times. Isolated incidents, if you will. Until she realized she'd started to like those incidents a little too much, to think of him a bit too often. Then she'd shut it down. "I was married a long time ago," she informed Ty. "And I was a completely different person back then."

That didn't seem to alleviate the concern that pulled at his mouth. He was likely cataloging back through their sexy encounters to figure out how he'd missed the fact that she was a widow.

"She's coming up on her ten-year anniversary," said Josie, aka the informant. "I was telling her that's one of the toughest."

Aaannd that was her cue. "Josie, why don't you go ahead and get into the car?" Darla found her keys and hit the UNLOCK button. "I'll be there in a minute."

"Right." Her friend suddenly seemed to realize she'd over-stepped. "Nice to meet you, Ty," she said as she scurried away.

"Yeah. Nice to meet you too." He didn't even look in Josie's direction. The man was obviously trying to wrap his head around the new information he'd learned, but Darla would stop him right there.

"You never said what you're doing here." Other than ruining a perfectly good secret eight years in the making.

"Oh." Ty seemed to shake himself out of his thoughts. "I had to get a part for my truck. This was the only location that had it in stock."

Of course it was. The universe loved her like that. "So what's it going to take for you to keep this quiet?" she asked, getting down to business.

"Keep what quiet?"

"The bereavement group. No one knows and I'd like to keep it that way." If her friends found out, they'd think she wasn't over her past. Then they'd wonder why she didn't talk to them about it, so they'd start trying to talk about it all the time.

Ty continued to stare at her with that damned frown. "I won't tell anyone, Darla."

God, even the way he said her name had changed. It was so solemn. They used to joke around, poke fun at each other, banter back and forth, but now he obviously felt sorry for her.

"I know you're surprised, but it happened a long time ago." In another life, it sometimes felt.

"You still attend a support group," he pointed out.

"Because they're my friends." She didn't know why she even tried. There was obviously no talking him out of the sympathy he suddenly felt for her. Which meant she would simply have to work hard to convince him—and everyone else—she was *fine*.

About the Author

Sara Richardson grew up chasing adventure in Colorado's rugged mountains. She's climbed to the top of a fourteen-thousand-foot peak at midnight, swum through Class IV rapids, completed her wilderness first-aid certification, and spent seven days at a time tromping through the wilderness with a thirty-pound backpack strapped to her shoulders.

Eventually Sara did the responsible thing and got an education in writing and journalism. After a brief stint in the corporate writing world, she stopped ignoring the voices in her head and started writing fiction. Now she uses her experience as a mountain adventure guide to write stories that incorporate adventure with romance. Sara lives and plays in Colorado, where she still indulges her adventurous spirit, with her saint of a husband and two young sons.

You can learn more at:
SaraRichardson.net
Twitter @SaraR_Books
Facebook.com/SaraRichardsonBooks
Instagram @Sarar_Books

Unbroken

A LOVELESS, TEXAS NOVELLA

JAY CROWNOVER

FOREVER

To my mom, who pretty much came up with the entire premise of this book on a flight home from Paris. I'm pretty sure she always wanted me to bring a cowboy home instead of a punk rocker.

Prologue

CREW

My ribs were no match for the set of heavy brass knuckles.

"Son of a bitch," I wheezed out.

I didn't hear the bones crack, but I felt them and nearly puked when blinding pain shot through my body from the blow. My eyes watered, and it was a struggle to breathe, but I managed not to face-plant on the cement in front of me.

"You ever been kicked by a horse? It feels almost the same." How I managed to hold on to the sarcasm while my whole side was on fire was a mystery. But I wasn't ever the type to let anyone else know they had the upper hand.

The cement floor in the basement of the bar I shouldn't have been at had questionable stains scattered from wall to wall. It looked like it was made to specifically withstand the bloodshed that came with the kind of beating I was currently taking. The man wielding the old-fashioned knuckles pulled back his fist and lined up his next shot with my face. I couldn't suppress the shudder when his arm started to move toward me. I knew my night was going to go to shit when they tied me to a chair, hands zip-tied behind my back. There was no way to block the blow or defend myself from the upcoming pain.

I'd suffered more than one broken nose over the course of my rodeo career. I'd had my head knocked around by an excited bronco and narrowly missed being stepped on by a pissed-off horse or bull on the regular. I'd always been lucky none of the damage was too serious and that I healed fast. But it was a known fact that everyone's luck eventually ran out. I'd been borrowing against mine for so long it was no surprise I was about to have my skull caved in by a guy who looked like a scary combination of The Rock and Vin Diesel. I'd been heading here, to this exact spot, this exact situation, for months.

I was a risk-taker, an adrenaline junkie, and a gambler by nature. I chased a rush, followed after danger and excitement like an eager puppy. My older brother wanted to save the world; I was the one who set it on fire. The need for a thrill, the longing for a challenge was what led me to the rodeo. I was a Central Texas boy through and through. I knew how to ride a horse almost as early as I knew how to walk. So it wasn't a surprise to anyone when I dropped out of high school and started chasing the amateur rodeo circuit in Texas. It also wasn't a shock to anyone that I had an instinctive knack for staying on the back of a twisting, turning beast that wanted nothing more than to drop me on my very fine ass. I found my calling and stuck with it, broken bones and all, until I reached pro level.

But in true Lawton fashion, once I was on top, the only way for me to go from there was down. My fall started slowly at first. I had too much money, and too many people putting tempting but no-good things directly in my path. The spike of excitement from breaking in a bucking, writhing bronc had started to wane, my senses numbed from too much booze and too many late nights with willing women. I needed something more, a different edge to walk precariously along.

When I slipped and fell, it was no surprise I'd landed with a thud, here in this dive bar. If you asked anyone who still loved me, this had been my destination for a long time coming. I forced myself to keep my eyes open. I might be a screwup, but I was a screwup who faced my repercussions head-on. There was no hiding from this. I was a little pissed that the last thing I was going to see before my face got smashed in was this snarling behemoth, not a pretty girl, or a blazing southern sunset. Those were things I wanted to remember.

The air whistled a sharp warning as the other man's tree trunk–like arm continued to swing toward my head. Sweat dripped into my eyes and down my temples as I tried to hold perfectly still and accept my fate stoically. Even though my older brother, Case, wasn't here, I still wanted him to be proud of me for taking what was coming my way like a man. As much as I resented him, he's always been my hero, the person I looked up to the most. Case was an annoying bastard, always questioning my motives and my integrity, but that never stopped me from trying to win his approval. I told myself, if Case were the one on his knees in a dingy basement out in the middle of nowhere, he wouldn't make a sound. So, I was determined to suffer through this in absolute silence, no matter how many bones were broken or how many teeth I ended up losing.

I braced for the impact, but right before the rings of the glinting, metal knuckles made contact, a hand reached out and stopped the momentum of the swing. The big guy grunted in annoyance but quietly stepped back as another man, this one dressed impeccably in a three-piece suit, stepped in front of me. I let out a pained breath and let my head fall forward. I felt sweat drip slowly down my temples as it mixed with blood. I knew this was far from over, but I was taking the reprieve to collect myself.

"Hello, cowboy. Seems like you're having a rough day." The voice was mocking and smooth. I hated it.

Looking up into the calm and completely unaffected face of Dante Vargas, I wondered if the brass knuckles would've been easier to take than whatever punishment the soulless gangster was bound to hand down. He was the man I owed over half a million dollars. I made good money; my problem was holding on to it. I spent it as fast as it came in, so while coming up with that sum shouldn't be much of a problem, it was in fact a huge problem. I didn't have the money, Dante knew that, but he let me keep making bets anyway. He had me over a barrel, and we both knew it. This beatdown was nothing more than a friendly reminder that he owned my ass, and the time was coming for me to make good on whatever scheme he had in mind.

I couldn't remember what I placed my first bet on, but I did recall the buzz that ran through me when I won a truckload of cash for nothing more than a lucky guess. I had money to spend, and it was a vice that was easy to hide from prying eyes, both the public's and my family's. I convinced myself it was harmless fun. But before I knew it, I was so deep in debt I lost my condo in Dallas, my truck, the entire college fund I'd been working on saving up for my sister, and my great-granddaddy's pocket watch, which was pretty much the only thing my old man had ever given to me.

"You lost your cowboy hat somewhere along the way, Crew." Vargas's tone was lightly sardonic and sent a shiver down my spine. It took every ounce of self-control I had not to flinch when he slid the blade of a very sharp knife right next to the skin on my wrists to cut through the zip ties keeping my hands behind me. He was setting me free, but there was also an implied warning in having the blade so close to my unprotected skin.

I tilted my chin defiantly and narrowed my eyes at him. The enforcer standing behind him let out a low growl of warning, and I wanted nothing more than to flip him off, but I refrained. "Must have fallen off when your boys hustled me into your limo."

I never went anywhere without a black Stetson on my head. It was part of my brand, a trademark of my public image, and a security blanket to hide behind whenever anyone tried to get close enough to look behind the mask I wore so effortlessly.

"That's a shame. It was a nice hat." Dante smiled at me, and the expression made my skin crawl. "You lose a lot of nice things, don't you, Crew?"

I grunted in response and tried to focus on his words and not on the pain radiating from my side. "I think you know the answer to that question, Vargas, seeing as you're the one who's taken most of those nice things away from me."

"Ahhh... well, that's not exactly accurate, now is it? You took risks, and they didn't pay off. That's hardly my fault. Unfortunately, you've got nothing left of value to barter with, unless you want to talk about your sister's bar back in your hometown. She seems to be turning a tidy little profit down there, and I'm always on the lookout for legitimate business opportunities to get my hands on." The way Dante watched for my reaction when he mentioned my sister should have been an indication he was prepared for me to react violently.

Which I did.

Cracked ribs and bruised body be damned. I was on my feet in a heartbeat, reaching for his throat. I forgot all about the brute with the brass knuckles until they smashed into my cheek and sent me flying backward onto my ass. The cement made for a rough landing, and the coppery scent of blood made my head spin, but I still managed to bark out, "Stay away from my family, Vargas." Especially my sister. She was the only one who still tolerated me most days.

I swiped at the blood on my face and narrowed my eyes at Dante as he started to pace back and forth in front of me with his hands laced together behind his back.

"Don't give me a reason to go anywhere near them, Crew. I have a way for you to earn back some of the money you owe me. The key word is *some*. Even if you do this, you're still going to have to come up with the balance, plus interest." He grinned at me again, and there was no mistaking the malicious gleam in his gaze. We both knew there was no way in hell I would ever be able to come up with that kind of money while the outrageous amount of interest continued to accrue. I was never going to get out of this mess. The hole was so deep and dark I was no longer sure which way was up and which way was down.

Sadly, this was a situation I'd created, and now the only thing to do was ride it out. It was a good thing I'd made a name for myself. Being able to hold on when the ride was brutal and rough was a rare talent. I knew today was coming. I even smiled at my last event and put up a charming, excited front when my new, unexpected endorsement deal had been announced to the media. I played the role of cocky, confident cowboy to perfection, acting like I was untouchable and unstoppable, all while knowing as soon as I stepped out of the arena in Vegas, it was time to pay up. Even with the endorsements and the second-place win for the night, there was no money. The debt was so much bigger than I was.

"What do you want me to do?" I pretended my voice didn't crack when I asked the question, and I acted like my heart didn't fall out of my chest when Dante answered....

Chapter 1

DELLA

I sneezed and tried to hide the gesture behind my hand. The woman sitting next to me gave me a dirty look and turned her nose up in my direction. I rolled my eyes in response and sneezed again. I couldn't care less what someone dressed in painted-on denim—covered in bejeweled embellishments—and a skintight plaid shirt thought of me. I sincerely doubted this woman had ever been to Fifth Avenue and suspected she couldn't spell *haute couture*. We were part of two very different worlds, and I resented the fact I was currently being forced to spend a sweltering afternoon in hers. Especially now that I realized I was allergic to straw, or maybe it was one of the animals that were making the arena smell like the inside of a barn? The closest I'd ever been to a horse before today was when one of my ex-boyfriends thought it would be romantic to take a ride around Central Park at Christmastime. I didn't remember sneezing my damn face off then, but that was probably because I was freezing and too busy fending off wandering hands. That particular guy was an ex for more than one reason, not just the typical one where I decided I was bored and walked away.

I sniffed again and turned when the bedazzled woman cleared her throat and wordlessly offered me a tissue. I took it with a weak grin and wiped my eyes. I was sure I had mascara smeared all over my face, along with a red nose. Dust covering my Louboutins. I was wholly unprepared and overdressed for a rodeo. I should have known my usual wardrobe wouldn't cut it in this kind of environment, but I'd been wearing designer duds and sky-high heels with an expertly applied face as armor for so long, I felt naked and exposed without the expensive trappings.

"Thank you. I think I'm allergic to…everything." I blinked my watery eyes and noticed the woman's return smile was much more genuine than mine.

"Yeah. You actually look like this *is* your first rodeo." She didn't bother to hide a snicker at my expense.

I nodded miserably. "It is." And it would be my last if I had anything to say about it.

The only reason my ass was parked in this arena was because my father's million-dollar investment was about to take my dream, my precious baby, my future, and my stake in my family's company under. I wasn't going to let that happen without putting up a fight. I'd never been on board with the plan to sign Crew Lawton as the face of our company's new men's skin care line. This product launch had been my idea, years of personal investment and work. It was set to be the project that would finally force my father to see I could take over the business and move our brand toward what was modern and happening now. I was targeting upwardly mobile men who were out to make an impression in both the boardroom and the bedroom. I envisioned suave and sophisticated gentlemen in Tom Ford suits who wined and dined heiresses and A-list actresses. Nowhere in any of my plans was there room for a man like Crew Lawton. And there definitely wasn't a rodeo with horses, bulls, poop, and mud anywhere on my vision boards.

"They're a good time, and you can't beat the scenery." The woman gave me a knowing look and inclined her chin toward the dirt-filled center of the floor in front of us. A blond man, tall and whipcord lean, was getting tossed around like a rag-doll on the back of a beautiful, rust-colored horse. The people seated around me seemed to be holding their collective breath as his body twisted and arched with every wild move the big animal made.

I couldn't see his face because my eyes were still itchy and watery, but I saw enough to determine the scenery was indeed no hardship. Unfortunately, the *scenery* was what got me into this mess in the first place.

I'd spent enough hours on social media stalking the man to know that there was no denying Crew Lawton was ridicu-lously good-looking. His pictures showed he was the perfect kind of cowboy—all rough and rugged in an effortless sort of way. He had the quintessential bad-boy image down pat. His dark hair was just a little too long. His chiseled face with its razor-sharp jawline and electric blue eyes were the stuff of secret daydreams and grown-up fantasies. His face, and the incredible body that went with it, were definitely worth a million dollars; they just weren't right for selling *my* products. I was searching for James Bond levels of so-phistication, yet I'd ended up with someone oozing raw masculinity and in-your-face sex appeal. Said sex appeal might work for women in the market for products to spoil the men in their lives. But I was banking on a target audience of men who had the desire, and the money, to buy my line to use in their everyday routines. Guys like Crew Lawton did not care about fine lines and wrinkles. He did not obsess over the sustainability of the ingredients in his body wash and shampoo. And there was no way in hell anyone could ever convince me he had a regular grooming routine he felt lost without. He was so far from the man I was trying to sell to it wasn't even funny, and again I wondered how my father could be so clueless.

Since the woman next to me was being nice and offered a diversion from how miserable and awkward I felt, I did my best to make small talk with her.

"Are you from around here?" I asked with fake interest.

She gave me a wide grin and replied with the last thing I'd expected her to say. "I'm from LA. I'm a location scout for TV and film." She grinned wider at my gasp and casually dropped the name of a huge big-budget movie she was getting ready to start working on.

"So the movie has to do with the rodeo?" I knew they could be popular on the big screen, but I tended to stick to films with subtitles.

My new friend snickered and bumped her shoulder against mine. "I'm here for the cowboys, Crew in particular. I met him a few years ago, scouting for another project. The director wanted him to sign on as an extra but he refused. I was smitten. I go and see him ride whenever I get the chance. He's unbelievable." She gave me another bump and laughingly explained she was what rodeo regulars referred to as a "buckle-bunny." Apparently, it was an actual *thing* to follow the rodeo circuit around chasing after the bull and bronc riders. I had no idea rodeo riders had their own groupies, and I remembered clearly arguing with my father over whether or not Crew was famous enough to attach to any project, let alone one the scale of mine. I was fascinated as the surprisingly well-spoken and obviously successful woman next to me gushed like a high school girl over the man I'd started to hate the minute my father mentioned his name.

"Crew's been the one to watch for the last couple of years. There's just something about him that fans can't get enough of. He has this swagger, this confidence that is totally sexy. It makes him come off as godlike and untouchable. And he's always up to some kind of trouble. Last year he was embroiled in a scandal with the newest star of the country music scene. The gossip rags said he knocked her up and then cheated on her with her best friend...who just happens to be the star of one of those vampire shows on TV. It was all over the media for days, and somehow Crew's the one who came out of it all with his reputation intact, if not emboldened by the claims. He has the golden touch, and it seems like he can do no wrong." She sounded absolutely dreamy when she talked about him, and the lascivious gleam in her eyes didn't go unnoticed. Crew inspired lust, but he did not inspire confidence.

"If he's golden, why has he been losing so much lately?" I asked the question quietly, worried I might offend her and her megasize crush.

I didn't know much about the sport, but I'd started keeping an eye on Crew as soon as he took the advance my father threw his way for agreeing to be the face of my product line. I had been clueless about anything rodeo related and still was, for the most part, but it was easy enough to read the headlines and follow the commentary about how the Texas-born cowboy had gone from the top of his game to the bottom of the barrel after each consecutive ride. Speculation ran the gamut from drug use to problems in his personal life. His concentration and dedication were both in question, and more than one article heralded the end of his, up to this point, stellar career.

He couldn't afford to keep losing, and I couldn't afford for him to take my brainchild down with him.

The glittery woman shifted uncomfortably, as if the man we were discussing might be able to hear her speaking ill about him. After an awkward pause, she sighed and pushed some of her curly blond hair over her shoulder. "No one really knows why he's riding like shit. At first, we all chalked it up to a few bad days. He likes to party and tends to be a little wild, plus he's getting older, and this sport is brutal on the body. Those of us who follow him just thought time was catching up with him. But each ride is worse than the one before it. It's like he's not even trying to stay on anymore. He won't answer questions when he's asked about what's going on, but he's passed all the mandatory drug screenings before each event, so it's not that."

I huffed out an annoyed sigh, which was immediately followed by a flurry of sneezes. I swore under my breath when they subsided and swiped angrily at my messy face. Of course, it couldn't be drugs or something else overtly obvious. There was a proprietary clause in the contract Crew signed with my father. If it had been something like an addiction, I would have been able to oust him with no fuss, but my luck wasn't that good. It never had been.

My new friend glanced over at me with genuine concern brimming in her eyes. "If he finishes anywhere out of the top three today, he won't be able to compete in Nationals. He'll lose his endorsements and so much money. It'll be a tragedy after how much work he's put into getting to this level."

I thought tragedy was a bit of an exaggeration, but the woman really seemed despondent over the possibility of how this might be the end for this infamous cowboy.

I was going to ask more questions, because I found her far more informative than Google, but she suddenly leaped to her feet, hands clapping, as she screamed Crew's name from the top of her lungs. Pretty much everyone seated around me climbed to their feet and followed her lead. Reluctantly, I also stood and tried to focus my blurry gaze on the arena floor below.

A hush fell over the crowd and there was a loud clang as metal hit metal when the chute opened, and man and beast were released. The horse was black, so dark it almost looked blue under the lights. The man perched precariously on its muscular back had hair to match. It was currently trapped under a dark gray cowboy hat, but it was long enough for the wild strands to be stuck to the back of his neck as he strained and fought to stay on the bucking horse's back. I'd researched enough to know he rode both with and without a saddle, depending on the competition. Today there didn't seem to be anything between his tight Wranglers and the glistening coat of the furiously thrashing horse underneath him.

People cheered, chanting his name over and over again. I knew the goal was for him to stay on for eight seconds and to encourage the roughest, toughest ride possible in that time frame. He had to keep one hand lifted above his head and make it all look impossibly effortless as a thousand-pound animal did its best to toss him to the ground. I could see why people were enamored with him. In the flesh, there was an air about him. It spoke to the recklessness of his profession, and the courage it took to climb up and ride day in and day out. He seemed fearless and impressive, even from this distance. I could clearly see the swagger my new glittery friend mentioned. I could also see why my father thought we should use his face to sell my products. He was mesmerizing, and I, like everyone else in the arena, couldn't tear my eyes off him as he writhed and rolled in a continuous glide with the horse. It was almost like a dance, graceful and elegant, but tinged with a hint of danger and brutality. I suddenly understood why Sparkles made it a point to follow him around, anxious for any of his attention.

Then, just as quickly as the excitement and exaltation began, it died a quiet death as the beautiful man seemed to suddenly lose all coordination and form. One second he was sitting tall and proud, owning the chaos he was tied to, and the next he was flying through the air and landing in an undignified heap and a cloud of dust on the ground. The horse continued to buck and thrash, while a murmur of disapproval and dissatisfaction worked through the crowd. Everyone sank back in their seats, but I stayed standing, watching as the dark-haired cowboy climbed to his feet, dejection evident in every line and curve of his muscled form.

"I can't believe he lost," I heard, and looked down at my seatmate. I was slightly horrified to see she had tears in her eyes.

With a sigh, I pushed a hand through my wavy blond bob and muttered. "I can."

Crew losing was why I was here. If he couldn't be the untouchable cowboy my father wanted, then I was determined to turn him into the debonair gentleman *I* wanted. I just had no clue how much work I was going to have cut out for me.

And I didn't think for a second that the sullen, rebellious man, who was walking away with his head down and his shoulders hunched in defeat, was going to make it easy on me.

Chapter 2

CREW

I threw my hat across the length of the RV. It served as my home away from home while I was on the road. Luckily, the luxe vehicle belonged to one of my sponsors, so I hadn't had the opportunity to gamble it away along with everything else of value I used to own. I kicked the wood of one of the kitchen cabinets and plowed my hands through my sweaty hair.

I lost.

My season was ruined.

So was my name.

And my career, for all intents and purposes.

It was all over.

I knew what people were saying. I'd lost my edge. Something was going on with me, and a lot of folks thought it was drugs, but they couldn't explain away my clean drug screens. They were all way off base. I was losing because I had to. I tossed away every single thing I'd ever worked for because that was the only way to keep Vargas away from my family in Loveless, Texas. He was stacking huge bets against me, knowing I was going to throw each and every ride for the rest of the season. Each ride I lost, Vargas took fifty to a hundred thousand off my debt, and won twice that from his unfair odds. He was making a fortune on my misfortune, and the entire situation left a sour taste in my mouth. The upside was that this situation finally dulled the gambling itch that lived under my skin.

When my older brother warned me I was on a dangerous path, I didn't listen. I never did. My younger sister was worried about me. But I brushed her concern off and went right on pretending that I was on top of the world. I was good at acting like I had my shit together. I was good at putting on a song and dance when the reality was this . . . me on the brink of paying the ultimate price for every bad decision I couldn't help but make. Sometimes I felt like I was compelled to fail, to screw up. At times I wondered if it was hardwired into my DNA. But then I remembered my perfect, heroic, and faultless older brother and realized it was just me, the only Lawton destined to be on his knees about to get his face permanently rearranged because I couldn't resist making one last bet.

The thing that pissed me off though was that even after the humiliation and horror of these last few rides, Vargas still wasn't calling us even. He insisted I still owed him over two hundred thousand dollars. Just the thought of it had me pulling at my hair in frustration and aiming another useless kick at the interior of the RV.

I was swearing up a storm, cursing myself and every move I'd made over the last five years when the door behind me swung open. Even though I was a loser, a failure, a man caught in a spiral downward, it hadn't seemed to hurt my appeal with the ladies. After every ride, no matter how poorly

I did, there was still a line of willing women waiting outside my trailer, eager to do their best to try and cheer me up. I hadn't been in the mood for frivolous moments that stroked my missing ego. I was too tired, too disgusted with myself to keep the mask of the carefree cowboy in place. The real Crew, the man who was vulnerable and incredibly damaged at the moment, was too close to the surface for me to spend time trying to charm an expectant stranger.

Without turning around, I laced my fingers behind my neck and looked down at the dirty, scuffed toes of my boots. Typically, after a ride, I was full of adrenaline and excitement. Even after a genuine loss, I could revel in the sound of the crowd and the determination to do better coursing through my blood. Now, all I felt was remorse and disgust. I was an embarrassment to the sport and to myself. I definitely wasn't fit for any kind of company at the moment.

"I'm busy right now. I don't have time to entertain guests, sorry." I was anything but. I wondered if my manager had let the woman in. I knew it was a woman without looking up because I could hear the click of her heels as she entered the RV, a light floral scent fighting to overtake the smell of sweat and horse that clung to me. My manager was under strict orders to keep everyone away from me after the event. I was too close to the edge and way too unpredictable to mingle with the masses right now. But the guy was sick of me losing and probably realized he was going to be out of a job soon, since my career was in the toilet. He might have let the intruder in as payback.

"I guess it's a good thing I'm not here for entertainment, Mr. Lawton. I'm here to talk business." The woman's voice was sharp, direct, and had a hint of an accent. Her words were also followed by a less-than-delicate sneeze, which had me turning around to face her.

She definitely didn't look like the women who normally circled my trailer looking for a way in. In fact, she didn't look like the kind of woman who ever crossed my path. No, she looked like the kind of woman who purposely walked to the other side of the street when she saw someone like me coming.

Who came to a rodeo in a pinstripe business suit, complete with a silk blouse and spiked high heels? Who lingered in a place full of dirt and dust with a face painted like it was going to be on the cover of *Vogue*, and with hair that had to cost a fortune to look *that* artfully messy and tousled? She was so incredibly out of place it was laughable, not to mention each time she sneezed it made her eyes water and turned her nose red under her flawless makeup.

She was so obviously miserable, I couldn't hold back a grin as I asked, "What kind of business could someone like you possibly have with me?" Because it was clear she wasn't here for a quick roll between the sheets. She looked like she didn't have a clue what sweaty, wild, uninhibited sex was like, or how good it could feel. I'd bet good money she was a strictly missionary type of girl, one who wouldn't let a man touch her until all the lights were off. Only, there would be no more betting, and I didn't have any money left.

I heaved a sigh as the woman moved farther into my personal space. She cast a look around the RV, her tiny nose wrinkling in obvious distaste. The place wasn't tidy, but it was far from a pigsty, and this particular model of RV was top-of-the-line and tricked out in all the best ways. It cost more than some people's houses, but it was clear, this woman was unimpressed with both the accommodations and the man who called them home.

"My name is Della Deveaux. I believe you know my father, Max." At my blank look her elegant, if somewhat messy, face pulled into a fierce frown. "He is the president and CEO of the Deveaux beauty empire. Recently, he signed you to an exclusive contract to represent our new line of products, Sophistiqué."

I blinked at her and lowered my hands to my hips as I wracked my brain, trying to remember doing business with anyone named Max, or talking to anyone who had anything to do with makeup. Those weren't the types of endorsement deals I attached my name to. I liked to represent only products and companies I actually had a use for. Sure, there was a random underwear ad here or there, and an occasional cologne or watch endorsement I sold out to represent when I started to get really desperate to pay Vargas back, but makeup...no way would I have agreed to anything like that. No matter how desperate I was for some quick cash.

"I don't know what you're talking about, lady. I've never heard of you, your father, or his company." I watched as she blinked at me in dull surprise and shifted nervously on those ridiculous shoes of hers. Reluctantly, I noted she had a pair of really nice legs underneath the tailored suit pants she was wearing. In fact, all of her seemed to be shaped very sweetly under the stuffy, inappropriate clothing. I was so used to flashy and in-your-face women, the type who knew they were sexy and did everything in their power to remind the world they had it going on. This woman's subtle, hidden appeal was a refreshing change of pace. When she wrinkled her nose at me again, I noticed she had a smattering of freckles across the bridge that she appeared to try and hide away, but they were too dark for her makeup to conceal. I found those little dots entirely more appealing than I should. They made her seem less stiff, less uptight and put together.

"Mr. Lawton..."

I lifted a hand and shook my head at her. "Crew. You can just call me Crew." Mr. Lawton was my old man, and Officer Lawton was my older brother. I was Crew, nothing more and nothing less.

She tilted her head to the side, and her slightly reddened eyes narrowed at me a fraction. "Fine, Crew, we've already paid you a sizable advance on the contract you signed. I have concerns about you being the right person for this campaign, and even though my father is convinced your face is perfect, I doubt your ability to follow through with a project of this scale after watching your performance today. I'm here because I want you to understand that every move you make, every word out of your mouth, every second of your day belongs to me now. You are my living, breathing paper doll until this campaign is under way. You are going to earn the balance remaining on your contract. It will not be handed to you."

It was my turn to blink at her in shock. "How much was the advance you paid, and how much is the remaining balance?"

Wordlessly, she bent and reached for a leather bag I hadn't noticed sitting at her feet. After a few seconds of rummaging around, she handed me a thick stack of papers with a fancy letterhead on the top and her last name in bold. Apparently, Deveaux was a name I should know, and I was starting to get an uneasy feeling as I flipped through pages and pages of legal speak, all of it initialed and signed by me. Only, it wasn't my signature—close, but not exact.

"Did my manager let you into this trailer?" I asked the question quietly, trying to keep my cool as I noticed the amount of the advance, three hundred thousand, and the remaining balance, seven hundred thousand. It took every ounce of willpower I possessed not to flinch when I noticed the account information on the contract wasn't mine, but the one where my manager's cut of my winnings and public appearance fees went. The man must have known he was on a sinking ship and taken the steps he thought necessary to keep his head above water while he watched me drown.

"No. I met a woman in the stands who had an unnerving amount of knowledge about all things Crew Lawton. She pointed me in the direction of this trailer. No one was around, and the door was unlocked, so I let myself in." She had the grace to blush over her clear lack of manners and decorum. "I wanted to make sure I had a chance to talk to you face-to-face. I apologize for being pushy." She didn't sound like she was sorry in the slightest.

"Did your father never once question why we never met in person when this contract was being negotiated?" I lifted an eyebrow, knowing the answer already. According to the paperwork in my hand, the US branch of the beauty empire was in New York, but the business was actually based in Paris, which explained her slight accent, a smooth hybrid between East Coast and Parisian. At least that's what I would guess, since I'd only been to New York once and had only heard someone speak French on TV.

She huffed out a breath and crossed her arms over her chest. "Your manager said you were too busy. He negotiated the contract with your lawyer and ours. My father appreciated how dedicated you were to your previous engagements. After watching your performance today, I have to question how wise he was to sign you without meeting you first. He was determined to bring you on board. No amount of arguing or persuasion would change his mind."

We'd all been had.

My manager, Marty, was good at his job and knew how to work a deal. He'd been with me a long time and knew I would probably turn down any offer coming from a froufrou company like Deveaux. It looked like he'd taken it upon himself to sign my name on the dotted line and commit me to the contract without any input from me, making some nice pocket change for himself along the way if he'd banked the advance. If he wasn't outside my trailer, I figured he was long gone after that final loss of the season. I could go after him for the money he stole if I wasn't in the poor house, and really, how could I walk away from something that very well might be the only way to get Vargas off my back and out of my life for good?

I dragged a rough hand over my face and looked at the woman who had barged uninvited into my nightmare. "What exactly do I have to do in order to fulfill this contract and get the rest of the balance?"

Her hazel eyes widened a fraction, as if she was prepared for me to put up a fight and not acquiesce so easily. Normally, I would have fought tooth and nail to get out of this mess, but right now, the prissy, proper blonde was actually the answer to my prayers. She was holding the light at the end of the very dark tunnel I'd been plunged into. And the only option I had was to move toward her.

She swallowed audibly and once again shifted her weight in those expensive-ass shoes. "You have to do everything I say and follow my instructions exactly."

I sighed. How hard could that be, and honestly, what other choice did I have?

"Alrighty, Ms. Priss. Do with me what you will."

Lord help us both.

Chapter 3

DELLA

A million and one questions were running through my mind after Crew agreed so easily to fall in line and play by my rules. It seemed out of character for him to be so passive and agreeable. At least from everything I'd read about him in the press and based upon his less-than-stellar first impression. The man was obviously wound so tightly, any little thing might cause him to snap. It was evident in every line of his tall, strong body. Every muscle he had, and there were a lot of them, was pulled so tight and tense that he almost seemed to be vibrating. After hastily throwing a few items into a worn, leather duffel bag and placing a frantic call to someone I assumed was his lawyer to change the banking information on the contract, he coolly informed me he was ready to go. He didn't ask where. He didn't ask how long we would be gone. He didn't seem at all concerned to be walking away from his entire life while I molded him into an entirely new person. I found it all unnerving and unsettling as I ushered him toward the car and driver I'd hired to chauffeur me around for the weekend.

I'd anticipated a fight. I thought I was going to have a much harder negotiation on my hands, so I wasn't as quick to skip town as Crew was. I had to go back to the hotel and pack. I also needed to call my pilot and make sure the company jet was ready to fly back to Manhattan ASAP. I spent the car ride to my hotel on the phone, sneaking sideways glances at the silent man seated next to me. His fingers tapped against his knee and a small tic in his razor-sharp jawline kept twitching. His bright blue gaze was trained on something outside the window, making him appear to be miles and miles away even though he was close enough to touch. At first, I thought he was being polite while I handled business over the phone, but I soon realized he was barely aware of my presence and he was totally indifferent to everything that was going to happen next.

I barely got a nod when we pulled up to the hotel, and I told him I would only be a few minutes while I packed and checked out. On my way up to my room, I called my father and wasn't surprised when I was told he was unavailable. Through gritted teeth, I left a message telling him I was on my way to New York with his cowboy in tow. I informed him the man's professional reputation was now in tatters, but I was going to do *anything* to keep my product launch on track. I sounded more like a whiny teenager at the end, but my father had an uncanny ability to bring that out in me, even though he never seemed to notice. It was a vicious circle, me trying everything to get him to pay attention, to acknowledge me, to appreciate me, only for him to treat me, alternately, like the furniture or one of the lackeys who worked for him. Not once in the six years that I'd overseen the entire product development team at Deveaux Beauty had my father ever given me credit for dragging the business, kicking and screaming, into the modern—and exceedingly profitable—beauty market. If it weren't for me, we would never have our own storefronts—brick-and-mortar shops that rivaled Sephora—from LA to Singapore.

Still grumbling under my breath about difficult men, I stopped short when I approached the car, tugging my Tumi carry-on behind me. I felt my jaw drop slightly and heard my breath make a soft whooshing sound as it rushed out of my lungs.

Crew was leaning against the side of the luxury car, one long leg bent so the heel of his cowboy boot was pressed against the black paint. His head was bent down, the brim from his cowboy hat casting shadows over his face, making him look dangerous and mysterious in the best way. He had a cell phone to his ear and his other hand shoved in the front pocket of his skintight jeans. The entire scene was a heady, sexy clashing of modern and classic masculinity. I felt my heart thud heavily in my chest as ideas started whirling in my mind.

"I don't care, Kody. I know you think you can take care of yourself and that you're the baddest bitch in all of Central Texas, but if these guys show up in Loveless, I need you to promise me that you'll tell Case. I don't know how long I'm going to be gone for, but I wouldn't put it past them to come looking for me. You cannot mess around with them. You cannot go up against them. Do you understand what I'm saying to you?" His deep voice was rumbling with irritation, and his already tense body seemed to tighten even more as whoever was on the other end of the phone obviously didn't tell him what he wanted to hear. "Goddammit! Don't make me call Case. That's the last thing I want to do, but I will if you can't stop being a brat for five minutes."

There was more grumbling, followed by some more colorful swearing, but eventually he seemed to get the reply he wanted, and he lowered the phone and pushed himself off the car. He dragged his hands over his face and suddenly realized he was no longer alone in the parking lot. Without a word he moved toward me, taking the handle of my small suitcase from me and hauling it to the trunk of the car. Someone had taught him manners somewhere along the way, and I felt a stab of guilt that I was surprised by that fact. I needed to stop being so judgmental and prickly. My entire campaign rested on this guy's brawny, wide shoulders. It would be so much better for me if we could work together without animosity and anger.

"Is everything all right?" I tried not to fidget under the sharpness of that neon-blue gaze as it snapped back in my direction. I wasn't prepared for him to be so intense. When I pictured a cowboy, a rodeo star, I imagined someone laid-back and easygoing. Crew Lawton was neither of those things. He was forceful and enigmatic. Way more intriguing and alluring than I was ready to give him credit for.

"Just my little sister being a pain in the ass as usual. She's got more attitude than me and my brother combined, and she tends to pick fights she knows she can't win when it comes to protecting her family." He opened the car door for me and ushered me inside.

I tried to hide the way I shivered when I brushed against him as I slid into my seat. He was in no way my type. He was, in fact, the opposite of my type completely. There was no reason for me to shiver. There was no reason the spacious backseat of the car seemed to shrink as he folded his big body into the seat next to me. There was no logical explanation for the way it was suddenly hard to breathe, and for my heart to be beating so hard and loud I was conscious of every single pump.

I cleared my throat nervously and made a big deal of smoothing out my blazer and pants. "So you have a fairly big family?"

He cocked his head to the side and his mouth quirked in a smirk at my obvious attempt to make small talk.

"I have an older brother who's a cop, and a younger sister who's a bar owner. They both still live in my hometown. My dad is around, but I don't have much to do with him. My mom passed away when I was a teenager, but her folks live in the same town where I grew up, and I go back to see them every now and then. My granddad was the one who got me into horses and eventually into rodeo. They're all good folks, except for my old man. I could never lay eyes on him again in this lifetime and be okay with it." The smirk on his face turned into a grimace. I wasn't sure if the change in expression was because of the reminder of his father, or the fact that he had given so much personal information away. "What about you? You have family you're tight with?"

I shrugged in a practiced move. I was used to hiding how touchy the subject of family was with me but figured, since he'd relented so easily to letting me drag him across the country and had been so transparent about his own history, I could give him a little insight.

"No. I'm an only child, and my mom also passed away when I was very young. It was always just my father and me, but when I was little, he was always working. He took over the company from his father when he was very young and was determined to make his own name in the industry. When my grandfather retired, he and my grandmother moved to the south of France. I didn't see them much before that, and never after they left. I was sent to a boarding school in Connecticut when I was eleven and only saw my dad on holidays and over breaks. When I went to work for Deveaux

Beauty, I assumed I would see him more and we would get to spend more time together, but the opposite happened. My father spends most of his time in Paris, and I spend most of my time in New York." There was no disguising the bitterness that colored my tone. "Now I hardly see him, even on holidays."

Crew made a sympathetic noise low in his throat and shifted uncomfortably on the leather seat. "Can't pick where we're from, or the people we're related to. Probably a good thing. My brother, Case, would have cut ties and thrown me back years ago if he had a choice. But because we're family he can't stop himself from being a protective big brother; he still pulls my ass out of the fire time and time again. And Kody, my sister, she's the only woman in my entire life who's ever been able to put up with my shit for longer than a week. They got the short stick in the sibling department, but I'm a lucky bastard, since blood makes it impossible for them to walk away from me."

I shifted on the seat and forcibly pulled my eyes away from his before I drowned in the endless blue depths. I fidgeted uneasily, noticing that now since I was no longer sneezing and sniffling, he smelled like leather and sunshine. Something very manly and fresh that I would never have thought I would find appealing, but suddenly did.

"Your family isn't proud of everything you've accomplished in your career? I don't follow your sport, but when my father decided to sign you I did some basic research. You're a big deal in the rodeo world. You've done well for yourself up until this season." I tried to speak with more authority than I possessed. It grated that he was a stranger, a virtual unknown, and yet my entire future was tied to him.

"Sure, they were proud. But they also know me well enough to know that no matter how good I was, or how much

I loved riding, I was bound to fuck it all up. They've been waiting for the other boot to drop, exactly like it did this season. I've let them down my entire life, so their expectations are pretty low when it comes to me." He puffed out a raspy laugh and turned his head to look out the window, effectively ending the conversation. He sounded resigned to the fact that he was nothing more than a failure.

"Well, if it makes you feel any better, I have no expectations. You are starting with a blank slate with me, Mr. Lawton." I folded my hands primly in my lap and watched out of the corner of my eye as a familiar smirk lifted the edges of his mouth.

"I highly doubt I'm going to be the man you need, Ms. Deveaux, but I sure am gonna do my best. At least until I get the rest of the money you owe me."

As long as he was willing to try, I could work with that.

Chapter 4

CREW

I didn't skip town, Vargas. I told you, I had to figure out a way to get the money I owe you now that my season is over." And probably my career, because of him. I glared out the window, taking in the blinding, chaotic lights from Times Square. This was a different kind of chaos than the type I was used to, but just as wild and just as entrancing. The flow of people, the energy emanating from the busy streets, even the heavy windows of the fancy hotel Della Deveaux had dropped me off at couldn't totally block the noise. It all rushed around me, calling to me, tempting me to do things that should be expressly forbidden. There was trouble down there, the kind that would be so much fun to find. The kind that would bite me in the ass and screw everything up as soon as the sun was back in the sky. "Stop threatening me, Vargas. I don't like it."

The other man snorted, and I could picture him narrowing his dark, beady eyes. My hand was wrapped so tightly around my phone, my fingers were starting to hurt. I wanted all of this to be over. I wanted out of this city that looked like it could eat me alive, and I wanted out from under the thumb of the blond dynamo who had effortlessly taken over my life. Owing Vargas was a pain in the ass and stupidly dangerous. Owing Della, well that was proving to have all kinds of complications I hadn't anticipated. I wasn't used to putting my best foot forward for anyone. Trying to impress the chilly, reserved woman who so clearly thought I was worthless was exhausting. I never realized how much effort being reliable and dependable took.

"I can threaten you, or I can have words with your family, cowboy. I can also raise your interest rate anytime I like. This is a dangerous game you're playing, son." The man's voice was smooth and the warning clear. Play nice or get my hand slapped, or knowing Vargas, get the whole thing chopped off.

"The money is coming, and for once it's a sure thing. Dante, if you go after my sister, you're going to have to face off with my brother. My old man might have been as corrupt as the day is long, but Case isn't like that. He takes his job seriously, and he's even more protective of Kody than I am. You roll into Loveless and start sniffing around either of them, Case is going to shut you down." It was a warning of my own. My brother didn't play around when it came to rules and regulations. He would take Vargas down, even if it meant I ended up crashing and burning right alongside him. I was a selfish man, thoughtless more often than I wanted to admit. But I would never let my siblings be used as pawns in this game I'd unwittingly started losing as soon as it began.

"I am not afraid of the law, cowboy. Especially not some backwoods, hick sheriff in a nowhere town." There was a sniff and then a low laugh that made my skin crawl. "I expect at least half of the balance you owe plus interest at the end of this week. Five days, cowboy. If I don't see it, the interest rate goes up ten percent, and I'm tacking on a ten-thousand-dollar late fee. Hope you come through, my boy; people are counting on you."

The call ended with him still laughing and me choking on swear words as I threw my phone in the direction of the pristine white bed. I was almost afraid to touch anything in this overly opulent hotel room. Everything looked like it cost a million dollars and would be irreplaceable if broken. I knew that probably wasn't the case, but I was still overly cautious as I moved around, throwing myself into one of the plush, velvet settees that sat near the windows.

I had no clue what a settee was. I asked Della why the couches were so small and useless-looking and she explained what they were. My long legs dangled over the side as I ran my hands through my hair and cursed the minute I placed my first bet. Of course, I was the guy who had to go all in. I couldn't do anything by half measures, which meant something that should have been inconsequential turned into a full-blown addiction before I could blink. I never knew when enough was enough until it was too much and I was being crushed under the weight of all my choices.

As my hair curled around my fingers, I looked over at the clock by the bed. I forgot that one of the many things Della had planned for me since my boots hit the ground in New York was a haircut. Yesterday, I'd spent the entire day at Deveaux Beauty's main office, signing a million different things after negotiating a partial payment for when the initial campaign images were shot and approved by the end of the week. I ended up getting a crash course in the seemingly endless number of products I was going to be hocking, and met Della's staff, which included the advertising and marketing people, who had all weighed in on everything from my hair to my slightly chipped front tooth. I was lucky I still had all my teeth, considering how often I was stepped on by hooves, and how often I ended up in situations where I took a fist to the face. I'd felt like a bug under a microscope, but I kept my opinions to myself because, at the end of the day, I was going to do whatever the reserved blonde in six-inch heels said as long as I got paid.

I was pushing to my feet just as there was a tentative knock on the door. Sighing and wondering if I was ever going to be back in control of my life, I wandered over to open the door. I flinched as it swung open before I could reach the knob. Della had given me a very clear set of rules before leaving me to my own devices. No women. No drinking. No drugs. No running amok in the city. No disappearing without warning. She told me she had her own key to my room and to expect the unexpected. I knew she was looking for me to give her a reason to forfeit the contract, so I was going to have to work extra hard not to give her the opportunity.

Those unusual, catlike eyes of hers widened when she practically walked into my chest. I watched as the yellow-gold colors flared brightly around the green and overtook the brown in her gaze as she skidded to a halt on those neck-breaking shoes she seemed to live in. She put her hands on my chest to catch her balance, and I didn't miss the way heat flooded into her face or the way her breath hitched when her palms landed on my pecs. I flashed her a grin and flexed under her touch, because I could, and because I was curious to see if I could crack some of the ice she was encased in. Her pale eyebrows lifted and before she could hide it, a spark of appreciation blazed through the lighter parts of her eyes.

It was gone in a second as the man standing behind her dramatically cleared his throat, and followed the sound with a low whistle as he pushed past me and Della into the hotel room.

"Nice digs, baby." I felt his gaze slide over me in appreciation as he tossed his platinum bangs out of his eyes. "You make this place look even better. Where do you want me to set up, Della Darling?"

I blinked at the guy and then at Della. There weren't a lot of flamboyant men in the circles I traveled in. In fact, I was pretty sure this was the first time I'd been in a room with a man who had a face full of flawless and artistically applied makeup. He was like a butterfly, flitting around the room in a colorful display.

"Crew, this is Sammy. He's one of the top hairstylists in the city. He works on all our big media launches. Sammy, this is Crew Lawton. I need you to make him fabulous. Give him a look that will make every man in the world want to emulate him." She took a step away as the smaller man moved toward me, sticking out his hand and offering a strong, sure shake when I put my hand in his.

He tapped his chin, painted mouth puckered into a thoughtful look as his eyes continued to rake over me. I lifted a self-conscious hand to my longish, normally unruly hair and shrugged as he continued to study me like I was a puzzle he was trying to figure out.

"I don't normally do much with it besides wash it. I wear a hat ninety percent of the time." I liked it long enough so whoever I took to bed had something to hold on to, but beyond that, I never gave the dark mop much thought.

"You've never used product?" The man asked the question with a lifted brow and an aghast expression.

I chuckled under my breath and shook my head in the negative. "Nope." I wasn't even sure I knew what *product* was referring to.

I was inspected some more, the stranger lifting onto the tips of the very pointed boots he wore to poke at my hair and rub strands through his fingers. Out of the corner of my eye, I watched Della stiffen as the stylist got closer and closer to me. I wasn't sure if she was concerned about my reaction to being pawed at by another man, or if she was worried the verdict was going to be there was no helping my shaggy, unkempt mess. I may have no experience in being around someone like Sammy, but I liked his upbeat demeanor and carelessly cheerful chatter. He was touching me more than I'd typically let a stranger while I was stone cold sober, but Sammy kept everything very professional and brisk.

"Della Darling, I don't think we should do much to him. He's got a beautiful head of hair. That blue-black is nearly impossible to come by without dye, and the slight wave... to die for." He smiled at me and turned to look at my keeper. Her spine stiffened even more. "If we give him an undercut or buzz him down to nothing he's going to look like every other gorgeous guy we've shot for every other campaign we've done. Right now he's special, wild, untamed. He looks like he just crawled out from between the sheets, and anyone who looks at him wants to take him right back to bed. Straight men are going to want to be him, gay men are going to want to do him, and I'm pretty sure all women will like looking at him. Most people have to work to have this level of sexy. Our cowboy comes by it naturally. I think we need to clean him up a little, give him an actual style and teach him how to use some product, but I wouldn't mess with perfection." The smaller man clapped his hands together in delight and looked over at Della for approval. "Less is more."

I swore I could hear Della's back teeth grinding together. Her eyes shifted from Sammy to me, and there was a fire inside of them. She wanted to argue. I could see it in the way her arms snapped up to cross over her chest, and how the patent leather tip of her toe tapped against the floor. I was far from perfect in her eyes. She wanted me to have a total overhaul to fit in with her stuffy, expensive vision. Hearing I was good enough as I was hadn't been part of her plans. It wasn't part of mine either. I'd never been good enough as I was.

She huffed out an aggravated breath and waved a hand in the air in front of her. "Fine. Do what you think is best. I just need him to smolder for the camera and sell my products."

Sammy laughed as he patted me on the shoulder, telling me it would take a second for him to set up. "Darling, he doesn't just smolder, he burns. And if you can't see it, you need to worry about more than your products."

She made an offended sound that was lost in the bark of laughter I let out. I gave Sammy a fist bump and decided I quite liked the sparkly, pretty man.

Chapter 5

DELLA

What a delightful creature. Wherever did you find him, Della?"

I lifted an eyebrow at the woman standing next to me, who was doing very little to hide the fact she was blatantly undressing Crew with her eyes. He was across the crowded ballroom, talking to not one, but two, supermodels, his dark head thrown back as he laughed at something one of them said. I'd spent a lot of time around beautiful women; very rarely did they ever say anything uproariously funny.

I tried not to scowl into my champagne flute and responded dryly, "In Texas. My dad actually found him. I'm the one trying to tame him." My fingers tightened around the delicate stem in my hand as the red-headed model lifted a finger and ran it seductively over Crew's well-defined chest. I'd wanted him to wear a suit to this event. He'd balked and put up enough of a fight I let him get away with black jeans, his boots, and a fitted black button-down. I put my foot down when it came to his Stetson, but now I was secretly regretting not letting him wear it. I found myself missing the way it added an air of mystery and danger to him. Maybe the dark hat would have kept a few of the more timid and image-conscious models at bay.

The older woman next to me who was lusting after the cowboy was also the editorial director for the top fashion magazine in New York. She was notoriously hard to impress, and if she didn't give the green light to my new advertising campaign, it wasn't even worth moving forward. The ball-room I was currently standing in was packed with the who's who of the fashion and beauty world to celebrate my companion's birthday. Tickets had been in the low six figures, and Father insisted I go and take Crew along with me. He informed me it was as good a place as any to get the man's face out there, and get him to schmooze with the people he was going to be selling my products to. I was convinced it was going to be a horrible idea. I just knew Crew was going to say the wrong thing or do something outrageous, and end up getting Deveaux Beauty blackballed.

I should have known better.

It seemed I was the only red-blooded human alive who wasn't immediately swept away in Crew Lawton's over-whelming charm and charisma. And, if I was entirely honest, I fought against his magnetic pull every single time we were alone together. There was simply something about him that drew all types of people in. I was furious my father could see it without even bothering to meet the man.

"Oh, my. So, he really does play around with horses and such? He cleans up very nicely." She turned to look at me with a lifted eyebrow. "I am intrigued how you are going to use him in this new product launch of yours."

I sighed. It would be great if I had figured that out myself. I was so ready to play fairy godmother and turn him into a princess—well, prince; but every instinct I had, and every person I encountered, seemed enamored with him just the way he was. I couldn't fathom how all his rough edges and abrasive bluntness didn't irritate them the way they irritated me, but maybe it was because they weren't looking beyond his very pretty face and unmistakably ripped body. Maybe the reason his deflection bothered me so much was because I could see the pain and regret hiding in his bright blue eyes...And both of those things called to me far more than his smooth words and effortless appeal.

"He doesn't play with horses. He rides them, and they try to throw him off. It's all very dangerous and surprisingly thrilling. Rodeo suits him." Far better than this swanky party with tiny amuse-bouche did. I gritted my teeth as the brunette model tried to outdo her friend in the laughing-like-a-hyena department. To his credit, Crew only appeared mildly amused by the reaction he was getting. He kept looking up to meet my gaze, almost as if he was making sure I took notice of the fact he was behaving. "I was looking for the next David Gandy and somehow ended up with Scott Eastwood in *The Longest Ride*. I'm not sure how to adjust."

Crew's admirer gave a gentle snort that was shocking coming from someone who prided herself on being dignified and proper. "Does it matter? Both are beautiful and unforgettable in their own way and made their own kind of impact. Count yourself lucky you found someone so memorable, someone who can do the same thing for you. Don't squander the gift you've been given. I'm off to mingle, my dear. Tell your father I said hello and I'd love to get together the next time he's in town. I loved the collection he released with that K-pop band earlier this year. So edgy and diverse."

She swept away in a cloud of Chanel No. 5 and swirl of silk. It was on the tip of my tongue to tell her that the collaboration was my idea, but I knew it was a waste of breath. My contributions to Deveaux Beauty always ended up lost under my father's reputation and overbearing personality.

A moment later, the smiling cowboy was standing in front of me, a hopeful expression stamped on his too-handsome face. "Can we go get some real food and maybe a beer? That was the lady you said you needed to talk to, right? I saw her checking out my ass. Did I pass inspection?"

He chuckled as I poked him in his rock-hard stomach. He playfully rubbed the spot, and I couldn't help but grin at his antics. I never behaved so spontaneously with anyone but him.

"You always pass, and yeah, we can go. If you don't mind leaving your fan club behind."

He flicked a grin toward the now-pouting women across the room and unceremoniously wrapped a rough hand around my elbow as he proceeded to drag me out of the ballroom. I hated the way my heart kicked up and the way my pulse fluttered under his touch.

"I asked them where to go to get real New York–style pizza that would blow my mind, and they thought it was a joke. What kind of man jokes about pizza?" He sounded horrified and slightly disgusted.

I smothered a laugh and waited while he opened my door for me, leaving the driver standing next to the car with nothing to do. Once he was seated in the back next to me, I told him quietly, "I know a place. I don't know if it's the best in New York, but I've always liked their pizza, and they're open late." It was a hole-in-the-wall pizza place in Little Italy I stumbled onto while I was in college. I hadn't been there in years, but if Crew was after an authentic experience, there was no better place to take him.

We chatted easily as we drove across town. Crew asked what it was like to go to college in such a big city, and I asked about growing up in a small town. He told me his mother passed away from breast cancer, and I shared that mine had passed from an undiagnosed heart condition. We both had fond memories of the women who left us too soon, and we both had issues with how the loss of those women affected our fathers. We had more in common than I think either of us would admit to, and that realization had both of us going quiet as we reached the restaurant.

I was greeted like an old friend as soon as I walked in the door. The restaurant was run by a couple from Napoli who had been married for over forty years. Back when I was in college I remembered thinking it was impossible for any relationship to last that long. But here they were, still together.

The wife, Carlotta, wrapped her plump arms around me and gave me a kiss on each cheek. "You are still so beautiful, Della. Always such a pretty, polite girl. Always too skinny and too lonely." It was jarring to be remembered in that way. It sent a flare of something uneasy shooting through me. The staff acted happier to see me than my father did when we'd been separated for long stretches of time. The way they worried about me when he never did was a stark reminder why I spent so much time here in my youth.

The husband, Luca, looked over to where Crew was hovering behind me.

A bushy, white eyebrow lifted and a smile split his weathered face. "You have company now. This is good. Always alone. Always so serious. Mama and I used to wonder if you would look up from your books to see the rest of the world around you."

I laughed to mask my discomfort, and moments later we were sequestered in a quiet booth where Crew ordered an entire pepperoni pizza just for himself. The conversation shifted to business as he asked what was expected of him in the upcoming photo shoots.

I fiddled with the straw in my drink and stared at him while I tried to put into words just how important this campaign was to me and how much the success of the whole thing hung on his broad shoulders.

"I've been trying to put together a new product line for the company for years. I've always had to prove to my father I'm capable and worthy of being his successor. I've come up with collaborations and expansion ideas that have paid off, but he's never trusted me with my own line before. This campaign, and your face, they mean everything to me, and to my future. You literally have my hopes and dreams in your hands right now, Crew. So it's a little more than standing there and looking handsome. I need you to convince men around the world they can't live without what it is you're selling, and you have to do it all with just one look." I quirked an eyebrow at him as he noticeably paled. "No pressure."

He let out a breath and slowly nodded as if he understood exactly how important his being here was, and how much he meant to me.

"I'm no model, but I have pranced around in my underwear in front of a camera before. I think it went okay." The joke was dry and I nearly choked on my water once that image popped into my head and refused to leave.

"I'm not the Lawton people usually put their faith in. That's my older brother, Case. He's always been the responsible one, the one who feel like he has to take care of everyone around him. He's the sheriff in the town where we all grew up. Took over the position from my old man, who never deserved to wear a badge because he didn't give a shit about serving or protecting anyone...ever." He cocked his head to the side and gave me a lopsided grin. "I'm gonna do my best to come through for you, Della. Not only because I have to for reasons I don't want to get into with you while we're having a nice night, but because I really want to prove I can be the guy someone relies on."

There was a sincerity in his tone that worked to settle some of the nerves that were still on edge about having to put so much trust in this very unpredictable man.

"Thank you, Crew." I cleared my throat and picked at the crust left on my plate. I was stuffed. It'd been a long time since I'd indulged in carbs and cheese the way I did tonight. To top things off, our waitress swung by when there was a lull in the conversation and dropped off a plate of homemade cannolis I knew came from Carlotta's kitchen. I'd loved them back in the day when I could afford to eat whatever I wanted without having a panic attack about extra inches. I'd forgotten how glorious the sweet confection could be. "I love these. They bring back a lot of good memories. Whenever I fought with my dad, or ended up working too hard, Carlotta seemed to know. She would put a couple of these cannolis in front of me without me having to ask. Italian comfort food at its finest. They always made me feel better." Or maybe it was the gesture of someone caring without being prompted that sent warm fuzzies shooting through me.

Scooping a dollop of cream out of the end of one with my finger, I popped it in my mouth and watched as Crew looked at his plate curiously.

"So your older brother is the responsible one, you're the wild one; what does that make your sister? I heard you talking to her on the phone the day we met. You seemed pretty tight with her."

Finally figuring he would just go all in, Crew stuck the end of the shell in his mouth and took a bite. It was fun watching his dark eyebrows shoot up as the sweet insides flooded his mouth. He chewed with an expression close to ecstasy for a full minute before answering my question.

"Damn, those are good. As for Kody, she's hard to define. She has all the best parts of Case and all the worst parts of me mixed up together. She doesn't take shit from anyone and never backs down, even when she should. She grew up in a houseful of boys, and had the biggest bully in the county for a father, so she's tough. Sometimes too tough. She has the biggest heart of anyone I've ever met. Unfortunately, whoever wants to get at it is gonna need a chain saw and probably some dynamite. She's the only person in my whole life who's never given up on me, even though I've given her countless reasons to write me off."

"Your sister sounds amazing. I would love to have someone talk about me the way you talk about her." I was envious he had people to share the good and the bad in his life with, people to set him straight and rein him in when he needed it. I'd never had anyone, not that I ever needed them, but it would be nice to not feel so alone all the time.

I stuck my finger back in the cannoli and collected another sweet bite. I gasped quietly when Crew caught my wrist before I could get my finger in my mouth. Slowly, deliberately, he tugged my arm across the table. I watched with wide eyes and a slack jaw as his tongue darted out and swirled across my fingertip. He licked the digit clean, leaving a warm, slick path behind. Also causing other parts of my body to tighten up and clench in heated awareness.

We both looked over when there was a round of applause coming from somewhere near the kitchen. The older married couple was watching us—Luca was smiling from ear to ear, his wife clapping her hands together in glee. I flushed in embarrassment but didn't jerk my hand away from Crew's strong hold. I wasn't alone right now.

The thought was enough to send my world off-kilter in the way only this man had been able to do. When I was with him I didn't feel the constant need to push forward, to prove my worth, to validate my existence. Being with him was as easy as breathing, and I enjoyed the freedom from expectations.

We left when the restaurant shut down, and the ride back to his hotel was spent in companionable silence as the city whizzed by. I jolted slightly when the car rolled to a stop. It was late, and I should've been tired and stressed-out about everything I still had to take care of for the campaign. However, minus the stuffy party, tonight had been one of the most enjoyable evenings I'd spent with someone else in a long time. There was none of the pretension I typically found on my dates. There was none of the dancing around who had the bigger portfolio, and which one of us made more money and had more connections. Crew didn't have to show off or work to impress. Just by being, he was the center of attention and the most interesting person in the room.

"Thank you for feeding me. It was a nice night once we ditched the stuffed shirts and Barbie dolls. You aren't so bad, Ms. Priss." He flashed me a grin in the darkened interior of the car and I swore it made my brain short-circuit.

"You're not a bad date yourself, Mr. Lawton."

I yelped in surprise as he suddenly leaned across the space separating us, one of his hands grasping my chin as his eyes searched mine. "If that was a date, then I get a good-night kiss. That's how all my dates end and you know how superstitious athletes can be. Don't want to mess with what works."

I couldn't think of a single argument to stop him. I wasn't sure I wanted to. I knew I should. He was all wrong for me. He didn't fit into my life. He was too pretty and too charming for his own good. But none of that mattered when his mouth settled over mine.

I would have guessed he would kiss like he did everything else, a little rough and totally uninhibited. I would have been wrong.

He kissed slowly, deliberately. His mouth moving with seductive intent as it slid purposefully over mine. He was slick and practiced, knowing just how to give just enough and where to take. I felt my head spinning, and my breath turning choppy as his tongue darted out to play with mine. I was the one who turned wild and unchecked. I was the one who slipped into the wanton skin, taking more and more, practically wrapping myself around his strong body and kissing him back like I'd never been properly kissed before in my life. And maybe I hadn't, because I couldn't remember a kiss turning me inside out, making me forget where I was and who I was with.

The way his palms rasped over my skin was hypnotic. I could feel his touch, because he used his hands for more than counting money and making phone calls. Who would have ever thought that rough palms would be a turn-on, but they totally were. I liked knowing he was there, liked feeling him in places other than where our mouths were fused together. I'd never lost so much of myself in a single moment. As he pulled back, blue eyes blazing in the dark, I silently wondered what else I'd missed out on by dating only men who were almost exactly like the man who had abandoned me when I needed him most.

Crew smiled at me, and I felt my heart turn over in response. All it would take was a return smile from me, and I knew he'd take me up to his room with him and change my life forever.

But unlike him, I didn't take risks and throw caution to the wind. I didn't ignore warning signs and grab life by the horns. He was a churning, thunderous storm, and I was a woman who never left home without an umbrella.

I swallowed, shook my head to clear my thoughts, and barely whispered, "Good night, Crew. I'll see you in the morning." And probably all throughout the night in my dreams, but he didn't need to know that. He already had too much power over me. Disappointment flashed in his brilliant gaze, but it was nowhere near as sharp as the needles of regret slowly shredding my stomach as I watched him slip out of the car and walk away.

Chapter 6

CREW

How long are you in town for? I would love to show you around if you have time," the young woman with her hands uncomfortably close to my cock said as she fiddled with the zipper on the sharply tailored pants I wore. She had been relentlessly flirting with me from the moment I stripped down to play dress-up. I was on outfit number twenty, or maybe it was twenty-five, and none of them seemed to meet Della's approval. Every ten minutes I was back in the fitting room with the bubbly blonde, who was making it no secret she would rather be taking my clothes off than putting them on.

I grunted and tugged at the vest covering the gray silk shirt I was wearing. It was all too fucking fancy. I looked like a teenager dressing up for prom. None of the expensive designer wear was anything I would typically be caught dead in...which I guess was the point. Della wanted me to be someone I wasn't, and all these designer labels were a good way to fool people into thinking I was better than I actually was.

"I'm only here a few more days. Doing a few photo shoots and some press until the end of the week, then I'm headed back home."

I was actually headed to Vegas to pay Vargas back, but no one needed to know that. I was acutely aware of the deadline approaching. Five days had never seemed like such a short amount of time before. A clock ticking steadily and noisily in the back of my head. Kody was getting sick of my persistent calls to check up on her, and Case knew something was up, because I broke down and sent him a text telling him to be extra vigilant if he noticed anyone who looked like they didn't belong in Loveless. Both the cop and the big brother wanted answers, and me telling him I had it under control didn't go over well. Once I had Vargas off my back, I was going to have to show my face in my hometown and come clean about all the things I'd screwed up. I was looking forward to that reckoning as much as I was looking forward to the girl in front of me, tugging on the crotch of my pants again to adjust the fit.

She was cute, with an easy smile and twinkling eyes that promised a good time. She was the kind of woman I had no problem falling into bed with, and forgetting about as soon as the sun came up. Only, Della was standing on the other side of the curtained-off area, and for some inexplicable reason, I didn't want to let her down. I didn't want to take this friendly woman up on everything she was offering because she simply wasn't the woman I'd kissed last night. Now that I knew how Della tasted, how sweet she sounded when I did something she liked, there wasn't a substitute able to fill the void she left when she walked away. Della said she had no expectations, but I wanted her to. I wanted to show her I could do this for her. I could prance around in too-expensive, too-tight clothes pretending to be the shit.

"Well, I'm sure you won't be working the entire time. I'll leave you my number, and you can call me when you're done with all the things Della has lined up for you." She was gliding her hands across my shoulders when the curtain behind us swished open and revealed the woman she just mentioned.

Della took in the scene with slightly narrowed eyes making the other woman fall back a step as she cleared her throat. I involuntarily lifted my hands, showing her I'd been an innocent victim of the wardrobe assistant's attentions. Hell, if any woman was going to paw at me and cop a feel, I wanted it to be the one watching me in the mirror with discerning, hazel eyes.

Our kiss was imprinted on my lips, and her taste was seared on my tongue. I foolishly thought putting my mouth on hers would be like rolling an ice cube around in my mouth. But there was nothing cold or soft about the way she responded to me. All the polish and shine that made her so hard to read fell away under the swirl of my tongue and the bite of my teeth. She moved like liquid under my hands, ice melting and turning into a river of want and need at the barest hint of a touch. That simple, playful kiss had me dying to strip her down so I could show her how much fun being dirty and wild could be. For a split second, I thought she was going to come upstairs with me; there was a flicker of hesitation in her gaze. Never had I wanted anyone to risk it all on me before, but I was silently begging Della to throw caution to the wind and be reckless with me.

She didn't. I couldn't blame her. But that didn't mean I hadn't spent last night dreaming about how her flawless skin would look under my hands, and how her long, elegant legs would feel wrapped tightly around me.

I bit back a groan and silently ordered my dick to behave. I didn't want to give either woman the wrong impression.

"This the one, Ms. Priss?" I turned in a circle, hating how restrictive and stiff the refined suit felt. There would be no staying on the horse for eight seconds in something like this. I doubted I could even bend over and pull my boots on in this getup. I failed to see how being dressed like I was going to high tea with the queen was going to convince normal men with a little extra cash to buy the junk in my hair. It felt like overkill, but I would chew my tongue off before telling Della that. I knew how much this campaign meant to her, and I needed her to keep me around so I could get paid . . . and get to kiss her again.

Della circled around me, eyes scanning from head to toe. A small frown tugged her perfectly arched brows down into a V, and her lush, soft mouth pulled into a pout I was becoming achingly familiar with. She lifted a hand and touched the knot of the silk tie where it rested at the base of my throat. She fingered the delicate material and heaved a sigh.

"You look perfect, but something is still off." She met my gaze with a scowl. "Can you try and look a little less like you're being tortured? That might help the overall image."

Her snippy tone and the upturn of her nose made me grin. I rolled my head around, causing my neck to pop and my shoulders to relax. Now that I wasn't being felt up and had some breathing room, I loosened up a bit. Della's expression softened when I was no longer standing at attention, but she still let out a dejected-sounding sigh and reached for my tie, releasing me from the expensive noose.

"You have a body made for designer clothes, but something is lost when you put them on. I feel like we're trying to wrap the *Mona Lisa* in silk or something. Frankly, it's annoying that you make denim and flannel look just as good as Versace and Prada." Once she had the tie off, she told me to go ahead and get back into my own clothes. I asked her what the plan was for the shoot tomorrow and a brief flare of panic and doubt lit up her catlike eyes. She forced a smile and told me she would figure it out.

Since I was totally a fish out of water in this scenario, all I could do was follow orders like a good soldier. I stripped out of the fitted vest and worked on the tiny buttons of the shirt. I was handing them both off to the flirty girl who was enjoying the impromptu striptease when Della's "Wait a second!" had both of us freezing on the spot.

She was looking at me in the mirror, eyes roving over my half-dressed form. She wandered over to where my jeans and boots were tossed in a haphazard pile on the floor. After a second of rooting around, she came toward me, my black wifebeater in one hand and my boots in the other.

"Put these on with the pants." She looked at the wardrobe girl with a lifted brow and had to snap her fingers in the woman's face to get her attention. "Go find me a pair of suspenders, leather if you have them." The other woman scurried off to do as she was told and I dropped to the seat to pull on my boots.

"I keep trying to turn you into something better." I looked up at Della as she snorted out a laugh. "But from the start, my father told me you were perfect the way you are. Maybe I need to stop fighting him so hard on every little thing."

A pair of suspenders were thrust into Della's hands, and I had to think very un-sexy thoughts as she worked to button them into the waistband of the tight pants. She lifted on the tippy toes of her heels to smooth them over my shoulders, and all I had to do was put a hand on the small of her back to pull her toward me. I could kiss her stupid and forget all about how I ended up here.

She rocked back on her heels, cocking her head to the side and checking out her handiwork. I was half me, and half the version of the man she kept saying she wanted me to be. It must have worked because she handed me the fallen tie and told me to wrap it around my neck but leave it hanging loose. I looked like I'd just crawled out of bed with a woman I couldn't afford, after having a really good time while I was there.

"That's it. I first thought of it when you were leaning against the car when we were in Texas. I need to stop trying to create an image that appeals to men who already have everything. I need to go with this one, the one that says this product line can make a man a little rough, and a little polished at the same time. I need to go right for the middle, hit the best of both worlds. I need the guy who rides in a chauffeured car, and the guy who willingly climbs on a bucking bronc. The crossover market should be amazing if we get the image right." She waved a hand in front of me. "This is right."

"He's perfect." The purr from the wardrobe assistant had my hackles rising and some of Della's newly found excitement dulling. She turned to look at the woman, but before she could tear into her, or make the moment more uncomfortable than it already was, I reached out a hand and grasped her shoulder, urging her back around to face me.

I gave her a crooked grin and absently lifted my hand so I could rub my thumb over the haughty arch of her sharp cheekbone. She was, without a doubt, the most fragile and delicate thing I'd ever put my hands on, and I was terrified I was going to break her.

"For what it's worth, I would love to be the kind of guy who actually slides seamlessly between those two worlds. I think most men would. I think you're on to something." I lifted my gaze and looked at the other woman in the room and shook my head at her. "I'm far from perfect, doll. I quit trying to be that around the time I learned to walk. There's always room for improvement, and I think that's what this campaign of Della's is going to show people. Those of us who roll around in the dirt need an excuse to spruce up every now and then, and the type of man that plays with money all day needs to remember what it's like to work with his hands and get rough once in a while. Ms. Priss is good at her job, and I'm happy to be along for the ride while she does her thing."

Della stared up at me, mouth hanging slightly open. The same flicker of hesitation that sparked in her gaze last night jumped to life while she stared at me. Only this time she gave in to temptation and threw herself into my arms, nearly taking me down with the force of her embrace.

"That might be the nicest thing anyone's ever said to me."

I squeezed her back and buried my nose in the top of her head. Her hair smelled like flowers. "Ahh. People should be telling you things way nicer than that, Della. You deserve to hear how awesome you are on a regular basis."

Just like I deserved to hear how much of a screwup I was over and over again, which was why I would never be the guy who fit into her world.

Chapter 7

DELLA

A true-blue cowboy, a Lamborghini, and an Arabian stallion walk onto a photo shoot...

It should be a joke. There should be a punch line, but I wasn't laughing because everything happening in front of the camera was magic. Crew was a natural. The camera loved everything about him. Every image captured made him seem larger than life. The wicked twinkle in his eye gleamed mischievously in every shot. He looked taller, stronger, just more everything than he already was under the bright lights. The mix of modern corporate raider and the untamed wild man had the temperature in the studio rising to nearly unbearable levels. The photographer kept fanning himself and muttered, "Dear Lord, if men in Texas look like him, I'm moving," over and over again. His assistant was practically drooling, and the makeup girl was taking far too much joy in touching Crew up every five minutes. The dark-haired cowboy seemed oblivious to the impact he was having on a roomful of jaded professionals. He was too busy being enamored of the massive, black stallion I'd miraculously found last minute for the shoot.

Crew chatted up the horse's handler between shots, asking about his lineage and other horse-type stuff that sounded like a foreign language to me. He touched the animal reverently but didn't seem at all excited when he got to climb all over the Lamborghini. It was evident he missed being on his home turf, but he was doing a damn good job of turning mine upside down.

"One more shot, Crew. Can you lean against the car and wrap the rope that's on the saddle around your arm? Put your head down a little, so we get some shadows across your face."

I gulped when Crew moved to obey the directions. I sighed inwardly when he inadvertently copied the pose from the first day we met, leaning against the car, one leg bent as he shoved a hand in the front pocket of the sharply tailored slacks he was wearing. All that was missing was his Stetson.

"He needs his cowboy hat." The sentence felt like it was wrenched out of me. The only way this was going to work was if I let Crew off the leash and let him be who he really was.

The photographer gave me a questioning look over his shoulder. "That's going to cover up his hair, and you're in the business of selling stuff to make those locks look flawless."

I cringed at the reminder, but my gut was screaming at me to put the damn hat on his head. "Just snap a few with the hat on. I have a feeling." Kind of like the feeling I had about this entire product line. I knew it was a good idea, knew it would be something special, even if the people I most wanted to impress thought I was crazy. "Crew, did you bring your cowboy hat with you?"

Those laser-like blue eyes lifted to meet mine and the corners of his mouth ticked up into a familiar grin. "Don't leave home without it."

I couldn't help but grin back. "Put it on and then get back in the same pose. We're gonna snap a few of you with the hat on, then we can call it a day. I actually have a check for you." He'd been very clear about getting paid as soon as the initial promo materials were shot. He'd seemed more and more anxious about getting the money as the week went on. I figured it was because he'd lost during his last several rides and thus lost out on his usual winnings. I was happy to hand over the next part of the payment I owed him; he'd more than earned it in the short time we'd spent together.

He tilted the hat on his head, and the shadows immediately shielded his expression, but there was something dangerous there. I barely caught a hint of it before he moved back to being the center of attention.

The photographer gasped when Crew was back in front of the lens, and this time the "oh my" was breathless and slightly stunned. I had to agree. Crew Lawton was impressive, but cloaked in his familiar garb, he was irresistible. It was easy to forget the car he was leaning on cost close to half a million dollars.

"The hat was a good call, Della. These are going to be extraordinary."

This time my sigh was audible. "He's extraordinary."

The photographer chuckled. "Not going to argue with you over that." He dropped the camera and clapped his hands together, declaring the shoot a wrap.

Crew made sure to thank everyone, then spent an extra minute scratching the horse's muzzle and exchanging pleasantries with his handler. By the time he made his way over to where I was waiting, we were the last two people in the studio.

He still had his mix of designer duds and western wear on, and his hat was still hiding his normally brilliant gaze.

"That wasn't nearly as bad as I expected it to be. I didn't feel like a bull at auction at all." It was a joke I wasn't entirely sure I understood, but I gave him a reassuring smile anyway.

I dug around in the Louis Vuitton tote hanging off the crook of my arm and fished out his check. I didn't ask why he didn't want the amount wired directly into his bank account but figured it had something to do with the contract amendments he'd made after learning about the deal his former manager had made on his behalf.

He looked at the envelope I held out to him like it might bite him. A muscle twitched in his jaw and his entire body stiffened in front of me. I pushed the paper at him and let out a little laugh. "Go on, take it. You've earned it. You did a great job. This campaign is going to do amazing things, and it's all because of you. You get the final payment once the product line launches and we go full steam ahead with the media blitz. You'll be required to do a public appearance here or there, but nothing that will interfere with your rodeo schedule once that starts back up."

Mentioning his return to his regularly scheduled life was a stark reminder how different our lives were. His was filled with dust and dirt. Mine with gray concrete and skyscrapers. We were so far apart from one another logistically. It made my wanting to reach out and touch him, to hold him close, seem silly. Even if I couldn't stop thinking about the kiss. Even if I wanted another one so badly I could taste it.

I thumped the check against his chest until he took it. With a lifted eyebrow I teased, "If you can convince some of your cowboy buddies to try the stuff I'm selling that would be even better. I think my dad would have a heart attack if we could officially become the product line of the Professional Bull Riders."

Crew let out a snort and stared at the check in his hand for a long, quiet moment. "PBR is bulls; I ride broncs, so that might be a hard sell. I don't know that most of those guys use any kind of product other than deodorant, but I can try to show them the error of their ways. That is, if I manage to qualify for any of the big rides this next season. I fucked up a lot at the end of this year. I lost most of my major sponsors. I'm not exactly sure where I stand in the sport right now. I sort of took off with you before facing the fallout of the end of my season. That's what I do. Make a mess and leave other people to clean it up for me."

I put a hand on his shoulder, muscle flexing enticingly under my touch. "There is always time to work on being less messy. Just like there is time to appreciate that being less orderly won't necessarily bring about the end of the world. Everyone has to find a balance, Crew."

He used a finger to push the brim of his hat back, and my insides fluttered at the motion. I never thought I would be the kind of girl who was turned on by something as simple as a hat tilt. But here I was, heart thumping, knees going weak, tummy twisting, and my mouth turning dry because even the simplest gesture from him was more of a turn-on than the most practiced moves from the men I typically dated. He had also proven to be more steadfast, harder working, and more committed to giving me exactly what I asked him for than I could have imagined. He was setting out to prove himself as reliable and worthy of carrying my dream on his back, exactly like he'd told me he was going to. I was impressed and not shy about showing him I appreciated all of his hard work and dedication.

"Balance is something I've never had. I've always been an all-or-nothing kind of guy. It's gotten me into a lot of trouble." He held up the check and grasped one of my hands. "This could get me in a lot of trouble. I need this money, Della. I need to do the right thing with it, but already I can feel the wrong thing burning under my skin and making me itch. Temptation is an ugly drug. It's my one habit I haven't managed to kick free of. I want to do the right thing so badly I can taste it, but I know there's a really good chance I'm going to do the wrong thing anyway." He sounded scared and almost desperate. His eyes were wide, pools of blue agony, and I was drowning with each word that rushed out of him. "Promise me something, Ms. Priss."

I blinked and nodded reflexively. "Okay."

A look of surprise crossed his face, only to melt into a soul-stealing smile that had my entire body heating up and leaning toward him.

"You don't want to know what you're getting yourself into before you offer up something you might not be willing to part with?" There was a warning there in his tone, but I was going to ignore it.

"You held up your end of the bargain we made, Crew. You made my dream into a reality, made it better than I hoped. Even if the product line flops, you helped bring my vision to life and helped me prove the idea was valid. I owe you." Plus, I kind of loved the idea of him needing me for something, since our entire acquaintance had been based on me needing him.

No one ever really needed me for anything. My father proved that to me time and time again, as did the men I tended to date. I liked the notion that someone like Crew Lawton could actually need someone like me.

The paper in his hand crumpled as he made a fist. His eyes practically glowed as they locked onto me and his voice was soft and serious, seemingly torn between anger and remorse as he practically begged, "Then don't leave me alone, Della. Don't let me out of your sight until I'm on that plane leaving New York tomorrow. Don't give me a chance to spend this money and screw up again. Keep me with you and make me do the right thing."

I gulped and tried not to shiver as he moved his hand to my waist and pulled me to him so my body was flush with his. It was a heady experience having all his hard pressed against all of my soft. He was so overwhelming, so all-consuming. I let my Louis drop to the floor without a second thought. The man was potent and went to my head far too fast for my own good. I couldn't help but stare at that clever, talented mouth as his lips moved, saying something I should have expected but was still shocked to hear.

"Spend the night with me, Ms. Priss. I need you."

I couldn't reply if I wanted to. I seemed to have forgotten how to speak. The "no" I knew I should say was trapped somewhere in my throat, along with every single reason why staying with this man was a bad idea.

Good thing my body knew exactly what it wanted. I nodded at him, agreeing to whatever he was asking, because somewhere deep inside of me, I knew I needed him, needed this, just as badly as he did.

Chapter 8

CREW

There was a beautiful woman in my hotel room. She was watching me with a mixture of fear and anticipation. It wasn't anything new. I'd been here many times before—it should be familiar, practiced; it should be easy. But nothing about this situation, or the woman who kept surprising me at every turn, was easy.

My hands were shaky. There was a trickle of cold sweat rolling down my spine, and there was a buzz under my skin that I was having a difficult time ignoring. I tried to convince myself it was because of the sweet-smelling blonde who had been on my mind nonstop since she invaded my life. Sadly, I was self-aware enough to know the reason I was so on edge was because of the money that might as well be burning a hole in my pocket. For being such a thin piece of paper, the damn thing felt like it was made of lead, weighing me down with every step, and the worst part was, I knew if I wasn't careful, one slip could drag Della down with me. She was the best thing that had happened to me in a long time. I liked the man she inspired me to be. I appreciated that I had to be at the top of my game in order to be even slightly worthy of her time and attention. I wasn't sure I'd ever worked as hard at anything as I had at trying to show her she could count on me this last week.

I flicked the lights on as I moved deeper into the room. I took my hat off and tossed it carelessly onto the big bed. I was back in my regular clothes, face and hair scrubbed down. I was back to being me in every way. My hands found my hair and pulled. However, the tiny sting of pain did little to distract me from the temptation of either the woman behind me or the paycheck and bad choices that were calling my name.

"Would you like me to order room service? Or we can raid the minibar." I glanced over my shoulder in Della's direction, expecting her to look nervous or apprehensive, but instead, her head was tilted to the side, curiosity alight in her multihued gaze.

"I'm fine." Since she'd been in the room several times before, she stepped around me and made herself at home on the settee. It was my favorite place in the room, even more so now that Della was draped over it, looking like a spread in one of the magazines she was determined to get my face in. At no point in my life did I ever think I deserved to have someone like her looking out for me, caring about what happened to me. She was so out of my league, so above the dirt and dust I always seemed to find myself rolling around in. I knew if I put my hands on her I was going to get her dirty in a way that wouldn't simply wash off. For once, the idea of leaving my mark behind like a stain didn't sit well with me. I created chaos and destruction and walked away from the wreckage. This time there would be no turning a blind eye to the outcome. I would carry the aftermath of whatever happened between me and Della Deveaux for a long time to come.

Della cleared her throat delicately and crossed her legs. One of those sexy shoes she was never without swung back and forth, and I found myself mesmerized by the motion. My tongue suddenly felt too big for my mouth, and for the first time since she handed it over, my attention was on something other than the check and all the damage I could do with it in a city like New York.

"I don't suppose you want to enlighten me as to why you need a babysitter tonight?" Her tone was kind, but her eyes were questioning, and I hated it.

So far I'd impressed her. The last thing I wanted was for her to see the real me. I grunted and flopped down on the edge of the bed. I stared up at the ceiling, lacing my hands together over my stomach.

"Do you have any bad habits, Ms. Priss? Is there anything out there that fires you up, gets you excited, makes you feel alive?" I heard the wistful quality of my own voice, and it made me cringe. My father had always insisted I was the weakest of his kids, I was too soft. I'd learned long ago to let his opinions roll off my back; after all, the man was a crook and a bully. But hearing the longing in my tone for something that almost got me killed, ruined my career, and threatened my family, I found myself wondering if he was right.

Della made a humming noise, and I closed my eyes, imagining her making it against my skin while I was buried deep inside of her. Just like that, the check wasn't the only thing hot and heavy in my pants. My cock throbbed as most of the blood in my body pooled low in my gut and groin. I shifted in what I hoped was a subtle way.

"No, I don't think I do, unless you count consistently trying to make relationships work with men who are just like my father. I can't seem to quit trying to find affection and acceptance from people who don't know the first thing about caring for someone other than themselves." She let out a breathy sigh, and I heard her shifting around on the seat by the window. "If that's a bad habit, it's one I would really like to break. I'd like a chance to finally be happy."

Her words made my gut clench and forced my hands into fists. She deserved to be happy. She was a tad high-maintenance (okay, more than a tad), and a bit prickly, but she was kind and forgiving. She was so much more than most of the people who drifted in and out of my life like tumbleweeds.

"I have too many bad habits to count. I drink too much. I like women too much. I can't turn down a challenge or a dare, so I end up taking too many risks. I don't take anything seriously, even the things I know I should. Other people end up getting hurt because of me. When I was younger, those things made me dangerous and sexy. Now, they make me pathetic and worthless. Most people grow out of their rebellious phase. Me, I've been stuck in mine for so long I don't know any other way to be." I blew out an aggravated breath and forced my hands to relax because my knuckles were turning white under the pressure. "I don't know if I can tell you what I'm rebelling against any-more. My father? The fact I'm always in my older brother's shadow? Small-town perceptions? I've lost sight of what-ever it was I thought I was trying to prove forever ago." And wasn't that pathetic? I was a grown man with no other purpose than to screw things up.

The bed suddenly dipped, and I heard the slither of her silky stockings against the comforter. Her fingers were cool when they ghosted over my face. She traced the arch of my eyebrow and brushed her fingertips over the rise of my cheek.

I opened my mouth when her thumb touched my bottom lip. I exhaled and watched as she leaned over me, her sunny hair falling around her face. There was a furrow between her eyebrows, but she had a faint smile playing around her mouth. Her usually artfully painted lips were bare, but they were still a pretty pink. They looked like they were made to be bitten and sucked on.

"I never had a rebellious phase. The most defiant thing I've ever done is fly to Texas so I could convince you to let me change everything about you, and that didn't even turn out the way I expected. Maybe we can help each other out, teach each other a few things. I've always been driven, focused on doing more and being better than everyone else. I can help you figure out something new, something good to care about, to be invested in, and you can show me what it's like to break the rules and throw caution to the wind." Della's voice had lost some of the polish I'd come to associate with it. I liked the rasp, the slight waver. It made my dick harder than it already was, and had my heart thudding loud between my ears.

I reached up so I could push some of her hair behind her ear. I wanted to see her eyes, to see if she was saying what I thought she was saying. It was there in the threads of gold shot throughout. She wanted to take more of a risk on me than she already had.

"Della." I lifted my hands and cupped her beautiful face between them. It was like putting my hands on an ancient work of art. I had no right to touch her, to want her the way I did. "I'm a bad bet. The worst, actually."

"Hmm…" Her thumb moved over my lip again, and her head started to lower. My breath caught, and something inside my chest started to flicker with heat, sending warmth shooting throughout my body. "Since I've never even thought about rolling the dice before, I probably have a whole lot of beginner's luck on my side."

If she wanted to blow her luck on me, who was I to argue? Because didn't that make me the luckiest bastard who ever lived?

"In my world, it's always better to be lucky than it is to be good." I winked up at her, which made her laugh. She was stunning when she forgot to be so serious and reserved.

I barely had to apply any pressure to get her to lower her mouth to mine. Our lips crashed together, breath mingling, teeth clicking, tongues tangling. We went up in flames in the first second. She went to my head so fast, I felt like I'd chugged a bottle of whiskey. The world narrowed to the feel of her slender body pressed against mine, and the only sound I could hear was the rasp of silk dragging across denim as she stretched over me, one hand braced on the bed above my head as her chest pressed into mine. I could feel the way her pointed nipples poked eagerly against my chest. One of her long legs worked its way between mine, and my hands automatically shifted to the back of her thighs. Her skirt had ridden up when she maneuvered herself over me and my brain short-circuited for a minute when I encountered bare skin above a complicated garter belt. I was no lingerie aficionado, but I knew this wasn't run-of-the-mill. This was special, just like she was.

Her mouth slid across mine, wet, seeking. Her free hand skated over my chest, a finger stopping to cover where it felt like my heart was trying to kick its way out of my chest. I felt the bite of her teeth against my bottom lip as she lowered herself and pressed into the steadily growing bulge between my legs. She was shockingly bold. There wasn't a hint of the chill that usually surrounded her. She was molten heat in my hands, and I ordered my excited body to behave. She was so damn responsive, it would be easy to get carried away. I wasn't stupid enough to believe we were ever going to have this one night, this single moment, ever again, and I didn't want it to be over before it started. I wanted to savor her. I wanted to get lost in the sensations she had churning inside of me. There was a familiar rush scorching through my blood. The only other time I felt that particular burn was when I was on the back of a horse doing my best not to be thrown off.

"You sure about this, Ms. Priss?" I didn't recognize the man trying to talk a beautiful woman out of sleeping with him for her own good, but here he was.

Della smiled down at me, a real smile. One that softened her face and made her eyes glitter with a lightness she didn't normally possess. A pang of longing shot through me. If I were a different kind of man, I could promise myself I would give her more reasons to smile, but the reality was we only had tonight.

Instead of answering me, her palm slid across the front of my jeans, fingers exploring the rigid length trapped behind the denim. I bit back a groan, her touch lighter and more careful than I was used to. She moved against me like I mattered. She touched me like she cared. I threaded my fingers through her hair, my thumb stroking over her temple and my hip involuntarily lifting to follow her hands as her fingers found the button on my jeans. I wanted skin on skin, her legs wrapped around me. I wanted to know how she tasted everywhere, and how my name sounded when she came apart under my hands.

I was greedy by nature, always wanting more than I was given, but with her, I held back. For once I actually tried to be a good guy.

"I want you, even though I know it's a bad idea. You have heartbreak written all over you in neon letters, Lawton." She squeezed the aching flesh beneath her hand and dropped a kiss on the end of my nose. It was playful and very sweet. It meant more to me than any other kiss I'd received in my lifetime. "You can be my bad habit, Crew. You can be the entirety of my rebellious phase."

I wasn't going to give her another out. I tugged her back down, so she was plastered to my front. After all, if there was one thing I could leave her with before we parted ways, it was the knowledge that being bad sometimes felt really damn good.

Chapter 9

DELLA

I was used to my sexual encounters being as polite and proper as the men I dated. Very rarely was there a rush, a need, to get naked and to touch every inch of the skin exposed. Normally the lights were off, and everything was very mechanical and practiced. If there was an efficient way to get someone off, the men I typically ended up with had figured it out so the whole encounter could be handled in the shortest amount of time possible, so they could get back to managing their money and flaunting their wealth.

Being with Crew was a totally different experience. He was overwhelmingly present. All of his attention focused on me. He was watching the way my body reacted to his every touch, listening to the sounds he was pulling from my mouth. His fingers chased every shiver and quiver across my skin. It was almost as if he didn't want to miss anything. The lights were on, highlighting every dip and curve of his body as he lost his shirt and ditched his jeans. He moved with an effort-less grace that was undeniably sexy. The way muscle pulled and flexed as he leaned over me and deliberately stripped me of my carefully chosen outfit, minus the silk stockings and garter belt, was enough to have me breathing hard and blindly reaching out to touch. Only he caught my hands together in one of his much bigger and rougher ones, holding them over my head as he braced his big body over mine.

Crew's dark head lowered, the tip of his nose touching the curve of my jaw. His warm breath puffed out in a gentle caress against my skin, making me shiver from head to toe. His body was hard in all the places it touched mine, especially his arousal, which rose proud and impressive between his legs. The tip was shiny and slick, the sight made my mouth water and forced a little gasp from me when he bent, and his cock knocked against his abs, leaving a sexy, wet trail. His lips landed on mine, his kiss devouring, consuming. It was the kind of kiss that seared its way into my memories and left its mark on all the soft, tender places I tried too hard to keep under wraps. This man with all his wild, reckless abandon got to me in ways I wasn't ready for but knew I would never be able to forget.

"There isn't any part of you that isn't perfect, Della." His voice was uneven and deeper than usual. It made me shiver, as did the compliment.

"I was thinking the same thing about you." He really was an outrageously good-looking man. It was hard to remember he was made up of all rough edges and sharp points when I was lost in the blue of his eyes, and falling under the spell of his hands dancing over my skin.

My hands found their way into his thick hair, the soft strands curling automatically around my fingertips. His mouth brushed across mine, a featherlight kiss I chased as he moved from my face down my neck. I felt the wet tip of his tongue flick over my fluttering pulse, and I shifted underneath him as his new position brought the heat of his naked cock in contact with my stomach. I lifted a leg and wrapped it around his lean waist, trying to pull him lower, wanting that contact in the place where I was wet and wanting.

Crew chuckled against the base of my throat as he let go of my hands. "I think I like your eagerness."

I liked it too, even if this was the first time I'd ever felt that way before.

I was going to respond, tell him I was never like this, never…hungry, needy, desperate…but I forgot how to make words when his mouth surrounded the tip of one of my breasts. My aching, tight nipple disappeared between his lips, and I felt the bite of his teeth. The sensation had my eyes slamming shut and my back arching off the bed. The motion pressed our hips together, and I felt every inch of his hardness grind and throb between my legs. Crew's tongue tortured one breast, while his fingers found the sensitive point on the other and started to play. All the nerves in my body felt like they were suddenly electrified. I writhed against him, wordlessly asking for more and less at the same time.

I let my hands skate over the taut plane of his back, fingers digging into muscle. One of his hands slipped down my ribs and curved along the slope of my hip. His fingers played with the edge of my stockings, the silk rubbing seductively across the outside of his strong thigh. I held my breath as the rough pads of his fingers traced tiny circles inward, moving up my thigh and targeting in on the part of my body that was obviously reacting to everything he did to me. I would never have considered myself a responsive lover. I was just as efficient and brisk as the men I'd been with in the past. Knowing I had other things I could be doing that would undoubtedly leave me more satisfied in the end.

With Crew, there was none of that. My attention was entirely focused on him, and the way he made me feel. I was cataloging it, keeping it close, because once he walked away, I knew the chance I would ever feel like this with another man was slim to none.

His fingers slipped through the moisture that painted the apex of my thighs, and I felt the back of his knuckles brush through swollen, slippery folds. A moan escaped my throat, and my head rolled to the side. My eyes wanted to drift closed, but I forced myself to keep them open. I didn't want to miss a moment of us being together.

"Nothing cold about you when I have you like this." Crew's words circled around my heart and pulled tight. He might be the only man I'd ever encountered who thought I was warm.

"You're hot, Della. You burn for me." His hands stopped playing around between my legs. I felt the blunt edge of his fingers breach my tender opening, my body stiffening at the initial intrusion, then going soft and liquid as his talented touch stroked oversensitized flesh.

He was right: I was on fire. It was in my veins. It was licking over my skin. It was burning inside of me, following every move his fingers made. When his thumb found my clit and started a slow, deliberate pressure, it felt like the flames were going to consume me.

Refusing to be a passive part of everything that was happening, I worked a hand between our straining bodies, fingers tracing his cut abs and the sharp V that arrowed down to the erection trapped enticingly against my stomach. He was long and hard in my hand. The tip slippery and hot against my palm. His hips rocked into my touch as I stroked up and down the rigid length. I could feel the way he throbbed and seemed to grow even harder as I tightened my hold and used my thumb to rub an erotic caress along the inverted V that pointed upward from the dripping slit.

"Shit." He panted the dirty word and moved so that his mouth was over mine once more, his tongue thrust into my mouth, mimicking the way his fingers were moving in and out of the wetness between my legs. The room filled with our labored breathing, and the unmistakable sounds of arousal and sex. I wiggled until his hand slipped away from the torment and torture it was causing inside of me. I hitched my other leg around his waist and purposely used the hold I had on his cock to drag the flared head through my quivering folds. I'd never had a bare cock this close to my center. It was foolish, risky, stupid, but I wouldn't give up the way it felt for anything in the heat of this moment. The stiff flesh in my hand kicked in response, and I could feel him leaking a steady flow of precum, making everything slip and slide in the best way possible. The kiss he was feeding me turned wild and messy as he ate his name from my lips.

Crew pushed himself up on the hand he had braced on the bed near my head. The fingers he had between my legs found their way back to my aching center, and the pressure he put on my clit turned frantic and less coordinated.

His words were choppy and strained when he told me, "We're about to hit the point of no return. Last chance to not make this mistake."

I shook my head and blindly reached for where his jeans had landed when he pulled them off. Luckily, they were half on, half off the bed, so it was easy enough to catch a handful of denim and pull them closer. But Crew reached for the wallet he had evidently already dug out and retrieved the thing we would need to move this "mistake," as he called it, forward.

I ran a finger over the arched line of his eyebrows, and told him honestly, "It doesn't feel like a mistake." It didn't feel like rebellion, or gambling either.

It felt right.

It felt perfect and special.

It felt better than anything had in a very long time.

My words must have been enough of reassurance because a moment later Crew had himself sheathed in latex and shifted his body over mine so his erection was lined up with my fluttering opening.

Eyes locked on mine, he watched closely as the first press of his body into mine turned my entire world upside down. I wondered if he could see it in my eyes, if it was stamped all over my face. It felt like there was no way to hide the effect his body had over mine. It was one of the most significant things that had ever happened to me. It was the first time I felt connected so intimately to another person. It was the first time I felt like I was more than an accessory or a convenience. I was more aware of all the things that made me feminine and womanly at this moment than I'd ever been in my entire life. I was so exposed, so open and vulnerable. That was my worst fear, not being able to hide just how sensitive and in need of love and care I really was. For a heartbeat, I worried it was too much, and I was going to freak him out, but as soon as he was fully seated inside of me, he lowered his head and gave me a kiss that might have healed all the fissures and cracks in my chronically abused heart.

"Ah, Della. You might burn, but we're going to go up in flames together." He was good with words, too smooth and slick for his own good. Lucky for me he had the moves and the confidence to back it up.

He wrapped a hand around the back of one of my thighs, pulled me closer, and started to move. I curled an arm around his shoulders, and let my free hand wander across my torso. I brushed across my nipples and gasped at the sensation. Crew growled in approval as his hips slung in a pounding rhythm against mine. I felt my body clamp down on his, felt pleasure pool and passion light up inside of me. His cock raged through tender flesh, the stretch and slide making me writhe underneath him.

He panted my name and told me how good I felt wrapped around him. I sighed and told him to go faster, to hit deeper. I wanted to be able to feel him when he was long gone.

I worked my hand down my body, brazen in a way that was totally new to me. There was something about being with someone who didn't believe the rules applied to them. It was freeing to know whatever I did, however I found pleasure, Crew would never judge me or look down on me for it. I let my fingers find their way between my legs and the backs skimmed over his pistoning erection as he dove inside of me over and over again. My fingertips feathered over the tight bud of my clit and my vision went white. There was so much desire, so much craving, I was ready to come out of my skin.

"Oh…my…" My words trailed off as his cock hit the special spot inside that made coherent thought impossible. How he found it when no one else I'd been with was able to was beyond me, but I was counting my lucky stars he had.

Reading me like an open book, and watching every minute response, Crew picked up on the fact he'd done something I really liked and repeated the move over and over again until I was breaking apart under his hands. I spiraled away on a cloud of bliss with his name on my lips, as my hand dug into his skin, leaving my own marks on him, hoping I would be as hard to forget as he was.

Lost in my own satisfaction, I hardly noticed Crew losing his steady rhythm as his thrusts picked up the pace and dropped any kind of finesse. When he found his own completion, he did it chanting "Della" in his soft drawl and with a look in his eyes that made promises I knew he didn't plan on keeping. None of those things mattered though, because he'd given me a night to remember and beautiful memories I'd hold close, and I'd kept him out of trouble. We could be good for each other if we were brave enough to take a chance on us.

Chapter 10

CREW

Neither one of us got much sleep that night. By some unspoken agreement, we both seemed to know we had to fit as much of each other into these few stolen moments together as possible. If I wasn't reaching for her in the dark, she was reaching for me, and I couldn't hold on to her tight enough.

When my phone went off in the early hours of dawn, my first inclination was to ignore it. I didn't want to burst the mellow, happy bubble I'd found in Della's arms. For the first time in my adult life, I actually felt some measure of calm and balance. She quieted the noise that was always screaming inside of me. She dulled some of the sharp edges that were always poking me, prodding me. The ones I did my best to run away from. However, knowing no one would dare call me before the sun was up unless there was an emergency, I quickly answered while slipping out of the warm bed and away from the even warmer body. A chill worked down my spine when I saw my sister's name on the screen as I padded naked into the bathroom, so the call wouldn't wake Della.

"Kody? What's wrong?" My sister owned a bar, so late-night and early-morning hours were nothing new for her, but I knew she wouldn't be calling unless something was wrong.

"Crew..." Kody was breathing hard and sounded furious. "I'm calling you before I call Case because the guys that just came in and trashed my bar told me to tell you 'time's up.' What in the hell have you gotten yourself into this time?" The disappointment in her voice shattered my heart.

I dragged a hand over my face and turned away from the mirror, unable to look at my own reflection. "Are you okay? They didn't hurt you, did they?"

Kody huffed out an annoyed breath. "No. I keep a shotgun under the bar for a reason, and I grew up with two older brothers who made sure I knew how to take care of myself. Stop changing the subject. What kind of mess are you in that these guys showed up in Loveless and messed around with your family?"

I could have lied, would have if I hadn't spent the last week with a woman who made me believe I could be better than I had always been, if I put my mind to it and finally gave myself the benefit of the doubt.

"I've got a gambling problem. Started out winning and it was fun, then I started losing. I got in so deep there was no way I was ever going to pay my bookie back. He threatened to come after you if I didn't pay him what I owed after throwing the last of my season. I had to lose so he could stack the bets against me. I have the money; I was headed to Vegas today to get rid of him. He must have gotten impatient or was trying to make a point." The confession tumbled out, and I knew for certain I would never feel as low as I did at this moment. My little sister was hurt because of me. What kind of man did that make me?

"Why didn't you tell me, Crew? Why didn't you let someone know what was going on before it got this bad? After all these years do you really think you don't have anyone in your corner? Because I've always been there and I'm not going anywhere, no matter what kind of stupid shit you get yourself into." She scoffed a little and dropped a bomb on me. "Plus I know a little about running numbers. You don't think a little town like Loveless with nearly zero tourist traffic is the reason this bar is so profitable, do you?"

I groaned and ran my hand over my face again. "Kody..."

"I don't want to hear it. Our dad is as much of a criminal as the guys who busted in and did this to my bar. I set up a spread on college football and let the boys bet against each other on the pro games. It's not a big deal, and it brings in enough money I can keep a roof over my head and my bar open. I'm not hurting anyone. I don't break legs and threaten families when people don't pay. I don't let my customers get in that deep." She sounded offended that I might even consider lumping her into the same category as Vargas.

"What about Case?" I couldn't imagine a scenario in which he was okay with our baby sister running an illegal gambling racket from inside of her bar.

She sighed, and I could picture the way her forehead furrowed and the way her mouth would slip into a perturbed frown. Case and I looked a lot alike. We were both tall and solid. Case was bulkier than I was, more intimidating at first glance, but we had the same dark hair and blue eyes. Our mother's eyes if you asked anyone who knew her before she passed away. Kody had our father's leafy-green eyes but took after our mother in every other way. She had pretty honey-colored hair and was built with much smaller and more delicate lines. Her petite stature was misleading. Kody was the toughest out of all three of us Lawton kids. She also had the biggest heart.

"Case and I have a *don't ask don't tell* policy in place. As long as he doesn't have confirmation anything illegal is going on, he lets me slide. He's made it known, if he ever receives a complaint, or has enough proof to show what I'm doing, he's going to shut me down. We don't talk about it. It's like the worst-kept secret in the world."

"You think he'd actually arrest you?" I'd like to think Case cared more about his family than upholding the law, but I wasn't sure. He'd had one hell of an uphill climb facing him when he took over our father's position as sheriff of Loveless. My older brother wanted to run a clean department, to clear out all the corruption and misconduct that had flourished under my old man's reign. Having most of his family lean toward the criminally inclined side of the street couldn't help his cause in the slightest.

Kody sighed again. "No. But I do think he'd let one of his deputies do it if they could prove what I had going on in here. And I don't blame him for that. Case isn't like you and me, Crew. We've always looked out for number one; Case has always looked out for everyone. He's always trying to save us all, and all you and I do is fight him every step of the way."

I blew out a breath. "Maybe it's time we learn how to save ourselves, so he doesn't always have to do it."

She laughed on the other end of the phone. "Maybe. But I'm still going to call Case and tell him thugs broke into my bar and threatened me. They couldn't have gotten very far out of town yet, and I'll happily press charges against them, especially if their boss is holding you by the balls."

I grunted in response. "No. I'll call Case. I'm going to come clean, let him know how bad I screwed up and that it bled onto you. I'm going to tell him about the guy who sent the muscle down to Loveless and see if, maybe, he can come up with a plan to get him off my back for good. I already told my bookie I had the money to pay him back; him coming after you means he's up to something. I don't think he's got any plans to let me simply walk away." It was time to bite the bullet and do the right thing, even if it was going to forever ruin the way my older brother saw me.

"I think that's a good idea. I think you being honest with Case, and yourself, is long overdue. Do you want to tell me how you managed to come up with the cash to the pay the bookie back so fast, or do I not want to know?" Kody's tone turned teasing, and I felt a smile lift the corners of my mouth.

"I don't know if you'd believe me if I told you."

"Oh, it's you, Crew. There isn't much I wouldn't believe."

I chuckled softly because she really did know me better than anyone else. "My former manager went behind my back and signed me on to be the face of a useless, high-end grooming product line for men. He bounced town with the advance, but the remaining amount on the contract was enough to pay off my debt and cover the interest. I pranced around looking pretty for the last week, feeling like an idiot. It wasn't anything I would have said yes to, but the stupid campaign saved my ass." And brought Della into my life, which I would be forever thankful for.

Kody laughed, and I was happy to hear that she no longer sounded pissed off or afraid. "I'm sure you rocked it, and it's a good thing the opportunity fell into your lap. Call me after you talk to Case, so I know what's going on. And stop acting like you are a lone soldier fighting a war you can't win. I love you, Case loves you, and we're not going to let anyone hurt you. Make good choices, Crew. I know that goes against your nature, but try."

I told her I loved her and promised I would be in touch after I talked to our older brother. I set my phone on the vanity and turned to look at myself in the mirror. The man facing me wasn't anything special, but he did have the ability to right a few wrongs. I took a deep breath and splashed some cold water on my face, preparing myself for a goodbye that was going to hurt.

I wrapped myself up in one of the fluffy complimentary robes hanging off the back of the door and made my way back into the hotel room.

"Hey, Ms. Priss. Do you want me to order breakfast? Get you a mimosa or something?" There was no way I was going to treat her like my usual one-night stands. I wanted her to know she had fundamentally changed the man I was. If someone like her had faith I was good enough, then there was no excuse for me to keep living up to my own low expectations.

I jerked to a stop as soon as I entered the room. It was exactly as I'd left it, bed rumpled, drapes still closed, the scent of sex and Della's expensive perfume still lingering in the air. It was all the same except the bed was empty. Della's clothes, which had been scattered across the floor, were gone, as was the woman I'd peeled them off of. There was no sign of her, no note, no lipstick message scrawled across the mirror. There was nothing to indicate she'd ever even been here.

I threw myself onto the bed, swearing under my breath and wondering if this was how all the women I skipped out on the morning after felt when I ghosted them.

I toyed with the idea of calling her. I wanted her to know that our night together was special, but just as I was levering myself up to go back to the bathroom and fetch my phone, I realized what I'd said to Kody when she'd asked about coming up with the money to pay my debts off. I called the product line Della worked so hard on stupid and worthless. I told my sister I felt like an idiot putting my face out there for the world to judge and find wanting. Once again I had acted without thinking, spoken without any thought about the impact my words and actions may have on someone other than myself. Della put everything on the line for this campaign, and took a huge risk on me, believing that I would do her vision justice. I belittled her passion, treated it like it was nothing.

It was unfair and in bad form. I was an idiot.

I remembered how uncomfortable she looked that first day when she tracked me down at the rodeo. She was so out of place, but she never tried to make me feel like what I did for a living was a waste of time or talent. She had more class and care in her pinky finger than I did in my entire body.

I swore again and knocked my fist against my forehead. I screwed up...again. But I had to take care of Vargas first. I needed to make sure my family was safe and I had to ensure the mobster never found out how important Della was to me. She was the ultimate weapon he could wield in order to keep me under his thumb forever, so I needed to find a way to sever all ties for good. I also needed to come up with something quick, something important and impactful to let her know I was leaving, but that she was still on my mind and I knew there were things I had to apologize for if she would let me. I didn't know if she would forgive me for speaking rashly, or if she would believe I didn't mean what I said. I was speaking through the stress of worrying about my sister and the upcoming conversation I had to have with my brother. I had to believe she knew me well enough to understand I was hotheaded and foolish even at my best.

Sighing, I shoved up off the bed and went and found my phone. I placed a local call and crossed my fingers, hoping the simple gesture would be enough to get through to the woman whose trust I'd just blindly betrayed. Then I called my brother.

It was time to go home.

Chapter 11

DELLA

I almost fell out of my chair when my office door opened and the last man I expected to see walked through it. Out of habit I sat up straighter, moved a hand to make sure there wasn't a stray hair out of place, and nervously fidgeted with my outfit. No matter how put together or professional I looked, this man standing in front of me always made me feel like I was lacking in one way or another.

"*Ma petite fille*, you look terrible. Are you not sleeping?" My father always spoke with an odd mix of French and English. Picking and choosing the words he used in a different language at random. But he always referred to me as his "little girl" even though I'd turned thirty several months ago.

Involuntarily, I lifted my fingers to the dark circles I knew were under my eyes. I hadn't slept well since sneaking out of Crew's hotel room at dawn a couple of days ago. The following evening a special delivery had arrived at my door. The married couple from the Italian restaurant where we'd gone on our first "date" were standing outside of my apartment door. I wasn't surprised they charmed their way past my doorman and were allowed up to my floor. Carlotta was holding a to-go container of those damn cannolis and Luca had a bottle of wine and a bouquet of flowers. They also recited a very sweeping and dramatic apology from Crew. I had no choice but to listen to it, since I wasn't rude enough to shut the door in their faces after they'd gone to so much trouble for the damn man. I listened as graciously as I could, promised I would hear Crew out should he call, closed the door when they left, and cried for two days straight. He sent a single text. All it said was *I'm sorry*. I'd yet to come up with a proper reply, so it sat unanswered, and the cannolis sat untouched. The gesture was grand and over-the-top, but the hurt he caused was bigger and impossible to ignore.

So was the worry that something terrible would happen to him and I would be none the wiser. I hated every single part of the conversation I'd overheard. But I agonized over the parts where he admitted he needed to deal with the dangerous man he owed money to. I lost night after night of sleep imagining what could happen to him when he confronted the bookie.

I did drink the wine and have myself a pity party for one. I'd reached peak pitiful at that point.

And now my father was here, so my already raw and tattered emotions were about to unravel.

"Just trying to put the finishing touches on the campaign for Sophistiqué. Everything goes to print next week, and the big launch in stores is only a few weeks after that. I want everything to be perfect." I sighed. "I don't want to let you down."

My father forced himself into one of the chairs that sat across from my desk and tapped his index finger against his lips as he looked at me without blinking. My father was not a big man, but every single inch of him was elegant and refined. He moved like a man who ruled the world and had no equal. Only now, after spending time with Crew, I saw he didn't seem nearly as imposing as he always had. I needed to stop viewing him as the man who shipped me off to boarding school because he had no clue what to do with me, and look at him as the CEO of the company I was bound and determined to take over.

"Tu travailles trop dur, petite fille." The same hazel eyes that I looked at every day in the mirror watched me closely as I stiffened at his gentle admonishment that I work too hard.

"I work as hard as I have to. What else do I have besides this company?" I rubbed my temples and tried to force back a headache I could feel starting to pound. "I didn't know you were coming to New York, Père. Are you checking up on me?" I was torn between being thrilled he cared, and annoyed he didn't trust me to handle things on my own.

My father made a noise and leaned forward on the chair. He put his hands on the edge of my desk, eyes flitting over the numerous pictures of Crew I had spread out before me. The man literally covered every inch of my work space, making clarity and distance impossible.

"He worked out better than I thought he would. *Il est très beau.* I'm happy to see you did not turn him into everyone else. I had my doubts how the two of you would work together." He reached for one of the candid shots the photographer had taken. Crew had his hands on the horse's mane, and there was a genuine smile on his too-handsome face. "I will buy whatever this man is selling." My father smiled, which totally caught me off guard. He was usually so stern and disapproving when we tried to work together.

Keeping the picture in his hands, he leaned back in the chair. A sigh drifted up between us as he seemed to get lost in thought.

"I loved your mother more than anything, Della. More than this company. More than any amount of money. More than my family name."

I bit my tongue before I could burst out that he obviously loved her more than me, since he shut me out of his life in all ways, except for business, as soon as she was gone.

"We were very different, your mother and I. No one believed we would work out in the long run, *mais notre amour était beau*. She was my everything, and when I lost her, I also felt like I had nothing." He held up a hand when I automatically started to protest that he had me, he made the decision to throw me away. "I know I was cold, distant, and not a good father to you after your mother was gone. I have many, many regrets, Della. You look so much like her, I hurt every time I looked at you. In the end, I forced you to end up just like me, and I know your mother would never want that for you. She would want you to have the kind of love we shared. She would want more for you than this company."

He tossed the picture of Crew back on my desk, and my heart skipped a beat when my eyes landed on his ruggedly handsome face. I swore I could feel the burn of those blue eyes from the picture.

"You are so much like me, I thought throwing you together with your opposite might result in the same kind of awakening I had when I met your mother. I searched far and wide for a man who would finally rattle the cage I unwittingly forced you into. A friend of a friend used this cowboy to model underwear. I watched him ride those wild horses and strut around in his boots and hat. I thought he would be perfect for you, and even if he wasn't, maybe he could show you there is more to life than work. I knew his manager was shady, and things were not on the up-and-up, but I brought him into your life anyway. I want you to have a chance to be happy like I once was. I want you to know the kind of love I've known. That is a far better gift I can give you than this company."

I took a deep breath and put my hands flat on the desk in front of me. I kind of wanted to strangle him, but so many years of perfect manners kept me seated, even though I was shaking. "You knew nothing about Crew. And worse than that, you know nothing about me. How could you gamble with something you knew was so important to me? This campaign means everything to me, and you risked it all to play matchmaker? Do you see him here? Do you think your scheme worked out?"

My father waved a hand in the air in front of him, as if to dismiss all the furious questions I fired his way. "I was hoping it would all work out between you and the cowboy. I never had a single concern about the new product line. *Tu es trop bonne dans ce que tu fais.* You are the best, and I never doubted this idea of yours was going to be a success. It is your heart I am now worried about. As a father should."

"I think this is all too little, too late." I got up and started to pace back and forth behind the desk. "I've waited my entire life for you to tell me I'm doing a good job, and the first time you do, you throw out that I should be concentrating more on my love life." I tossed my hands up in the air and let them fall uselessly to my sides. "I'm never going to win with you, never going to make you proud."

My father climbed to his feet and made his way around the desk. I froze in shock when he pulled me into a tight hug. I could count on one hand the number of times this man had willingly been affectionate with me. I gulped and looked up at him through suddenly watery eyes. "Are you dying? Is that why you're suddenly so concerned about me being alone?"

My father chuckled and kissed both of my cheeks in a very French way. "*Petite idiote.* Of course I'm not dying. I would not keep something like that from you. What I am is lonely, and I do not want that for you. I have watched you seek out men who will not bring anything new into your life. No adventure. No light. No love. You deserve all of those things and so much more, Della."

I sniffed and wiped at my eyes. I don't know when I started crying, but the tears were rolling down my cheeks unchecked. "It's sweet, you trying to set me up, but I don't think Crew and I were meant to be. There is different, then there is impossible. We were impossible. He doesn't take what I do seriously. I thought he cared about how important this campaign was to me. He called it stupid and useless, and said he felt like an idiot participating." The words hurt just as much the second time around when I was the one saying them. "He also has some pretty dangerous hobbies." I'd heard him confess to the gambling and all the destruction it led to.

"*Oui.* His manager may have alluded to there being some problems, which is why he was so desperate to sign the deal. None of us are without fault. When you first learned of the cowboy, you had some very harsh words about him and his lifestyle. If he overheard you then, how would he have felt?"

I cringed and pulled away from his embrace. I wiped my face with the back of one hand, noticing my eye makeup was smeared. It reminded me of the first encounter I had with Crew. The one where I told him he was going to have to change everything about who he was to be good enough. Then I slept with the man I thought I knew, the one who was still wild, but thoughtful and considerate, only to have him reveal he hadn't changed all that much from the man I pegged him as from the start.

"Okay. So I'm old enough and wise enough to know sometimes people think without speaking, but I haven't actually talked to him. He left without a goodbye. He sent an apology, not an explanation." The silence after the best sex I'd ever had felt vast and echoing. It didn't help when I closed my eyes: I could still picture his strong body moving over mine, and feel his hands running all over me. Which was why sleep had been hard to come by lately.

My father scoffed. "As I said, you are like me, Della. In business and in your personal life. When do you find it acceptable to accept defeat without trying every possible option? When do you give up on something you are passionate about and believe in? Did you know, your mother did not want to date me? She claimed I was too out of touch with the 'real people.' She viewed my wealth as something ugly and problematic. I had to court her. Woo her. Charm her into going out with me. She did not agree to a single date until I proved how serious I was about her. I had to donate money to charity. I had to volunteer to help the homeless. I had to spend time with the real people to show her I was worth her time."

I wrinkled my nose and gave him a narrow-eyed look. "You think I need to learn how to ride a horse or something?"

He laughed and put his hands on his stomach. "No. I think you need to decide what is more important, your pride and hurt feelings, or the person who hurt them." He nodded at me and pointed at the desk. "Everything you are and everything you have become went into this campaign. Look at those pictures, Della. I see you in them just as much as I see him. Do not live the life I've lived. Live the life your mother would have wanted for you. The company and your place in it will never go anywhere. Your last name is on the damn building. I may not have gotten much right, but I have always known you were going to carry my legacy on. But there is nothing in the fine print that says you should do it alone. I'm in town for a few weeks. I can take care of whatever you need me to if you need a few days off."

He kissed my forehead and disappeared as quickly as he appeared. I swore under my breath and rubbed the heels of my palms into my eyes. It was so much to take in, and I had no clue what my next move should be.

"Qu'est-ce que je vais faire?"

Chapter 12

CREW

Sitting in the wreckage of my sister's bar, it was everything I could do not to leap across the space separating me from a smirking Dante Vargas.

The huge mirror that ran behind the bar was smashed into a million pieces. Several of the tables were broken, and it was obvious a chair had been used to bust out almost all of the windows in the building. There were burn marks on the floor, and the entire room smelled like spilled booze and old blood. There were bullet holes in the ceiling and a couple in the front door. My sister wasn't joking around about keeping a shotgun under the bar and knowing how to use it. Kody had definitely downplayed how extensive the damage was.

My hands were curled into fists on top of my bouncing thighs as I glared at the man who had become the bane of my existence. I didn't spare Vargas's muscle a single look. All my focus was on the Vegas gangster who had pulled my strings for far too long.

"Are you positive you can convince your brother to let my men out of jail? He does not strike me as a forgiving man." I hated that Vargas looked so smug. He'd had the upper hand for too long. It was past time I took him down a notch.

I narrowed my eyes and ordered myself to relax. I had one shot to get this right, and if I screwed it up, there was no walking away from Vargas, no getting my life back. It was also more than just my neck on the line this time, and I refused to drag anyone else into this muck and mire with me.

"I told you, as long as someone posts their bond...in cash..." I lifted my eyebrows and gave him a knowing look. "Case will let them go, and their paperwork will magically disappear. After you fucked with Kody, all he wants is to get your guys out of town."

Vargas chuckled and lifted a dark eyebrow. "So your older brother is taking a page out of your father's very dirty playbook, is he?"

I held in a curse and tapped my fingers against my knee. "Case is cleaning up my mess for a price. He's sick of doing it for free. Look, Vargas." I leaned forward. "I gave you your money, with the inflated interest. I'll make sure you get your guys back. We're square. You need to walk away."

The other man laughed and clapped his hands together. "Oh, cowboy, I think it is adorable that you think you get to decide when we're done, or when you have paid enough." An ugly glint flashed in his beady gaze, and his tone took on a sinister quality I'd never heard him use before. Even when he was ordering his brute to beat the crap out of me. A prickle of fear poked at my skin and I took a deep breath, trying to keep my face blank and my temper in check. "You are a particularly handsome man, Crew Lawton. A rodeo star, and now a full-fledged supermodel. I made a lot of money off you when you were getting dropped off those horses of yours, but I will make so much more selling that pretty face of yours to the highest bidder. Doesn't that sound like fun?"

I stood up so fast my chair toppled over, making a huge racket. The monster guarding the mobster took a step forward but I was so pissed I kept moving until I felt his massive paws hit me dead center in my chest. Vargas had insisted on inspecting me for a wire before uttering a word. Being paranoid kept him out of jail and alive.

"You're out of your mind. I'm not going to whore myself out for you, Vargas. We're even. I don't owe you anything else." I shoved the giant's hands away and pointed at the other man, who was still smirking at me like he knew something I didn't. "You're out of your damn mind."

"I'm a brilliant businessman, cowboy. You've proved you are willing to do just about anything to keep me away from your family. And you've proven to be remarkably resourceful when it comes to coming up with ways to pay off your debts. We both know you won't be able to stay away, so it's just a matter of time before you owe me more than you can repay. I can always make plans to take your sister and sell her in your place. My guys told me she's feisty, likes to put up a fight. Some people like that. They enjoy breaking that kind of wild spirit." Vargas winked, and I let out a howl of outrage that could probably be heard all the way in Vegas. I lunged at him and ended up getting clotheslined by his bodyguard before I could get close enough to touch.

I pushed at the massive hands holding me in place and swore up a storm. "Fuck you, Vargas. I'll kill you before you get anywhere near Kody again." I took a right hook to the side of my face, and immediately tasted blood and heard bells as my head practically spun around. I spit out a mouthful of blood, a sense of déjà vu settling over me as this scene between us played out once again. I wiped the back of my hand across my mouth and looked at the mob boss from under lowered lashes. "I'm done. Done playing fast and loose with right and wrong, done doing stupid shit that puts the people I care about at risk. I don't care if I have to check myself into rehab if I have to drag my ass to group meetings, or even if I have to join a goddamn monastery, I will never be in a position where you, or anyone else like you, has any power over me again."

I scrambled back as Vargas suddenly stepped around the hired muscle and reached for me. His hands, adorned with more jewelry than most women wore, tightened on the front of my shirt. He used his grip to jerk me toward him, dragging me closer until we were almost nose to nose. I'd never really been scared of Vargas, even knowing he was ruthless when it came to his business. But right now I felt fear. It slithered down my spine and settled like lead in my gut.

It wasn't that I was scared of what he had planned for Kody. I knew Case wasn't going to let Vargas anywhere near my sister. I was terrified that whatever he had planned for me was going to make it so much harder for me to get Della back if I convinced her to accept my apology. The last thing I wanted was to end up six feet under before making things right with the beautiful blonde. That was a wrong I was determined to right no matter the cost.

"You are done when I say you're done, Lawton. You've been a pain in the ass since the beginning. Acting like you deserve special treatment. Acting like you're better than the rest of the bums who come to my house and lose everything. You are nothing but a pawn, and I own you." The other man gave me a little shake. "The sooner you realize that, the easier it will be on you." Vargas gave me another one of those malicious grins that made him look devilish. "We can talk about the pretty executive you left behind in New York if you want. Something tells me she won't put up as much of a fight as your sister did. I play to win, cowboy. Do not challenge me."

I saw red . . .

Everything moved in a swirl of furious, desperate color and all I could think about was getting my hands around Vargas's neck so he would shut up, so he would never be able to even hint at hurting Della.

He was stupid and got close enough for me to grab, and I was pissed enough I barely felt the behemoth on my back pounding and kicking as he tried to dislodge me from his boss.

I wasn't letting go.

If it was Della or Vargas, there was no choice which one was going to be left breathing at the end of the day. Distantly, I wondered if Case would actually be able to throw his younger brother in the slammer for murder as Vargas rapidly started to turn a startling shade of blue. I clutched my hands tighter, even as blows landed on the back of my head and across my shoulders. I yelped as the chair I'd kicked over was shattered across my back, but I still kept my fingers clamped down around Vargas's windpipe.

The man's jeweled fingers clawed frantically and painfully at mine, and his dark eyes bulged as he struggled for any kind of air. I wanted to gloat. I wanted to let out a victory shout, one declaring I'd finally managed to protect everyone I loved. But the relief was short-lived when a starburst of pain, so bright and all-consuming, bloomed over my lower back. I gasped as the metallic scent of fresh blood filled the air. I rolled off of Vargas, hands numb and my vision going blurry. I reached for my left side where the pain was radiating from, and groaned when my fingers encountered the cool blade of a knife sticking out of my body right above my jeans. I'd been kicked in the same spot enough times to know the blade had to be right by my kidney if it wasn't embedded in one. This wasn't good. Not good at all.

I flopped on the floor like a beached fish and belatedly whispered, "Case, I need you." I wasn't sure if I actually got the words out because everything got hazy. I could hear my breath whooshing in and out. My heartbeat sounded extraordinarily loud, and it felt like I could feel each and every beat.

Groggily, I tried to lift my head off the ground as the front door of the bar suddenly burst open, and the entire sheriff's department of Loveless, Texas, flooded the room, led by my brother. Vaguely, I was aware of flashing lights and the sight of guns being pointed at Vargas and his man whose hands were covered in my blood. Knowing Case was there, I let my eyes drift closed and fought back the darkness, which was doing its best to take me under.

"You weren't wearing a wire! I checked!" Vargas was screaming, demanding a lawyer and telling Case he was going to be sorry.

I tried to peel an eye open, so I could watch my brother put cuffs on the man who had threatened Della and roughed up Kody, but my body wasn't obeying my commands.

"Your guys were too stupid to disable the security cameras my sister already has in place. We tapped into the feed. We have every threat you made on tape. I've got you dead to rights on extortion, Vargas. Not to mention attempted murder. You're never going to see the light of day again, and if my brother dies, I'll make sure your time in lockup is as agonizing as possible. I play to win too, asshole." Case's growl was oddly reassuring and for once not directed at me.

I winced when a big hand tapped my cheek. "Everything was going as planned until you jumped him, you crazy bastard.

You just had to go and get yourself stabbed, didn't you? Why can't you ever do anything the easy way, Crew?" I felt his hands skate over me and heard him swear. "Shit! Guys, I need an ambulance here NOW. Someone call Westwood General and tell them we have a stab wound coming in."

I had no clue who Case was talking to, but I was glad he was here and taking charge of everything. I groaned when someone tried to move me and pain shot through my whole body like a fireball. I wanted to scream at them to be careful, but I couldn't get words out. Instead, I floated away in a haze of agony and regret.

I whispered "I'm sorry" over and over. I was sure my brother thought the words were for him. I owed him those words and so much more, but I knew they were for Della. All I could do was hope someone passed the message along for me as I succumbed to the void of nothingness closing in around me.

Chapter 13

DELLA

I was waiting for my connecting flight to Austin, the city closest to Loveless with a big airport, when my phone rang with a number I didn't recognize. My first inclination was to ignore it. My nerves were stretched thin, and I was second-guessing every decision I'd made since booking a flight from JFK yesterday. I wasn't even certain Crew was back in his hometown, or if he wanted anything to do with me. I'd let my father's sudden flight of fancy get to me, but with every minute that crawled by I was having a million doubts and scolding myself for being rash and reckless. That was how Crew acted, and look where it landed him.

Shaking my head at my own foolishness, I answered the call, thinking maybe something was wrong with the campaign. My father had already given all my images and marketing materials the green light, but who was to say the confusing old man hadn't had a change of heart.

"Hello." I shifted my laptop bag on my shoulder and tried not to tap the toe of my Jimmy Choo impatiently. I was working on presenting an outwardly calm and collected appearance, figuring I could fake it until I was face-to-face with the man who'd wrecked me. I gave myself permission to fall apart if Crew sent me on my way without an explanation or apology. I was determined to keep my head held high, regardless of the outcome of this little adventure.

"Is this Della Deveaux?" The voice on the other end of the call was female and had a distinct southern twang to it.

"This is she. Who is this?" I couldn't bring to mind anyone I worked with, or knew casually, who spoke with the slow drawl. Aside from Crew.

"My name is Kody Lawton. I'm—"

"Crew's sister." I cut in before she could finish. Suddenly the anxiety wrapped around me found a whole new reason to try and choke the life out of me. "He talked about you quite a bit. Is everything all right?"

She sighed, and I heard her make a hiccuping sound, indicating she was probably fighting back tears. Something cold and dark swirled inside of my chest, and my fingers turned white where they were clutching my phone like a lifeline.

"Crew was injured while participating in a police sting last night. He needed emergency surgery." She hiccupped again, and I heard her working to get control of her emotions. "It was touch and go there for a while. He needed a massive blood transfusion, and there were complications from an old injury he had from riding rodeo all these years."

"Oh my god." My computer bag slipped off my shoulder and landed with a thud by my feet. I didn't notice. It took every ounce of concentration I had to keep breathing and stay focused on Kody's words. "Is he okay now?"

The other woman cleared her throat. "They're going to move him out of ICU later today. He's on all kinds of painkillers, and antibiotics, and blood thinners, but he was awake for a short period of time this morning. He asked for you repeatedly. My other brother, Case, thought he was delirious from the drugs, but I know Crew. He never asks for help. He does everything the absolutely hardest way possible. If he wants you here, I swear I will sell my soul to get you here for him. I will do anything if you agree to come and see him. You obviously mean something to him if he wants you when he's flat on his back and completely vulnerable. I stole your number out of his phone." It was obvious this woman wasn't used to asking anyone for anything. It must be a family trait.

"I'm on my way to Loveless right now. I'm in Dallas, waiting for my connection to board. I should be there within the next couple of hours." My voice shook, and I couldn't get the image of Crew, injured and helpless in a hospital bed, out of my mind. It made all the insecurity and reservations I'd had about going to him fade away. "Can you tell me the quickest way to get to the hospital from Austin?"

Another sigh, this one full of relief, met my ears as the woman told me she would text me directions and promised to keep me updated on Crew's status. I wanted to ask how in the world Crew ended up involved in a police sting, especially one that had the potential to put him in such a dangerous position, but I figured all of that could wait. I still had to keep it together so I didn't melt down into a hysterical mess. They wouldn't let me on the plane if I shrieked and pulled at my hair the way I wanted to. Luckily, we boarded shortly after Kody's call. It was also a short flight to Austin from Dallas. It was going to take an hour or so to make the drive to the small town of Loveless.

When I finally got to the hospital, it was easy to spot Crew's family. There was a man who so closely resembled my wayward cowboy there was no question they were related. He was a little bit taller, a little bit wider around the shoulders, and it was obvious he was older by the faint lines fanning from familiar blue eyes, and the touch of silvery-white at his temples. He was also dressed in a tan uniform and held a bone-colored cowboy hat in his hand as he faced off with an older man who was creating some kind of scene. A young woman was standing between the two men. She had a hand on each of their chests and was physically keeping them apart. She was a tiny little thing, with a riot of caramel- and bronze-colored hair, and enough attitude I could feel it all the way across the room. She didn't look like the older version of Case or my cowboy. But her stance, and curl of her mouth as she ordered the other two men to behave, reminded me so much of Crew I had no doubt this was his little sister.

"Knock it off. Both of you. This isn't about either of you, and if you can't behave, I'll throw both your asses out of this hospital. I don't care if you're the sheriff or the former sheriff." She huffed and gave each chest a purposeful push as I tentatively made my way closer, my heels clicking loudly against the linoleum under my feet. The woman looked up and met my gaze, but the men were oblivious.

"If Case had a clue as to what he was doing, his little brother wouldn't be in here fighting for his life." The older man, who I figured was the patriarch of the Lawton clan, sneered at the big guy in the uniform. "Always acted like you were so much better than me, boy. Always up on your high horse. Where were you when your brother needed you? What kind of cop are you?" It was nasty. The old man was clearly unpleasant, and I could see why Crew had so much animosity toward him.

"I'm an honest cop, which is more than you could ever say, old man. You're out of your mind if you think Crew wants to see you now. You haven't been in his life unless it was to guilt him into giving you money for years. I'm going to let Kody throw you out on your ass if you don't step away from me right this second." The sheriff even sounded like Crew. He had the same low, raspy southern drawl. Voices started to rise once again despite Kody's interference, and I found myself impatient with the family drama.

"Excuse me. Can someone show me where Crew is… please?" I asked. If they didn't stop bickering, I was going to find him without their help.

The woman stopped mid-argument and blinked at me in surprise. The two men turned and looked at me with matching shocked expressions. The man in the uniform was the first one to speak. He lifted a dark eyebrow and let his gaze wander over me from head to the tips of my designer shoes.

"You're real?"

The gruff question caught me off guard, so I looked at Kody for help. She maneuvered toward me, a strained smile on her pretty face. "Of course she's real. She's standing right in front of you, you dumb ass. Thank you so much for getting here so quickly."

The old man gave me the same once-over his son just had, but his made me feel icky and had my skin crawling uncomfortably. "Where did Crew find a fancy piece like you?"

I stiffened. I couldn't recall ever being called a "piece" to my face before. Kody stepped in front of me, blocking her father and brother from view. "Ignore them. Come on, Crew was in and out of consciousness a little bit ago. I think seeing you might be exactly what he needs right now. You're much prettier to look at than either of those two jackasses." She grasped my elbow and all but hauled me down a long hallway until we reached one of the patient rooms. "I'm sorry about that. Case is usually all right, but get him and my dad together, and it's never a good time. He's dealing with some major guilt about Crew getting hurt so badly on his watch and has always taken on too much responsibility when it comes to protecting both of us." She gestured to the door. "Go on in. He may be out of it, and he looks terrible, so brace yourself. I'll be back after I deal with my dad and brother." She marched off like a tiny soldier, and I felt a grin pull at my mouth. It was easy to see why Crew had such a soft spot for her. She was a dynamo.

I entered the dimly lit room and jerked to a stop at the sight that greeted me. For being such a large, expressive man, Crew looked incredibly small and frail in the hospital bed. A monitor above his head beeped every few seconds, and a tangle of tubes and wires seemed to be surrounding him. His normally golden skin tone was now an ashy gray, and the purple smudges under his eyes were visible even in the low light. He did look terrible, but I could see his chest rise and fall with each breath he took, and his long, sooty lashes fluttered, letting me know he was wounded, but still alive. The flood of relief I felt was enough to take me to my knees. I probably would have fallen if a scratchy "Hey" hadn't floated up from the bed.

I practically ran across the room, hovering at the side of the bed, barely touching the back of his hand with my fingertips. His skin was dry and cool to the touch. All the vitality and life I associated with this man was currently missing. I gulped back too many emotions to name and forced a weak smile. "Hey back."

It was obvious he was struggling to keep his eyes open, and the bright blue was dull and flat. "Are you real?"

A laugh escaped as I curled my fingers around his hand. "Your brother just asked me the same thing. I am very real, and I'm sorry it took me so long to get here."

He moaned low and long, and not at all in a good way. I could see him struggling to speak, to get his fuzzy thoughts in order. I smoothed a caress over his forehead and told him to relax.

"I wanted to apologize. Didn't mean it." His words were stilted but intent.

I shushed him. "I need to apologize for being so scared of everything, scared of you as well. But all of that can wait until you're feeling better. I want you out of this bed, and maybe an explanation of how you ended up here. I'm not going anywhere until you're better." The campaign was the furthest thing from my mind with him out of commission like this.

"All or nothing. Everything in my life is all or nothing. Want it all when it comes to you, Della."

Getting that out must have taken a lot out of him because his eyes drifted closed as soon as he was done talking and his breaths turned from choppy and jagged, to even and steady. I stroked my thumb over the back of his hand and dropped a kiss on his forehead.

We were so different. We hardly knew each other. We lived very different lives, but I couldn't deny that if there was a way to make it work, I wanted it all with him too. Nothing was no longer good enough; I wanted more than that. I wanted everything.

Epilogue

CREW

Eight months later

This RV was a hundred times better than the last one I'd been given.

Not because it was bigger, or flashier, or more high-tech, but because Della was inside of it. Not just her body, which was currently sprawled underneath mine on the flat surface I used as a dining table. It was her lingering presence that had seeped deep into the walls and splashed through all of the elegant and sophisticated touches she'd used to decorate the space after my new sponsor handed over the keys. Even when we weren't together, which happened far more often than I liked, I still felt her inside this space. This RV had become my safe haven, the place I retreated to when life got overwhelming or my vices started to rear their ugly heads. Inside this tin can of a home, I remembered it was no longer just me I was accountable for. My actions could hurt some-one I never, ever wanted to bring harm to.

Della moaned as my mouth moved between her legs. Her toned calves were up by my ears, and I hadn't gotten around to pulling her lipstick-red heels off her feet yet. I'd been all over her the minute I picked her up from the airport. The long-distance thing sucked, even if we had a rule that the longest we went without seeing one another was two weeks. We were two busy people with active careers, and making our schedules and lives mesh took more work than I'd ever put toward anything. I wasn't sure she was going to stick around after I came clean about the gambling and everything with Vargas, but she had. She told me she would stand by me, as long as I did the smart thing and looked into getting help. She found me a rehab center in Colorado, where I spent a little over a month. Della visited every single weekend and acted as my own personal cheerleader. I felt like we were invincible after that.

"Crew." My name came out on a gasp as her eager fingers knocked my hat off my head so they could rake through my hair. It was getting long again. I was leaving it until she asked me to cut it. For now, she seemed to like that there was more than a handful she could get her fingers in and tug on. "God, I missed you."

"Missed you too, Ms. Priss." She flew in from France to watch my qualifying round this weekend. Getting back on the horse, literally, meant starting from the bottom and working my way back up to world champion status. I'd had to pay my dues, ride in smaller competitions with the new up-and-comers, but I'd qualified for one of the big rides in California, and Della promised she would be there to cheer me on. When today's rides were over, we were both headed back to New York for a couple weeks so I could shoot some new promo for Sophistiqué. The line had taken off like crazy, selling out all over the world, so being the face of it had really become my second job. A job I loved, because it kept me close to the woman whimpering so sweetly beneath me. This trailer was only one of the ways I proved to Della her passion was mine and seeing her dreams come true was the most important thing in the world to me. I kept a part of her with me always in the bright colors and flashy logo painted on the outside, even when we were forced to spend time apart. Having her stand by me, no matter what, gave me the strength to stand next to her and support her in the same way.

She lifted her hips and pressed herself insistently against my open mouth. I had my tongue buried deep inside her sweet heat and was using my fingers to tease and torment her. It was gratifying; she'd started to strip and pull at my clothes with frantic hands as soon as the RV door closed behind her. Della still didn't dress like she was going to the rodeo, but I liked it. It made her easy to pick out from the crowd, and I always felt a surge of pride when people realized the best-dressed woman in the entire place was there to support me. She did come armed with allergy meds now, so I didn't have to worry about her sneezing all over the place.

I swirled my tongue through the moisture pooling inside of her. Her thighs quivered next to my head, and her long, lean body writhed beautifully before me. She was tracing erratic designs across each breast with her nails. Her head was tossed to one side, blond hair fanning out like a halo. Her colorful eyes locked on mine as she wordlessly asked me to give her more.

I nuzzled deeper into her wet heat, trying to chase every drop of her desire. She muttered my name again, and her hips bucked up like one of the horses I rode. I knew she wasn't trying to throw me off, but I held on just the same.

"Want you inside of me, Crew. Everything always feels so empty and hollow when we're apart for too long." Her eyelashes fluttered, and a pretty, pink flush crawled up the long line of her neck. "I need you to fill me back up and remind me I'm always going to be yours."

I leaned back so I could nibble along the inside of her smooth thigh. "Always gonna be mine. Doesn't matter where you are or where I am. You're always right in the center of my heart." They were more than practiced words. I meant them. I meant everything I said to her. She was the center of everything. She was the thing that finally set my whole world right. I was no longer constantly off balance, because Della kept me upright, steady, and focused on the future.

She'd already pulled my big belt buckle open and had my jeans hanging off my ass. All it took was a small wiggle and a quick shift of the hips to send the denim down to the floor. Della's hands found the waistband of my boxer-briefs and had my straining cock free of the damp cotton in no time. Her touch felt like silk and fire as she stroked along the rigid length. She used her thumb to spread the pearly moisture pooling at the tip around, and we both hummed in satisfaction.

I gritted my teeth, leaning forward to drag the swollen head through her soaked softness. During my last visit to New York, we'd taken the time to get tested and gotten the green light to ride bareback. It was a first for both of us, and the amount of trust she put in me to allow me inside of her like that was humbling. We spent as much time apart as we did together, so her belief in me, her trust, was something I worked every single day to keep. I wasn't going to screw this up. She meant everything to me.

As always, the first press of my body into hers felt like coming home. She was always tight and so warm. She slid like silk around every aching part of me, and I could feel her body flutter excitedly around my cock. We fit together perfectly, two broken pieces bonded together to become whole and completely unbroken. We were strong together, unbreakable.

"Ohhh...you feel so good." She moaned and arched her back, straining to get closer as I set a steady, slow rhythm. Making sure I dragged my hardness across every sensitive spot I'd found inside of her over the last few months.

I nibbled on the side of her neck, knowing I was going to leave bruises and my rough stubble was going to turn her fair skin red, but I didn't stop. I got off when she couldn't hide the way I ravaged her and she had to walk around with my claim on her, visible for others to see.

"You feel better than good, Ms. Priss. You feel perfect." She opened so sweetly for me, melted under my hands and mouth. I loved how supple her skin felt and how welcoming her body was. She was liquid want and need, rippling and flowing around me.

We pushed and pulled against one another, hands moving with urgency, mouths panting out each other's names. Sweat slid down my spine and dotted her forehead, as the sound of skin gliding against skin filled the small space. Della looked as good spread out on a fold-down RV table as she did on one-thousand-thread-count sheets. She was flawless, and the way she begged for me, the way she broke into a million pieces around my pounding cock, was perfect no matter where we were or how long we had to wait to make it happen.

I growled in satisfaction and started to move faster, hips pistoning, as if it was a race to the finish. Her body fluttered with small pulses around my still iron-hard dick, milking my orgasm from me in an irresistible way. I shouted my completion and shook over her. I let her legs drop so they were hooked around my waist and lowered myself down, across her, so our hearts were pounding in time, our slick skin pressed together. I kissed her slowly and thoroughly.

Loving the way she smelled and tasted like me. I rubbed my nose across her velvet-soft cheek and kissed her ear. She yelped when I got a handful of one toned, round ass cheek and squeezed.

"I think we need to make this a good-luck tradition before every ride." I dropped a hard kiss on her parted lips and nipped at her smile.

I pushed off of her spent form and ran shaky hands through my messy hair. Della worked her way into a sitting position and blinked those unusual feline-like eyes at me. *"Tu n'as pas besoin de la chance quand tu es le meilleur, mon amour."*

I was never going to understand what she was saying to me when she slipped into French, but I did know what the last part meant. I ran my knuckles along the line of her jaw and dropped a kiss on the top of her head. "You're my love too, Della. The only one I've ever had." She blushed adorably and took the plain denim shirt I handed her to cover up in. It looked ridiculously hot with her red heels, and I knew that was an image I was holding on to for the next time we were separated.

"How's my new sponsor feel about the start of the season?" I helped her off the table and sighed when she fit herself along my back, her lips landing on my neck.

She laughed lightly and gave my waist a squeeze. "Dad's very happy you've been winning. He's even more delighted that you've managed to talk so many of your rodeo riding pals into give Deveaux products a try. Dad is taking full credit for the sudden influx of properly groomed cowboys in the rodeo circuit. He likes being involved. He's happy we're happy."

Nothing was more shocking than Max Deveaux showing up in Loveless while I was still in the hospital, claiming he wanted to help me get back on my feet. The RV we were currently in had Deveaux Beauty's logo on the outside, and I didn't give a shit that it was painted in hot pink. I was touched both Deveauxs had so much faith in me. Plus having a personal connection to my biggest sponsor had me more determined than ever to win...to be the best.

"We are happy, aren't we?" Sometimes I had to check because it was such a foreign feeling, one I wasn't sure I deserved to have.

Della kissed the back of my neck again and squeezed me tighter. *"Oui. Tu me rends si heureuse. Je t'aime,* Crew."

I knew that one too. Even if the words made no sense, my heart knew what love sounded like however she said it. "I love you back, Della."

The fact that I had her, and she loved me, made me feel like it was still better to be lucky than good. Because being with her made me the luckiest guy alive.

Author's Note

Hi, everyone!

Welcome to Loveless and the wild, wicked world of the Lawtons.

I hope you enjoyed this quick introduction to our complicated, difficult, stubborn southern family. I've been playing around with the idea of this town, and these characters, for a very long time! I have to give a huge THANK YOU to Forever Romance and my new editor, Lexi, for giving me the chance to *finally* bring this family to life. I think we're in for a wild ride.

If you enjoyed my Getaway series, then the Loveless, Texas series is going to be right up your alley.

If you have a thing for opposites attracting, sort of my stock in trade, then these books will absolutely deliver.

I keep saying this series is a lot like if my Getaway series and my Saints of Denver series had a baby.

There is a lot of fun family dynamics, as well as having one of the characters in a position to significantly help...or hinder...the other. It's gonna be a damn good time.

If you want to keep up-to-date on all the Jay-like happenings, or if you're a new reader and want to see what I'm all about, you can find me at any of the links that follow.

I strongly suggest joining my reader group on Facebook. I'm super active in there. Also, my monthly newsletter is great for a one-stop shop for all updates and deals. I also write a free book for subscribers you can only access through the newsletter.

Happy reading!

All the Places to Find Me

Website: jaycrownover.com
Newsletter: www.jaycrownover.com/subscribe
Bookbub: bookbub.com/authors/jay-crownover
My store: shop.spreadshirt.com/100036557
Facebook: facebook.com/AuthorJayCrownover
Twitter: @jaycrownover
Instagram: @jay.crownover
Pinterest: pinterest.com/jaycrownover
Spotify & Snapchat: Jay Crownover
Reader Group: facebook.com/groups/crownoverscrowd

Welcome to the wild world of Loveless, Texas. Are you ready to meet the lawless Lawtons and the rest of the residents of this volatile small town?

Keep an eye out for the rest of the Loveless, Texas series, and keep reading for a preview of Case's book, *Justified*, coming in Summer 2019.

Prologue

ASPEN

I feel it is in the best interest of the child if full custody of the juvenile goes to the mother. I also approve her request for the increase in child support. The father will be allowed supervised visits overseen by a representative of the court. We will revisit the issue in a year." An animalistic growl sounded from the table opposite the one I was sitting at with my client.

The former Mrs. Lawton dug her manicured fingers into my forearm hard enough to draw blood, and I fought back a wince.

"We won. Aspen, we actually won. You're amazing. Worth every penny." Her voice was breathy and high. It matched her very blond hair and huge blue eyes. She looked like a Barbie doll, but she was far from a useless, plastic toy. The woman was a viper. Cunning and poisonous. I hated representing her.

Unfortunately for the father, I was very, very good at my job and had just wiped the floor with him and his attorney. I'd gotten everything my client asked for, which included her ex-husband losing all parental rights to their nine-year-old son. It wasn't that my client was the best parent in the world, or actually concerned about her kid. The little boy was the only thing her ex had shown the slightest interest in fighting for, so she'd latched on and thrown everything into keeping father and son apart. Like I said, she was a snake.

Right now I was wondering if I was any better. I cast a look out of the corner of my eye to the man silently seething on the other side of the courtroom. Our eyes met briefly, and I had to look away almost immediately. If looks could kill, he'd have to arrest himself for murder. He hated me.

It shouldn't hurt, but it did.

Because Case Lawton had always been *that* guy.

You know the one. The guy who was always taller, bigger, stronger, faster, smarter, and more handsome than any other. He was witty, unfailingly polite, and full of good ole southern charm. He seemed completely untouchable, unstoppable. He never had a problem getting whatever it was he wanted, be it a football championship, a nearly perfect score on his SATs, or the prettiest girl in the entire county. His constant good fortune and the ease with which he had the entire small town of Loveless, Texas eating out of the palm of his hand should've been annoying. It should have built up loads of resentment in the rest of us who didn't have the same kind of unwavering luck.

It never did though. Because it was no secret that, as perfect as Case's life had looked on the outside, on the inside, it was far from flawless. Case's father was the sheriff of Loveless. He was also a bully who used his position and his badge to abuse the locals. He had a very loose definition of law and order. Rumors had floated around for years that Sheriff Lawton was a bigger criminal than half the people he put away. No one missed how Case tried to make up for all of his father's blatant shortcomings. It was almost as if he was trying to save the entire Lawton name from disgrace, and because he was *that* guy, most of the people in town applauded his effort and encouraged him to be the very best of all of us.

But everyone, including me, knew Case wanted to leave Loveless right after graduation. He had a football scholarship locked down for a Big Ten school up north, and he didn't hide that he was ready to leave Texas, and his father, far behind.

It was right before graduation when his precariously built house of cards came tumbling down around him, and Case fell from grace in the way only idols and gods can.

His mother passed away suddenly. He broke his leg in two places during the last game of the season. His father lost all the restraint he pretended to have, and all the Lawton siblings started showing up to school with obvious bruises and marks all over them. And last but not least, the prettiest girl in the county ended up pregnant. There would be no escape, no bigger and better things for Case Lawton. He joined the military days after graduation and minutes after putting a ring on the finger of the girl who'd effectively trapped him. He served his four years and returned to Loveless harder, colder, and so much angrier than before. He also came back to a very young wife who was practically a stranger and to a son who hardly recognized him. The rushed marriage was not one anyone would call happy.

Instead of being the town's favored son, he was no different from any of the other young men who couldn't find their way out of the city limits. Soon, Case gave up all pretense of ever wanting more and went to work as a deputy for his father in the Sheriff's Department.

I didn't have a logical reason as to why his giving up affected me so deeply—all I knew was that it did. I'd harbored a passionate infatuation with Case from the first moment I saw him. My family moved to Loveless from Chicago my freshman year of high school. To say I was a fish out of water in the small Texas town was an understatement. I stood out like a sore thumb, had trouble making friends and fitting in. I mostly kept to myself, watching the new people and the world around me. Case was impossible to miss, so he immediately became the center of all my focus. Obviously, he never noticed me or returned my avid attraction, but I didn't mind. I was so used to being ignored, I might die if I ended up in the center of his attention.

After high school, while Case was busy doing exactly what everyone expected, I was doing the opposite. I graduated from law school and decided to move back to Loveless, even though my parents had long since retired and moved to Florida. When I went away to college, my father fully expected me to go into environmental law, the way he had. But I wanted to help families and kids, those who felt left behind and discarded. I was there for the underdogs, not the winners, and eventually, I ended up lost inside my own status quo, building a business, getting married, trying to start a family, and finally feeling like I belonged in the adopted small town I proudly called home.

It was all going pretty smoothly, if not boringly and predictably, until the day I happened to be at the wrong place at the right time.

I was walking into the Sheriff's Department to speak with one of my clients. She was a young woman who was a victim of domestic violence. Case's father had arrested her instead of her husband, even though she was the one with black eyes and a broken nose. It just so happened I was walking up the steps and Case was walking down when a process server shoved a set of familiar documents into a surprised Case's hands.

"You've been served, Deputy Lawton."

I knew they were divorce papers before Case did. I'd sent plenty of them out in my few years practicing. I should've kept moving—my client needed me—but I couldn't get my feet to cooperate. Instead, I was frozen on the spot as Case read through the pages and pages of documents, pale blue eyes widening in an almost comical way as he learned exactly how done with him his wife was.

When he got to the last page, he lifted his head and looked right at me. I doubted he even realized I was there, but when he whispered, "She wants to take my boy," I couldn't stop myself from reaching out and putting a hand on his tense forearm. It was the first time I'd ever been brave enough to touch him.

"It'll be fine. Get a good lawyer." It was the advice I would give to anyone in his shoes. And, by a good lawyer, I obviously meant myself, but we didn't know each other well enough for me to be that bold. He still intimidated the hell out of me, and I still questioned his sincerity and trustworthiness, since he knowingly went to work for a crook like his father.

In a split second the man morphed from a confused spouse and scared father to a fire-breathing dragon. He shook my hand off his arm and glowered at me from underneath lowered, dark brows.

"Do I know you?" His tone was icy and every line in his big body locked as if he was ready for a fight.

I fell back a step. Again, it shouldn't hurt to be so forgettable and unremarkable, but it did. "I'm Aspen Barlow. We went to high school together."

His eyebrows twitched, and his mouth shifted to an emotionless line. "The weird girl who moved here from New York? That's you?"

I bristled and locked down any scrap of emotion that might betray how badly his words stung. I'd lived here for years, built up a solid reputation. I thought I was finally fitting in and had shaken the "weird girl" reputation.

"Yep. That's me, the weird girl, but I moved here from Chicago, not New York." I nodded to the papers in his hand. "Trust me. Don't fight her without a good attorney. Courts always tend to give mothers the benefit of the doubt." I was speaking from experience.

"What do you know about it?" Case sounded confused. I felt for the guy, especially considering his marriage was about to implode.

"More than I want to. I'm a family attorney. Divorces and custody agreements make up about eighty percent of my case list." I jumped down a full step, not easy in heels, mind you, when he let out a bark of disbelieving laughter.

"People actually let *you* represent them? Most lawyers in town grew up here. I'll go with one of them. They have to know there's no way Becca is a better parent to Hayes than I am. Thanks for your advice, but I've got this." He rolled the papers into a tight tube and stuck them in the back pocket of his tan uniform. Face set in a scowl, he walked away without another word, dismissing me as inconsequential.

I thought it was all said and done until the senior partner at my practice, who also happened to be my father-in-law, walked into my office and informed me I would be representing Becca Lawton in her divorce.

Before I could tell him there was a conflict of interest, Becca Lawton was sitting in front of me, airing years of dirty laundry between her and Case. She wanted to bury the poor man. She wanted everything he had. And she really, really wanted to break his heart by taking away his son. She did have some valid points. Case worked too much. Drank too much. He had an unpredictable temper, and his family was a volatile mess. She suspected he was unfaithful, but there was no proof of it. Mostly, she was tired of pretending to be happily married when she was anything but. She claimed she wasted her youth on Case, and her resentment was evident.

It was on the tip of my tongue to tell her I couldn't represent her. Sure, Case had issues, but nothing worthy of separating father and son permanently. But then she looked me dead in the eye and told me she could convince the court Case was abusive if she needed to. It made my blood run cold. She was vindictive and sympathetic at the same time. If she ended up in the hands of a less scrupulous attorney they would take her offer and run with it, so I pushed every reservation I had down and promised her I would get her everything she wanted. I promised myself I could do it without completely ruining Case's image and dragging his name through the mud.

Case foolishly hired an old football buddy, an attorney I knew relied more on charm and flashy theatrics in court, rather than on any actual skill. I almost felt sorry for him. *Almost.* If he hadn't smirked at me like his victory was guaranteed the first day, I might have even extended more effort into trying to convince Becca to be reasonable. Instead, we battled it out for months and months, and in the end, it was Case's father who finally swayed the judge to give Becca everything she asked for.

It seemed Sheriff Lawton thought he could use his usual intimidation tactics on the presiding judge. Threats were made, weight was thrown around, and for once, the patriarch of the Lawton clan ran up against someone who wasn't scared of him. The judge was concerned about young Hayes being under the influence of such a morally questionable man. He advised Case to take a good hard look at his life choices over the next year, and the case was closed.

At least it was supposed to be.

I should've known a guy like Case Lawton wasn't going to let such a catastrophic loss go without a word.

When I noticed he was waiting in the hallway, I foolishly hoped it was for his former spouse. When Becca breezed by him with a tiny wave and a wink, his entire face flushed and his cheeks turned a furious red. I told myself to keep moving, my job here was done.

His massive arms crossed over his wide chest, and his eyes cut through me like twin lasers.

"Are you happy? Do you feel good about what just happened, weird girl?" His words were cutting and blunt.

I cleared my throat, tightened my hand on the handle of my briefcase, and refused to flinch away from the absolutely murderous look in his eyes.

"I told you to get a *good* lawyer, Mr. Lawton." I kept my voice calm, but the sarcasm in my tone was unmistakable. I wasn't a woman prone to sass, or particularly standing up for myself, but something about him pushed every button I had.

He growled an ugly string of swear words in my direction and leaned forward. He loomed over me, and I had to suppress a full-body shiver.

"You ruined my life, Aspen Barlow. Everything that matters to me you've ripped away. I would give what little I have left for you to have never stepped foot in this town. You better hope to God our paths don't cross again." He gave me one last scathing look before marching off down the hall, rage evident in his stride.

After that day it was common knowledge that Case and I were enemies. I went out of my way to avoid him, and he made it a point to make my life a living hell whenever the opportunity arose.

If there was one person I didn't expect to lean on when my own house of cards went up in flames a few years later, it was the newly appointed sheriff, Case Lawton.

About the Author

Jay Crownover is the international and multiple *New York Times* and *USA Today* bestselling author of the Marked Men Series, the Saints of Denver Series, the Point Series, the Breaking Point Series, and the Getaway Series. Her books have been translated in many different languages all around the world. She is a tattooed, crazy-haired Colorado native who lives at the base of the Rockies with her awesome dogs. This is where she can frequently be found enjoying a cold beer and Taco Tuesdays. Jay is a self-declared music snob and outspoken book lover who is always looking for her next adventure, between the pages and on the road.

Learn more:
  www.jaycrownover.com
  Twitter @JayCrownover
  Facebook.com/AuthorJayCrownover

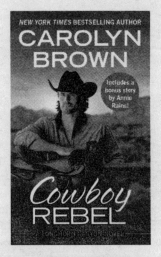

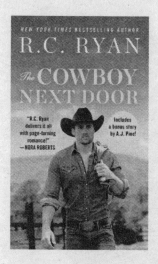
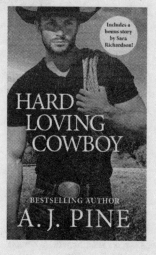

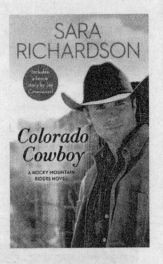
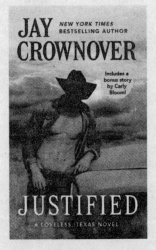

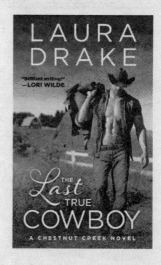